ESSEX CC LIBRARIES

D0279814

A BETTER QUALITY of MURDER

By Ann Granger and available from Headline

Lizzie Martin and Ben Ross crime novels
A Rare Interest in Corpses
A Mortal Curiosity
A Better Quality Of Murder

Fran Varady crime novels
Asking For Trouble
Keeping Bad Company
Running Scared
Risking It All
Watching Out
Mixing With Murder
Rattling The Bones

Mitchell and Markby crime novels
Say It With Poison
A Season For Murder
Cold In The Earth
Murder Among Us
Where Old Bones Lie
A Fine Place For Death
Flowers For His Funeral
Candle For A Corpse
A Touch Of Mortality
A Word After Dying
Call The Dead Again
Beneath These Stones
Shades Of Murder
A Restless Evil
That Way Murder Lies

Campbell and Carter crime novels
Mud, Muck and Dead Things

A BETTER QUALITY of MURDER

Ann Granger

headline

Copyright © 2010 Ann Granger

The right of Ann Granger to be identified as the Author
of the Work has been asserted by her in accordance with the
Copyright, Designs and Patents Act 1988.

First published in 2010
by HEADLINE PUBLISHING GROUP

1

Apart from any use permitted under UK copyright law, this publication
may only be reproduced, stored, or transmitted, in any form, or by any means,
with prior permission in writing of the publishers or, in the case of
reprographic production, in accordance with the terms of licences issued
by the Copyright Licensing Agency.

All characters in this publication are fictitious and any
resemblance to real persons, living or dead, is purely coincidental.

Cataloguing in Publication Data is available from the British Library

Hardback ISBN 978 0 7553 4908 1
Trade paperback ISBN 978 0 7553 4920 3

Typeset in Plantin by Avon DataSet Ltd,
Bidford-on-Avon, Warwickshire

Printed in the UK by CPI Mackays, Chatham, ME5 8TD

Headline's policy is to use papers that are natural, renewable and
recyclable products and made from wood grown in sustainable forests.
The logging and manufacturing processes are expected to conform
to the environmental regulations of the country of origin.

HEADLINE PUBLISHING GROUP
An Hachette UK Company
338 Euston Road
London NW1 3BH

www.headline.co.uk
www.hachette.co.uk

Author's Note:

A visitor could walk all over London's Green Park, but he or she won't find the great oak tree claimed by Park Constable Hopkins to have been planted at the command of King Charles II, nor the adjacent clump of bushes. That is because I have planted both tree and bushes there in my imagination and trust I'll be excused taking a liberty with a royal park. Similarly, the visitor to Piccadilly would search in vain for the location of Sebastian Benedict's art gallery. The whole block is now occupied by the imposing mass of the Ritz hotel.

Chapter One

Inspector Benjamin Ross

I ONCE met a man on his way to commit a murder. I didn't know it at the time. Perhaps no more did he. What was to become a crime could still have been no more than a hazy thought, a sick dream in his mind. If he had formed the resolve, then he still might have been frightened by the horror of it, a natural revulsion driving him back from the brink. A word would have been enough. I might have detained him if only to ask where he was going and told him to mind how he went; as police officers are always supposed to advise the public. He had still enough time to think it over. He might have changed his plans, had I spoken. But we passed by one another 'like ships in the night', as the saying goes, and a woman died.

I made the transition from uniformed officer to plain clothes when I'd not been long in the force, only a couple of years. The occasion was the Great Exhibition of 1851. The idea was I should mingle with the crowds and catch pickpockets and passers of bad coin among visitors to the great Crystal Palace in Hyde Park. I was moderately successful, although I soon learned that the criminal fraternity (and sorority) spots a policeman within seconds of his arrival on the scene however he's dressed.

Be that as it may, I've been with plain-clothes branch ever since, based at Scotland Yard and eventually rising to the rank of inspector. That, even if I say so myself, isn't bad for someone who began his working life as a pit boy in his native Derbyshire, before coming down to London to try his luck. But I'll never forget the Great Exhibition. I'd seen machinery at the pithead but nothing like the Crystal Palace had to offer. All kinds of gadgets and contrivances were on display: splendid furniture and household requirements fit for the Queen to use, everything you could think of, and even a steam locomotive to take you around the site.

One product wasn't on show back then but was well on display as I walked homeward that Saturday evening sixteen years later, in early November 1867 to be precise. It's something I'll swear London must be unrivalled for throughout the world. It isn't made of metal, wood, china clay or cloth, nor has it sprung from the ingenious mind of an inventor or craftsman. It doesn't come clanking past you belching steam and spilling oil. It isn't painted every colour of the rainbow, but instead is a dirty yellow or dingy grey in colour. It's silent and formed from the dank breath of the city itself. It is fog.

The London fog is like a living beast. It swirls around you and attacks you from all sides, sneaking into your throat and crawling up your nostrils. It blinds your vision. Sometimes it appears so thick, it tricks you into thinking you can reach out and grab handfuls of it, like cotton waste. But, of course, you can't. It slips mockingly through your fingers leaving only its tarry smell sticking to your clothes, hair and skin. Even when you try to shut it out behind your own front door, it is still there in your living room with you.

That day the fog descended in mid-afternoon and by four o'clock had wrapped its clammy embrace round central London and even stretched its damp fingers as far as the city's outer fringe. Things had been pretty quiet all day. The weather had a lot to do with that: even crooks are kept at home by fog. Through the windows of my tiny office at Scotland Yard, I'd watched it thicken and now the sun – wherever it was up there above the grey blanket – was going down and darkness creeping in. Indoors the gas lighting made the world bright and clear; but the murk pressing against the window-panes mocked our efforts to keep it at bay. Officers came in coughing and swearing you could scarcely see a hand in front of your face. By the time I set off for home, you certainly couldn't unless you held it in front of your nose.

Superintendent Dunn took himself off homewards at four, muttering about a dinner party he and his wife were to attend, though how on earth was he to reach home in time to get ready? What was more, after that, how were he and Mrs Dunn to make their way to their hosts' house in Camden?

'And you might as well go home, too, Ross,' he concluded.

So I took him at his word and left the building not long after him. My intention was to cross the river not by Westminster Bridge as I normally did, but by Waterloo Bridge. It wasn't really so very far to walk if the weather had been clear. But it took me three-quarters of an hour and near-disastrous collision with a dozen obstacles before a worsening of the smell told me I'd reached the great embankment under construction along the Thames. Fog had put paid to work on that, too, for the day.

As for the stench, that rose from the Thames itself. Unable to escape upward and trapped at low level, the watery miasma mingled with all the other odours. Everything goes into the river, even though Mr Bazalgette's wonderful new sewer system, part of it under my feet and the embankment, is designed to remove one source of pollution. But the river traffic discharges its own debris and if anyone living in the area wants to get rid of something, household or trade refuse, legal or otherwise, the easiest way is to take it to the river and throw it in.

Bodies, mostly animal but occasionally human, also find their way into the river. Murderers roll their victims silently over the edge by night. Suicides fling themselves from the bridges. I am glad I don't serve with the River Police. The smoke from the engines entering and leaving the great rail terminus of Waterloo on the south side added a whiff of their distinctive odour to the rest. I was used to that. I came home to it every night.

I found my way to the great nine-arched granite bridge and stepped on to it. There was no attendant in the toll-booth. I dare say he thought no one would cross in this weather. The cabmen had as good as given up plying their trade. At the best of times, the traffic using the bridge is limited by the fact that Londoners with their natural thrift object to paying the toll so, if they can, they cross elsewhere. I understand that the original investors in the bridge have never got their money back. They even say the government will have to take it over eventually and that will be the end of the toll and the taxpayer will have to pick up the bill.

I set out, keeping prudently to the stonework on the left-hand side, reaching out to touch it every few minutes.

In no time I felt quite alone in that silent world. The only occasional sound was a muffled blast of a foghorn. But mostly the river traffic had heaved to and was riding out the fog at anchor. Warning lights were of no use now. At intervals the gas lamps along the bridge glowed uselessly, doing no more than lend a saffron hue to the few inches of air around them. I could hear my own footsteps echoing off the parapet. Although I'd muffled my scarf round the lower part of my face, covering my nose, the wretched fog still found its way into my throat and made me splutter.

I must have reached the halfway point, as far as I could judge, when I had warning I was no longer alone. Footsteps pattered towards me. Fog plays tricks with your hearing; so I stopped in case all I heard was the echo of my own cautious tread. But these were quick footsteps. The other person was running; there was no doubt about that. This was someone heedless of the lack of visibility and not afraid to pelt headlong into it.

Now the police officer in me was alert. It isn't only fearlessness that makes someone risk his neck. Sometimes it's fear itself. The other didn't care where he or she ran, or what obstacle might lie ahead, because he – or she – was running away from something behind him – or her.

I waited where I was, straining my ears. I guessed it was a woman. The impact on the cobbles was light, not made by a man's sturdy boots. *Tap-tap-tap* came the rapid footfalls, ever nearer, seeming to me to signal desperation. A woman made them: alone, afraid, and running headlong and heedless across the bridge through the enveloping ochre mass.

'Damn this fog!' I muttered into my scarf. I felt disorientated. I thought she was directly ahead of me, on the same side of the bridge. But she might be approaching to my right or even rushing straight down the middle. I moved out a little to the centre of the roadway. In the unlikely event wheeled traffic rattled on to the bridge, I could scuttle to one side. But from a central position, if she passed me either to left or right, I would know and with luck be able to intercept her. There was only the width of the bridge, after all. I debated briefly whether to shout out to let her know I was there. But if she were already terrified enough to risk life and limb, the sound of a disembodied and unfamiliar voice ahead of her would only panic her more.

Biff!

Before I could do anything about it, a dim shape materialised an arm's length from me. I'd only time to realise it was wearing skirts, and the top of its head was crowned with something like a cockerel's comb, before the figure cannoned full tilt into me. The breath gushed out of me. The world turned topsy-turvy. I staggered back and almost fell, yet managed to keep my footing and to reach out. By purest luck, I grasped a handful of light material – a woman's gown – and, as I did, a dreadful screech right in my ear almost led me to release it again, but I hung on.

'Madam!' I shouted to the unknown, still only a silhouette, 'I am a police officer! Don't be alarmed!'

She let out another screech and began battering my chest and head with blows of her clenched fists. In with the smells of the fog, I sniffed another: cheap scent.

'You let me go!' she yelled. 'I never done you no harm!'

'I'm not going to do *you* any harm!' I shouted back as we wrestled.

She realised I wasn't going to let her go. I had even managed to get hold of her arm. She suddenly stopped struggling and in a weaker, pathetic voice, begged, 'Don't hurt me!'

'I am not going to hurt you.' I wanted to bellow at her but that would only have produced another panic on her part, so I tried my best to sound like a reasonable human being. 'I told you, I'm a police officer.'

Her free arm came out of the murk and a hand patted my chest in a rather familiar fashion.

'You ain't the law,' she said accusingly. 'You ain't got no uniform! Where's your brass buttons?'

I realised that the peculiar crest on her head was formed by some kind of hat decorated with sprays of silk flowers or feathers pinned to it. I was now pretty sure that what I had here in my grasp was one of those women who plies her trade on the streets.

I could be wrong. She might be a respectable girl, of course. But the flowery scent, the unseasonably lightweight material of her dress and summery nature of her headwear, to say nothing of the rapid way she'd checked my statement by examination of my clothing, suggested otherwise.

'I am in plain clothes,' I said.

'Oh, yes?' Now she was sarcastic. 'Well, that's a new one on me. They tells me all sorts of things, but it's the first time a man's told me he's a plain-clothes rozzer.'

'My name is Inspector Benjamin Ross,' I said firmly. 'And you are running away from someone.'

'No, I ain't!' she retorted immediately. 'Let go of my arm!'

'Certainly not!' I said. 'You may have stolen someone's wallet or watch and chain, and be running from justice.'

This time her free arm swung at me; and her clenched first struck me a forceful blow in the middle of my chest.

'I ain't a thief! I'm an honest girl.'

'You are a ladybird,' I said. I could have said 'common prostitute' but I suspected that would earn me another barrage of blows. 'And you have just struck an officer of the law. For that alone I can arrest you.'

She had been trying to tug her arm free of my grasp, but now she relaxed, which was an odd sort of reaction to my threat. There was a silence. Perhaps she was only thinking it over, but I sensed she was also listening. For pursuit?

'All right,' she said suddenly. 'Arrest me.'

'You want me to arrest you?' I tried not to sound surprised.

'Yus! Go on, arrest me!' She had leaned towards me as she spoke and mixed with the cheap scent came a blast of beery breath.

'Ah,' I said. 'You think you will be safer in my custody than free and risking a meeting with *him*.'

'Who?' she demanded immediately. But there was fear in her voice again.

'The man you are running away from. Who is he?'

I was loath to arrest her. She sounded very young. That was to be expected. The girls working the streets are mostly young, some distressingly so, only children. But I hadn't caught her soliciting. I had only stopped a very frightened runaway girl. To haul her off to a police station and put her on a charge seemed uncalled for.

'What's your name?' I asked.

'Wouldn't you like to know?' she retorted sullenly.

'Yes, I should like to know. I told you my name. Come along now, speak up, a fair exchange is no robbery.'

'Daisy,' she said, after a pause.

'Surname?'

Another pause. 'Smith.'

'I don't think so,' I said.

'Think what you like. If I say I'm Daisy Smith, you show me proof I'm not.'

'Well, Daisy Smith,' I replied, 'tell me what has scared you so.'

'You did!' she retorted at once. 'Grabbing hold of a girl like that. You gave me a very nasty fright.'

'Perhaps I did, but someone else had already given you a nastier one.'

Another silence ensued. In it, a foghorn echoed mournfully across the river. There was a creak of wood beneath our feet and a man's voice shouting a warning. Someone was foolish enough to try navigating the river in these conditions.

'It was him,' she said suddenly in such a quiet voice I almost missed it.

Just as softly I returned, 'Then tell me who he is, Daisy. I can protect you from him.'

She gave an odd forced little laugh. 'Ain't no one can do that! He's beyond your grip, Inspector Benjamin Ross. Beyond yours and mine!'

'Why?' I asked.

Another waft of beer breath and of flowery scent so strong that it made my nose itch. She had placed her lips close to my ear.

'Because he's dead already, ain't he? It was the River Wraith. He crawls out of the Thames on foggy nights and prowls about the streets. He's wrapped in his burial shroud and hides in doorways and alleys. You never see him nor hear him until you feel the touch of his hand and you smell him. Like the grave itself he smells, of dead things and blood. That's what got a hold of me, back there. His cold hands came out of the fog and grabbed me by the throat. But I got away from him.'

'How?' I asked sceptically. Although the girls spin all kinds of tales when they're arrested, this was a new one on me.

In a voice suddenly briskly practical she said, 'I shoved me fingers up his nostrils!'

Ah, yes, a girl plying her trade on the streets has to learn all those tricks. But she had supplied my next line of argument.

'Daisy,' I said, 'he's no ghost or wraith or whatever you care to call him. Not if he can feel pain. Whoever had hold of you, he's flesh and blood.'

'So why does he only come out in the fog?' she demanded.

'It hides him,' I said simply. 'And he wants to be hidden. So do most criminals or people with bad intentions.'

'They don't all walk round wearing their shrouds,' countered Daisy.

I was determined to persuade her to abandon this fanciful version of her attacker and challenged, 'You *saw* him in this shroud?'

That did make her hesitate but then she came back as confidently as before with, 'I haven't. But others have. A friend of mine, she saw him clear. She was waiting about for custom but, the night being so bad, she hadn't found any and she was afraid to go home without any money.'

This had the ring of truth to it. I know there is usually some lout who takes the girl's money. The same 'man friend' is also quick with his fists if she comes back with nothing to show for her efforts. I wondered if this girl, Daisy, also had a 'protector' or had managed to survive without falling into such unsavoury hands.

'Go on,' I said.

'Well, she heard footsteps and thought maybe, here's one! So she stepped out in front of him. The fog parted sudden, like it sometimes does, and there he stood right in front of her. She told me all about it, the shroud, everything. All white, it is. It covers him all over, his head as well except for his eyes. Only he doesn't have any eyes. Only big black empty sockets where eyes ought to be. So there!' she finished triumphantly.

I didn't believe in shrouded ghouls in any weather. But there was a mystery here and I wanted to get to the bottom of it, preferably in more comfortable surroundings. I was getting chilled standing there and my companion, in her light gown, must be nearly frozen.

'Let's go back across the bridge to the Strand side,' I suggested. 'We can find a coffee house. You could do with a hot drink and you can tell me all about it.'

She squirmed in my grip. She had changed her mind about accompanying me. Perhaps she was confident she had shaken off her pursuer or thought my presence had frightened him away.

'I ain't going anywhere with a policeman, not even an inspector! It's no coffee house we'll go to. I'll end up down the police station and find meself up in front of the magistrates in the morning!'

'I'm not arresting you, Daisy. I want to help! Listen to me. Have you been attacked by this so-called wraith before? When did he first appear?'

'Perhaps as long ago as six months,' she said vaguely, adding with more spirit: 'You can ask the other girls. More than one of them's been lucky to escape him. I'm not making it all up. You can ask any of them that works near the river, Waterloo side or Strand side.'

'And you say these other girls have actually been attacked, some of them as long ago as six months?'

'Yes, they have! But only on nights like this, when the fog comes down and you can't see him. But he can see you, just like it was a clear sunny day! That's why he's no human being like you and me. Here I am standing right by you. Yet you don't know what I look like; nor do I know what you look like. I can't see clear in the fog. You can't, neither. *But the River Wraith, he can!*'

With that she suddenly twisted like an eel, her arm escaped my grasp and before I could grab it again she was off, running full pelt again to the Strand side of the bridge.

'River Wraith!' I muttered furiously. 'The girl's brain is addled.'

But someone had attacked her. Someone or thing had frightened her into headlong, blind flight.

I resumed my walk across the bridge. I could smell the massive locomotives distinctly now and hear them growling and clanking as they negotiated the tracks in and out of Waterloo Station. The engine drivers were taking it slowly and wouldn't pick up speed until they had cleared central London and visibility improved. That meant I was nearly home. I'd just about reached the other side when I again heard a footfall coming towards me, but this time a measured tread, a man's boot. This pedestrian was making prudent progress. He had no cane. I would have heard it tap on the ground or against the balustrade. Perhaps, as I had done, he felt his way by hand.

Another silhouette loomed up: male, on the short side, wearing a long dark coat and carrying some kind of bag. I guessed he was a traveller, just arrived and come from the railway station.

'A poor evening, sir!' I called out sociably to him.

A grunt was the only reply. He quickened his step and hurried past. I was able to make out that he held his handkerchief to his face against the bad air and was obviously not inclined to remove it to return my greeting.

Or perhaps, with the best will in the world, I couldn't help sounding like a policeman.

But if he realised I was a policeman, he also knew I was walking in the opposite direction to his. With every step the distance between us lengthened. Perhaps a little thing like that settled his mind.

It's something to be making for your own front door and my step quickened and lightened and I quite forgot about my encounters on the bridge for the moment until, would you believe it, it happened again!

A second figure cannoned into me and again a female voice let out a cry of surprise and then, from the fog, came a familiar voice.

'I'm so sorry, I didn't see you!' it gasped.

The speaker scuttled to one side to get round me but I reached out and caught her arm.

'Lizzie? Is that you?'

'Oh, Ben,' gasped my wife. 'It's you! What an awful evening!'

Chapter Two

Elizabeth Martin Ross

BEN'S FIRST question, when he realised the identity of his catch in the fog, was to demand what on earth I was doing out and about.

I told him I was looking for Bessie.

'What's Bessie doing out in this murk?' he demanded.

'I'll explain later,' I told him, 'it has to do with apples.'

I heard Ben give a gusty sigh which turned into a cough as fog seeped into his throat.

'Let's go home,' he said. 'You won't find her in these conditions and she may have made her own way home by now.'

I wasn't sorry at the prospect, so home we stumbled, holding on to one another like a pair of blind people.

When we married we invested what money we had in our little red-brick terrace house not far from Waterloo Station. We were able to do this because the previous owner was my former employer, my godfather's widow, 'Aunt' Parry. It had been among the many properties she owned and one of the best of them, built only twenty years before. (Other buildings she owned were frankly slums and no one would choose to live in them, but the rents kept Aunt Parry in comfort!) However, she generously allowed us to purchase our new home at a very good price.

Having laid out our capital for the house, however, there was no question of us being able to furnish it down to the last saucepan and also pay servants of the better sort. (Although Ben is in receipt of a very respectable salary with prospects of it being increased.) Anyway, the house wasn't large enough to warrant 'staff'. But if I were to be spared the rough work, I would need help. In Dorset Square, where I had been living with Aunt Parry, Bessie had been the lowliest staff member, the kitchen maid. She was more than willing to escape the eagle eye of the Parry cook, Mrs Simms, and come to be our maid of all work. So we moved into the house, all three together.

I had always thought, when I was at Dorset Square, that Mrs Simms was unduly strict with Bessie. But then, I had never had charge of a fifteen-year-old girl; and after a very short time I began to have some sympathy with Mrs Simms.

Bessie was hard-working and loyal and I knew her to be intelligent and quick-witted. But she also possessed an independent mind and was certainly not shy of giving her opinion. In addition she proved unexpectedly artful. The problem had been exacerbated, not long after we set up house, by Bessie discovering temperance.

My first knowledge of this came when Bessie, after we had been only a month in the house, meekly asked if she might have permission to go to a regular prayer meeting at five p.m. on a Sunday.

I hadn't expected Bessie to develop an enthusiasm for religion but it seemed a reasonable request, even laudable. Nevertheless, I asked one or two questions. One of Mrs Simms's recommendations, when she handed Bessie over to my charge, was a darkly whispered, 'You want to watch out for followers, Mrs Ross!'

I must admit Bessie isn't the prettiest girl. She has a scrawny but wiry frame and, given that the poor child has been employed to scour pots and scrub floors since the age of twelve, her hands are roughened and red enough to belong to a forty-year-old. Add in frizzy mouse-coloured hair and crooked teeth, and 'followers' wasn't the word that first sprang to my mind when she begged her permission. But I did ask what kind of prayer meeting it was, where it was held and who conducted it.

I learned it was run by a Reverend Mr Fawcett in a nearby hall and was an offshoot of the temperance movement. I consulted Ben.

'I've seen enough violence and crime originating in drunkenness,' said Ben, 'if Bessie wants to "sign the pledge" it's fine with me.'

It would have been acceptable to me, too, but Bessie's new-found interest extended to a desire to 'spread the word'. In a nutshell, Ben and I were expected to shun the Demon Drink, too. It wasn't that we did drink very much. Ben had an occasional glass of porter with his supper. During his time in London he had come to like this strong dark ale, very popular with the porters at London's meat and fish markets. A bottle of porter on the table is unsightly, so on the rare occasions we had guests I removed the porter and substituted a bottle of inexpensive hock. You can see, we hardly kept a cellar! Porter or hock, it had to be drunk with Bessie looming in the background like a Greek chorus. She didn't wring her hands, but she had mastered the sorrowful shake of the head and the reproachful look.

'Ignore her,' said Ben, who was amused by the pantomime, 'she'll soon get tired of it.'

So Bessie got away with that and moved on to a more openly expressed criticism.

I found her in the kitchen, standing over the washing-up, gazing at a pair of wine glasses, and shaking her head dolefully.

'I can't do it, missus,' she said as soon as I approached. I did wish she wouldn't call me 'missus' and had suggested various alternatives, but Bessie had decided in her own mind what my title should be. Ben was always referred to as 'the inspector' and addressed as such.

'You can't wash up, Bessie, why not?' I asked.

'I can wash the pots and dishes,' said Bessie, 'but not them glasses as have had strong drink in them. If I do, I'm encouraging you and the inspector in what I know is wrong.'

My instinct was to shout, 'Rubbish! Get on with the dishes!' But for once I managed not to say the first thing to come into my head. I had a better idea how to deal with this.

'Oh, I see, Bessie. Well, yes, I have been thinking it might be better if you left the glassware to one side and I'll wash that. The glasses were a wedding present from my Aunt Parry and I shouldn't like them broken.'

Bessie turned to me, her face a picture. She opened her mouth but, for once, no retort came out. I picked up the offending glasses and put them to one side. Bessie washed up the dishes with much clattering and clanging of the pots but otherwise in a mutinous silence. For some time after that I was repeatedly asked, 'Are you sure you want me to wash this plate, missus? I might break it.'

She would gaze at me innocently when she put the question, but I had won that round and she knew it.

On that day, the day of the fog, we were to have pork chops for supper and I discovered, when I went into the kitchen to prepare the meal, that we had no apples for the accompanying sauce.

'There were two apples in the bowl, Bessie. What happened to them?'

'The inspector put them in his pocket, missus, when he went off this morning.'

'But they were cooking apples, sour.'

'I did tell him,' was the serene reply. 'But he took 'em just the same. He'll have a horrible ache in the guts. Do you want me to run to the greengrocer and get some more?'

'Stomach, Bessie, not "guts",' I corrected automatically and hesitated. The fog, gathering fast all afternoon, was now a real pea-souper.

'It ain't far,' said Bessie. 'I know the way. I'll keep close to the wall.'

Against my better judgement, I agreed. In normal weather it would have taken her fifteen minutes at the most. The shop was only just round the corner. Even adding on time for the fog, she should have been back easily in half an hour. But when there was still no sign of her three-quarters of an hour later, I threw a shawl round my shoulders and went out to look for her. Instead I'd found Ben.

We hurried back to the house as fast as we could. As soon as we were through the front door I was listening for Bessie, in the kitchen, but there was no sound. I made sure the kitchen was empty and came back to Ben.

'No luck?' he asked, 'I'll go and look for her.'

As he turned back to the door I detained him.

'There's no chance of finding her in this, Ben. You've only just arrived home. Sit down and warm yourself by the fire and if she's not back in another twenty minutes, perhaps, well, I don't know what we can do.'

Ben looked unhappy. 'She would choose tonight of all nights!'

'Why? What's so special about tonight?'

Ben hesitated but eventually told me about his encounter with the girl on the bridge. 'It doesn't mean any harm has come to Bessie, but I don't like her being out so long.'

'That sounds terrifying,' I said, worried. 'But is it true? Do you believe the girl? About the shrouded figure, I mean?'

Ben hesitated before answering. 'I know it sounds fanciful, but she swears the other girls working in the area know about him and one of them, she says, actually saw his face.' He gave a hiss of frustration. 'I wish I could find that girl and get a description, *any* detail would help. First, though, I have to find Daisy Smith, *if* that's her real name, and ask her the name of the girl who got a glimpse of the Wraith's face. But I know nothing about Daisy, other than she's a street-walker and wears a hat with feathers on the top of it.'

The gaslight gleamed on something stuck to the lapel of Ben's overcoat. I stretched out my hand and gently detached it, holding it up. It quivered in the draught, a single thread of a colour almost scarlet in its intensity.

'We know one thing,' I said. 'She has bright red hair.'

Ben uttered an exclamation and took the hair. He hurried into the parlour to the desk where we kept writing materials and, taking a fresh sheet of clean letter paper, carefully folded the hair inside it in a little packet. On this he wrote, 'Daisy Smith' and the date.

'Preserving the evidence, Inspector Ross?' I asked with a smile.

'As yet we have no crime,' he replied. 'But we may well end up with one.'

At that moment, a faint click from the ground floor rear told us someone had just closed the back door very gently indeed.

We both dashed into the kitchen to find Bessie, still in bonnet and shawl, gripping a basket with apples in it.

Together we demanded to know where she'd been for so long.

'It's the fog, missus,' said Bessie defensively. 'It took me longer than I thought it would.'

'It's taken you an hour, Bessie!' I reached out to take the basket from her. She was unwilling to relinquish it and I saw why. 'What are these?'

From underneath the apples I retrieved a stack of cheaply printed leaflets. ' "Beware the danger of strong drink!"' I read aloud. 'What on earth is this, Bessie? Where did you get them?'

Bessie looked miserable. But she was a truthful girl. 'I got to the greengrocer's shop real quick, and I thought I had time to go on just a little bit further and collect them pamphlets from the hall. Mr Fawcett asked us last week to give out the pamphlets, when they came from the printer's. There's a meeting at the hall tonight, so instead of waiting till tomorrow, I thought I'd collect them now, and give some of 'em out before I went to the meeting tomorrow, Sunday.'

'Give them out!' I cried. 'Does Mr Fawcett expect you to stand about on street corners handing out these things?' I shook the stack of paper sheets at her.

'Oh, no,' said Bessie earnestly. 'Just give 'em to people we know, to tell 'em about temperance.'

'I don't know about temperance,' said Ben, 'but if there should be a bottle of porter in the larder, I'll have it with my supper.'

'Oh, good heavens, supper! Bessie!' I ordered, 'we must get on with that now. There's no time to discuss this. But we'll talk later.'

'Yes, missus,' said Bessie unhappily.

'What are you going to do?' asked Ben later, over the pork chops.

The fire burned cheerily in the grate and glinted on the brass fire-irons and fender. It was a sight to make anyone feel more relaxed.

'It's partly my fault,' I said, 'I should have found out more about these meetings before now. I thought they just sang hymns and listened to this fellow Fawcett preach about temperance. I think, I think that tomorrow I'll go with Bessie, meet this preacher for myself and tell him that distributing leaflets is completely out of the question as far as Bessie is concerned.'

'Fair enough,' said Ben, pouring out the last of his bottle of porter.

'Ben,' I asked, 'do you really eat sour cooking apples?'

'Certainly,' said my husband, 'I've always liked them since I was a child.'

Ben was snoozing in front of the fire when Bessie and I left the house late the following afternoon. There was no sign of the previous day's fog, though every chimney belched out grey clouds to hang above the streets. These were emptier than on a weekday and in a Sunday silence. Those few people to be seen were dressed in their best, although as always, there was a scattering of street urchins in rags. They ran alongside the Sunday strollers asking for pence, trusting that it being church day, Christian charity would make the target feel obliged to part with some small coins.

The hall where the meeting was to be held was wedged between two taller buildings and looked as if it might have begun its existence as a storehouse of some kind. Its brickwork was coated with the normal layer of soot but its tall narrow windows had been cleaned and a noticeboard outside had a paper sheet pinned to it, advertising that evening's meeting 'with an address by Reverend Joshua Fawcett. Tea and biscuits to follow'.

'Sometime I help with the tea and biscuits,' said Bessie proudly as she led me over the threshold, 'and sometimes I mind the little ones.'

Inside, the hall was warmed inadequately by a smoky stove. It was sparsely furnished with rows of wooden chairs and our boots clattered on the bare boards. At the far end a stage had been built and in the middle of it stood a lectern. On the right-hand side, near the threadbare curtain, lurked a scratched piano in need of a polish. Below the stage and to the left, as we looked towards it, was a table with a large urn hissing gently on it, presided over by a pair of ladies, one short and plump and one taller and thinner.

'The little fat one,' whispered Bessie impolitely, 'is Mrs Gribble and the tall one is Mrs Scott. Mrs Scott is a widow lady. Her husband was a soldier, but he didn't die in no battle. He went out to India and took a fever.' She frowned. 'It don't look like Miss Marchwood's here today. I wonder where she is. She's always here, doing the teas. I wanted you to meet Miss Marchwood. She's like you were, missus.'

'Like I was?' I asked, puzzled.

'Before you married the inspector. She's a lady's companion,' explained Bessie.

'Indeed?' I murmured. But I was studying Mrs Scott. Though soberly clad, her fine green mantle was trimmed with fur. It was worn with a skirt of some Highland plaid, such as Her Majesty has made so popular. I noted that her crinoline was of the newer style, with more fullness behind and less at the sides. A round astrakhan hat of vaguely Russian style was pinned atop a chignon of dark hair. I suspected the chignon to be false, and put her age at a little over forty. I wondered what such an obviously well-to-do woman of fashion was doing here, supervising the making of cups of tea at a temperance meeting.

Mrs Gribble was by contrast colourful, in a maroon skirt with tiers of flounces, stretched over a perfectly round crinoline, green bodice, paisley shawl and bonnet adorned with silk flowers. As I watched, Mrs Scott drew her attention to some irregularity in the line of pottery teacups set out ready for the promised refreshments. Mrs Gribble, flustered and red-faced, hastened to correct the fault so that the cups stood as straight as a line of guardsmen.

I took a seat to the rear of the hall in order to observe everything.

'You want to move a bit nearer the front, missus!' urged Bessie.

I thanked her but said I would do very well where I was.

Bessie looked disappointed. I fancied she wanted to show me off.

Gradually the hall filled. A group of infant abstainers was placed at the front under the command of a short, stocky, wan-faced middle-aged man in a tight suit of hound's-tooth tweed. I suspected his hair was thinning early, because he had brushed it all forward over the top of his head and arranged the resulting fringe in a row of carefully constructed curls across his brow. The whole lot was plastered into place with a liberal application of some pomade that made his whole coiffure shine.

'Is that Mr Fawcett?' I asked Bessie, taken aback.

'Oh no,' replied Bessie dismissively, 'that's only Mr Pritchard.'

A lugubrious gentleman with muttonchop whiskers appeared and handed out dog-eared hymnbooks. Bessie identified him for me as 'Mr Walters'. There certainly seemed to be no shortage of helpers.

But an air of suppressed excitement had been growing and the buzz of whispered chatter mingled with the soft hiss of the gaslights around the walls. Anticipation was written on every face. Clearly Mr Fawcett was 'a draw'.

But still we were not to see him yet. Whiskery Mr Walters climbed on to the stage and requested us to stand for the first hymn. As we obeyed, he made his way to the piano and struck an opening chord that demonstrated the piano not only needed a polish, it needed tuning. Nevertheless we all gave voice lustily.

We then sat down. Mr Pritchard ushered his infant charges to the centre, facing us down the hall, and with much arm-waving conducted them in a cheerful ditty promising us that they would never touch 'wine nor beer, nor even apple cider'.

Then they scrambled back into their seats and Mr Pritchard, his pale cheeks flushed with triumph and sweat trickling from his curled fringe, turned round to take his bow and receive our polite applause. I clapped the children's efforts, though not approving of them performing this sort of turn.

But the main moment of the evening had come. Mr Walters brought his whiskers back on stage and begged that we would all give an enthusiastic welcome to Mr Fawcett, our speaker this evening.

Everyone burst into renewed applause, Bessie with particular energy, and on to the stage strode the Reverend Joshua.

I had had no idea what to expect. I hadn't wanted to quiz Bessie too much to avoid having to listen to his praises sung in my ear. He now proved much younger than I'd expected. I doubted he was much over thirty and if he was in holy orders, it was not in the Church of England. He was tall and slender and elegantly clad in a well-fitting dark-blue frock coat and dove-grey pantaloons. His linen was snowy white and the only black he wore was a silk cravat with a diamond pin. He was clean-shaven, but had long hair like a poet, and was altogether far more a dandy in appearance than a minister of the cloth. I understood now why the larger part of the audience consisted of ladies. Indeed, at his appearance on stage, a collective sigh of appreciation went up all around me.

'Dear friends,' began Fawcett, gripping the lectern between his hands, his bright gaze sweeping across our ranks. 'My dear, dear friends . . . What a very great pleasure it is to see you all here this evening. It makes my heart rise in my bosom to know that so many are anxious to support our truly noble cause. I see in your faces that you have given your own hearts and minds to our great task.'

His voice was mellifluous, but his eyes sharp. He had marked me in the back row as a newcomer, I was sure.

Then, in an abrupt change of tempo and style, he was off. My goodness, as I told Ben later, I had to give the man his due. He was a formidable preacher. His voice swooped low and rose again, grew louder or hushed, as required. He led us through the story of Noah in the vineyard. He reminded us that wine and all strong drink dulled the senses, was the cause of all kinds of physical ailments (including loss of teeth) and premature ageing. It led to violence and terrible errors of judgement. Most of all, addiction was a first step on a slippery slope to all kinds of sin, leading from foul language and lewd behaviour in public to forbidden desires and adultery in private, to greed and envy, from the hatching of criminal plots to murder.

He went on to explain there wasn't one of the Ten Commandments we couldn't easily be led to break if we took enough drink. As for the seven deadly sins, we'd fall into all of those head first.

'Lust!' cried Fawcett, his voice echoing around the hall.

The ladies in the audience all shivered. Every one of them had been gazing at him, rapt. No one fidgeted, not a chair scraped, no one even coughed. I thought the infant abstainers at the front might get restless, but they seemed as fascinated by him as everyone else. Beside me, Bessie's eyes shone. I began to feel uneasy.

'Go out into these streets!' cried Fawcett, flinging out a manicured hand to indicate the world outside the hall. His long dark hair flew around his head. For one wild moment I was reminded of some stained-glass image of the Archangel Michael about to spear the dragon of evil. 'You will find dens of vice, every kind of vice, my friends! You will see men brought low, workless, devoid of all self-respect, and begging in the streets! You will see women selling themselves openly! You will see wastrel young men of good family throwing away their fortunes! You will see starving mothers cradling miserable babies, waiting at the doors of public houses and calling for their husbands to come out before every penny has been spent. And what has brought them all to this? Drink!' he thundered.

The word fell into silence. We waited. After a pause, Fawcett resumed in a more moderate but no less expressive tone, sinking into pathos and rising to indignation as he recounted a dramatic tale of a drunkard in charge of a horse and cart. Befuddled and heedless, the fellow had run down a virtuous young female escorting her elderly and infirm father across the road.

Fawcett gripped his hands as if in prayer. 'Imagine the scene, dear friends, if you will. "My dearest daughter!" cried the poor old man, kneeling at her side, "speak to me!" But his child lay lifeless and could not, while the drunken carter stood by, overwhelmed by horror at his deed. But too late!'

Several ladies were by now weeping decorously into lace-trimmed handkerchiefs.

My reaction, I am afraid, was different. Of course, the story was a dreadful one and I know these tragedies do happen. My father was a doctor and was sometimes called out suddenly from his surgery to attend accidents in the street, or at places of work. Drunkenness was the cause of many of them. I have myself seen wretched women and half-naked children waiting at the doors of public houses and drinking dens, knowing that when the man of the family does stumble out it will probably be to rain blows on them. But I am ashamed to tell you that, as Mr Fawcett's ringing tones fell silent, and he put a hand to his sweating brow to brush back his disordered locks, I suddenly had a desire to giggle and was forced to look down quickly at my lap. My father would have explained the impulse as an emotional response to a speaker who made no bones about appealing to his audience's feelings. But I was sorry for it and mastered it. When I looked up again, Mr Fawcett was staring straight at me and I was certain he guessed. To my mortification, I felt myself blush.

'Those in a better station of life,' Fawcett began silkily (I swear he was still looking at me), 'need not think they are not at risk. What gentleman sees no harm in a glass or two of port wine after a good dinner? What otherwise respectable lady may take a glass of sherry?'

He shook his head sorrowfully and his long hair floated cross his face. He plucked the offending strand away. 'But before we know it, the gentleman is drinking an entire decanter of port of an evening and lying senseless most of the night. As for his wife, the bloom of virtuous womanhood soon deserts her. Her cheeks are mottled with broken veins, her dress is careless and hair pinned up anyhow. Her servants lack direction and soon begin to shirk their tasks. In no time at all, the entire household has gone to rack and ruin.'

Did Fawcett look in my direction? Had Bessie told him of Ben's innocent glass of porter or our occasional bottle of hock? My earlier unease began to turn to anger.

But the address was over. Fawcett's tone became practical. He reminded us that much work was to be done among the drink-addicted poor and begged us to give generously in order to support the many projects under his eye. Our money would not be wasted and we would be laying up treasure in heaven.

Then, mopping his brow with a crisp white handkerchief, he strode off stage, presumably to recover. Mr Pritchard invited us in a high-pitched voice to come forward and sign a pledge promising never to touch a drop of strong drink again. The document lay on the lectern. Three or four people went up to him. As they put their names down Mr Walters took his seat at the piano. We stood for a final hymn, during which Mr Pritchard, still perspiring, came round with a wooden bowl collecting offerings. By the time it reached me, it was almost full. Moved by Fawcett's eloquence and his final pleas, people had been generous. I dropped a modest shilling in it and, seeing that Bessie was about to add two pence, tapped her hand and said, 'I have put in for us both!'

Mr Pritchard gave me a reproachful look but I met his eye directly and he scuttled away. Not before, however, I had time to realise that it wasn't scented pomade that glued his fringe in place: it was lard. The melting fat trickled across his brow and made it shine as if it had been polished.

People began to gather around the tea urn. Mrs Gribble, in a flurry of shawl and flounces, sprang into action under the direction of Mrs Scott.

'You sit here, missus,' said Bessie, 'and I'll bring you a cup and a biscuit.'

'No, no,' I said serenely, 'I want to meet everyone!' I sailed forward with an apprehensive Bessie in tow.

I saw when I neared the urn that, although the notice outside promised refreshments, on the table stood another wooden bowl into which, if we were so inclined, we might drop a few extra coins for our tea. But Bessie had secured me tea already in one of the thick pottery cups. She had also attracted the attention of Mrs Scott and whispered to her. Mrs Scott approached, looking me over as she did, and making an unconcealed assessment of my station in life and the likely income of my husband.

'I understand,' she said, 'you are Bessie's employer, Mrs Ross. You are most welcome.' She inclined her head graciously.

'I have come to see for myself where Bessie goes,' I returned crisply, 'I am responsible for her.'

Mrs Scott acknowledged this with a thin smile. 'I'm pleased to see you take your responsibility so seriously, Mrs Ross. Bessie is a good girl and very helpful here in the hall. Do you feel you have gained from this evening?'

'Gained?' I asked, taken aback.

'Have you learned what you came to find out?' There was something in her tone that wasn't quite sarcastic, but just a little dry.

'I think so,' I said. 'As to Bessie being helpful, that's all well and good, but there's the matter of some pamphlets –'

But Mrs Scott was no longer listening to me. She was looking at someone behind me and a faint pink stained her pale cheeks. I felt a breath on my cheek and the scent of violet cachous wafted past my nose. I turned.

'Dear madam,' said Mr Fawcett. 'Am I to understand you are Bessie's employer?' He stretched out a hand and placed it briefly on the top of Bessie's best bonnet.

Bessie looked as though it were Christmas. Fawcett was smiling at me benignly in a way I thought ill befitted his youth . . . and he *was* young. My original guess had been about right. He wasn't more than thirty. His skin was good, his eyes large and widely spaced and his nose slightly aquiline. He had taken time to comb back his long hair. Once again I was put in mind of some archangel in a stained-glass window.

'Yes,' I said abruptly. I didn't know why, but my mind had gone quite blank. All the things I had rehearsed had fled. I made an effort. 'You are a powerful speaker, Mr Fawcett.'

He leaned forward slightly. I couldn't look away from his eyes, which were an extraordinary colour, almost aquamarine. 'It is a powerful subject, Mrs Ross, and one we should all be mindful of.'

I rallied. 'Mr Fawcett, I'll be frank with you. I came today because of the matter of some leaflets – pamphlets.'

He raised his eyebrows.

'Bessie collected them here yesterday, which made her return home very late on a foggy night and caused me and my husband some concern.' I could hear myself gabbling but I couldn't help it.

Mr Fawcett shook his head sadly and gazed at Bessie in reproach. Bessie's expression went from elation to dismay. That brought me to my senses.

'It is not her fault!' I said briskly. 'She had been persuaded it was her duty. But I have no intention of allowing her to pass round printed leaflets, no matter what their content may be.'

'Then she shall not pass them round,' said Fawcett blandly. 'You need not distribute the leaflets, Bessie, since your employer doesn't wish it. You should have obtained her permission first.'

'Yes, sir,' said Bessie miserably.

'Perhaps you can help collect the cups, Bessie,' I suggested.

Bessie sidled away, her eyes fixed on us.

'I don't blame Bessie,' I continued to Fawcett, 'I want to make that clear. I was impressed by your address, but I don't agree with playing on people's emotions and I certainly think it is inappropriate to involve children and young people.'

I heard an intake of breath from Mrs Scott, but I was not distracted and kept my eyes on Fawcett.

To my surprise, he gave me another of his benign smiles. Then he reached out and had the effrontery to take my hand. His own was long and slender with tapering manicured fingernails.

'Dear madam,' he said, leaning forward again so that I was once more aware of his almost hypnotic gaze. 'You do not believe.'

'I haven't come to discuss my faith!' I snapped, snatching away my hand.

'Indeed not. I meant that you do not believe *in what we are doing here*. I hope you will come again and be persuaded to join our cause.'

With that and another smile he gave a little bow and moved away to address a hovering admirer.

I met Mrs Scott's eyes. They were fixed on me, filled with dislike.

There was a private carriage waiting outside when we left the hall. I wondered for whom and guessed Mrs Scott.

'Ain't he something?' Bessie's question took my attention.

'He certainly is,' I replied.

'And a fine-looking gentleman, too,' went on Bessie in wistful tones.

'Yes. He will have to watch out he doesn't fall into the sin of vanity!' I said sharply.

Bessie looked startled but fell silent.

Just then came a clip-clop of hooves and rumble of wheels and the private carriage I'd seen waiting outside the hall passed by us. I had time to catch a glimpse of Mrs Scott and Mr Fawcett within.

I wondered if the lady was taking him back to his lodgings, in an act of kindness, or taking him with her to her own house, perhaps to address some smaller, more select, group there. I suspected Fawcett, with his dove-grey pantaloons, flowing locks and diamond stickpin in his cravat, might be quite an attraction in a fashionable drawing room.

Later at home I recounted everything to Ben.

'Do you intend to forbid her going to the meetings?' he asked, when he had heard me out.

I hesitated. 'I don't know. No, not at once. She would be resentful and inclined to admire him all the more. I've spoken my mind and I think they will be more careful what they ask her to do, now they know I'm watching them.'

Ben leaned back in his chair. 'Come on, Lizzie, what is it troubles you about this fellow Fawcett?'

'I think,' I said slowly, 'he has it in him to be a dangerous man.'

Ben raised his black eyebrows. 'Dangerous?'

'Oh, not in the way you usually deal with,' I went on hastily. 'I don't think he's going to attack anyone. It's just that he has such power over his audience when he speaks. Believe me, Ben, those women, and even the men there, would have done anything he asked them to. This afternoon he was asking them to abstain from strong drink. There is nothing wrong with that, I suppose, although I found his posturing on the stage rather tiresome. My father always recommended his invalids to drink a little port wine. Whisky in hot water, he once told me, is the best thing for colds in the head, better than any medicinal powders. Fawcett certainly knows how to encourage people to empty their pockets. But I suppose it is a very good cause. No, my worry is that he could make *any* crowd agree with him on almost any subject; and do anything he asked it to.'

'Let's hope he never takes up politics,' said Ben.

Chapter Three

Inspector Benjamin Ross

SERGEANT MORRIS was lurking in wait for me on Monday morning. His substantial form materialised as I set foot through the door and I guessed at once what he was about to say. Sure enough, he put a clenched fist to his moustache, cleared his throat delicately behind it and rumbled, 'Superintendent Dunn would like to see you, sir. Right away.'

'What is it?' I asked, because Morris probably knew what was going on.

'Body,' returned Morris lugubriously. 'Body of the quality sort.'

'Found where?' I had set off already for Dunn's office with Morris on my heels.

'Green Park,' he informed me.

'Quality scene of the crime!' I observed, startled.

Murder, and I supposed we were talking of that, is no joking matter. But I was right. Green Park occupies a site between the larger Hyde Park and the rather more distinguished St James's Park. More importantly, to the east lay Buckingham Palace, its grounds and gardens. I could understand Dunn's urgent summons. People don't get murdered in a royal park every day, and certainly not virtually on the doorstep of Her Majesty's residence. I quickened my own step.

Superintendent Dunn was pacing up and down, rubbing a hand over his head and scowling. He was a burly man, in appearance more like a country squire than a police officer. He always arrived in the morning with his short wiry hair brushed ruthlessly flat. But before long it stood up on end. Dunn always reminded me of one of the larger sort of terrier. He came to a stop at my entrance, wheeled round and fixed me with his slightly bloodshot gaze.

'Here's a rum do,' he said.

'Good morning, sir,' I returned.

'No, it ain't a good morning!' snapped Dunn. 'Here's a well-dressed woman's body found lying in some bushes in Green Park.'

'Where is the body now?' I asked.

'Oh, over at St Thomas's,' Dunn told me. 'Carmichael will be doing the necessary.'

Dr Carmichael regularly conducted any necessary post-mortem examinations for us. I respected him and was glad he was to do it. I was also pleased to hear the body had been taken to the hospital mortuary. During my time, I have been obliged to attend the proceedings or view corpses in a variety of improvised locations, on one occasion in a garden shed and on another in the back room of a third-rate hotel where the overpowering smell had been that of onions rising from the kitchen beneath. At the time, I had been grateful for it. It had masked the other smell of clotted blood.

Dunn sat down heavily at his desk and gestured to me to take a chair.

'The body was found very early on Sunday morning by one of the park constables, making his first round of the day,' he went on.

'He noticed broken twigs and scattered leaves in a clump of bushes and went to investigate. He thought some homeless wretch might have crawled in there to spend the night. He found the body, already stiff.'

'Cause of death?'

'Strangulation.'

If rigor were that far advanced when it was found, then the body had been there since Saturday evening, probably early evening. Carmichael would confirm the time. Saturday . . . the fog . . . strangled . . . An uneasy feeling rippled along my spine. Green Park was nearer to Westminster Bridge than Waterloo Bridge but no great distance. Had the River Wraith, on his prowls, got that far?

'There is something I should tell you, sir,' I said.

'What now? In the middle of this?' Dunn exclaimed. 'This is a serious affair, Ross! Don't keep interrupting! You can ask questions afterwards, when I've given you the facts.'

'Yes, sir, but what I have to tell you may – or may not – have some bearing on it.'

Dunn sat in silence while I told him of my encounter with Daisy Smith in the fog and her tale of the River Wraith. When I had finished he rubbed his hands furiously over his head and said soberly, 'We must keep this quiet, Ross, do you understand? At least for the time being. Only you and I and those officers involved in the investigation must know of it. The last thing we want to do is to provoke a panic on the streets of London. Once the story gets about, there will be a stream of women arriving at our door declaring they have seen, or heard, or been attacked by this "Wraith". The press will get hold of it. We won't be able to move for reporters.'

'I agree with all, sir. Can you tell me, was the body robbed?'

Dunn rubbed his chin. 'There was no purse or reticule but she wore a wedding ring and another diamond ring, and pearl and gold earrings. She wasn't robbed, that doesn't appear to have been his motive. But your River Wraith may have his own sick motives. She doesn't appear to have been a prostitute, however.'

'Certainly not, sir. Sergeant Morris described her as "a body of the quality sort". But if this was a woman walking alone in the park, her attacker may have thought her a drab. Remember the fog. She couldn't see him until he was upon her, but neither could he see her very clearly. He saw only an unaccompanied female form. We don't know why she was there but we can take it she was lost. She may have hailed him to ask directions and he assumed she was about to offer herself.'

There was a silence while Dunn thought it all over. I ventured to prompt him.

'What happened next, sir, when the body was discovered?'

Dunn roused himself. 'Oh, yes, Let's see . . . He, the park constable, felt that dead bodies went beyond the normal policing of the park. He ran out to find the first regular beat officer he could and by luck ran at once into PC Wootton, of C Division. He blew his whistle to call up help. Inspector Watkins at Little Vine Street was informed and went there directly. By that time an inspector of the Parks Police had also arrived and there was some dispute as to who was in charge.'

While the body lay on the ground? I had a mental image of them all standing round it, arguing about precedence. Would they have bothered so much about whose case it was if the body had clearly been that of a prostitute?

My mind turned back to Daisy and a thought occurred to me. 'We ought not to jump to any conclusion about her station in life, just on the grounds that she was well dressed. The better class of prostitute might venture into the park. If she were to evade the park constables any ladybird who wished to ply her trade there would have to be fashionably turned out and show no obvious sign of her calling.'

'That may be true, but there is no doubt that this unfortunate woman was as respectable as she appeared,' rumbled Dunn. 'We know who she is.'

'Already?' I exclaimed.

'Yes, a Mr Sebastian Benedict has already claimed her to be his wife; Allegra is her name. The Benedicts live outside London, in Surrey, near to Egham. On Saturday afternoon Mrs Benedict, together with a female who lives with them in the capacity of lady's companion, came up by train to London on some errand. They were caught by the fog and separated in Piccadilly. The companion searched as best she could for her employer, enlisting the help of a Mr Angelis who works for Mr Benedict at his London establishment. It's nearby to where she lost touch with her employer. When they couldn't find her, the companion made her way back to Waterloo and took the down train home to inform Mr Benedict. They waited for Mrs Benedict to also find her way home, but in vain. Only the employee, Angelis, arrived by an evening train to tell them he had not found a trace of the lady and had informed the police. He then returned to London, as there was nothing more to be done.

'So on Sunday morning early Benedict came up to town himself and went straight to Little Vine Street. As he was talking to the desk sergeant, as luck would have it Inspector Watkins walked in, having just come from the scene of the murder where he'd seen the victim for himself. The descriptions seemed to tally. So naturally they all feared the worst. Benedict was taken to see the body and immediately identified it as that of his wife. He then broke down. They had to render him assistance.'

'What do we know of him?' I asked. 'What's his line of business? He must be doing pretty well if he keeps some sort of establishment near Piccadilly.'

'Benedict shows all the signs of a very wealthy man,' was Dunn's rather dour response. 'He is a dealer in fine arts, whatever that might mean, with a shop – he calls it "a gallery" – in Piccadilly itself.'

'Then he's certainly got money,' I muttered to myself. 'And knows a lot of other wealthy men, his clients and others.'

'He probably does,' said Dunn. 'It has now been agreed that, although the crime took place within the precincts of the park, the remit of its constabulary ends at the park's gates and they can hardly investigate something so serious . . . and with such possible ramifications. C division, likewise, don't want to handle it. So the whole thing has been passed to us.'

And Dunn was passing it to me, literally, in that he was holding out a folder of papers.

'You'll find details of Benedict, his address and so forth, in there. There is also a statement of a sort from him, confirming the body is that of his wife. He was in too much of a state to say more. You'll also find the account of the park constable, who is anxious to point out that, but for the fog the previous evening, the body would have been found earlier, on Saturday evening. They check the park very thoroughly before nightfall when the gates are locked.'

'I'll speak to him again, sir, and to the others who were there, and I'll have to speak to the companion, the woman who was with Mrs Benedict until they lost touch with one another in the fog. Do we know her name?'

I was riffling through the few papers in the file as I spoke, searching, but Dunn answered.

'Yes, her name is Marchwood. Isabella Marchwood.'

'I can have Morris, I hope?' I asked.

Dunn nodded and waved a hand to dismiss me.

'Nasty business, this. How do we go about it, sir?' Morris asked as we left the building.

'I'll go over to St Thomas's and have a word with Carmichael, if he's available, and take a look at the victim. While I do that, you get yourself off to Little Vine Street and if Constable Wootton is there, go with him to the park and seek out the constable who found the body. I'll join you there.'

'Well, well, Inspector Ross, sir, what a pleasure to see you again.'

These words, hardly suitable in the circumstances, greeted me as I entered the mortuary. They were spoken by a pasty-faced, lank-haired individual wearing a rubber apron. His sleeves had been rolled up and he stood with his bare forearms hanging limply at his sides. He peered at me with eyes of such pale blue they almost seemed to have no iris.

'Good day to you, Scully,' I replied briskly, trying to hide my dislike of the man. He was Carmichael's assistant and factotum and I supposed he was indispensable. I couldn't help wishing, not for the first time, that Carmichael – for whom I had the greatest respect – would find someone else. But who would be willing to do such a grisly job as stand by while Carmichael carved up corpses?

'You'll have come to view our newest arrival,' Scully went on in his soft voice. 'Perhaps you'd care to follow me?'

'Is Dr Carmichael here?'

Scully paused on his way to a door on the further side of the room and turned his head. 'I expect him very shortly, Inspector Ross.'

'Has he . . .?'

'We haven't begun yet, sir.'

Thank goodness for that. I wanted to see Allegra Benedict while she was still in one piece.

I followed Scully into the further room. As I neared the door I was surprised to hear a hissing noise, and a pungent smell of carbolic filled my nostrils. To my great astonishment the air, when I entered, was full of falling drops of moisture. I felt I had stepped outside again into a rain shower. But this shower was certainly indoors; and originated with a contraption pumping away to spill fine droplets in an endless stream over a table on which lay the marble-white body of a young woman. The corpse's skin glistened from the drenching it was receiving and the tarry smell was even worse. I was getting wet, too, and probably I'd smell of carbolic until I got home that evening.

'What on earth is that?' I demanded, pointing at the water-dispensing monster chugging away in the corner. With my other hand I was trying to shield my face.

'I'll switch it off, sir!' called Scully, raising his voice above the hiss and growl of the infernal machine.

He turned a tap; the hissing stopped and, thank goodness, so did the deluge, reduced to a few obstinate drips.

'The machine's only just been installed,' said Scully proudly. 'It dispenses a carbolic spray as you saw, and it's reckoned to reduce the risk of infection. We're giving it a trial run.'

'Infection? That poor woman's not going to catch anything!' I said indignantly, wiping my hands over my hair.

'It protects Dr Carmichael and myself, sir, not the unfortunate deceased.'

I still couldn't quite see why an old-fashioned professional like Carmichael would want to experiment with the thing, or what benefit it could have. Fortunately Carmichael himself appeared, dapper in his black frock coat, silk top hat in hand.

He shook me warmly by the hand. 'I thought you'd be down, Inspector, or one of your colleagues, and I waited a little before examining the deceased internally.'

'Scully here,' I said, 'has been explaining your use of the carbolic spray.'

'I am willing to be persuaded as to its efficacy,' Carmichael nodded judiciously towards the silent machine. 'We must not have closed minds, Inspector. I have been reading articles by Dr Lister in *The Lancet* and elsewhere. He has used it to great success in Glasgow in his operating theatre. So I thought I would conduct a few experiments of my own here. You will, no doubt, wonder at it, since I am not conducting operations upon the living. But I'll explain my interest.

'I well remember when I was a medical student, Ross. I had a very good friend and fellow student. His name was Robert Parkinson. He was a jolly fellow, always good company and given to fooling about, as young fellows will, medical students probably more than most.

'We had attended a dissection and Robert and I between us sewed up the cadaver afterwards. I put the needle I had used away carefully but Robert, in his heedless way, stuck his in the lapel of his jacket. A little later, while engaged in some tomfoolery or other, he scraped his hand against his coat and the point caught it. It ripped a great tear across his palm and wrist. We all knew what it meant, of course, and I shall never forget the look on the unfortunate fellow's face. I remember how we all fell silent. Everything possible was done to get the wound to heal and not turn septic. But, well, when you have been sewing up a corpse amid a miasma of putrefaction . . . Blood poisoning took poor Robert off within days.'

Carmichael finished his dreadful tale with a shake of his head. With Scully's assiduous help he divested himself of the smart frock coat, which was hung in a cupboard. To replace it, Scully brought out Carmichael's 'dissecting coat' with its stains of dried blood and worse, and helped the doctor into it.

'Now, then, Inspector,' said Carmichael briskly, 'enough of wandering down memory's lane. Let us take a look at the poor young woman. Take care not to slip. The tiles are wet underfoot.'

We approached the naked body on the table. I heard my own intake of breath. She was, or had been, beautiful. Death had drained away expression, her face was blotched and eyes glazed and bloodshot, but you could still see the fine-looking woman she must have been. Her spray-dampened hair was long and thick and jet black. It was swept back and disordered around her head. Her parted lips revealed perfect teeth.

'How old?' I asked quietly.

'Her husband has informed us she is twenty-seven. You will have noticed the neck, Inspector?'

Carmichael's tone was testy. I fancy he thought I was gawping. I leaned towards the corpse and for a second time, heard my own sharply drawn breath.

This was not a manual strangulation, a throttling. This was true strangulation using a ligature. No wonder Dunn had sounded so certain about the cause of death. Round the woman's neck, cutting cruelly into the white flesh, was a thin cord.

'How is it secured?' I asked quietly.

'Knotted at the back of the neck.'

'Can you remove it without damaging the knot?'

'Scully!' ordered Carmichael briskly. 'The scissors, if you please!'

Scully came up with the scissors and Carmichael carefully snipped the cord. Scully raised the dead woman's head awkwardly. A trace of rigor was still present. Carmichael drew the cord free, revealing a scarlet imprint on the neck where it had been, and handed it to me. I found myself holding a length of fine cord of the sort used to pull window blinds. For that purpose it usually has a tassel or wooden toggle on the end. This just had a knot in the middle.

'It's a double knot,' I said with a frown.

'It suggests to me,' Carmichael offered, 'that he meant there to be no chance she would survive. I would guess he tied it once to form a loose loop, slipped it over her head, pulled it tight and, when she collapsed, tied it again before abandoning his victim. He may have heard tales of strangled victims coming back to life.'

That certainly had occurred before. On rare occasions it had even been known for a body hanged on the gallows to be revived. That was in days gone by, of course. Now we are much more scientific in matters of execution.

'In due course,' Carmichael went on, 'I shall expect to find the hyoid bone fractured, possibly the larynx. There should be some internal bruising. If so, it will confirm my first diagnosis.'

'He went out intending and equipped to kill,' I murmured, more to myself than to Carmichael.

Yet Daisy said the Wraith had *his hands* on her throat. There had been no mention in all her tale of a cord. But Daisy had escaped him. Perhaps the Wraith didn't mean to give the next woman the chance. He had the cord ready this time.

'He came across that woman alone, lost, and wandering in the fog, frightened. Did he offer to help, guide her, lure her in that way into the park?' I mused aloud.

'My skills lie in the medical examinations of cadavers, Inspector, I leave the detection of crimes to you,' was all Carmichael replied.

'Then can you tell me how long you think she has been dead? When she died?' This was important. A park is a public place. The fog would have emptied it in late afternoon, of course.

He pursed his lips. 'That is not an exact business, Inspector Ross, as you will know. I'm informed she was found early on Sunday morning. I would say she died in the late afternoon or early evening of Saturday. Let us say, between four and six o'clock.'

That certainly put the time of death within the period of the fog.

'There is just one more thing I need to ask you, Doctor,' I said. 'Were you present when Mr Benedict saw the body?'

'No,' replied Carmichael, his attention now turned to a tray of instruments. 'But Scully was.'

So I had to talk to Scully again and retreated to the outer room to find him.

'Oh, yes, Inspector Ross, sir, I remember Mr Benedict very well. I conducted the gentleman to the body.' Scully smiled unpleasantly and rubbed his hands together.

I felt my nerves twitch. There is an expression 'to make the skin crawl' and that was exactly the effect Scully had on me. How could Carmichael work almost daily with the wretch? But Carmichael would be absorbed in his dissections.

'I hope,' I couldn't help saying, 'you didn't have that wretched spray going when you took him in.'

'No, sir, I had laid out the lady nicely, covered with a sheet except for the face. I didn't want to distress him more than necessary.' Scully had replaced his ghoulish grimace with an expression of suitable gravity.

'Distress him more . . .? Good heavens, man, you were showing him the body of his wife!' I exclaimed.

'Oh, yes, indeed, but I wanted him to see we were treating it with respect.' Scully's tone became reproachful. I had questioned his professional competence.

'All right, yes, of course, but he was very distressed, anyway, wasn't he? I understand he collapsed.'

'He fainted away,' said Scully with a shrug. 'Straight out, went down like a skittle, flat out on the floor. I brought him round with some smelling salts. I keep a little bottle ready. Relatives have been known to pass out, but usually it's the ladies. I bring 'em round and say a few words to console them.' He gave me a coy smile.

I struggled again to conceal just how repulsive I found this fellow. 'How was the gentleman when he came round?'

'Confused, well, he would be, finding himself sitting on the floor. They always are. Like most of them he asked what had happened, and I told him he'd passed out.'

'Did he say anything else?'

Scully screwed up his unlovely features and gave his answer some thought. 'He mumbled a bit,' he went on at last, 'but he was still very confused. I couldn't make head nor tail of it.'

'All right, so it didn't make much sense, but tell me anyway, exactly if you can, what he said!' I urged.

'He said that death had galloped past the old again and was chasing the young. He said that they wanted to shut the gates but it would do no good.'

'Gates, what gates? The park gates?'

'I don't know about that,' Scully retorted defensively. 'I'm just telling you what he said to me. I warned you it didn't make any sense. That's not my fault,' he added, aggrieved.

I apologised. 'You've been very helpful, Scully. It is very important for the investigation that we know the first reactions of the bereaved spouse.'

'Think he done it?' asked Scully with a gleam of interest in his normally lacklustre gaze. 'Think the husband croaked her? What would he do it in the middle of a park for? He could strangle her at home.'

'I'm not suggesting he did it,' I snapped.

'Oh,' said Scully, clearly disappointed.

'Are those her clothes?' I asked.

'Yes, Mr Ross.' Scully led me to a table on which the dead woman's garments lay in a neat row.

'Bit torn,' offered Scully, picking up the skirt. 'Here, see?' He pointed to an area halfway between waist and hem.

The skirt was of a brown woollen cloth and it was certainly torn. I spread the length out flat and it revealed a jagged hole about three inches long and a little over an inch across.

'Tell you anything?' asked Scully, his pale eyes fixed on my face.

'It may do,' I replied. 'If I can find the missing piece. Where is the jewellery?'

I was handed a battered card box. I opened it and saw the items Dunn had listed lying in a forlorn little heap.

'I'll take these with me; wait, I'll sign a receipt for you.' I scribbled out that I had taken charge of two rings, one yellow metal, one silver metal with a white stone, and one pair of yellow metal and pearly earrings. It is as well to be prudent in describing such items. Paste jewels and rolled gold can be very convincing to a layman's eye. Besides, I did not want Benedict claiming we had substituted valuable jewels with lesser ones. 'Thank you, Scully.'

He recognised dismissal, and tucked the receipt into his waistcoat pocket.

'Oh, well, if I've helped you all I can, Inspector, I'd better get along and help Dr Carmichael now, hadn't I?'

As arranged, I went next to the Green Park where I found Morris waiting for me with PC Wootton, and the discoverer of the body, Park Constable William Hopkins. We also had with us an inspector of the Park Police whose name was Pickles. It was a pity he had that surname as he had a remarkably sour expression and looked very much as if he might suffer from indigestion. Even his wispy moustache drooped in a dispirited way. In contrast, there was a look of the retired military man about Park Constable Hopkins. He stood very straight, as if on parade, and his luxurious waxed moustache put Inspector Pickles's meagre growth of upper-lip hair to shame.

The Green Park is an area of open lawns, avenues of trees and broad walks. A little over a hundred years before, when still quite a rural spot, it had been notorious for footpads and even highwaymen. But now it was a quiet retreat, a place of leisure, with its own constables to keep it in order, and not a place to expect murder. The more I looked around me, the more extraordinary it seemed. How on earth had Allegra Benedict come to be here? I could understand her walking in the park in sunshine. I couldn't explain satisfactorily what could have lured her into it on such a bad evening. The obvious explanation was, of course, that she was lost. After all, it was adjacent to Piccadilly. But still . . .

We had gathered at the place where Hopkins had made his gruesome discovery. It lay on the far edge of the park and its appearance was a little less orderly than that of the main area.

There were some bushes growing here. Nearby a huge old oak tree spread its venerable branches over us. Morris was staring up into its tangle of limbs.

'Very fine tree, this,' he observed.

'That tree,' Constable Hopkins informed him proudly, 'was planted here in King Charles the Second's day. He took a great interest in the park, did King Charles. He would come here, with his lords and ladies in attendance, and walk around, talking to the common people. That was after his Restoration to the throne, of course. Long before that, in the time of the Civil War, gentlemen, when the king was fleeing his enemies, he hid in an oak tree. The Roundhead soldiers hunting him searched all round but never looked up. Very likely, the king was very fond of oak trees after that and may have ordered that one be planted to commemorate his blessed escape.'

I had heard the story that the fugitive young king had escaped detection by hiding in an oak tree. But I had never heard that he went around for the rest of his life ordering the planting of oak trees in memory. I suspected Hopkins told this story to impressionable visitors to the park; they probably thanked him for the information and pressed shilling coins into his hand.

'All right, Hopkins!' ordered Inspector Pickles, annoyed at his underling's garrulity.

However, Morris and I looked properly impressed and turned our attention to the disturbed bushes. A rope cordon had been set up and an improvised wooden notice hammered into the turf, reading, 'Keep Off'.

I told Inspector Pickles I was pleased to see the scene so well secured.

Pickles looked, if anything, even more out of sorts. 'We did everything necessary. I had a couple of fellows get over here straight away and make sure the public knew to stay clear.'

'Yessir, absolutely, sir!' the park constable supported him.

His importance as finder of the body had given Hopkins the urge to communicate with us, risking Inspector Pickles's displeasure, and he chose, unwisely, to elaborate on his superior's words.

'Once the news gets round – and get round it will, you mark my words – that a body has been found in them very bushes, well, half the world and his wife will be trampling over the place, keen to see the very spot. They'll do even more damage to the grass,' he went on wrathfully, 'probably go carving their names on that very oak tree that was a sapling in good King Charles's day, because they've got no respect. We had to cordon it off and put that notice there. Not that it will do much good,' he concluded in a resigned voice.

'*All right*, Hopkins!' said Pickles testily.

I thanked them both again, although it wasn't clear whether their priority had been to preserve the scene of the crime, or protect the damaged greenery. I didn't doubt Hopkins was correct about the visitors who would come to the spot, and wondered briefly at the public's morbid interest. But Hopkins was only saying much what Dunn had said earlier. The press would seize on this story avidly.

I stepped over the rope, watched mistrustfully by Pickles, and examined the ground and the bushes. The broken twigs and branches were fairly obvious and I wasn't surprised Hopkins had spotted them on his round.

'Could you see anything of the dead woman or her clothing from here on the path?' I asked. 'Or did you just notice the damage?'

Hopkins shook his head. 'Not at first, sir. I saw that someone had gone trampling through. Then noticed that there was a scrap of brown cloth, caught on the bushes.'

'Where?' I asked, peering in eagerly.

'I got it here, sir,' said Hopkins producing it. 'I can show you just where I found it.'

I took the scrap of cloth from him and had little doubt it had come from Mrs Benedict's gown and would fit into the damaged area I'd seen at the mortuary. I did wish Hopkins had left it undisturbed, but at least he had kept it.

'No bag, reticule or purse?' I asked.

'No, sir, I looked very carefully. But the villain will have made off with that.'

'Assaults upon the public are as good as unheard of in the park!' snapped Pickles with a glare. 'This is quite out of the ordinary, absolutely!'

'Quite, Inspector. Go on, Hopkins,' I invited.

Hopkins squared his shoulders, took a deep breath, and resumed his tale.

'He'd made a sort of path so I followed it. I hoped he'd still be there, lying drunk perhaps, and I could collar him!'

Hopkins's waxed moustache quivered and his eyes gleamed at the thought of what he might have done to the miscreant if only he'd been able to lay hands on him.

'Unfortunately, sir, he wasn't. But she was, lying there, right in the middle and as dead as a doornail. Inspector Pickles not being immediately available, sir, I ran out and found PC Wootton.'

Wootton cleared his throat and intoned, 'That's right, sir.'

'I was in my office at Marble Arch at the time,' Pickles interrupted. 'I came as soon as a message was brought to me.'

'And Inspector Watkins came down, sir, from Little Vine Street,' added the C Division man.

No wonder there had been some confusion, with two senior officers arriving at the scene at about the same time.

I turned my attention back to the forced entry into the bushes, obviously recently made by the murderer, dragging his victim's lifeless body under cover.

A thought occurred to me and I turned to the others. 'Has any search been made of the surrounding area, to see if there is damage to any other plants or trees, or if the grass is scored by boot marks? Any small articles dropped on the ground? I understand there was no purse, but either victim or assailant might have dropped something and if he was waiting here, the murderer might have enjoyed a cigarette and even something as small as a spent match might place him further away from this spot.'

There might have been a struggle, I was thinking. He could have waylaid her and killed her a little way off and then dragged her here.

Pickles scowled at me. 'There most certainly has. Hopkins and another constable conducted it under my personal direction. You can be confident we were thorough!'

'Yes, sir,' confirmed Hopkins. 'Constable Jasper Billings and I, we looked all around, as directed by Inspector Pickles. We were afraid we'd find more damage, but thankfully, whoever he was, he only lumbered about in there . . .' Hopkins indicated the path beaten into the shrubbery. 'Not caring what a mess he made!'

Hopkins's priorities were clearly divided. I thought I understood. He and his colleagues were expected to keep the park free of unsuitable visitors, unseemly behaviour, and damage to grass and trees. They would be held to account for the damage to the vegetation and any future inconvenience in the running of the park. As for crime, they would normally keep a sharp eye open for the many pickpockets who would see the park's strollers as easy prey. But murder? Oh, dear, no. That was *not* to be expected. Not in a royal park. There would be questions from on high, demanding an explanation as to how a killer could operate in the park and hide the body of his victim, not to be found until the next day. The authorities might accept the explanation of fog, or they might seek to blame the Park Police.

However, the Park Police had done all the right things and rendered our investigation sterling service. I was satisfied the body hadn't been dragged or carried here from elsewhere in the park. Allegra Benedict had died here, or very nearby.

I made a little speech to that effect, thanked Pickles, Hopkins and Wootton for the last time and told them we need take up no more of their time. I shook Pickles by the hand.

Unmollified, Pickles sniffed and walked off immediately, an air of pique about him.

'The villain what did this ought to be made to pay for it!' growled Hopkins, lingering to survey the damaged bushes one more time.

'He will pay for his crime, never fear,' I assured him.

'It'll cost money to replant that, you know!' said Hopkins.

'What do we do now, sir?' asked Morris.

'We go back to the Yard and explain that we must travel out of London to pursue our enquiries at Egham. There must be several trains a day.'

Morris looked glum. 'The Yard will allow it as expenses, I hope, sir. You'll be aware, sir, that a sergeant's daily expenses don't run to much.'

'That's why I'm getting Superintendent Dunn's agreement beforehand. I'll also ask him to telegraph the local police in Surrey and clear our activities in their area with them. At Egham I shall interview Miss Isabella Marchwood and Mr Sebastian Benedict. You, Morris, will make your way round to the kitchen and beg a cup of tea of Cook. Make yourself comfortable and get her gossiping. There is a special relationship between the lady of the house and her cook. Find out Cook's opinion of the state of the marriage. It shouldn't be difficult.'

Chapter Four

Inspector Benjamin Ross

MORRIS AND I had no difficulty in obtaining directions to The Cedars, as the Benedict house was named. The stationmaster at Egham knew the name and the owners and was only too pleased to direct us; but explained the house was not in the town.

'It's right up the top of the hill, just before the village of Englefield Green. A steep climb that will take you the better part of half an hour, gentlemen. You had best find some conveyance.'

'Where from?' growled Morris.

'Billy Cooper will be outside with his trap,' said the stationmaster, 'if you move quickly, that is. He's always in demand.'

We were in luck. Waiting outside the station we found a pony and trap awaiting business in the yard. We hailed its driver seconds ahead of a stout gentleman with a large portmanteau. The stout gentleman made his displeasure clear, but I assured him that we were on official business, and Mr Cooper promised he would be back within twenty minutes.

If the stationmaster were right and the climb a steep one, I thought that an optimistic forecast, even given a pony and trap. It didn't console the stout gentleman, who was still shouting after us as we rolled out of the station yard.

'Outrageous! I shall write to my member of parliament, sir! The police are supposed to be the servants of the public. They are not supposed to use their authority to commandeer all available hackney carriages!'

I didn't doubt he would write to his MP, but I was happy enough that a murder inquiry took precedence over a portmanteau.

We clattered briskly through the small neat town and out into countryside where a signpost indicated we were on the road to Englefield Green. The surroundings were green and leafy and Morris observed that it must be a very nice place to live. The stationmaster was certainly correct in the steepness of the climb and it was lucky The Cedars was only about halfway up. I doubted the pony could have hauled us the entire way and we should have been obliged to get out and walk. But as it was, the driver set us down at the gates. We stood there, Morris and I, as the trap rolled away back down the hill to collect the stout gentleman (if he were still waiting). We surveyed the scene before us.

The house was a large one built, I guessed, around 1800. Its exterior was rendered in white stucco, giving it a slightly Italianate look. Manicured lawns surrounded it and there were indeed a pair of beautiful cedar trees, one on either side of the building.

'Very nice,' said Morris, even more convinced that we found ourselves in a most desirable part of the country.

We crunched across the gravel and saw, as we approached the front door, that this was a household in deepest mourning. All the curtains were drawn and a large bow of black silk ribbon adorned the doorknocker. Visiting the bereaved is always the worst part of the job. It is bad enough to lose a loved one, but to know that person has died as a result of a violent crime for which there is no apparent explanation, that seems almost random in its horror, must be the worst of all. Benedict would be in shock and grappling with his grief and here was I, come to quiz him about his wife and his marriage. I had to set aside my qualms, however. I was, as I had told the stout gentleman, on official business.

'Off you go to find Cook, Morris!'

'Yessir!' said Morris, making for the back of the building.

I raised my hand to the black silk bow and tapped briskly.

After a few moments I heard a rattle from the other side of the door and it was opened by a red-eyed parlourmaid.

'The master is not receiving, sir,' she said, before I could speak.

I nodded sympathetically but said, 'I'm sorry, but I must speak to him. You see I am Inspector Ross from Scotland Yard and it is my sad duty to discover the truth of what happened to your mistress.'

I could hardly say, 'who killed her', but that was what I meant and the girl knew it.

She burst into tears and dabbed them away with the corner of her starched pinafore. 'Oh, sir, it's such a dreadful thing! I'm sure none of us will ever get over it! Mrs Benedict was a lovely lady. All the staff loved her, me and Cook and Milly –'

'Milly?' I asked.

'The housemaid, sir.'

'That is all the staff? A cook and two maids?'

'Oh no, sir, there is Mr Benedict's valet and madam's personal maid, Henderson. Then there's the boot boy, of course, and the skivvy.'

'What about outdoor staff?' The gardens had appeared well tended.

'There's the gardener and his boy, and the groom . . . Oh, sir, you may ask *any* of them, they will all tell you they can't believe what's happened.'

'Who is this, Parker?' a woman's voice asked sharply from within the hall. 'What are you doing, standing there and gossiping?'

Parker turned bright red. 'Beg pardon, Miss Marchwood, but it's a police inspector, all the way from London, Scotland Yard, wanting to speak to the master.'

'Mr Benedict is not receiving visitors,' said the woman, whose form was still indistinct behind the girl, in the recesses of the dimly lit hall.

'I told the gentleman—' Parker began.

It was time for me to take control.

'I am sorry to intrude at this very difficult time for the whole household, Miss Marchwood, but I am afraid I must insist. This is a murder inquiry.'

'Ow – ow – ow . . .' wailed Parker and abandoned us, fleeing into the house.

I was left face to face with Miss Marchwood and looked at her with some interest. This was the companion, then, who had travelled up to London with Allegra Benedict on a shopping expedition, and returned alone.

She was a woman in her early forties, plain to the point of ugliness, wearing a black silk dress in mourning for her late employer and a black lace veil, like a Spanish mantilla, over her mousy brown hair. She wore no jewellery but a string of jet mourning beads. The only touch of colour in her whole appearance was the gold-rimmed pince-nez clipped to the bridge of her large nose. Behind the lenses of the pince-nez, muddy brown eyes peered at me. So we studied one another and eventually Miss Marchwood spoke in the same clipped voice.

'Then you had better come in. Mr Benedict is in his study. I will tell him you are here. But I should advise you that he is in a very bad state. If you could make your visit brief, it would be appreciated. Or perhaps you could come back another day?'

If Miss Marchwood thought Scotland Yard's policy on an inspector's daily expenses would allow me repeatedly to ride up and down the railway to Egham, in order to visit The Cedars, she was mistaken.

'I understand and will be tactful,' I said (not that the circumstances allowed for much tact), 'but it's important to get our investigation underway as speedily as possible. I should also like to speak to you, Miss Marchwood. I know you were companion to Mrs Benedict and were with her last Saturday.'

Behind the pince-nez her eyes blinked rapidly. But Miss Marchwood was not the sort to burst into tears. That kind of unseemly behaviour was left to the parlourmaid, Parker. Miss Marchwood, like all companions, had had plenty of opportunity to learn to control her feelings. My wife, Lizzie, although she had been companion to her Aunt Parry before our marriage, would never have turned into a Miss Marchwood. Lizzie has great difficulty in concealing her feelings and opinions.

As for Isabella Marchwood, with the death of Allegra Benedict she must now be out of a job. She would have to seek a new post and I wondered if Benedict would be willing to allow her to remain in the house until she found one. It must be painful for him even to see her and know that if only she had stayed with her employer, and not been parted from her by the fog . . . Did he blame Miss Marchwood for what had happened?

'I was,' the companion said briefly, in reply to my question. 'Will you speak to me first or to Mr Benedict?'

'I should perhaps see the owner of the house – and the bereaved husband – first.'

'Then please wait here one moment.'

With a swish of silk skirts she turned and began to climb the staircase. Mr Benedict's study was on the first floor, then, well away from disturbance from callers and household coming and goings.

I waited below, taking the opportunity to have a good look round. Everywhere I saw more signs of mourning. All pictures on the walls were veiled, as was a large mirror. I made bold to open a door and peer into what was obviously a drawing room. Again, windows curtained, pictures and mirrors veiled . . . even the legs of a grand piano had been decorously girded about with black silk skirts. No wonder the place was so dark.

But then I spotted a picture that wasn't covered and went to investigate. It stood on the piano and was a photographic study of the deceased woman. In it she was dressed in white and appeared to be very young. She was posed against a classical pillar and some draperies and I was struck again by how beautiful she must have been in life. Before this photograph had been placed a single rose in a ruby-red glass vase. I picked up the heavy silver frame to look more closely and saw, stamped in gold across one corner of the picture, the words 'Studio Podestà' and beneath them 'Venezia'.

'Inspector?'

Miss Marchwood was back and stood by the door, watching me with undisguised disapproval. Well, policemen snooped. It's what we're good at. Nobody in the house would like it but they would have to get used to it.

'Mr Benedict will see you. I'll take you up to him.'

Benedict rose from a leather wing chair to greet me as I entered. The room, like the rest of the house, had been plunged into mourning but the window drapes had been pulled back sufficiently to admit a thin beam of light, bisecting it. As elsewhere, mirrors and windows had been veiled. But there was a single exception and it echoed that below. Above the mantelpiece hung a large oil portrait of Allegra, seated in some sort of garden. In it, as in the photograph on the grand piano downstairs, she looked very young. The background was of blue skies, bright sunshine and what appeared to be a trailing vine across a pergola. In this picture too she wore a white dress and nestling in her lap, higgledy-piggledy, were assorted flowers. The intention, I supposed, was to suggest the sitter had been gathering them.

'My wife was a great beauty,' Benedict said quietly.

I was embarrassed enough to show it. 'I'm very sorry. I didn't mean to ignore you or to stare so openly at the portrait. Mrs Benedict was, as you say, a very fine-looking lady . . . and all the other paintings in the house are covered.'

'I could not order that one veiled,' said Benedict in the same quiet voice, 'it would be like burying her. I shall be doing that soon enough. Won't you sit down, Inspector?'

He gestured towards a chair and sat down again himself in the winged chair from which he'd risen when I'd entered. His back was to the window and the shaft of light so that I couldn't see him clearly. What little light there was fell on me, so that he had the advantage. I wondered if that had been intended. He seemed a slightly built figure, certainly some years older than his wife. As my eyes adjusted to the dim light, I saw that his hair was thinning. When he had stood up, I had noticed that he was of only medium height. I thought of the woman I had seen, still a beauty though disfigured by a dreadful death.

I opened my side of the conversation by extending my condolences. He received these in a lacklustre way. He did not care whether I sympathised with him or not. His own grief was sufficient.

'Mrs Benedict was an Italian lady?' I ventured next.

He inclined his head. 'Yes. If you find there are a large number of paintings in this house, it is because I specialise in fine arts, Inspector, as you may already know. I have a gallery in Piccadilly, on the south side, near . . .' He broke off, paused, and recommenced, 'Near to the Piccadilly limits of the Green Park.'

'Were you at your gallery on Saturday last?'

He shook his head. 'No, I never go up to town at weekends. Most of my clients, you see, go down into the country on Friday night.'

'To their country houses and estates?'

'Yes,' he said simply.

'But the gallery is open on Saturdays?'

'Yes, I have an excellent manager, George Angelis. He is there on a Saturday until six o'clock. The gallery is then closed until the following Tuesday.'

It did no business on a Monday, then. But, of course, the clients were returning to town from the country on Mondays. I took my notebook from my coat pocket and wrote in it that the gallery closed at six on Saturdays.

'May I ask how you met your late wife, sir?'

He raised his eyebrows at what he obviously found an unexpected question. But he replied easily enough, 'Of course. We met in Italy. I visit the Continent every year, looking for items of interest for the gallery. I also have a great love of the country. I first went there as a very young man, not much more than a boy. I was making the usual European tour, you know.'

I knew this was a habit among the wealthy. Young men would be sent off to finish their education, probably with some tutor in tow to keep an eye on them. Young men of my background, however, were busy earning a living at a similar age, and had been doing so from childhood.

'My wife's father, sadly now deceased, was also in the fine arts business,' Benedict was saying. 'I called on him regularly when in Italy and became a friend of the family. When I first met my wife she was no more than a child, a girl of fourteen. She was exquisite . . . lovely and vivacious, full of life and laughter, intelligent . . . to know her was to adore her.'

He looked towards the portrait and fell silent.

'Was that her age when it was painted?' I prompted.

Benedict turned his head and looked at me as though he had forgotten who I was. 'Oh,' he said at last. 'No, she was a little older when she sat for that. Fifteen, I think.'

'And, forgive me, sir, but I have to ask intrusive questions: how old was the lady when you married?'

'Eighteen.' Benedict gave me an ironic smile. 'I see how your mind is working, Inspector. Yes, I am – was – somewhat older than my wife. Fifteen years older, in fact.'

So when the portrait of fifteen-year-old Allegra had been painted, her future husband had already been a man of thirty. Had the portrait been commissioned at his request?

'When, may I ask, did you acquire the painting?'

He raised his eyebrows again and this time replied with a touch of impatience. 'It was painted for me. I had already spoken to her father. He agreed to our marriage, once his daughter should reach the age of eighteen. Until then, I should have to console myself with the possession of a portrait in oils in place of the sitter.'

Had fifteen-year-old Allegra been as enthusiastic, I wondered, at the prospect of a husband so much older? I was beginning to feel a little dissatisfied by some of the words Benedict used.

'Adore' not 'love', for example. You might say they meant the same thing, but there again, in human terms, they might not. 'Possession' of the portrait, instead of the living girl . . . that also niggled at me.

'May I ask a question in my turn, Inspector?' Benedict's voice broke into my musings. I realised with a shock that I had been silent for two or three minutes.

'Certainly, sir.'

'What has all this to do with finding the fiend who killed my wife?'

'Probably nothing, sir, but we have to know the background of the victim.'

'Then now you know it,' he said simply.

'You have no children?' I got in one last personal question.

'No,' he said coldly. It was an intrusion too far. 'I am finding this very difficult, Inspector; perhaps you could come again? Or I would be happy to come to Scotland Yard and we can discuss all this further. I really feel . . . my doctor has given me some powders, to calm my nerves. I am in need of a draught now.'

That led neatly to my last enquiry. 'I understand, sir. I was told that you collapsed after identifying the body.'

His face twisted in pain at the memory. He nodded.

'The assistant, Scully, who conducted you to see your wife, said that, when you were recovered enough to speak, you spoke of some "gates". I understood that you said words to the effect, "They want to close the gates but it won't help." I may not be accurate, or Scully may not have told me accurately.'

'Oh, he was correct enough,' said Benedict brusquely. 'You want to know what I meant? Let me show you!'

He got up and went to a table on which was stacked a pile of leather folders. When he came back he was carrying one which I saw was a sketch album. Benedict opened it and found what he sought. He turned the open pages towards me, so that I could see the picture.

It was a watercolour, signed S. B. I supposed it must be a copy of something he had seen, perhaps on his original Italian tour, perhaps later. The scene was mediaeval in style and quite terrifying. It showed a landscape. Across it raced a ghastly figure on a spectral horse in pursuit of a fleeing group of young men, also on horseback. The figure, which could only be Death, had galloped past a very elderly couple, ignoring them. The crone of a wife was pointing at him in amazement, unable to believe she and her aged husband had not been his chosen victims. But Death had other prey. He wanted the youngsters. The young men were finely dressed. They had golden curls. Their companions at the rear of their party had already fallen victim and were slung lifeless across their saddles, carried onward uselessly by their panicking steeds. The young men at the front of the group looked back in horror and desperation. Their intention was clearly to squeeze through the open gates of a walled city, as if, once inside, they could close them against the pursuing apocalyptic figure and escape. But they were doomed, and knew it. It was written on their faces. Even their horses knew it, eyes rolling and nostrils flared. They had reached the gates, but the earthly refuge would save none of them. Youth, beauty, wealth . . . nothing would cheat the pursuer.

'I copied that,' Benedict said, 'from a wall painting in a chapel of the Dominican church in Bozen, as the Austrians call it, in the South Tyrol. The Italian name of the city is Bolzano. The mural is generally called "The Triumph of Death". Death takes pleasure in seizing the young and fair, you see. He ought to take the old, but he . . .'

Benedict closed the book.

'So he took my wife, Inspector. I am fifteen years older than she, but he took my wife first. No one can stop him. No gates can shut him out.'

'Your wife didn't die in the ordinary way of things . . .' I said awkwardly.

'Death is death,' he replied. 'We can none of us escape it and to rail against it is useless. But to destroy so wantonly, so needlessly, something, someone, so beautiful, that can never be forgiven.'

I uttered a few more words expressing my regrets, both for his loss and for my intrusion. I doubt if he heard them.

Miss Marchwood was awaiting me in the hall below. When I reached the bottom of the staircase she turned silently and led the way into the drawing room with the grand piano. I shut the door behind us and went to the nearer window to draw back the curtains. I like to see a witness's face and Benedict had already outmanoeuvred me in that. I saw in hers that she disapproved of my action, but probably understood. Still in silence, we sat down facing one another. The ticking of a porcelain clock on the mantelshelf sounded far too loud.

I realised that she was waiting for me to begin our conversation and, to break the ice, I observed, 'That is a pretty clock.'

'It is from the Meissen factory,' she said. 'Mr Benedict acquired it on his travels.'

As, indeed, he had acquired Mrs Benedict, another beautiful possession.

How long, I asked Miss Marchwood, had she been the lady's companion?

'Since Mr Benedict brought his wife to England from Italy, almost nine years.' Behind the pince-nez lenses her eyes blinked rapidly. She would not shed tears in front of me.

'Then you and Mrs Benedict must have grown very close. This has been a very bad experience for you,' I sympathised.

She inclined her head but said nothing. I had a feeling that getting information from Isabella Marchwood would be like drawing teeth. Because of loyalty to the dead woman? Or from a misplaced sense of propriety, a feeling that my very presence here sullied the house? I was supposed to be making my sordid enquiries far from this middle-class drawing room with its polished grand piano, silver-framed photographs and Meissen clock, was that it?

'Before this tragic event, Miss Marchwood, were you happy here?' I asked.

'I have been very happy here!' she snapped. Then she clasped her hands tightly in her lap and pressed her lips together.

'Very well, then, tell me about last Saturday.'

I thought I might meet with more reticence but she began to speak quite fast. I wondered if she had rehearsed this, anticipating my visit. But I couldn't help noticing that, as she spoke, her clasped fingers tightened, relaxed, and tightened again repeatedly.

'Mrs Benedict wished to take a piece of jewellery, a brooch, to a jeweller's shop in the Burlington Arcade. She knew the jeweller well. Tedeschi is his name. He is Italian by origin, I fancy, and so Mrs Benedict liked to visit his establishment. She – and Mr Benedict – had bought various items from Mr Tedeschi in the past.'

'Why did she take the brooch there? Was something wrong with it?'

'No, only that she didn't much care for it and so didn't wear it. She wanted to know whether it could be made into a ring, using the gold and the stones. She was told that it could be. We – she – left the brooch there.'

'You had no notion, when you left home, that the weather in London would turn so unpleasant?'

Miss Marchwood took off her pince-nez and pressed the bridge of her nose where a faint red mark showed it had rested. 'No, although the weather was overcast here. Of course, it's not unknown for the London fog, when at its worst, to reach out as far as this. But there was nothing to indicate we shouldn't make the journey.'

She replaced the pince-nez and continued more briskly. 'We went up after lunch on the two-thirty train. As we drew near to London we realised that a thick fog, yellow with smoke, was gathering. It had already reached the outskirts of the city. By the time we got to Waterloo, it was very unpleasant. We stepped down from the train to find it swirling round us. It smelled disgusting. I suggested to Mrs Benedict that we turn back. We had only to walk to the down platform and take the first return train. But she said it wouldn't take us very long, if we could get a hackney carriage, to take the brooch to the Arcade. So that is what we did.'

'You had no difficulty finding a cab?'

'At the station? No. We took a growler,' she added, 'not a hansom cab.'

I nodded my understanding. A growler was a closed vehicle, more suitable for ladies. For a pair of ladies to travel across London in an open-fronted hansom cab would have appeared improper.

'But it still took us a long time to reach Piccadilly, as the cabman could only drive very slowly. He had to stop frequently. The traffic had become quite entangled. Some of the other cab drivers and coachmen almost came to blows. Pedestrians could not be seen until the very last minute and several were nearly run down by vehicles. Both Mrs Benedict and I were quite frightened.

But at last we got there, to Piccadilly. We were both very pleased, I can tell you, to descend from the cab outside the entrance to the Burlington Arcade.'

'I am sure you both were. I was out in the fog myself,' I told her. 'I know how difficult progress was. There could not have been many visitors to the Arcade.'

'There were some, apart from ourselves, but no one was dawdling. All were concerned about how they should get home, I imagine. I was beginning to be very worried, too. We visited the jeweller's and spent some time there, discussing the design of the ring that was to be made. We looked at one or two other items he had on display. When we came out of the Arcade we were horrified, truly, horrified.' She leaned forward to emphasise her words. 'It was so thick! We were both alarmed and asked a beadle to hail us a cab.'

The Arcade was, I knew, guarded by its own uniformed beadles.

'But he was unable to do so. There were no cabs to be had by that time, and almost impossible to see if there were any about, even! We discussed what we should do.'

'What time was this?' I interrupted her to ask.

'It was well after four. It must have been nearly five. I cannot tell you more exactly. We decided we would cross the road and walk the very short distance to the gallery. We could wait there in comfort and hope the fog lifted.'

'Ah, of course, The Arcade's main entrance is on Piccadilly and Mr Benedict has his shop in that street.'

A tide of red flooded her features. 'Gallery, Inspector! Mr Benedict is not a shopkeeper!'

'My error, please go on,' I apologised.

'We were more than a little afraid of being run down, while

crossing the road, by some vehicle that hadn't seen us. As we talked, discussing what we should do, a boy suddenly appeared, just materialised out of the fog. He startled me.'

'A boy?' I asked, startled. 'What sort of boy?'

'A street urchin, a crossing sweeper. He held his broom in his hand so I knew what he was. He'd heard our voices and what we said. He offered to take us safely across. He assured us he would know if anything approached. We agreed. He did guide us safely across. Then . . .'

For the first time Isabella Marchwood faltered in her account. 'We were on the pavement on the south side of Piccadilly and I told the boy to wait, I would give him something for his trouble. I searched in my purse for a sixpence and found one. I paid the boy and he vanished, just melted back into the fog. I turned to speak to Mrs Benedict and she was no longer there.'

She fell silent and, when she showed no sign of resuming, I prompted her, 'You called her name?'

'Repeatedly!' She leaned forward again. 'I thought she had walked on ahead of me to the gallery.'

'The gallery closes at six, I understand, on Saturday.'

'Yes, but I didn't think it was anything like so late. So I hurried on, as best I could, keeping to the wall, until I reached the gallery. It wasn't easy even then to make sure I was at the right place. I went in and found the assistant. He is relatively new there but he recognised me. He was surprised to see me come through the door on such an afternoon, and alone. He denied seeing Mrs Benedict. We could not understand it. Surely she could not have missed the door and walked on too far? She would soon have realised it, if she had, and turned back. The assistant (his name, I think, is Gray) went to tell Mr Angelis, the manager. He came running from the back office, with a pen still in his hand. I asked again for Mrs Benedict. Mr Angelis confirmed the assistant's claim. He said she had not been there. He hadn't seen her at all.'

Miss Marchwood was still clasping and unclasping her hands as she spoke.

'We were by now all three of us very concerned. We didn't know what to do. Mr Angelis told me I should stay in the gallery. It was almost six and certainly there would be no more clients in such foul weather. Both he and the assistant would go out and search, locking the door with me inside. They were gone quite some time, half an hour at least. But they could find her nowhere. However, Mr Angelis had found a cab still willing to take a fare. He insisted I take it to Waterloo and catch the train back to Egham. He and the assistant, Mr Gray, would continue to look for Mrs Benedict.'

She fell silent. The Meissen clock ticked on loudly.

'I didn't want to leave without her,' she said quietly. 'But I couldn't find her. Mr Angelis said there was no question of my wandering around alone in the fog. I would get lost, too, he said; Gray and he would find themselves searching for both of us. So I came back here and left it all to him.

'When I reached the house here and told Mr Benedict what had happened, he was very alarmed. You can imagine it. We waited for news of her, hoping all the time to see her arrive home. We were both of us in a wretched state. Neither of us could eat dinner. We had a little soup and – and coffee, I think. The meal Cook had prepared quite went to waste. Of course she understood. The servants, too, were all very upset and worried. They loved Mrs Benedict.

'Then – very late, it was gone nine o'clock at night – Mr Angelis himself arrived on the doorstep here at The Cedars. He was very distressed. He had been quite unable to find her. Mr Benedict and

I were sitting in this drawing room, just waiting, you know, and hoping. When we heard a visitor arrive, so late, we naturally hoped that it was Mrs Benedict, home at last. Mr Benedict leaped up and ran into the hall. I followed behind him, just praying it would be Allegra. But it was only Mr Angelis. There was no Allegra and Angelis's face told it all.'

She paused and looked down. I waited for her to compose herself. I could well imagine the scene. I knew how I would feel, if it were Lizzie who had gone missing in such a way.

'Mr Benedict showed great courage,' Miss Marchwood said. 'He pulled himself together, brought Angelis in here and insisted he have a glass of brandy to restore his nerves.'

'Had Angelis informed the police?' I asked.

'Yes, at Little Vine Street police station. He did not know what else he could have done. Mr Benedict thanked him for his efforts and for bringing in the police. He said it was quite the right thing to have done. I think Mr Angelis was a little worried . . .'

She broke off and gave me an embarrassed look.

'Not everyone wants the police brought into their private lives,' I said, 'I understand.'

Miss Marchwood gave me a look of gratitude. 'Yes, that was it. People talk, as you know. But in the circumstances, Mr Angelis had taken upon himself to inform them – you. Then, when he had told us all this, he hurried back to Egham to catch the late train back into London. The cabman, who had brought him from the station to the house, had been waiting all the time outside for him, to drive him back down the hill. It must have been a great expense. But I think I heard Mr Benedict go out and ask what the total fare would be and so he must have paid it. I have never spent such a dreadful night in my life. I couldn't sleep at all and I know Mr Benedict stayed all night in his study, just waiting. In the

A Better Quality Of Murder

morning, Sunday, he went up to London straight away, and went first to Little Vine Street . . . You know the rest.'

She was losing her self-control at last and beginning to shake.

'I know this is difficult for you,' I told her as sympathetically as I could. 'But although we are confident the motive was not robbery . . .'

She gave a convulsive start and stared at me wild-eyed.

'Mrs Benedict still wore her jewellery,' I explained. 'Yet no purse or bag was found. Did she carry one that day?'

'Purse?' She shook her head as if she had something lodged in her ear. 'No purse? But there should be . . .' The question seemed to have quite bewildered her. At last, with an effort, she said, 'Yes, she carried a little pink suede drawstring bag. It looped over her wrist with a silk cord. She carried a little money, her handkerchief, a bottle of sal volatile and the brooch in it; that is to say, she had carried the brooch up to town in it. But the brooch had been left with Tedeschi, the jeweller, as I told you. I don't know why you didn't find the bag, Inspector. You should have found the bag . . .' She was beginning to shake again. 'It should have been on her wrist . . . I don't know, this is so terrible . . .'

This last detail had broken down her defences. I decided that I should cut short the questioning for the time being, and asked if she would be so good as to call down Henderson, the lady's maid, so that I could have a word with her.

Henderson proved to be a dumpy middle-aged woman, red-eyed and tearful.

'It's a terrible thing, a dreadful thing, sir! I swear I've hardly slept a wink since it happened. Who would ever have believed it? Poor Mrs Benedict. She was such a kind lady.'

'Was she in her usual spirits that morning, when you helped her dress?'

73

'Oh, yes, Inspector! In fact, she was in very good spirits. She was looking forward to the trip up to London, I fancy. I put up her hair with extra pins, so it wouldn't come loose when she was away from the house.'

'Would you say Mrs Benedict was a happy woman?'

Henderson looked bewildered. 'Why should she not be, sir? She had beautiful clothes. It was a real pleasure to have the care of them.'

'Mr Benedict was a generous husband?'

'Oh, yes, sir. She could have whatever she fancied. She had only to express the wish . . . and he'd buy it for her.'

'She didn't have her own allowance?'

Henderson seemed bothered by the question. 'Well, yes, sir. She had her pin money, to be sure. I couldn't tell you much about that, sir.' Her homely face crumpled and tears began to trickle down her plump cheeks. 'Oh, whatever shall I do now?'

She, like Miss Marchwood, had lost a good place and was now faced with having to find another at a time of life when she was no longer young.

Morris and I made our way back to the railway station on foot, down the hill and across the town. It was pleasant walking and it gave us plenty of opportunity to exchange what information we'd learned.

'All the servants said they were very happy working at The Cedars,' Morris told me. 'They're very distressed. They were fond of Mrs Benedict, it appears.'

'I've been hearing the same. It makes me wonder . . . How about Benedict himself, their employer? Much sympathy for him? Did you get the feeling he was as popular as his wife?'

'Plenty of sympathy, sir. Perhaps not much—' Morris hesitated and searched without luck for a word. 'I got the impression they have a lot of respect for the gentleman, but are a bit in awe of him, as you might say,' he concluded. 'They perhaps don't like him as much as they liked her.'

There was evidence of a real affection for the lady of the house, but not for the master.

'And do the staff think the Benedicts had a happy marriage?'

Morris hesitated. 'Cook called it a "good" marriage. That was the word she used. They said Mr Benedict thought the world of his wife.'

This tallied much with what Henderson had said to me.

'Did she appear to think the world of him? Did she appear to love her husband?'

Morris reddened. 'I don't know about love, sir. How do you tell? I mean, people like that, well, they're very formal, aren't they, in the way they talk to one another? They don't go kissing and cuddling in front of others.'

True, and I couldn't imagine Sebastian Benedict indulging in such playful behaviour, whether in privacy or not. But no outsider ever really knows what goes on in another couple's marriage. However, Henderson, the lady's maid, had not doubted how Benedict felt about his wife. The character of the victim was beginning to fascinate me.

'How did the staff describe the deceased?' I asked next.

'A very quiet, dignified lady, was all they said. She was musical, played the piano very well. She'd sit for hours playing, just for herself.'

The description bothered me. What happened to the spirited, intelligent Italian girl of eighteen, full of laughter, that nine years of marriage to Benedict had turned her into a quiet, dignified British matron, sitting alone in her drawing room, playing the piano for herself? What had extinguished all the fire?

'How did *you* find the husband, sir?' Morris asked.

'A bit of an odd character,' I confessed. 'I don't doubt he loved his wife. He is genuinely distraught. But he seems to have been obsessed by her beauty. I couldn't help feeling that he would have been almost as upset by the loss of some highly prized painting or statue. It occurs to me, Morris, that, from Mrs Benedict's viewpoint, it must have been very tedious, not to say depressing, to have a husband who appeared to love you primarily for your beauty, saw you as an objet d'art, and not love you for yourself, with any imperfections you might have. Also, she was very young when they married, eighteen, although they had known one another since she was fourteen. He was fifteen years older than her. The marriage seems to have been agreed between her father and Benedict. Benedict himself hardly strikes me as the type to sweep a young girl off her feet.'

'You're thinking she might have had a fancy man?' Morris suggested.

I am afraid we police officers develop sordid minds. We see too much of human nature's weaknesses and private vices. I couldn't have denied the thought had ever entered my head. It had been there since I set eyes on the husband. But I expressed myself more cautiously.

'She might have been very bored and lonely here in England. The only company she had was that of the woman Marchwood – and she's hardly a lively sort of person. There are no children. Marchwood was with her nine years and was the lady's only confidante. If there was anything scandalous in Mrs Benedict's private life, the companion must know of it and have turned a blind eye to it. She won't now confess her complicity in a love affair. Or tell us anything else that reflects on her own behaviour.

She was engaged to look after Mrs Benedict but Mr Benedict paid her wages, and still does at the moment, it seems.' I allowed myself a wry grimace. 'She is quick to tell me how she came to lose Mrs Benedict in the fog. But any other questions won't, I think, get ready answers.'

'Very likely you're right, sir,' rumbled Morris. 'Sad thing that, Mr Benedict having to hire a friend for his wife. The staff did not have much to say about Miss Marchwood, only that she's rather stiff in her way with them. I fancy Cook gets along with her best.'

'I am not happy about the whole thing, to be honest with you, Morris,' I muttered discontentedly as we turned into the station yard. 'Marchwood was too glib in some ways and too reticent in others. She had the explanation of their trip to London and how they came to be parted, all off pat. But she is vague as to times. They left the jeweller's premises in the Burlington Arcade, she says, a little after four. She quickly corrects that to "almost five". But that is nearly an hour's difference.

'And there is another matter. I can't help thinking of that oak tree, standing alone.'

'Oak?' asked Morris, startled. 'You mean that one King Charles the Second ordered planted?'

'King Charles no more ordered it planted than my granny did, but yes, I do mean that tree in Green Park. Most of the other trees in the park are in avenues. So let us say you are right, and Mrs Benedict had an – an amorous interest. Well, if I were her, and I wanted to arrange to meet someone in the park, discreetly, I might suggest a tryst at the oak tree, tucked away at the back of the area and not to be confused with any other tree.'

Morris sucked his teeth and finally offered, 'There's this chap, Angelis.'

'There is, and I'll seek him out tomorrow. You, Morris, will go to Burlington Arcade and find the jeweller called Tedeschi. Get him not only to confirm Mrs Benedict was there on Saturday afternoon. Try to get him to remember what time she and Miss Marchwood left his shop. Try and find the beadle they asked to call a cab for them, and a crossing sweeper who guided them across the road. Miss Marchwood said the boy had heard them talking in the fog. I would like very much to know exactly what he heard them say. Crossing sweepers generally patrol the same stretch of street watching out for custom. They don't trespass on one another's beats. You should find him.'

Several things were bothering me, buzzing about my brain. 'What happened to the pink suede drawstring bag Marchwood says the victim was carrying?'

'Anyone could have picked that up,' said Morris. 'She might have dropped it in the street, or anywhere in the park, and not been able to find it in the fog. Later, when the fog cleared, someone found it before Park Constable Hopkins found her.'

They were possible explanations. An expensive pink purse, of the sort described to me by Miss Marchwood, wouldn't lie unclaimed in a London street or park for long.

'Here's our train, sir,' said Morris as it puffed into view and filled the air with sulphurous steam.

We climbed aboard, fortunate enough to find ourselves alone in the carriage. The guard on the platform blew his whistle. We lurched and, with a grinding of metal and hurried huff-puff-puff, were underway.

'Why no butler?' I asked, as another troublesome thought sprang into my head.

'How's that, sir?' Morris found the rocking of the carriage soothing and was having difficulty not closing his eyes.

'Altogether there are seven indoor servants at The Cedars,

including a valet and a lady's maid. I do not include the companion, who occupies a higher status and is not a servant, although paid a respectable salary. But there is no butler. I would have expected a butler in such a well-set-up household, to supervise the staff, be arbiter of their disputes and judge of their behaviour. He would be the link between them and the master of the house – and he would open the door to visitors. I was greeted by a tearful parlourmaid. A nice girl, no doubt, but in my experience a household like that of The Cedars always has a butler.'

'Oh, that,' mumbled Morris, 'there was one, but he left.'

'You didn't mention this, Morris!' I turned to him, surprised.

He looked embarrassed. 'It wasn't recent, sir. When I asked Cook if there were any servants I hadn't met, she said I'd seen them all. She added they managed without a butler now since Mr Seymour left six months ago. Mr Benedict had been very put out about it at the time. He hasn't taken on any one else to replace Seymour.'

'If Mr Benedict was very put out at Seymour leaving, it suggests the butler handed in his notice. He wasn't sacked. Why, I wonder did Seymour leave when the work could hardly have been arduous and all the other servants were so happy? Morris! When you have been to the Burlington Arcade tomorrow, and also found the crossing sweeper, you have another job. You can go round the agencies that place domestic staff of the superior kind. Seymour has had plenty of time to find another post. I would like to know where he is working now and, if possible, talk to him.'

'Yessir,' said Morris with a sigh. 'Might I suggest, sir, that Constable Biddle go out to look for the crossing sweeper? It might make things move a little quicker. Biddle would like the chance, sir. He's very ambitious.'

'Send young Biddle, by all means. I suppose he can't make a complete muddle of it.' I knew Constable Biddle to be enthusiastic and well-meaning but his keenness sometimes got him into a pickle.

We were nearing our terminus at Waterloo.

'Excuse me, Mr Ross,' said Morris diffidently, 'but what exactly is an obzhaydar?'

At home that evening, as I sat with Lizzie at our modest dining table, I told her that we had a new murder on our hands at the Yard. I described Allegra Benedict as she would have looked before her death; and said I'd been all the way out to Egham to visit the bereaved husband. Knowing she was a doctor's daughter, I even told her about Carmichael's carbolic spray.

'Goodness,' said Lizzie. 'I didn't think Dr Carmichael would be so open to new ideas. What an awful business. That poor woman. I wonder if she was happy in England, so far from her own country. I wonder if she had many friends.'

'She had a companion who had been with her all the time she'd been in this country and who travelled up to London with her that day, a Miss Marchwood. Rather a peculiar female – why, Lizzie, what is it?'

Lizzie had put down her knife and fork and was staring at me.

'Did you say Marchwood? It can't be the same – but you say she was Mrs Benedict's *companion*? It must be the same one.'

'You know her?' I asked, astonished.

'No, not at all. But I know of her and Bessie knows her.'

'Bessie!' I exclaimed so loudly that Bessie appeared and asked what I wanted.

'Bessie,' said Lizzie to her. 'The lady who normally comes to the Temperance Hall and helps with the teas on a Sunday is a

Miss Marchwood, so you told me, isn't that right?'

'That's right, missus,' said Bessie. 'Only she wasn't there last Sunday when you came along. I was really sorry about that. She always is there, along with Mrs Scott and Mrs Gribble. Miss Marchwood brings shortbread biscuits. I don't think she bakes them herself. I think she gets the cook where she lives to do it. They're very good biscuits.'

'Never mind the biscuits!' I interrupted. 'Do you know the name of Miss Marchwood's employer? Did the lady ever come with her? Do you know where they live?'

'She don't live in London,' said Bessie. 'She comes on the train. I mean Miss Marchwood. The lady she works for doesn't come.'

'She would be a very beautiful lady, Italian,' I told her.

Bessie looked impressed. 'My, fancy that, and Miss Marchwood so plain.'

I was sure now that we did have the same woman in mind. Of all the staff at The Cedars, Marchwood, we had learned, got along best with the cook. That same cook who didn't mind baking shortbread biscuits for the companion to carry up to London and the meetings. 'The name Benedict means nothing to you, Bessie?'

Bessie shook her head. 'I don't know any one called that. Do you want me to take that vegetable dish?'

When Bessie had gone, I observed to Lizzie, 'It seems the reason you didn't meet Miss Marchwood last Sunday was because with Mrs Benedict first being missing since the Saturday afternoon before, and then the discovery that she was dead, the household at The Cedars was in turmoil.'

'She might be there this coming Sunday,' said Lizzie, adding casually, 'I was thinking of going again with Bessie to hear Mr Fawcett speak. It was quite entertaining.'

'Lizzie!' I said as sternly as I could, knowing that any objection on my part would be useless. 'I don't want you to be involved in this!'

'But you would like to know if Miss Marchwood shows her face on Sunday; and what sort of state of mind she's in, if she does,' Lizzie pointed out.

'Would she know who you were?' I asked, after a pause. 'I mean, would she know you are married to me and what I do for a living?'

'If she doesn't then either Mrs Scott or Mr Fawcett himself will tell her, I dare say. I think Mrs Scott does know who you are. I fancied she was a little suspicious of me.'

'Well, don't go rousing more suspicions. Just go and see if Marchwood is there and how she seems. No quizzing her, mind, or referring to the murder directly!'

'As if I would!' said my wife indignantly. 'Really, Ben.'

'Of course, I know you will be tactful,' I hastened to say. 'But I don't want Marchwood more frightened than she is.'

Lizzie's sharp ear caught my choice of word. 'You think she is afraid? Not just very shocked and distressed?'

'Yes,' I told her, 'I have been thinking it over and I am sure Isabella Marchwood is very afraid. But I don't know of what or of whom.'

Chapter Five

Inspector Benjamin Ross

BY THE following morning, much to Superintendent Dunn's anger, the gentlemen of the press had found out about the River Wraith. Together with the discovery of the body of a beautiful woman, lying strangled in Green Park (and one whose husband owned a gallery in Piccadilly), it must have given them more material than they could have dreamed of in their wildest moments. Naturally the two stories were linked. I was as irritated as Dunn was. In my mind there was still no proof that the River Wraith had killed Allegra Benedict. The press, however, was in no such doubt.

The resultant story was splashed prominently across the newssheets beneath banner headlines. Nor was it only the popular press which made such a furore about it. The *Daily Telegraph* ran to half a page. It even earned a long paragraph in *The Times* (with an observation from a leading churchman about lawlessness on the streets). The hullabaloo was set to last until we made an arrest. In the following days there were letters to the papers; a Question was even asked in parliament. The Home Secretary, no less, was forced to rise to his feet to try and answer it. He insisted that the streets of London were quite safe for respectable women. This brought more letters to the press. The image of the River Wraith depicted by several artists with varying degrees of imagination, but invariably lurid, appeared everywhere. The idea of such a strange prowler seized all imaginations.

Of course the police force was somehow blamed for the whole thing, as was usual. The writers of the letters to the newspapers were particularly anxious to point out that we were never around when needed. The words 'taxpayers' money' were much used.

'How do they know?' demanded an exasperated Dunn, thumping his fist on the outspread newssheet on his desk. 'They know of a woman found dead in the park, that's to be expected. But how do they know about this so-called River Wraith?'

'If I had to guess, sir,' I offered, 'when the story of a woman found strangled in the park was printed, one of the street girls went to a reporter and sold him her story of the River Wraith for a guinea. Now it's open season and reporters are all hunting girls who have a story about the River Wraith to tell.'

'Just what I feared!' groaned Dunn, rubbing his head. 'We can increase the men on foot patrol in the river area. But if this deviant is seeking his prey in the parks as well . . .'

'We still don't know, sir, that he really does exist, or that he is our murderer. Daisy Smith, the girl I spoke to, told me the Wraith had his hands on her neck. There was no mention of a cord.'

'So he has changed his modus operandi,' grumbled Dunn.

'Why should he do that, sir?'

'Why, man, because the girls had been escaping him! He meant to make sure of his next victim.'

The possibility had already occurred to me, but I had had time to think it over and to dismiss it.

'In that case,' I objected, 'why should he use the two different methods on the same night? He put no cord round Daisy's throat.'

'Do I know what's in his head?' roared Dunn. 'We are dealing with a madman! The next victim may be attacked with a knife, for all we know. He's not a rational being, Ross.'

The River Wraith, to call him that for want of a better name, might not be rational in a normal way of thinking, but he would have his own reasons for doing what he did. Perhaps he hated prostitutes or just enjoyed frightening the girls with his macabre charade. Perhaps his object was only to scare them half out of their wits. Placing his hands on their necks was meant to terrify, but not to kill. It was a line of thought. The murderer of Allegra Benedict, on the other hand, had left home carrying a length of cord in his pocket. It was in his mind to commit murder.

Aloud, I agreed that it wasn't the action of a rational man to dress up in a shroud and creep round in the fog, attacking street women. But I still doubted he'd use his hands on one and a prepared cord noose on another, on the selfsame night. I didn't tell Dunn that, or any of my other conjectures. He was in no mood to listen.

I made the acquaintance of George Angelis that same day. As arranged, Morris went off to find the jeweller, Tedeschi, and to try and find the whereabouts of the former butler to the Benedict household, Mortimer Seymour. Biddle, his youthful face shining with enthusiasm, began to scour Piccadilly and surrounding thoroughfares for crossing sweepers. I went to the Benedict Fine Arts Gallery.

It had a discreet frontage on the south side of Piccadilly, not far from the park. The proximity of the gallery to the place where the body had been found was certainly significant in some way. But quite how, I didn't yet know. I had decided there was a lot that I didn't know. As for the gallery, it might have been an undertaker's establishment such was its discretion and the amount of black lacquer on the door and window cases. There was nothing on display in the shadowy plate-glass window but a single landscape in oils, propped on an easel, showing a view of a large city with a great domed baroque church, painted from a standpoint across an intervening river. The easel was surrounded by velvet drapes.

The door was locked, although there was no 'closed' notice hanging in it. I guessed the manager, George Angelis, found it necessary to deny entry to all but bona fide clients, though possible buyers were probably avoiding the place to avoid being trapped themselves by reporters. To gain admittance I had to jangle the doorbell repeatedly until a young assistant appeared on the other side of the glass and gestured that I should go away. Clearly, I thought ruefully, my appearance was not that of a prospective customer. On the other hand I did look rather like a reporter. I mouthed the word 'police'. The young man's face took on a look of resignation but he unlocked the door and let me in.

'Thank you,' I said. 'I am Inspector Ross, from Scotland Yard.'

'Yes, sir,' he said courteously and waited for me to explain what I wanted.

I was disconcerted, because he surely knew what business brought me. His grimace on learning my profession had told me that. But also because now that I saw him close at hand, without the intervening glass panel in the door, I was struck by his appearance. He was very young; I supposed him not more than two and twenty. Moreover, he was beautiful. I was startled at finding myself applying this adjective to any man, yet it was apt.

His features were of a classical regularity seldom seen other than on antique statues and his complexion very pale. His expression was both serene and sad as he stood patiently before me, his hands folded one over the other. I was reminded of a carved angel presiding over a tombstone. Had he not been employed here, he might have done very well working for an undertaker. No! I dismissed the idea immediately. An artist's model, surely that is what this youth should be. Perhaps he had been?

'Mr Angelis?' I asked hastily. 'Is he here?'

The assistant's sorrowful look did not change. 'Mr Angelis is in the office, sir. I'll tell him you're here.' He turned away.

'One moment!' I detained him. 'What is your name?'

'Gray, sir, Francis Gray.' He inclined in a graceful half-bow. 'I have been assistant to Mr Angelis for the past six months.'

'And you were here on Saturday last when Miss Marchwood came to the shop – gallery – seeking Mrs Benedict?'

'I was, Inspector. I went out with Mr Angelis to look for the lady. It was a hopeless task.' Tragedy seemed to sit naturally on this young man's shoulders. Perhaps it was allowable in the circumstances. Even so, I couldn't imagine him ever telling a joke in happier times.

'Did you go into the park?'

He looked hurt. 'Why, no! I didn't think she would have gone into the park. Besides, in that fog, I could have wandered all over the park and not found her. I assumed it would be empty of visitors.' His tone was one of polite reproach.

We had reached the door of the office and I decided to let him off the hook.

He seemed relieved, as people are when the police stop taking an interest in them, and disappeared inside to inform the manager of my arrival.

I took a look around. There were some paintings tastefully hung on the walls, mostly oils but a few watercolours. The latter were collected together and to my eye appeared to be by the same artist. Standing right behind me, so that it gave me quite a start when I turned, was a statue. It was of a singularly unpleasant-looking satyr and because of the plinth on which it stood it looked me directly in the eye. I can't tell you how malicious its gaze was. I couldn't imagine anyone wanting such a thing in his home.

Gray had returned. 'This way, sir.' He flung open the office door and announced, 'An Inspector Ross, Mr Angelis, from Scotland Yard.'

Why 'an' Inspector Ross? I wondered. Did he fancy Scotland Yard had more than one of us of that name and rank?

Angelis was a fine figure of a fellow, that's the best way to describe him. He was tall, perhaps in his forties, and of Levantine complexion. His thick black hair was grown long, curling over his collar, and had a distinguished touch of silver at his temples. He had deep-set large, dark eyes and thick black brows. His black frock coat and trousers were only slightly relieved by a maroon satin waistcoat, but this sombre attire hardly did him justice. He seemed somehow to belong to a more ancient and exotic time. I could imagine him striding about the court of some long-ago Byzantine emperor, clad in golden robes.

He received me with dignity, seated me in a comfortable leather chair and offered me a glass of sherry. I suspected I was being treated with the courtesy offered to clients. I thanked him but declined the sherry.

'I am very sorry, Inspector,' began Angelis smoothly, 'that my own efforts to find Mrs Benedict were unsuccessful. The news, when we heard it, was terrible. I can't imagine how Mr Benedict is coping with it. I have not seen him since I called at his house that sad evening.'

'Previous to that, when had you last seen him?' I asked.

Angelis placed the tips of his fingers together. I thought the nails were polished. 'Let me see, that would have been Wednesday of last week. Normally Mr Benedict visits the gallery on Tuesdays, Wednesdays and Thursdays. He seldom if ever comes in on a Friday, and never on a Saturday. We are not open on Mondays.'

That tallied with what Benedict himself had told me. 'Did Mrs Benedict come with him very often?' I asked.

Angelis gave that question the same careful consideration. 'I hadn't seen the lady for at least three weeks. I would not say she came often. But occasionally, yes. Mr Benedict sometimes brought her to see some acquisition he was particularly proud of. Or, if she had been in town shopping, she might call by if she knew her husband would be here.'

He emphasised the last words to let me know there was no suggestion of Mrs Benedict being guilty of any impropriety – or that he might have behaved incorrectly.

'Would Miss Marchwood be with her on these occasions?'

'Yes, Inspector, Miss Marchwood was always with her,' said Angelis reproachfully.

How very proper it all was. Had Benedict, I wondered, been a jealous husband?

The thing was, I did suspect poor Allegra of impropriety. Angelis had wished to make it clear it wasn't with him. But if she had been meeting an admirer clandestinely, Marchwood would know of it. It seemed Allegra never left the house without her. Not so much a companion as a guardian! She must have helped to conceal the affair from the deceived husband . . . if affair there had been. It would explain Miss Marchwood's reticence and possibly her fear. If Benedict found out, she would have to face his anger alone. He would never give her a reference. If future prospective employers contacted him, he would certainly tell them Miss Marchwood was unreliable.

'You have a landscape painting in the window,' I said.

Angelis was surprised into showing it. 'Yes, we do!'

I didn't know if his surprise was because I had noticed it at all, or whether he thought I might be going to ask how much it was. I certainly had no intention of doing that.

'It seems to be of a foreign city.'

Angelis raised his thick dark brows but bestowed a much less reserved look on me. As a policeman I had stood low in his esteem. As an art lover, I'd now climbed a few notches.

'Why, yes, indeed it is, Inspector. It is a view of Dresden by Bernardo Bellotto.'

'You have the advantage of me,' I said. 'I don't know the name.'

'Bernardo Bellotto was the nephew of the great Canaletto,' Angelis said.

Thank goodness I had heard of him, so could look properly impressed.

'Bellotto,' Angelis was continuing, 'was not above occasionally signing his own work "Canaletto". One can generally tell the difference between the two at first glance, if one knows what to look for. But a few of his paintings in museums and collections around Europe claim to be by his illustrious uncle. I don't mean that Bellotto is not a fine painter. However he lacks the same lightness of touch.'

'What would be the provenance of the painting?'

Any goodwill I'd earned vanished in a trice. Angelis stiffened and said in an icy voice: 'You are not suggesting any irregularity? Any item bought in this gallery always has impeccable provenance!'

I held up a hand and apologised. 'Forgive me, I didn't mean to suggest otherwise. I only wanted to ask where Benedict acquired it for sale.'

He relaxed. 'Oh, as to that, Mr Benedict brought it back from his last visit to Europe. He goes every year and makes a tour, seeking out works of art.'

'Did Mrs Benedict accompany him on these visits?'

Angelis shook his dark curls. 'They were business visits, Inspector.'

So Allegra, who probably would dearly have loved to go travelling, had been left at home in Surrey with nothing to do but play her piano.

I returned to the matter of Saturday afternoon. 'What time did Miss Marchwood arrive here, looking for Mrs Benedict?'

'It will have been a minute or two after five thirty,' said Angelis at once. 'I know because I had just consulted my watch before I heard voices in the gallery. They turned out to be those of Miss Marchwood and Mr Gray. Mr Gray came here, to the office, to tell me that Mrs Benedict was not to be found. When I went out into the main area, I found Miss Marchwood in a very agitated state. She was sobbing uncontrollably. I took her into the office and gave her a large glass of sherry. It seemed to help, although she was still incoherent. She babbled out the story she had told Gray, about Mrs Benedict being lost. "She's gone, she's gone!" she kept wailing.

'I had been thinking of closing the gallery early, because of the bad weather. As soon as I realised the seriousness of the news, I did close the gallery – leaving Miss Marchwood inside with the sherry decanter for support – and Gray and I went out to look for the missing lady.'

'Mr Gray tells me he didn't go into the park during his search. Did *you*, Mr Angelis?'

'No, Inspector, I took the other direction and went down as far as Piccadilly Circus on this side of the road. Then I came back on the other side of the road.'

'Passing by the Burlington Arcade?'

'Just so. The fog was atrocious. I could hardly see where I was going. I realised there was little hope of finding Mrs Benedict. I did come across a cab, so I asked the cabbie to return with me. I put Miss Marchwood in the vehicle and sent her off to Waterloo. I went out a second time to try again, leaving Gray here in case Mrs Benedict should find her way here after all. Eventually I gave it all up as hopeless. I came back, sent Gray home, locked up the gallery, and went to Little Vine Street to report the lady missing at the police station there. They took details of her appearance. I had taken the precaution of asking Miss Marchwood how the lady was dressed. She told me she was wearing a brown skirt and mantle. I also . . .' Angelis put his fist to his mouth and coughed delicately. 'I also told them she was uncommonly handsome. Then I went to Waterloo Station and took a train to Egham. I made my way to Mr Benedict's house and told him of the situation.'

'He must have been very alarmed,' I said.

'Very!' said Angelis curtly.

I thanked him for his help and returned to the main part of the gallery where Gray waited. He preceded me to the door and showed me out with the graceful courtesy that seemed natural to him. I mumbled my thanks and exited into Piccadilly, quite glad to be out in the hurly-burly of the street. The passers-by looked reassuringly normal, in contrast to the exotic pair I'd left behind me in the gallery. You do not belong in the art world, Ross! I told myself. You need not be embarrassed at finding it a rum set-up.

As I neared the entry to the Burlington Arcade, I saw Morris was there (surely no more welcome figure than his sensible bulk!). He was talking to a top-hatted, uniformed beadle.

'This is Harry Barnes,' Morris told me when I joined them. 'He was on duty on Saturday last, but he doesn't recall the two ladies.'

I looked at the beadle. He touched a finger to the brim of his hat and peered at me with eyes remarkable for the yellowness of the 'whites'. His skin also had an unhealthy ochre tinge. Did he suffer from jaundice or some liver disease? He appeared otherwise healthy. More likely he had spent many years in hot and unhealthy climes, suffering there from the ailments that afflict Europeans. An ex-soldier, I thought, as the Arcade's beadles mostly were.

'You are certain about the ladies?' I asked him. 'You don't recall them? One of them was very handsome.'

'Visibility very poor, sir!' barked Barnes at once, as if making a report to his superior officer. Then his manner grew less certain. 'It doesn't mean they weren't here, sir. But there are a lot of visitors to the Arcade, you understand.'

'They would have asked you to find them a cab,' I prompted him.

'It's very possible they did, sir. But I can't say as I recall it. Several people asked me to find them cabs that afternoon, gentlemen and ladies. A lot of ladies come to shop here in the Arcade. But there wasn't one single cab of any description to be had anywhere. There were people coming out of the fog and asking me all manner of questions, most of them lost and some of them not able to tell north from south. Sorry if I can't help you further, gentlemen.'

We moved away a little.

'Pity about that,' rumbled Morris.

'What about the jeweller?' I asked in some exasperation. 'How is his memory?'

'He does confirm Mrs Benedict and her companion were in his shop on Saturday afternoon, sir. He knows Mrs Benedict and there is no doubt it was her. I asked him if he could remember why they were there and he said it concerned a brooch belonging to Mrs Benedict. I asked him what time they left and he said it was about half past four, as well as he can remember. He's sorry but he can't be more precise.'

'But Angelis tells me Miss Marchwood didn't arrive at the gallery until half past five, and he is sure of the time. The gallery is what, ten minutes from here, if that?'

'In good weather, sir,' Morris agreed. 'But it would take longer in the fog, and the ladies dithered a bit about crossing the road and so on.'

I gave an exasperated sigh. 'I wish Tedeschi could be as precise as Angelis. But it looks more and more, Morris, as if there is a period of time unaccounted for. I'll have to ask Miss Marchwood again. But I don't think it will get me anywhere. You had better begin your trawl of the domestic agencies. Perhaps we can at least find Seymour!'

I returned to Scotland Yard with the intention of writing up an account of my interview with George Angelis for the benefit of Superintendent Dunn. When I walked into the outer office I saw that there was a visitor.

He sat on a chair devouring a large hunk of bread with some cheese, tearing the bread apart as if he hadn't eaten all day, as perhaps he hadn't. He was a ragged, unwashed urchin of some ten or eleven years of age, wearing boots too large for him. A battered felt hat lay on the floor at his feet.

Constable Biddle was sitting at a desk staring gloomily at the boy. When he saw me, he scrambled to his feet and said, 'The crossing sweeper, sir, from Piccadilly.'

'Well done, Biddle!' I said, pleased.

Biddle turned puce under the praise.

The urchin collected up the last crumbs of bread carefully and put them in his mouth. Ignoring me, he addressed Biddle.

'Aven't you got any more?'

'No, I haven't,' said Biddle crossly. 'You've eaten my dinner as it is. This is Inspector Ross, so stand up and mind your manners!'

'Come into my office,' I told the sweeper.

He collected his hat, tucked it under his arm and followed me into my office. There he unashamedly took stock of his new surroundings.

I sat down at my desk and hoped he was impressed. I had the strong feeling he wasn't.

'What's your name?' I asked him.

'Charlie,' said the boy.

'Charlie what?'

'No!' returned the boy in disgust. 'You've got the wrong one. You're thinking of Percy Watt. He sweeps the crossings in the Strand.'

'I meant,' I said as patiently as I could, 'what is your surname? Your family's name.'

'Got no family,' said the boy promptly.

'But you must have another name besides Charlie.'

'Oh, that,' said the boy at last. 'They calls me Charlie Tubbs.'

'Then your name is Tubbs. Where do you live?'

'Nowhere,' said the boy.

'Well, where do you sleep at night?'

'Doorways mostly.'

He was probably telling the truth.

'Now then, Tubbs, I understand you sweep the crossings for pedestrians.' The boy frowned, and I quickly changed that to 'for people walking in Piccadilly'.

'Between the Circus and St James's Street,' said the boy, with a nod.

'It's a good place to work?'

'Yus,' agreed the boy. 'It's where the swells do their shopping.

They go walking up and down in polished boots and ladies with their crinolines all made of shiny material and lace. They don't like crossing the road in all the muck and mud. So I run up and offer to sweep them a clear path and very pleased they are, too!'

'You were there last Saturday afternoon?'

'Always there,' said the boy.

'It was very foggy.'

'*Don't* I know it?' said Charlie Tubbs with deep feeling. 'There weren't no people walking about at all. I didn't think I'd make any money. It was cold, too, and *damp*. I thought it would be nice to have a hot pie. There's a pie stall in the Circus. I kept thinking about them pies.'

'Then what happened? After the fog came down and you were wandering up and down Piccadilly hoping to find a customer?'

'I heard voices, women's voices. Very ladylike, they was. So I moved up nearer, because ladies in particular don't like to cross the road. Especially where you get a lot of horse traffic like you get in Piccadilly. Hard to get across without putting your foot right in—'

'Yes, yes, Tubbs! Could you hear what the ladies were saying?'

'Yus,' said Tubbs and then stopped, looking at me expectantly.

'Well, go on,' I urged him.

'What's it worth?' demanded the wretched child.

'A clip round the ear if I think you're being impudent,' I snapped. 'Or I'll tell Constable Biddle to lock you in the cells until you learn better!'

Tubbs was unabashed. 'I could be out there in Piccadilly, sweeping crossings and making money. I've been sitting out there I don't know how long.' He jerked his head towards the outer office behind him.

'You've been fed. Come on, Tubbs, what did the ladies say?'

Tubbs decided it would be better to impart his information and try for remuneration later.

'One of them was saying they should go home. But the other one, she said . . .' Tubbs drew a deep breath and made a passable imitation of a lady's voice. 'But we are so near.'

'What kind of voice did she have?' I asked. 'No, don't, please, try and imitate it again! Just tell me. Was she soft-spoken? Loud? How did she sound? Alarmed? Worried?'

'She spoke very quiet. I could hardly hear her,' said Tubbs, 'and in a funny sort of way. I don't reckon she was a Londoner. I know most London voices. She was foreign. She sounded like old Martini who runs a coffee stall in Old Bond Street.'

God bless all London urchins. They missed nothing. One of the speakers had certainly been Allegra Benedict who hadn't lost her Italian accent! *We are so near* . . . Near to what? Benedict's gallery?

'Go on,' I invited Tubbs.

'The other female,' continued Tubbs, 'she started moaning about the fog and how it was hopeless. But the one with the funny accent, she said they could get there. "It's so near," she said again. "And he will be waiting!"'

I nearby jumped off my chair and tried to hide my emotions from Tubbs. I didn't want him to start elaborating from his imagination.

'Are you sure she said that, Charlie?'

'Yes,' said the sweeper. 'I was standing right by her at the time. She didn't see me. Fog was really bad.'

'"But we cannot even cross the road safely," says the first female. So that was when I jumped in, see? "You want to cross the street? I'll take you!" I says. She gives a little shriek, on account she didn't know I was there. Then the one with the funny voice, she says, "Yes, yes, Isabella! The boy will take us across and we can find our way from there." So I took 'em across, sweeping a nice clean path for them. The first lady, she gave me sixpence. I went straight off and bought a pie with it.'

'And the other one, the one with the funny voice, as you call it?'

Tubbs shrugged, 'I don't know about her. She walked off into the fog. She was in a hurry, I reckon.'

'Why do you reckon that?'

'She was sort of jumpy. The first one, she was worried. But the one with the foreign voice, she was like a cat on hot bricks.'

I gave Tubbs a shilling, which he tested with his teeth to make sure it was a good one. Then I took him back to Biddle, sat him down and requested him to tell his story again, just as he had told me.

'The constable,' I said, 'will write it down and read it back to you. You will make your mark to agree it's a true record. Do you understand?'

'Do I get another sixpence for that?' asked Tubbs hopefully.

'No, you do not. If you do it nicely, you might get a mug of tea.'

Biddle gave me a reproachful look.

'It was an assignation,' I told Dunn a few minutes later. 'I'd wager a pound to a penny. Wherever those two women were going, it wasn't the gallery. They were making for the park and that oak tree. Or, more likely, Allegra Benedict was to meet someone at the oak tree. Isabella Marchwood was to wait in Piccadilly, perhaps at the park gate or just walking up and down inside the park near the gate, until Allegra came back. That accounts for the period of time about which Miss Marchwood is so vague. She spent it waiting for her employer to return. But Allegra didn't come back. Eventually so much time had passed that she realised Allegra was not going to rejoin her and that something had obviously gone wrong. She may even have tried to search for her in the park, but in the fog it was impossible. So by the time she turned up at the gallery, she was understandably in the very distressed state described by Angelis. Not only had she lost Mrs Benedict, but she would have to explain somehow why she had not been with that lady all the time . . .

'That, too, is why Charlie Tubbs described the foreign-sounding woman as being "like a cat on hot bricks", worried about being late and someone waiting. That, sir, is why what Harry Barnes had to say is important.'

'Who on earth is Harry Barnes? Do stand still, Ross!'

By now I was marching up and down in front of his desk, jabbing the air with my forefinger. Understandably the superintendent was beginning to look bewildered. I came to a halt and apologised.

'Sorry, sir. Harry Barnes is a beadle employed by the Burlington Arcade. On Saturday afternoon last he was on duty at the Piccadilly exit of the Arcade. Isabella Marchwood told me that she and Mrs Benedict asked the beadle to find them a cab but he was unable to oblige them. When we asked him, he told Morris and me that he couldn't recall two ladies asking him to find them a cab. But he was anxious to point out that a lot of people had asked him to do them that service on Saturday but owing to the fog, he hadn't been able to find a single cab. It had been a confused situation and his memory was correspondingly patchy.

'But, just let us suppose his memory isn't poor but quite the opposite. The reason Barnes could not recall two ladies asking for a cab was because *they didn't make any such request!* The patrons of the Arcade are wealthy people and not to be offended. Barnes's job, apart from making sure undesirables don't enter the Arcade, is to keep the paying customers happy. He wouldn't say that one of them was telling a lie. Or he may genuinely not even remember. It was an afternoon of confusion. Either way, he doesn't back up the story Isabella Marchwood told me, that they asked the beadle to find a cab. I thought Barnes had nothing to tell us but, by that very fact, he did.'

'Will the woman Marchwood admit all this?' asked Dunn simply, when I had run out of steam and argument. He was looking singularly unimpressed by my logic, not to say downright sceptical.

That poured cold water on my enthusiasm. I had to confess it was extremely unlikely.

'I doubt it, sir. How can she? Not without compromising herself, and leaving herself defenceless before Benedict's anger. She'll say the beadle has forgotten . . . and Barnes himself says he has. She'll say the boy misheard them. She'll say they were worried about being late returning to Cedar Lodge where Benedict was waiting. She'll say they were talking of going to the gallery, and she did go to the gallery.' I thumped my clenched right fist into the palm of my left hand. 'She will have a ready answer for everything. But I knew Marchwood was holding something back!'

'No, Ross, you have a theory that she is. Now, now, I am not saying you aren't on the right track . . .' Dunn waved a solid palm at me to forestall any further outburst. 'But you will have to restrain your alarming enthusiasm, you know. We shall have to be careful. Keep it to yourself for the time being, there's a good chap. We don't want Benedict storming in here to accuse us of blackening the name of an innocent woman. We shall have to be very sure, Ross.'

But I was sure of very little, except that I was only just at the beginning of this mystery. I nodded glumly.

Chapter Six

Elizabeth Martin Ross

'NOW THEN, Bessie!' I said, 'we shall have to be discreet, you and I. Do you know what "discreet" means?'

We were seated at the kitchen table. Between us stood a brown earthenware teapot with a curl of steam spiralling from its spout, two cups (pottery, for day-to-day use, not best china), two plates and fruit cake. The recipe for the cake was a special one of Mrs Simms, my Aunt Parry's cook. It had been divulged to Bessie, with injunctions not to pass it on, when Bessie had left Aunt Parry's staff to join our small household.

'Yes, I do,' said Bessie loftily. 'Of course I know what "discreet" means. It means, we don't tell anyone what we do.' She gave me a look from beneath lowered eyelids. 'And 'specially, we don't tell the inspector what we do.'

'Yes, no, I mean,' I went on hastily, 'I will decide what we tell the inspector.'

'And I says nothing,' said Bessie cheerfully. 'Shall I cut us a piece of that cake, missus, or do you want to do it?'

'I'll cut it. You have made it very nicely, Bessie.' I carefully cut two neat slices and put one on each of our plates.

Bessie smoothed down her apron and smiled at the cake. 'It's nice us having a tea party like this.'

'It's a council of war,' I said. 'We are making a plan of campaign, you and I, Bessie.'

'Whatever you say, missus,' was the indistinct reply through a mouthful of cake.

'From now on, we put together what we know. For a start, you tell me all you know about Miss Marchwood and anyone else who attends the temperance meetings.'

Perhaps it was wrong of me to encourage her to gossip, but as Ben says, detectives have to ask questions, and can't be fussy about observing the rules of politeness, or they'd never learn anything. But it did strike me that I'd just told Bessie we must be discreet and here I was, encouraging her to be anything but.

'I told you already,' said Bessie. 'Miss Marchwood comes up to London on the train and brings biscuits. I don't know any more about her, only that she's a lady's companion, like you used to be before you married the inspector.'

'But how do you know she's a lady's companion?' I asked. 'Did she tell you?'

Bessie gave a snort. 'No, she don't talk to me. Only to say, "Fetch more milk, Bessie!" But she talks to Mrs Scott, see, and I listen. That's how I know Mrs Scott's husband was a soldier and died of a fever in India, in some place with a funny name. Lucky something.'

'Lucknow?'

Bessie nodded. 'Could be. I thought it strange and a bit sad that the poor man died at a place called Lucky.'

Had Scott died at the infamous siege of Lucknow during the Mutiny, some ten years earlier? I wondered. If so, Mrs Scott had been left a young widow. Had she too been caught up in the siege as had many army wives? I felt inclined to forgive her being so suspicious of me, if she had been through so much trouble and danger.

'Does Mrs Scott often take Mr Fawcett with her in her carriage when she leaves the meetings?'

'Quite a lot,' said Bessie, 'I seen them a few times, going off together in the carriage. I think Mr Fawcett lodges not far away from Mrs Scott's house.'

'How about Miss Marchwood? Does Mrs Scott ever take her in the carriage?'

Bessie shook her head. 'Not that I've seen. Mrs Scott lives at Clapham.'

'How do you know that?'

'Because,' said Bessie calmly, 'I heard her tell Mr Fawcett once, "I hope you will be at my next swarry in Clapham."'

'Swarry?' I asked cautiously.

'It's a party,' explained Bessie.

'Oh, a *soirée!*' I exclaimed.

'That's what I said,' repeated Bessie, growing a little impatient at all my interruptions. 'A swarry. And I know she's got a big house, very fine, because Mr Pritchard told me so.'

'Mr Pritchard has been invited to these soirées?' I was surprised. I could easily imagine Mr Fawcett, with his dove-coloured pantaloons and silk cravat, enchanting the guests at such a gathering. But not little Mr Pritchard with his kiss-curls plastered fast with lard across his sweating brow.

'Oh, no!' Bessie gave a hoot of laughter. 'He's tradesman's entrance, he is! He don't get invited. He's her butcher, delivers her meat.' Bessie leaned forward confidentially. 'He says it's a really fine place and full of beautiful things.'

'I would expect Mr Pritchard to have got no further than the kitchen,' I objected.

'He's looked through the windows. And one day when he was leaving, he saw a cab drive up and a really swell-looking feller get down. He had long black hair curling over his collar and looked, said Mr Pritchard, like a pirate. He was carrying a big square flat parcel, all done up in brown paper. Mr Pritchard thought it was another picture. The house is full of pictures. He saw them when he was looking through the windows.'

Now this Ben would be interested to know.

'You're doing very well, Bessie,' I said. 'Let us have another slice of cake.'

Ben was certainly very interested. 'Good Lord!' he said, when I told him about the picture.

'Of course,' I warned, 'we don't know Mrs Scott bought it at Benedict's Gallery. But suppose she did? Do you think it could have been Benedict himself delivering it by cab? To a favoured customer?'

Ben looked doubtful. 'Benedict isn't a fine-looking fellow with curling hair and piratical good looks. He's an insignificant sort of chap, medium height, balding, slender in build. But Angelis, now, I'd describe him as a swell, a man who wants to be noticed. There's more than a touch of a Barbary corsair about him! If you saw Angelis getting out of a cab with a large parcel, you'd remember.'

He scratched his chin. 'Well, well . . . I had dismissed Angelis from all this. Perhaps I was wrong to do so. But we mustn't be hasty in our conclusions. We don't, as you say, know that the painting, if the mysterious parcel *was* a painting, was bought from Benedict, even though its delivery by Angelis strongly suggests it was.'

'But you could find out,' I said. 'Angelis will keep a record of all sales at the gallery.'

'Obviously I have to talk to Angelis again, and to Isabella Marchwood. That woman has deliberately concealed a good deal from me! But even if Angelis lets me see the record of sales and Mrs Scott is in it, what does it prove?' Ben tapped his fingers on the table top in an irritated way. 'We could be jumping to conclusions, seeing connections where there are only coincidences. I have to have more than this, Lizzie, before I take it all to Dunn. The superintendent is already as nervous as a cat with only one of his nine lives left. Is there anything else?'

'Not yet,' I confessed. 'But I might learn more at the temperance meeting this Sunday. I do know that the meetings seem to provide a link between all these people. It's all the more curious because they are such a varied group and would seem to have nothing else in common.'

I began to tick off the points on my fingers. 'Mrs Scott, a soldier's widow, knows Miss Marchwood, a lady's companion. She also knows Mr Pritchard, a butcher by trade with a clientele among the better-off, including herself. He delivers meat to her house regularly. Both Marchwood and Pritchard help at the temperance meetings, as does Mrs Scott. So does that mean that one of them encouraged the others to come along?

'Miss Marchwood was companion to Allegra Benedict. Mr Benedict owns a business dealing in fine arts and Mrs Scott has a house full of paintings. She acquired a new one not so long ago and it was delivered by a man who might – I know it's guesswork now –' I said apologetically, 'but he *might* be Angelis, the manager of Benedict's Gallery. Someone who looks very like him, at any rate. If he was, and Mrs Scott buys works of art from the gallery in Piccadilly, then it's possible Mrs Scott knew Sebastian Benedict himself. In fact it's very likely. She could have met him at his gallery. You say he goes there three days a week. He would want to establish a personal rapport with a good customer. Allegra Benedict sometimes went to the gallery with him, or called in when she knew he was there. Mrs Scott could well have made her acquaintance, too.' I paused, working out the next link in the chain.

'You say Angelis was anxious to tell you that Miss Marchwood always accompanied Allegra when she called at the gallery, so Mrs Scott could have met Miss Marchwood there as well. She may have suggested the two women attend the temperance meetings. Bessie is keen to spread the word about abstaining from alcohol and perhaps Mrs Scott is, too?' I paused again. 'What do you think of my reasoning so far?'

'Plausible,' said Ben. 'But far too many "perhapses".'

'There is a weakness, too,' I admitted, 'because Allegra Benedict didn't accept the invitation to the temperance meetings; only her companion did. Bessie never saw Allegra there. She didn't go.'

'That simply means Isabella Marchwood was interested enough to go along, and her employer was not. Perhaps we are being led down the wrong path by concentrating on the Temperance Hall. Allegra Benedict was Italian and grew up in a country where everyone drinks wine and thinks nothing of it,' Ben observed. 'I can't imagine she would fancy going to a temperance meeting.'

'No,' I said, leaning forward in my excitement as the idea entered my head, 'but she might go to a soirée at a fine house in Clapham.'

There was a silence. Then Ben said slowly, 'If your mind is travelling along the same track as mine, then there may be another link between them – between Allegra and Mrs Scott, I mean. I am thinking that they were both lonely women: one widowed, possibly when young, and one an exile from her native land and married to an older man whose only interest seems to be paintings and his art business.'

He paused. 'Angelis would have an excuse for calling on Mrs Scott. He would be advising her about her purchases in the art world. She might, if lonely enough, encourage his visits; even invite him to her soirées. He'd cut a fine swashbuckling figure there.

'But Allegra was lonely too. I have no doubt at all about that. We know for certain that Allegra and George Angelis knew one another. They met at the gallery. I don't know Angelis's origins, but even if he was born in this country, his ancestors weren't, that's clear. Perhaps he and Allegra shared the fact that they were *both* exiles in a strange land. They both hailed from countries full of sunshine and vineyards . . . and they both ended up living in rainy, foggy England where demon drink is shunned. I think,' concluded Ben with a smile, 'that would be enough to make any two people form a friendship. It could be furthered by meetings at Mrs Scott's house.'

'It's a splendid theory, Ben,' I told him, 'but it has a fatal flaw. For that to be the case, Allegra would need to be friendly with Mrs Scott.'

'It was you who suggested she might be,' he pointed out. 'You said she might attend these soirées given by the Scott woman out at Clapham.'

'I know I did. But I can't be sure of it. Give me time,' I told him. 'Bessie and I will work on it.'

He looked at me soberly. 'Be very careful, Lizzie. Don't forget, someone out there in that circle is a murderer.'

Inspector Benjamin Ross

Of course I was very interested in everything Lizzie had told me. It made me even surer in my own mind that it was not by some unlucky chance that Allegra Benedict went into Green Park that foggy afternoon. She had arranged to meet someone and was so desperate not to miss the appointment that she decided she could find her way to the oak tree, despite the fog. That suggested to me she and the unknown person she was to meet had rendezvoused at the oak tree before. It, and the way there, were familiar to her. Even with such poor visibility, she was confident she could find it.

It seems I am too well known. The gentlemen of the press certainly know me and I had to run a gauntlet of them before I reached my office the next morning. One wretch trapped me a good hundred yards away. He was a tall, lean, eager-looking fellow with a long thin nose, who reminded me of a greyhound.

He loped alongside me, pestering with his questions. 'Oh, come on, Inspector! You know, the press can help you a lot in this. Look at the number of people we reach! Everyone wants to know more about the River Wraith! Is it true he's a known lunatic who's escaped from a madhouse? You must have something you can tell me. I'll see my paper gives you full credit.'

Superintendent Dunn would love that, I thought sourly.

'Are you making any progress? Are you about to arrest anyone?'

'Yes, you, for impeding me in my duty!' I snarled at him.

He gave a high-pitched giggle and his eyes gleamed at the thought of what a good story that would make – if I should be so foolish as to arrest him. He knew I wouldn't.

'My, you are a wit, Inspector. Come on, now, anything . . .' he coaxed.

I walked on, ignoring him until I realised a different voice spoke in my ear and saw that another member of the Fourth Estate had taken his place. This one was of middle height and stocky with a red jowly face, more a bulldog than a greyhound.

'Perkins, Inspector, of the *Daily Telegraph*. You know me, sir. We're a reputable newssheet, Inspector, as you know well. We're not a penny rag. Our readers include important people and respectable citizens in all walks of life. Just let me have something. Is it true the Wraith's a foreigner? There's a rumour he's a Russian anarchist. How about an exclusive?'

I escaped into the Yard with a sigh of relief.

'I'm going down to Egham again,' I told Dunn. 'I need to have another talk to the Marchwood woman. She must tell me the truth. She isn't doing so at the moment, I'm sure of it.'

'Taking Morris?' he asked. 'Bear in mind that there is a limit to the amount of expenses you can claim . . . and Morris can claim even less.'

'Morris is still trying to find the butler, Seymour, and I don't need him for this,' I assured Dunn. 'I am doing my utmost to keep within my expense allowance.'

I managed to give the reporters the slip and get to Waterloo Station unobserved by them. I reached Egham and toiled up the hill on foot to The Cedars. Dunn would approve my wearing out my boot leather, but the fact was that the pony and trap that had conveyed Morris and me on our first visit was already taken. It was rolling away as I emerged from the station into the yard. Was it, I wondered, the same vehicle as had taken Angelis from the station to The Cedars to report his failure to find Allegra? If I had managed to secure the trap I could have asked Billy Cooper about that. He would remember a fellow like Angelis and being asked to wait for quite some time outside the house and take the visitor back to the station. He must have been curious about an errand of such importance that a man would travel from London and back on the same evening, late and in poor weather. (Interviewing a witness would have allowed me to bring the cost of the trap within my expenses, too.)

Oddly enough, given the foul weather we had been having, it was a mild day for my second visit, quite warm, as sometimes happens late in the year. The trees were bare of leaves yet the scenery was not wintry. I was halfway up the hill when I saw a walker coming towards me. He was dressed in a dark frock coat and wore a black top hat with a black silk scarf tied round it, its two ends fluttering behind him as he walked. It was Benedict himself.

He was as close as fifteen feet away when he recognised me and I wondered how good his eyesight was without spectacles.

'Inspector!' he exclaimed. 'You have news? You have arrested the fiend who murdered my wife?'

'I'm afraid not, sir,' I apologised. 'But we are leaving no stone unturned.'

He looked dissatisfied. 'Then what are you doing here again? You are not going to find him here. There is nothing more I can tell you. You are wasting your time travelling out here again, when you could be on his track in London!'

'I had hoped,' I said, 'to speak to Miss Marchwood again. Is she at The Cedars? I hope she hasn't left.'

'No, no, she's still there,' said Benedict impatiently. 'I can't stand the sight of the woman. I have told her to keep to her room. She failed in her duty. I will give her a week or two to find a new place, and then she must go.'

'How did she fail, sir?'

He gaped at me and then a tide of red crept from his neck up his pale face. 'Are you a fool, Inspector? She was hired to be Allegra's, my wife's, companion! Yet she was not with her when – when it happened.'

'Forgive me, sir, but a companion is not a gaoler, nor a bodyguard.'

'You are impertinent, sir.' From red, Benedict's face turned white. 'I shall report this matter to your superiors at the Yard. I do not expect to be insulted by someone supposed to be a public servant! For your information, I did not keep my wife a prisoner. She came and went as she pleased. But she was young, and when she first came to this country everything was strange to her. I engaged Marchwood at that time to take very good care of Allegra. I expected her to do that. Yet she didn't! I would be entitled to throw the woman out of the house immediately. But, because Allegra was fond of her, I am allowing her a period of grace. She does not deserve it.' He raised his hand to touch the brim of his hat with his cane. 'Good day to you, Inspector.'

Hum! I thought. I might have handled that better. But in the end, I needed to shake up a few people in this matter. Everyone had his or her story off pat to tell me. When Allegra Benedict died, everyone was somewhere else: Benedict at home, Miss Marchwood ostensibly looking for her or at the gallery. Angelis, also, was either at the gallery or out looking for the missing woman. Gray, the assistant, likewise. The beadle at the Arcade did not remember the ladies. Tedeschi, the jeweller, had confirmed to Morris they had been there. I'd have to talk to him again. But he was in his shop at the time of the murder. The only person to speak frankly and supply me with important information had been the crossing sweeper, Charlie Tubbs.

The same parlourmaid, still weepy, opened the door to me and told me that Miss Marchwood was upstairs in her own room.

'She won't come down, sir. I know she won't. It's very bad here. Everyone's so upset. Mr Benedict . . . well, you can understand how he feels, poor gentleman.' She dropped her voice to impart a confidence. 'Miss Marchwood won't want to meet him, sir, because the sight of her seems to irritate him.'

'Mr Benedict has left the house,' I said. 'I met him halfway down the hill. I am sure it will be in order for me to talk to Miss Marchwood in the drawing room in his absence.'

The parlourmaid, whose name I belatedly remembered was Parker, looked unhappy and dithered for a moment, but as I remained firmly where I was on the doorstep, gave way.

'You'd best come in, sir. I'll go up and ask the lady if she can come down and have a word with you. She's very distressed, too. I'm sure we all are!'

With that, and a sob, Parker showed me into the room I'd been in before, where the piano stood. As I waited by it for Isabella Marchwood to appear, I spent the time re-examining the photograph of Allegra Benedict. In it she looked so very young, beautiful and innocent, but perhaps also a little unpredictable. Behind those eyes staring so frankly at the camera, those lips turned up in a slight smile, perhaps intended for the photographer, what was running through her mind? Everyone, it seemed, had loved her. But what did she, still half a child, expect of her life? A passionate romance? Certainly Sebastian Benedict was no dashing hero of one of those tales. Travelling to England, now, that must have seemed an exciting prospect to a youngster. What had been her expectations of her new life? Rather more than she had found here, I suspected.

I sighed in sympathy with that young girl in the silver frame and touched the ruby vase. Italian glassware, perhaps. The red rose of my last visit had been replaced with a pink one. This was not the season for roses. This one and its predecessor had been forced under glass in some way and must be expensive.

A faint click behind me caused me to turn and I saw that Isabella Marchwood had come into the room and stood by the door, watching me apprehensively. As on the previous day she was dressed in black with the lace mantilla. She had been a very plain woman when I saw her then. Now she looked ill, white, drawn and with a nervous tic at one corner of her mouth. I wondered how far she was from complete collapse.

'Your employer will not disturb us,' I said reassuringly. 'He has gone out. I saw him myself, walking down the hill towards Egham. Please, sit down.'

She came forward hesitantly and seated herself not far from the door so that, I presumed, she could bolt out if she heard Benedict return . . . or if I frightened her too much.

'I am afraid I must trouble you again,' I began.

'Have you found him?' she asked eagerly, leaning forward with clasped hands pressed against her flat bosom.

'Not yet,' I admitted, wondering if I was to be subjected to the reproaches Benedict had heaped on me.

But she only sighed, shaking her head. With her gaze averted, she asked very quietly, 'Do you think it likely that you will find him?'

'It is my job to find him, Miss Marchwood. I shall do my utmost. Perhaps, although I know it will distress you, you could tell me again about the events of that Saturday afternoon?'

She didn't protest but began to recite her story again in a low, monotonous tone. I use the word 'recite' advisedly. She used very nearly the same words as before and it confirmed my suspicion that she had rehearsed all this in readiness for my first visit. When a person is afraid to deviate by so much as a phrase from an account, it often means they are afraid they will let slip something they mean to hide, contradict themselves, or become in some other way inconsistent. I have experienced the same with many witnesses. It is not what they are telling you that counts. It is what they are not.

When she had finished I asked, 'There was no other reason for travelling up to London on that Saturday afternoon, apart from wishing to take a brooch to the jeweller?'

'We did take the brooch to the jeweller!' she said at once, sounding frightened and insistent at the same time.

'Indeed, you did. An officer has spoken with the jeweller, Tedeschi.'

At this she looked up and blurted, 'What did he say?'

'That Mrs Benedict, with you, had visited him and left a brooch at his shop.'

'Yes, yes!' she said quickly. 'That is what we did. I told you so. Why are you asking about it again?'

'Because, Miss Marchwood, I have a problem. It is this. You left the jeweller's about four thirty, but did not arrive at the gallery until a little after half past five. Mr Angelis is certain of the time. So, there is a period of an hour unaccounted for. Where were you both during that time? Or, more to the point, where was Mrs Benedict?'

'But I don't know!' she wailed. 'I don't know what time we left Tedeschi's shop. We were separated in the fog. I wandered up and down looking for her. I have no idea how long it took me!' She scrabbled at her sleeve and dragged out a lace-trimmed handkerchief. 'How can I tell you where poor dear Allegra was? I had *lost* her, lost her forever. She may already have been lying dead on the cold ground . . . oh, it's more than I can bear!'

I felt sorry for the poor little woman but I had to ask my questions.

'Then let me ask you bluntly, was there any other reason for travelling up to London on that afternoon? Some other errand? Did either of you hope to meet someone?'

'No, no!' she cried, looking terrified. 'It's just as I said. You don't believe me, but it's true, I swear it! I lost Allegra in the fog. Mr Benedict blames me, of course he does. After you came here yesterday, he flew into a terrible rage. He said some dreadful things but nothing could be worse than the things I've said to myself in my head. I blame myself! Since your visit, he won't see me. I am to stay in my room and take my meals there. If I go out into the garden, then I am to walk out of sight of his study windows. If I am in the garden and see him coming, I am to turn back and go some other way. I have written letters to all the ladies of my acquaintance, asking if they know of a situation. I want to leave. I don't want to stay here! He hates me! I hate myself! It is all my fault, all of it!'

Tears had begun to roll down her cheeks as she spoke. Now she was sobbing uncontrollably, just as according to Angelis she had been when she arrived at the gallery to report Mrs Benedict's apparent disappearance. The tiny lace-edged square was inadequate to stem the flow.

A sobbing witness can't give any kind of coherent account. I attempted to soothe her. 'Come, come, it is not your fault a murderer was at large. But I must know how it came about that Mrs Benedict was in Green Park. That she was wandering up and down Piccadilly, yes, I can understand that. But that she should go into the park in such dreadful weather and when, as you tell me, the intention of the pair of you was only to go as far as the gallery . . .'

There was a scurrying outside the door and it opened to reveal the parlourmaid, Parker.

'Sorry, Miss Marchwood, and sorry, Inspector. But the master is coming up the drive. He's just stopped to have a word with the gardener, but he'll be here directly.'

Isabella Marchwood jumped to her feet. 'He mustn't see me. He will throw me out on the spot! I have nowhere to go! Please, Inspector, leave now. I can't talk to you any more!'

With that, she rushed out of the room and I could hear her running up the staircase.

I picked up my hat and walked out of the front door as Benedict arrived at it.

'I trust,' he said when he saw me, 'that this journey has proved worth your while, Inspector. The next time you come, I shall expect you to have news of some progress to report to me.'

He stalked past me into the house. The door was shut and I was alone on the doorstep.

'Damn, damn, damn . . .' I muttered to myself as I walked away. 'Another ten minutes and I might have got something useful from that woman. She's terrified of him, that's clear. If she had been helping Allegra to do something Benedict would not have approved of, she'll be determined he won't find out. She'd rather the murderer went undiscovered!'

All the way back to the station and on the train back to London, I turned over in my head every word spoken by Isabella Marchwood that afternoon. The first time I'd spoken to her, she had been much more in control of herself. This time she could barely keep from breaking down. Surely, in that distressed state, she must have said something, if only one word . . .

Then there was Benedict's attitude towards her to be considered. When I had first called at the house, Miss Marchwood had been the one to go up to his study and tell him I was downstairs and to conduct me to him. She had seemed to be in charge of the household.

All this had changed dramatically after I'd left. Benedict had, so she'd just told me, flown into a rage and ordered her to keep out of his sight. Why the sudden change in his attitude towards her? I couldn't help but think it was because of my visit. What had I said? Was it just that his rage had initially been muffled by his sorrow and shock? But with my presence and my questions, he had realised this was now a police investigation and all that meant? He would not be permitted to grieve in private. There would be the attendant publicity engendered by our investigation, his relationship with his wife put under a microscope, his privacy invaded not only by us, but also by the press. That, in turn, might affect his business. He needed someone to blame. He could not blame himself; I suspected it was not in his nature. So he had turned on Isabella Marchwood. She had been hired to keep Allegra from harm and she had not done so. For Benedict it was as simple as that. That a murderer wandered in the fog did not excuse her lapse.

Or had I, despite my caution, planted the notion in his mind that this sorry affair might be down to more than unlucky chance? It was not simply that his wife, lost in the fog, had met a dangerous man out to kill. Such dreadful coincidences happen. But had Benedict now allowed the suspicion that there was more to it to take root and grow? That his wife's presence in the park, still unexplained, was not due to her taking a wrong turn in poor visibility. That he might have been deceived and that Marchwood must have been party to it? It would explain his rage.

I reflected that Isabella Marchwood had been afraid from the first. Distressed, shocked, grief-stricken, all of those things . . . but also afraid. She had good reason to fear Benedict; and me, too, if she was hiding something. My questions that afternoon had clearly terrified her. But what else frightened her? *Who* else? What had I missed?

'The brooch!' I exclaimed, startling my fellow train passengers who looked at me with some apprehension.

'Excuse me!' I muttered and they returned to their newspapers or books or to studying the passing scenery, but keeping a wary watch on me at the same time.

Isabella Marchwood had been alarmed when she heard we had checked with Tedeschi that the two women had indeed visited his shop. She didn't fear the jeweller would have contradicted her story, because he had already confirmed it. The women had been there. Why, then, so frightened? *What did he say?* That had been her question to me. What had Tedeschi *actually said* to the police? What could he possibly have said that would have invalidated her story in some way?

There was only one way to find out. I must call on the jeweller without delay. I went to the Burlington Arcade as soon as I got back to London, but Tedeschi had already left the shop for the day. He would not, the assistant told me, return until around eleven o'clock the next morning. I left word that I would call then to see him.

I stepped out of the Arcade into Piccadilly and consulted my watch. It was a quarter to five, the light fading fast. But Angelis should still be at the gallery. I turned my footsteps in that direction.

Chapter Seven

Inspector Benjamin Ross

CHARLES GRAY, still wearing his expression of otherworldly serenity, greeted me in the gallery and said that Mr Angelis would be pleased to see me in the office.

'Things are quiet?' I remarked, looking round. I was the only visitor.

'Apart from the press, very quiet,' agreed Gray. 'Though even those gentlemen seem to have found somewhere else to be today.'

'Your usual clients don't care to be associated with vulgar crime, I suppose,' I remarked.

He nodded. 'We won't see any business until all this is over.'

'How about the owner, Mr Benedict. Has he come into the gallery since the sad event?'

'No, sir. But one wouldn't expect it, would one?' was Gray's cool response. 'Mr Benedict is in mourning. Come this way, sir, if you would.'

Put in my place, I followed him.

Angelis greeted me civilly but this time I wasn't offered sherry.

'How can I help you, Inspector? I really can't add anything to what I told you on your last visit.' He sat back in his chair and folded his manicured hands over his waistcoat, today made of black and gold brocade. A thick gold 'Albert' chain was draped across it to secure his pocket watch. He wore rings, too, I noticed, also gold. As before, he struck me as far too exotic for smoky London.

'I am wondering,' I said casually, 'whether among your clients you number a Mrs Scott, who lives in Clapham. She is a widow. Her husband, I understand, was a military man.'

After some lengthy pause Angelis inclined his head. 'The name is familiar.'

'She has bought pictures here?' I asked him.

He raised a thick black eyebrow. 'May I ask the reason for your interest, Inspector?'

It wasn't for him to ask me questions, as I could have pointed out. But I didn't want to antagonise him.

'You'll appreciate, Mr Angelis, that our enquiries seldom proceed in a straight line,' I explained apologetically. 'All kinds of tangential matters crop up. Most can be disposed of quickly and dismissed from the proceedings.'

It was as good an answer as he was going to get and he knew it.

'Mrs Scott has bought here. Not often, perhaps, but on a few occasions.'

'She has a good eye for a painting?'

He pursed his lips but he could not but answer frankly. This was the area of his expertise and he had a reputation to maintain.

'I will be frank, Inspector, trusting it will go no further than these walls?'

I nodded. Whatever he had to tell me, I doubted it would ever be necessary to reveal Mrs Scott's taste, or lack of it, in court.

'The late Major Scott was, as you rightly said, a military man.

Both he and Mrs Scott were among those Europeans trapped for five whole months when the garrison at Lucknow was besieged during the Indian Mutiny of fifty-seven and fifty-eight. Major Scott took a fever during the siege and died. Mrs Scott had also taken the fever but recovered when the garrison was relieved and better medical care could be had. She travelled with her husband throughout their marriage and, despite her terrible experience at Lucknow and the death of her husband there, she has retained a liking for pictures of oriental scenes: caravan halts, nomads camped in a desert among the ruins of ancient civilisations, bazaars, the women of the seraglio, that sort of thing. There are plenty of examples to be had. It is a fashionable subject. But not all are of the best quality. Mrs Scott . . .' Angelis put his fist to his mouth and cleared his throat delicately as he sought the words. 'The lady cares for the scene depicted and is generally indifferent to the brushwork and ability of the artist, shall we say?'

'I see,' I said.

Hastily, Angelis added, 'We don't sell daubs here, Inspector. I beg you won't think that! But the lady has a liking for certain artists, not necessarily ones I would recommend. But I have her instructions that if a work by one of them should become available, I am to let her know.'

'Money is not an obstacle, then?' I observed.

'I don't think so, Inspector, although I have no knowledge of the lady's fortune. There are no children.'

'You've visited her house at Clapham yourself, perhaps, delivering some work?'

Angelis was no fool. The heavy lids drooped over his lustrous eyes and then opened again. If I asked this, it was because I already knew the answer.

'I have done so on occasion,' he agreed.

'Could you tell me when was the last occasion?'

He didn't want to do it, but he couldn't break off the conversation now. He rose from his chair, made a majestic progress to a shelf, and returned with a stout ledger. He turned the pages carefully. 'Here, you see, Inspector, I delivered "Bedouin tribesmen before the Great Pyramid", by a minor French artist, to her two months ago. I do not undertake to deliver the paintings to everyone, you understand. But Mrs Scott likes my advice on hanging the subject.'

'She takes your advice on that, but not on the quality of the painting!' I said with an attempt at humour.

But for Angelis it was a serious matter. 'Quite, Inspector. In this case I did explain to her that if she would wait a while, it was more than possible that a better work with a similar subject would come on the market. But she was in a hurry to have a replacement painting on her wall.'

'Replacement?' I asked.

Angelis flushed. He had said more than he intended. Good, that's what I wanted a witness to do.

'A painting had been taken down. It left a gap. Mrs Scott was less interested in the quality of the painting than the size of the frame. The absence of the previous one left a paler rectangle on the wall covering. She wanted to disguise it.'

I felt that prickle run up my spine that always signifies something of real interest is about to be revealed.

'Why?' I asked simply.

He gave a rueful smile. 'So that her friends would not notice the other one had been sold, I dare say.'

'Sold?' I exclaimed.

'Yes, by us.'

'For how much?' I asked tersely.

'That is a very private matter . . .' he began feebly. But then he sighed and went to fetch a second ledger. 'Here,' he said.

I looked at the entry beneath his pointing finger.

'That is a great deal of money,' I said, when I found breath.

'It was a very fine painting.' Angelis gave a kind of muted growl. 'And she replaced it with a bread-and-butter piece by a virtual unknown!'

I sat for a moment digesting the implication of all this. 'You said she had no money problems,' I said at last.

'I told you I have no knowledge of the lady's fortune,' he corrected me gently. 'But even if a person is in comfortable circumstances, he – or she – might want to raise an extra lump sum of money for something special. Something, let us say, that she would not wish her usual financial advisers to know about?'

'And you think that is what she was doing when she sold the good painting and replaced it with a cheaper one?'

'I had that impression. But I repeat, only an impression. I can give you no details. I may have been wrong.'

No, I thought, you weren't wrong. I'd wager my month's wages on it, and I think I can guess where that sum of money was going.

'May I ask,' I began and Angelis looked wary, 'if you have ever called at her Clapham house socially? She holds soirées, I understand.'

'Never, Inspector,' Angelis said coolly. 'Have you further questions? Because if not, I think I shall close the gallery for the day now, and let Gray go home.'

I left the gallery well satisfied. Now I knew the question I had to put to Signor Tedeschi the following day.

I arrived at the Burlington Arcade promptly at eleven the following morning. Harry Barnes was on duty and greeted me by name. He was the sort of employee who would remember all regular customers by name – and an inspector of police, if he should turn up. If Mrs Benedict had asked him to call her a cab that fateful Saturday afternoon, Barnes would have remembered that, too. I was surer than ever that she had not.

Tedeschi was waiting for me in his private sanctum, a tiny room above his shop. It was a pity the room was not larger because the jeweller himself was a big man. Whereas Angelis presented a well-built but elegant figure, Tedeschi was simply fat, with curling grey hair and sharp, pouched eyes. He didn't attempt to rise from the chair in which he was wedged. Perhaps it would have been an ungainly action and he didn't wish me to see his struggle. Instead, he waved a podgy hand at the one other chair. I sat down.

'They told me,' he said, 'that you would be coming today. I have already spoken to a Sergeant Morris.'

'Yes, sir, but matters have progressed a little since then.'

Tedeschi's chest wheezed faintly as he expelled his breath. I thought he was probably asthmatic. But he said nothing, waiting for me to go on.

'Mrs Benedict came with her companion to visit you last Saturday afternoon, the afternoon of the fog. She brought you a brooch.'

'She did,' he agreed.

'You still have the article?'

'I do.'

'May I see it?'

In reply, Tedeschi reached for a bell pull. From beneath our feet I heard a jangle and then footsteps on the spiral stair. A middle-aged assistant appeared.

'You wish something, Signor Tedeschi?'

'Open the safe,' ordered the jeweller.

The man went to a steel safe in a corner and opened it as bid. Kneeling before it, he turned his head and looked at his employer.

'The Benedict brooch,' said Tedeschi.

The man brought over a rather worn blue velvet case and placed it reverently before the jeweller. Tedeschi nodded, and the man returned to the shop below.

I watched as Tedeschi opened the case, took out a brooch from it and placed it carefully in the centre of a square of black velvet laid on his desk. He put the case to one side and sat back, looking at me. When I hesitated, he gestured towards the brooch.

I leaned forward and studied it.

'You wish a glass?'

I realised Tedeschi was offering me a jeweller's magnifying eyeglass.

'Thank you,' I said. 'I am, alas, not well enough versed in gems to make good use of it. I take it these are real gems, and not paste?'

'They are real gems, Inspector. Three small medium-quality rubies and one larger, very good stone. A ring of small diamonds, also of medium quality. Three small freshwater pearls. Excellent craftsmanship.'

'Of your own workshop?'

A faint smile crossed the jeweller's soft white countenance. 'The brooch is at least sixty years old, or even a little more. I would say it was made shortly before eighteen hundred. After the establishment of the Directoire in France, in the seventeen nineties, Roman and Greek antiquity was very much in fashion. There is no assay stamp on the gold because it is not of British manufacture. I suspect it is Italian.'

I looked down at the thing. It was larger than I'd expected. An intricate net of woven gold strands formed a shape like a Grecian

urn, which was ornamented with gems. Three small pearl drops
were attached, one to the base and one either side where, if it had
been an urn, there would have been handles or rings. The
resulting impression was vaguely classical; some Italian admirer of
the new French Republic had ordered this made for the lady of
his affections. I hoped she'd liked it. It was a very fancy piece but
not one that appealed to me.

'I see in your face that you don't care for it,' Tedeschi observed.
'It is old-fashioned.'

'I can't tell if it's old or new in style,' I admitted. 'Mrs Benedict
wanted a ring made of this? Could that be done?'

'It could. It would mean destroying the piece.'

'It would make a very good-sized ring,' I murmured.

'Yes, or even two rings,' Tedeschi agreed, 'or a ring and a pair
of small earrings.'

'Did you discuss the design of the ring, or rings, with Mrs
Benedict?'

'No, that was to be done at a later date.' The jeweller's voice was
curt. His chest wheezed more audibly. He took out a lawn
handkerchief and mopped his brow.

'So what will you do with it now?'

'At a suitable moment,' Tedeschi said, 'I shall write to Mr
Benedict and ask him what he wishes done. But the time is not
right.' He paused. 'He is in mourning. It would be inappropriate
to ask him about it now.'

'It would be even more distressing, perhaps,' I said, 'to tell him
the real reason why his wife had brought you the brooch.'

The silence was broken only by the wheezing from the other
man's chest. Then Tedeschi said quietly, 'There is no need. The
lady brought me the brooch for it to be converted into something
else. She was entitled to do so. The brooch is part of a collection

of jewellery, family jewellery, which she inherited on the death of her mother. As her mother had died when Allegra was only twelve, her father kept it in safety for her until her marriage. When she became Mrs Benedict, the casket of jewellery was handed to her and she brought it to England. I doubt Mr Benedict has ever known exactly what it contained.'

'So he would not miss one item?'

The jeweller sat very still. 'Possibly,' he admitted at last. 'I hope you are not going to suggest that, in these unexpected circumstances, I would *not* return the item to Mr Benedict, simply because he doesn't know I have it?'

'Of course not, Signor Tedeschi. Any jeweller who trades in the Burlington Arcade has a reputation above reproach!'

Tedeschi inclined his head graciously at the vote of confidence.

But I was about to upset him again. 'But possibly the true situation is somewhat different. You would not be obliged to return the brooch, let us say, if it belonged to you.'

Tedeschi twitched an eyebrow.

'May I suggest that the story about the brooch being made into some other item of jewellery is a convenient fiction? The motives for it are of the best. You wish to protect the lady. I believe Mrs Benedict wished to sell the brooch. You bought it from her. A condition of the sale was that no one should know of it. In fact, any knowledge of it would really put the cat among the pigeons. Her husband would be horrified, furious.'

I gestured at it. 'It is your property now and there's no need for you ever to write to Mr Benedict about it. Am I right?'

Tedeschi tucked away the handkerchief and tugged at the bell cord. The assistant ran up the spiral staircase again, and was dispatched to fetch coffee.

As we waited, Tedeschi began to talk. 'Let me tell you a story,

Inspector. It concerns a beautiful young girl. And she was, believe me, a great beauty. Please don't think me impertinent in my observations. I knew Allegra from babyhood. Her father Stefano was my old friend. He was very worried what would become of her should he die. He was not a young man. There was no suitable relative to whom he could turn in Italy. When Benedict made an offer for her hand, Stefano was delighted. He trusted Benedict. He knew his daughter would have a comfortable life.'

'But she wasn't happy here in England,' I suggested.

He shook his head and sighed. 'No, she was not happy. She didn't complain. But she liked to come here and talk to me about her childhood, her father, the family home she'd left on the shore of Lake Garda. Benedict was a generous husband, please don't doubt that. He liked to buy her presents, jewellery. He bought several expensive items here, in my shop. He liked to see her wearing his gifts. He did not want to see her wearing her mother's jewels or her grandmother's. He was . . .' Tedeschi waved a hand. 'He was a little jealous, I think, a little possessive. That, I believe, is why he did not give her a great deal of "pin money", isn't that what you call it? He paid all her bills, dressmaker and so forth, without a murmur. But he wanted to be the one to pay. He wanted her to depend on him.'

The coffee arrived and there was a short break in our conversation. I thought I understood exactly what Tedeschi meant. It tied in perfectly with the impression I had had of Benedict and his attitude towards his young wife, and also with what Henderson, the maid, had told me.

'She had no fortune of her own, apart from the jewellery?' I asked. 'No dowry or inheritance from her father? The family property you mention on Lake Garda? What of that?'

'Oh, there was a little money, but not a great deal.'

Unexpectedly Tedeschi chuckled. 'My dear friend Stefano liked to live well: fine wine, fine dinners, to spoil his daughter, to make merry with his friends . . . There was not much money, no. The house was sold on his death to pay his debts. Allegra's husband took charge of what inheritance there was; and invested it on her behalf. He controls it. The law in England does not protect married women well in such matters. She has – had – no access to it without his permission. No independence, you understand.'

I did understand. 'You had bought items of her mother's jewellery from Allegra before?'

'On two or three occasions,' Tedeschi admitted. 'A string of pearls and, I recall, a hair ornament. Neither was of great value.'

'And on last Saturday you bought this brooch?'

Tedeschi nodded. 'This . . .' he gestured at the brooch on its velvet bed. 'This is of greater value than either of the other pieces. She expressed some urgency about its sale. I was a little concerned for her.'

'She didn't tell you what she wanted it for, I suppose?' I could guess the reason. It had been destined, I had no doubt, for the same recipient who had benefited from Mrs Scott's secretive sale of her painting. But I needed confirmation of the fact. However I was not to get it from Tedeschi.

He looked shocked. 'No, and I could not ask her why she needed the money! That would have been highly indiscreet, impertinent. In any case, she would have not been obliged to reply.'

I was suitably chastened. 'Of course, but how did she seem to you?'

He pursed his plump lips. 'She seemed . . .' he hesitated.

'Worried?' I prompted.

'No, no!' The jeweller leaned forward. 'Not at all worried.

Excited, perhaps. Yes, that's the word. She seemed excited as if she were embarking on some adventure. I confess, I did suspect what form such an adventure might take.' He pulled a wry face. 'I guessed a *bel ami*, as the French so charmingly put it.'

Like a cat on hot bricks . . . Charlie Tubbs had called it. Tragic Allegra, rushing full of hope towards a dreadful death.

I tried to put emotion from my mind and asked briskly, 'May I ask how much you paid her for it?'

Tedeschi told me. As when I learned from Angelis what Mrs Scott had been paid for her painting, I was left temporarily speechless.

'Cash?' I croaked at last.

'Cash, Inspector.'

'And she left these premises carrying this money?'

'Yes. She put it into her bag, a little pink leather bag, suede.' Tedeschi took out his handkerchief again and wiped his eyes. 'I begged her to be careful, carrying such a sum. I feared some rogue might snatch her purse. I did not fear for her life.'

Elizabeth Martin Ross

The investigation into the death of poor Allegra Benedict was worrying Ben. He had given me a detailed description of George Angelis and of Francis Gray, and that evening he told me about his meeting with the jeweller, Tedeschi.

'I feel I hold the pieces of a puzzle in my hand,' he said, 'but I can't put it together, Lizzie.'

'You will!' I told him confidently. But he did not look reassured.

That night I woke up and lay, as I did by habit already, listening for the sound of Ben's breathing on the pillows alongside me. But I heard nothing. I stretched out a hand. He was not there, the sheets cold. He must have got up and gone downstairs at least an hour earlier.

I slipped out of bed and lit a candle. With a shawl round my shoulders and candlestick in hand, I made my way cautiously downstairs. Ben was not in the kitchen so I peeped into the parlour.

The fire still burned low in the hearth; he must have added some coals to its dying embers. They glowed red and made the brass fire-irons and fender gleam like gold. The air was warm. Ben was slumped in his chair so still I thought he must have fallen asleep there. But he became aware of me and stirred, asking, 'Lizzie? What are you doing?'

'I might ask the same of you,' I said. I went to put my candlestick on the mantelshelf. Its flame allowed me to see the face of the clock standing there. It was almost two o'clock.

'Oh, Ben,' I said. 'You'll be so tired in the morning.'

'I think I fell asleep here for a while,' he mumbled. 'I've been thinking over the case.'

'Shall I make us some tea?'

'No, no, Lizzie. There is no need for you to stay awake. Go back to bed.'

In answer I pulled up the little footstool and sat down on it by him. The fire rustled and sank down on itself as the underlying ashes compacted. A tiny red and purple flame flickered into life and was quenched.

He made no protest at my remaining, but began to talk as if I had been there all along and he was continuing the conversation we had been having over supper.

'Allegra intended to give the money to a man, just as Mrs Scott wanted to raise a sum of money quietly, without the knowledge of her bankers, to give it to a man. And, in Allegra's case, that man was either Angelis or . . .'

'Or Joshua Fawcett,' I finished his sentence for him when his voice tailed off. 'For his good works among the drink-addicted poor! *Pah!* I sensed that man was a hypocrite when I first set eyes on him.'

He looked down at me with a faint smile. 'Except,' he reminded me, 'that we have no evidence that Allegra even knew Joshua Fawcett.'

'Miss Marchwood, her companion, did. Perhaps she was going to be her intermediary? Perhaps she had suggested to Allegra that some money could be raised by selling unwanted jewellery?' I felt I had to do something and picked up the poker and rattled it in the grate despite the danger of making the struggling fire go out completely. 'Allegra was going to meet him in Green Park and hand it to him herself!'

'Marchwood must be persuaded to confide in the police,' Ben said forcibly. 'I have told Dunn it's the only way. Otherwise it's all speculation, as Dunn is fond of reminding me.'

'She might confide in me,' I suggested. 'If I go to the next meeting, she might well be there. She missed last week's because of the murder, but I'm sure she'll return. I could meet her there quite in the normal way of things.'

That sparked another vigorous reaction. 'It would be dangerous for you to raise the subject with her! We are dealing here with a killer, whoever he is. Besides, Superintendent Dunn dislikes your medd— helping me.'

'Superintendent Dunn can't object to my attendance at a temperance meeting,' I argued.

After a silence he replied, 'Nor can I, but for pity's sake, do be careful!'

'Am I not always careful, Ben? I don't want to upset Superintendent Dunn.'

'You don't worry about upsetting me, then, and my fears for you?'

I reached up and took his hand. 'I will make sure no one is nearby to overhear me if I talk to Isabella Marchwood.'

'I don't know how you are going to manage that at a crowded meeting.' He squeezed my fingers in his. 'Benedict believes his wife was conducting an affair. I am afraid I put the idea in his head. The jeweller, Tedeschi, who took a fatherly interest in her, admits he thought the same. But with whom? Or was she? Perhaps we are all wrong.

'And we don't yet know the destination of the money got from selling the brooch. It may not have been intended for Fawcett and his campaign to save the world from the demon drink. It's so easy to think that and consider no other possibility. Some other person may have asked her for money or suggested that he needed some.'

'If the suspicions of both Benedict and Tedeschi are right, the recipient was a lover,' I said firmly.

'Or a very close friend. We must not jump to conclusions,' Ben warned. 'I leave that to Superintendent Dunn! But Allegra had few friends. I think she must have known Angelis quite well, meeting him in the gallery so often over the years. There is also that pretty boy assistant of his, Gray. He is a relative newcomer, only working there for six months, but he is what you might call an inhabitant of the art world and she may have encountered him before that time.' Ben gave a hiss of irritation. 'That young fellow annoys me. I would give a lot to know what goes on in his mind. His face is too much of a mask. He has to be hiding something behind it.'

The fire had almost gone out and above it on the mantelshelf my candle was guttering.

'You have made no mention of the River Wraith,' I said.

'Perhaps he did kill Allegra. In the end, whoever she intended to give the money to, it is who *killed* her that is important and they do not have to be the same man.'

As I spoke the dying fire found one last scrap of coal and sent up a sudden yellow flame.

'Oh, I have not forgotten our will-o-the-wisp, the River Wraith,' Ben said. 'He is out there somewhere prowling around in his shroud, and so, I fancy, is his next victim.'

The fire had been vanquished, exhausted by its final effort. Now only a glowing layer of ashes remained.

'Power,' Ben said softly. 'Anonymity grants power, freedom to act in a way otherwise unacceptable or impossible. The Wraith hides behind his shroud as Gray hides behind his extraordinary looks. Fawcett hides behind his tub-thumping and Benedict lurks like a spider in a lair stocked with dainties in that house in Surrey. Even little Miss Marchwood is not what she seems. Bear that in mind, Lizzie, if you do meet her. Too many people in this matter have secrets.'

Chapter Eight

Elizabeth Martin Ross

WHEN BESSIE and I arrived at the Temperance Hall the following Sunday, little Mr Pritchard, kiss-curls larded in place across
his brow, was greeting people at the door. When he saw me he
looked startled but rallied very well. He hurried forward, bowing.

'Dear me, Mrs Ross. Now this is very nice, very nice indeed.
You are very welcome, dear lady.'

'You didn't expect to see me?' I asked blandly.

'Well, now,' admitted Pritchard, reddening. 'I felt – and I am
the first to admit I was wrong! I felt you didn't quite approve of
us.'

'I have no idea why you should think that, Mr Pritchard,' I said,
sailing past him with Bessie in tow.

He watched me go into the hall with some apprehension on his
face. But then more people arrived and he returned to his greeting
duties.

'Is his infant choir going to sing again, do you think, Bessie?' I
whispered.

'Bound to,' said Bessie at once. 'He's very proud of the choir.
Mr Pritchard is very musical.'

'Did he write the dreadful ditty the children sang last time?'

'Don't know,' said Bessie. 'I'll ask.'

'Don't bother,' I told her.

There was some commotion at the door. Mr Pritchard was practically falling over backwards in his efforts to welcome the latest arrivals.

Two ladies swept in, one leading the way. The foremost one was Mrs Scott, still wearing her Cossack hat, but with a purple skirt and mantle. The lady behind her was in deep mourning. A veil draped over a black bonnet concealed her face. Once she was inside the hall she turned the veil back to reveal a countenance quite ravaged by grief. I could also see she wore a gold-rimmed pince-nez.

I felt excitement rising in me and made an effort to quell it and ask Bessie as casually as I could, 'And is that Miss Marchwood, by any chance?'

'Yes, and don't she look sad?' Bessie sighed deeply in sympathy. 'Poor lady, she'll be out of a position, won't she, missus?'

'Perhaps her friend, Mrs Scott, will find her another post. She can't be without influence in her circle,' I said.

'Perhaps she will!' Bessie cheered up.

The hall had filled. There seemed to be even more people here than the week before. Mr Walters handed out his hymn-books and the proceedings followed the pattern of the previous week. We were treated to the infant choir again, singing a song with words much the same as the previous week. Then Mr Walters asked us to welcome our speaker and on to the stage came Mr Fawcett.

His speech, too, followed the same pattern. He greeted us mildly enough, his compelling aquamarine gaze sweeping the audience. It rested briefly on me; a flicker of some emotion showed before he passed on to the next row. What was it? Surprise? Amusement? No, I thought, it is mockery.

All the suspicions I had about the man flooded into my mind. He knew he hadn't ensnared me as he had Mrs Scott, Miss Marchwood and all the other ladies here – and the very few men. All of them he had captured with his charm and his oratory. I had not been taken in, but there was nothing I could do about it. No criticism of him I voiced to anyone in that hall would get a hearing. His loyal followers would rise up in horror. I would be driven away with imprecations. My heart set hard against him.

He began to preach to us again on the familiar subject, illustrating his message with several dramatic stories of men ruined, women lost to respectability and every kind of daily disaster. Miss Marchwood seemed very moved. She removed her pince-nez to dab at her eyes with a handkerchief. Mrs Scott, beside her, leaned towards her and murmured something, but it did not strike me as words of comfort. Rather, she appeared to be ordering the poor woman to bear up and not make an unseemly display. Miss Marchwood nodded, put away the handkerchief and fixed her gaze on Fawcett, her face now set in a mask of petrified unhappiness.

When time came for the tea, I made for the urn. I wanted to speak to Miss Marchwood, but Fawcett had come down from the stage and engaged her in earnest conversation in a far corner. Again, I had the uneasy feeling he was not giving her words of comfort and encouragement so much as telling her to pull herself together. She was listening and nodding.

'Well, Mrs Ross, we did not expect to see you here again,' said a cool voice by my ear.

I looked up to see Mrs Scott holding out a cup of tea to me.

I took it. 'Thank you. Why ever not?'

The directness of my question seemed to take her aback. She paused before answering, then said in the same cool manner, 'I received the impression, last week, that you did not altogether approve of our gathering.'

'I didn't approve of Bessie handing out leaflets,' I countered. 'I made that clear at the time to Mr Fawcett.'

'Was that your only objection?'

There was something in her gaze that was both detached and yet relentless. I thought of a cat, toying with a mouse. Well, she would find I would not oblige her by playing the mouse's part.

'Should there be any other?' I asked her, my tone as cool as hers.

Now her look turned to one of plain dislike. 'Certainly not!' she said curtly and turned aside. 'Mrs Gribble! How is the hot water in that urn?'

I looked back to the corner where I'd seen Miss Marchwood talking to Fawcett, but to my surprise both had disappeared.

Mrs Scott had her back to me. I was annoyed with myself; if I had been cleverer, I would have tried to make a friend of the odious woman and with luck received an invitation to the Clapham house and one of the 'swarries'. But it was pretty clear to me that would never happen.

She didn't like me. Why, though? Because I had had the effrontery to complain to Fawcett's face about the matter of the leaflets? Because she realised I was less than impressed by the man? She was shrewd enough to know it, I was sure of that. Or because I was married to the man investigating the murder of Miss Marchwood's employer and she had me down as a spy? Scandal, I thought sourly. That is the answer. She fears scandal and that somehow or other it will taint the meetings here and interfere with Fawcett's so-called charity work. I am not welcome.

She means to make that clear enough. The murder of Allegra Benedict must not be permitted to cast its shadow over the Temperance Hall.

People were beginning to leave. 'Come along, Bessie,' I ordered and we slipped out ahead of Mrs Scott. A little further down the street, a wide entry led under an arch into a tunnel between buildings to either side. At the rear it opened into a stableyard lit by a couple of swinging lanterns; but between that and the street, in the tunnel, the darkness formed a black mass. I drew a reluctant Bessie beneath the brick arch into the tenebrous depths where, unable to see each other, we huddled close together for contact and comfort as we waited.

'I don't like it here,' muttered Bessie, wriggling in the gloom. The accompanying rustling of petticoats told me she was drawing her skirts around her. 'It stinks something awful of horses.' Her voice trembled nervously. 'Can't we wait out in the street?'

'I want to speak to Miss Marchwood but she has not come out yet, so I must wait. I promised Mr Ross I would not let anyone see what I was about. A good healthy smell of horses need not trouble you, Bessie. It won't do us any harm.'

'Rats might!' warned Bessie in a dire tone. 'There's always rats in stables and they run up your skirts.'

Despite myself, I strained my ears for the skittering of claws in the darkness.

'Don't talk nonsense!' I commanded as firmly as I could.

'What if she sees us, missus?' hissed Bessie next.

'Then it will confirm her in her suspicions. But why should she look this way? Besides, it's too dark for her to see us.'

Before us, in the street, the light was fading fast and the shadows lengthening. The gas lighter had made his round already and lit his street lamps, but they cast no luminous glow beyond the entrance. From behind us I could hear the muffled stamp of stabled animals and an occasional soft snicker. Horse sweat and manure, saddle soap, hay, hoof oil mingled in an odour that announced their unseen presence. But did they somehow know we were here? Had our presence made them restless – or something else?

'I also want to see if Mrs Scott takes Fawcett with her in the carriage again. It's waiting for her,' I murmured, perhaps to justify our presence here to myself, rather than to Bessie. My eyes were now becoming accustomed to the darkness and I could make out the walls of the buildings to either side. But I still didn't like it here.

Fortunately at that very moment Mrs Scott came out with Fawcett in attendance. They didn't so much as glance in the direction of our hiding place. Fawcett handed her into the carriage and climbed up himself. The coachman put up the step and closed the door. But as the man was clambering back on to his perch, there was a diversion.

Miss Marchwood suddenly hurried from the hall. She ran to the carriage, just as it was about to drive off, and gripped the frame of the opened window as Mrs Scott made to pull up the sash.

'Jemima, please, I must speak to you!'

I saw Mrs Scott lean towards the opening from within and caught her reply.

'This is not the moment, Isabella. Come and see me in Clapham. Drive on!'

The carriage with its two occupants rattled away and Miss Marchwood was left disconsolate on the pavement.

'A few coppers, lady? For some hot soup to keep out the cold?'

I jumped and Bessie squeaked. The request, uttered in a hoarse voice, seemed to come from my very feet. To all the other odours was added that of unwashed humanity and stale ale. What I had taken for a sack of rubbish propped in the shadows of a corner formed by the wall and the rear of the arch now moved. A pale claw-like hand was extended in our direction. We had neither of us realised a homeless wretch had bedded down there.

I scrabbled for a few pence in my bag and hastily dropped them into that skeletal hand. Then I darted from the doorway with Bessie on my heels, and approached the solitary figure still on the pavement just as she was about to turn and walk away.

'Miss Marchwood! Please wait!'

'Yes?' she replied automatically, ignoring my request. She began to walk on at a brisk pace, clearly in no frame of mind for social chatter. I had to scurry alongside her and address myself to the veiled bonnet.

'I am Mrs Ross. You have met my husband, I think. He's investigating the death of your late employer.'

At that she did stop. She turned back the veil and I saw the expression of panic on her plain features, livid in the gaslight. 'What do you want?' Her agitation was such that the pince-nez fell from her nose and dangled on the black silk ribbon by which it was pinned to her pelisse.

'Don't be alarmed,' I soothed her. 'I only wanted to express my condolences. It is a sad loss. This is a dreadful experience for you.'

'What are you doing here?' she demanded, fumbling with the pince-nez and putting it back crookedly on her nose. My sympathy had passed her by as if unheard.

'I accompanied Bessie here to the meeting. Bessie is our maid. We were a little behind you, towards the back of the hall.'

'Bessie, oh, yes, Bessie . . .' Isabella Marchwood stared vaguely at Bessie. 'Yes, she is a very good girl.'

'And if there is anything I can do to help . . .'

'You?' she exclaimed. 'No, nothing! No one can help!'

'Please,' I urged her. 'Have confidence in the police. They will find the murderer.'

'Find the murderer?' she cried, looking at me wildly again. 'What good will that do? Will it bring back poor Allegra?'

'No, of course not, but the killer will be brought to account before the court and receive his punishment.'

'A trial?' she cried. 'How can that do anything but harm? The courtroom crowded with vulgar onlookers, every dreadful detail revealed and Mr Benedict obliged to sit and listen to it! To say nothing of the newspapers, and they are already bad enough. Have you seen them?'

'Yes, I have,' I confessed. I had gone so far, the previous day, as to buy a copy of an evening sheet that featured the murder, together with the story of the River Wraith and a dramatic illustration. This showed a woman starting back in horror as a hideous shrouded creature with burning eyes reached out its elongated hands to her. I had shown it to Ben when he got home and I wouldn't like to tell you what he had to say about it.

'A trial would see the courtroom packed with reporters. That can only make things worse . . .' Isabella Marchwood repeated desperately. Then she snapped her mouth shut. After a moment she began again, more calmly, 'Hasn't poor Mr Benedict suffered enough?'

'To know the murderer went unpunished would surely make him suffer more?' I suggested.

She shook her head. 'You don't understand. How can you?' She turned away and began to walk off down the street,

I hurried to catch up with her. 'Miss Marchwood!' I said urgently. 'Believe me, I want to help you. If there is something you feel you cannot tell my husband or any other police officer, but perhaps could confide to another woman, to me . . .'

She stopped and fixed me with a look so cold it might have been her friend Jemima Scott who looked at me. Although what kind of 'friend', possessed of a carriage, left a woman to make her way alone on foot to Waterloo Station where I imagined Miss Marchwood must now be going? It would not have been such a diversion, surely, to have taken her up in the carriage with Fawcett?

'I have nothing to say to you. Please, don't attempt to delay me. I have to catch my train back to Egham.' Miss Marchwood pulled the veil down over her face.

'Waterloo is almost half a mile from here,' I protested. 'Is there a cab rank nearby?'

'I am accustomed to walk,' she said, setting out again with a brisk step.

'Then at least allow Bessie and me to come with you. It is already quite dark . . .'

'I do not need your company, Mrs Ross. Good night.'

She hurried away and there was no purpose in following her and arguing it out any more.

Bessie and I set off homeward through the gaslit streets. I was startled when she spoke to me with an unexpected question.

'You don't like Mr Fawcett, do you, missus?'

'I think he is a charlatan,' I told her frankly. 'I'm sorry to distress you, Bessie, but that is what he is. His professed cause is a good one. I know drink to be the reason for all kinds of sorrow and crime. But men such as he are quick to attach themselves to a good cause and turn it to their own purpose. And that is what your Mr Fawcett has done. He harms the just battle against drunkenness, not helps it, and that is unpardonable.'

'Funny,' said Bessie sadly. 'I don't think I like him as much as I did. He didn't come and speak to you, did he, missus? That wasn't very civil of him.'

'He was more anxious to speak alone with Miss Marchwood and I would give a lot to know what he said.'

'She's bereaved!' said Bessie, shocked. 'Of course he wanted to talk to her in private, say all the right things, you know, what the clergy say at times like that.'

'I don't believe he is what you call "clergy". It wouldn't surprise me if he awarded himself whatever kind of theological qualification he lays claim to. Nor do I believe he only wanted to give Miss Marchwood solace and support. If you really want to know what I think, Bessie, it's this. He is alarmed that a member of his congregation, Miss Marchwood, is caught up in a murder investigation. Police investigations tend to range far and wide in such matters, going down all manner of paths, some ending in a dead end, some, with luck, offering up some clue. Mr Fawcett has something to hide. I am not suggesting it is anything to do with the murder – don't think that. But when a man has something to hide, he doesn't like any questions, for fear of what they may bring to light.'

My observation of Mrs Scott, and subsequent unsatisfactory conversation with Miss Marchwood outside the hall, had taken a good half an hour. That meant it had grown even darker. Decent folk were sitting indoors by their own firesides. Bessie and I made our way through streets now empty of all but those setting out for an evening's entertainment. I stepped out briskly, anxious to be home.

'The inspector will be wondering what's become of us, missus,' said Bessie, as she scurried along beside me.

'I'm sorry we haven't more to tell him,' I replied. 'If only I could have persuaded Miss Marchwood to confide in me. But perhaps I'll get another chance.'

On the other side of the road, on a corner, a public house was beginning to do good business. People jostled in the doorway and from within came a glow of gaslight and the sound of voices and a tinny piano. Suddenly there was a commotion. Voices inside, women's voices, were raised, in fierce argument. It was followed by sounds of a scuffle, breaking glass and falling chairs.

'Come on, missus!' urged Bessie, pulling at my arm. 'Likely as not there's going to be a punch-up.'

She was right. The door flew open and two female figures were propelled through it by a burly barman, to the accompaniment of raucous cheers from customers.

'And stay out!' he roared at them. 'Settle your differences somewhere else!'

The women ignored him, far too busy in grappling with one another. They hurled accusations and abuse, swearing all the while like the proverbial troopers, grabbing handfuls of clothing and hanks of hair, tugging and pushing, swinging their fists and scratching.

'Why does none of those men in there pull them apart?' I demanded.

'It's street girls, missus,' explained Bessie. 'They're always quarrelling over something. One of 'em will have strayed on to the other one's pitch, most likely.'

'Pitch?' I exclaimed.

'Yes, missus, they divides the streets and pubs up between them. One of them will have been trying to get the other one's business. It's nothing for you, missus!' finished Bessie severely. 'You come along.'

But at that moment one of the brawling girls yelled, 'Now look what you done! You bent me feathers!'

They had momentarily broken apart and were standing a few feet from one another, both breathless and for the moment unable to continue their battle. One of them was holding out a ridiculous little hat topped with a sadly battered plume of garishly dyed feathers. Her uncovered hair had been torn loose from its pins and tumbled in profusion over her shoulders. From the light pouring through the glass windows of the pub's doors, I could see the colour was a brilliant scarlet.

To Bessie's dismay, I darted across the road, calling, 'Daisy! Daisy Smith!'

The girl paid no heed to me; she was still holding out the hat towards the other girl. Her face was suffused with fury and what I can only describe as bloodlust.

'I'll make you pay for this, Lily Spraggs! It's me best hat!'

Such was the rage and desire for vengeance in her face and voice, and the obvious intent to do some serious harm to her opponent, that Lily Spraggs wisely chose the better part of valour and fled.

The scarlet-haired girl was left in possession of the field, still muttering furiously as she turned her hat this way and that, and tried to straighten the damaged feathers.

'Daisy Smith, you are Daisy Smith, aren't you?' I shouted at her, to gain her attention.

The girl looked up at last, from me to Bessie and then back again. 'Who wants to know?' she demanded, putting her hands on her hips in a challenging attitude. 'And who might you be?'

I was alarmed to see she was getting ready for battle again and Bessie caught my arm and hauled me back a few steps.

'Missus! Leave it alone!'

Daisy advanced on us. 'I've seen off Lily Spraggs and I can see off the pair of you, too! I've worked this pub for nearly a year. I got good customers in there! You ain't muscling in, you hear me?' She paused. 'Although I don't know what kind of business the pair of you think you are going to do, dressed like you was going to a funeral.'

This was too much for Bessie who erupted like a small volcano. 'Here! I'm a respectable girl! So is my missus, I mean, she's a respectable married lady!'

'Oh, yes?' said Daisy sarcastically, 'so why are the pair of you hanging about outside the pub? And you were last in line when they were handing out the good looks, weren't you?'

I flung both arms round Bessie to prevent her hurling herself bodily at Daisy and the scrap beginning all over again with a new contestant.

'I am Mrs Ross!' I gasped, as I struggled to hold the writhing Bessie. 'You met my husband, I believe, last Saturday – keep still, Bessie! On Waterloo Bridge, Daisy, in the fog. Inspector Benjamin Ross – no, don't run away, please!'

Daisy had started back and was turning to flee. I released Bessie and darted after her.

From behind me I heard Bessie yell, 'At least my hair's its own natural colour! It's not all come out of a bottle of henna!'

'Daisy, wait!' I panted as I raced along in the girl's wake. From behind I could hear the pattering of Bessie's footsteps and her increasingly desperate pleas for me to come back. 'My husband is most anxious to speak to you! He is investigating a murder. You have met the River Wraith—'

Daisy stopped so suddenly I cannoned into her. Bessie arrived and pushed herself between us bodily to protect me. Daisy looked at her with contempt, then at me with pursed lips. 'Hold me hat,' she said at last and handed it to me.

I realised that she would go nowhere without this prized item so didn't mean to run off again. Instead she began to put up her disordered hair. 'Most of me pins has fallen out,' she grumbled. She took her hat back from me and surveyed it disconsolately. 'Look at that! The hatpin's lost, too.'

'I've got a hatpin, wait, you can have it.' I pulled out the pin and handed it to her.

Daisy turned it this way and that and remarked approvingly, 'Got a silver knob on the end. That's really swell, that is.' She pinned the little hat back on top of her head. 'Is it straight?'

'Yes,' Bessie and I assured her together. 'It's perfect.'

Daisy folded her arms and fixed me with a stern look. 'You're not ragging me? You're married to that "jack" I met on the bridge, Saturday before last?'

'Yes, and he wants so urgently to talk to you about the Wraith. You know the other girl, the one who saw the creature plainly. He'd like to find that girl and speak to her, too, but he doesn't know her name.'

Daisy bit her lower lip, then said shrewdly, 'I heard about the woman who was murdered in Green Park. So your husband thinks it was the River Wraith who done it, does he? I never heard the Wraith went that far from the water. All the girls what have met him, met him by the river, like I did, the night I bumped into your old man. Bloomin' bad luck, that was.'

'It was very bad luck to meet the prowler,' I agreed, 'and you were fortunate to escape.'

'No! It was my bad luck to run straight into the law!' snapped Daisy. 'He didn't believe me then, I could tell that. I'm just nothing. But now some rich lady has got herself croaked, it's a different matter. Now it's all, "We must find the River Wraith!"' Daisy gave a sardonic chuckle.

'My husband isn't certain the Wraith killed Mrs Benedict,' I said cautiously. 'But he really does want to find him. Any help you can give—'

'I ain't interested in helping the police,' she interrupted me. 'They only end up giving you grief. So just like I told your old man before, I'm telling you now. I'm not going near no police station.'

'Then come with us to our house. It's not so very far away and my husband is there now,' I pleaded.

'Make it worth my time, will he?' asked Daisy, after pause for thought.

'I'm sure he will, or I will,' I promised her.

An impish grin crossed her face. 'Well, *won't* he look surprised when you turn up with me in tow! It'll be worth it, just to see him. And your neighbours!' She gave a hoarse chuckle. 'Well, go on, then, lead on. I'm behind you!'

'You know what, missus?' muttered Bessie as the three of us set off. 'I don't think this is a very good idea. We'll take her in the back way, through the yard, into the kitchen. Neighbours won't see her then, and if you keep her in the kitchen, she won't be able to pinch anything.'

'Oi! I heard that!' called Daisy.

Our terrace of houses all had backyards with a door in the far wall giving access on to an alley which ran the length of the street. It was mostly used by coalmen delivering sacks of fuel, to avoid having to carry them through the house from the street. That was the way we took Daisy, up the path between coalhouse and outhouse, and through the kitchen door.

Bessie shut this with a sigh of relief. 'Cor, I was afraid someone would look out of an upstairs window and see us!'

'See me, you mean,' said Daisy. She looked round the kitchen and then settled herself at the table. 'This is very cosy, I must say.'

Bessie folded her arms and looked mutinous. 'I know how many spoons there are, you know,' she said in dire tones.

'All right, Bessie!' I said hastily, 'I'll fetch Mr Ross.'

I have to confess I rather cherish the memory of the moment I went up to Ben, comfortably nodding off in his chair before the fire, and told him we had a visitor.

'In the kitchen, Ben. It's that girl, Daisy Smith, the one you said you wanted to find again.'

His jaw dropped. '*What?* Where did you find her?' But he was already running towards the kitchen as he spoke.

Daisy was already seated at the table there and Bessie standing over her, arms still folded.

'Bessie,' I suggested, 'why don't you make us all some tea?'

'Me?' squawked Bessie. 'Make tea for the likes of her?' She pointed at Daisy.

'I like it nice and strong,' said Daisy maliciously, 'with two sugars in the cup.'

'Please, Bessie,' I said hurriedly. 'We shall all feel the better.'

Bessie stalked to the range and dragged the kettle from it.

'You'll have heard the news, Daisy, about the woman's body found in Green Park?' Ben asked her.

'He killed her, then, did he? The River Wraith?' Daisy demanded.

'He might have done,' was Ben's cautious response. 'But until I find him I can't make any progress in that direction.'

'You rozzers do like a mouthful of words,' observed Daisy, 'and 'specially a plain-clothes "jack" like you, I suppose. Can't make any progress? Do you mean you're stumped?'

'Well, since you put it that way, Daisy, yes, we are. That's why I need to talk to the girl who saw the Wraith. I'm very anxious to know his exact modus operandi . . .'

'What's that then, when it's at home? You swallowed a dictionary or something?' demanded Daisy.

'I beg your pardon,' Ben smiled apologetically at her. 'I mean I want to know exactly what he did, not just to the other girl, but to you. You say he put his hands on your throat?'

'Yes, he did!' said Daisy. 'Nasty clammy fingers he'd got.'

'He didn't try and put a string or cord round your neck?'

'No, I told you. He had horrible cold dead man's fingers.'

'And the other girl? She had much the same experience?' Ben asked.

'I suppose so,' said Daisy. 'You'll have to ask her yourself, won't you?'

'That's what I want to do,' Ben reminded her.

Bessie put the teacup down with a clatter in front of our guest. Daisy sniffed at it, sipped it, nodded and poured some liquid from the cup into the saucer. She held the saucer to her lips and slurped appreciatively while we waited. She was clearly enjoying her moment of attention and being able to make us all dance to her tune.

'Well, Mr Inspector Ross,' she said at last, 'it sounds like you believe me now, doesn't it?'

'About the River Wraith? Yes, I do.'

'Because he killed a fine respectable lady, I suppose. You wouldn't be so interested if he'd killed me or someone like me, would you?'

'Yes,' said Ben simply, 'I would.'

Daisy blinked. Her manner changed from sarcastic to thoughtful. 'Swelp me, I believe you would, and all.' She paused, studying him carefully and then said, 'If I tell you all I know, you'll do something for me?'

'You'll be paid for your time,' Ben promised.

To the surprise of us all, especially Bessie, Daisy shook her head, sending the poor battered feathers on her hat bobbing.

'I don't want your money. I want you to find someone. Well, you'll have to find her if you want to talk to her! The girl who saw the Wraith clearly, her name is Clarrie Brady. That's Clarissa, but everyone calls her Clarrie.' Daisy folded her arms and leaned them on the table. 'See, I work the south side of the river, just around where your missus found me tonight. Clarrie she worked the north side, up as far as the Strand. Only there's a lot of girls working the Strand, so mostly Clarrie worked nearer the river.'

'Why do you say "worked"?' Ben asked sharply. 'Where is she working now?'

'That's it,' said Daisy. 'No one's seen her since Friday before last. When I met you on the bridge that Saturday night, I was running across to try and find her and warn her that the Wraith was about, tell her I'd just met him myself. But I couldn't find her. She was still working the district; I knew that, because I'd seen her meself on the Friday morning. There's a coffee stall just over the bridge and that's where I met her, drinking a cup on her way home from work. We had a bit of a chat because we're friends. We've been friends since we were kids. Ever since that time she saw him standing right in front of her, in his shroud, she's been scared of meeting him again. She told me she was sure he knew who she was; and he was looking for her. She's not working another pitch. I asked all the girls I could find. None of 'em's seen her.'

She shook her head sadly and I realised how very young she was, certainly little older than Bessie. I didn't like to think how long she had been at her present trade.

'When you told me about her, that evening on the bridge,' Ben said slowly, 'you mentioned she had a man friend.'

Daisy gave a snort of disgust. 'Jed Sparrow. He don't care. He's not even looking for her now. He did look for a couple of days. Now he's got himself another girl.'

'Where can I find Sparrow?'

'The pub, the Conquering Hero, just where your missus saw me tonight. He was drinking in there earlier, might still be. Only if you go looking for him, don't you tell him I told you where to find him – or he'll find *me!*' Bessie finished warningly.

'I won't tell him. What does she look like, Clarrie Brady?'

'She's short, little runt like her . . .' Daisy pointed at the bristling Bessie. 'But she got a pretty face, not like her –'

'If you says one more thing about my looks,' shouted Bessie, 'I'll tip that pot of hot tea right over your dyed hair and silly hat!'

'Bessie, go and make up the sitting-room fire,' I ordered. 'I'm sure Daisy is only teasing you.'

'No, she ain't,' growled Bessie. 'She means it.' She pushed her face into Daisy's. 'Well, I ain't on the streets, am I?'

'Shouldn't think so,' said Daisy, 'not looking—'

I jumped up, grabbed Bessie's arm and bundled her out into the hall. 'Just listen, Bessie, I know she's being very rude to you. But she does it because you react. She prods you, you snap back. Leave it all to the inspector and me. The inspector really needs her information.'

Bessie removed her arm from my grip. 'I'll go and make up that fire,' she said icily.

Back in the kitchen, Daisy was making herself at home, pouring herself another cup of tea.'

'So, she's short and she's pretty,' Ben was saying, a touch wearily. 'So are hundreds of girls in London.'

'She's got a mole on her forehead, right here.' Daisy touched her left temple. 'And a scar under her eye, here.' She put a forefinger on her right cheekbone. 'That's where Jed Sparrow smashed a glass into her face one time. He was sorry he done that,' she added.

'So I should think!' I said indignantly. 'The poor girl was defenceless!'

'It's 'cos he was worried it'd spoil her looks a bit,' explained Daisy. 'That's why he was sorry. But it healed up nice and you don't see it much. She puts greasepaint over it, the stuff the actresses use. It covers it up really well.'

She turned her attention back to Ben. 'So where is she? I can't find her. But if the bobbies on the beat was to look out for her, one of them might find her.'

'I'll put out the description to all of them,' Ben promised.

'And you won't give up if they don't find her in a couple of days? Supposing you find the Wraith first, you'll still go on looking for Clarrie, like you'd look for some fine lady if she went missing? You promise that? It's what I want in return for my information.'

'Yes, I will,' said Ben. 'You have my word, Daisy.'

Daisy stood up. 'Thanks for the tea, then. I'll let meself out the back way, like I come in.' She paused by the door and looked over her shoulder. 'You give me ten minutes to get well away before you going running round to the Conquering Hero, if that's what you're going to do.'

'I will,' promised Ben.

'And if ever you want to find me, you can leave a message with Sally, the barmaid at the Hero. I'll be off, then.'

When Daisy had gone, I sat down at the table again. 'What do you think has happened to Clarrie Brady, Ben?'

Ben hunched his shoulders. 'She may have been so frightened by her encounter with the Wraith and so sure he was looking for her – or so frightened of that lout, Sparrow – that she's run right away, out of London. Or . . .'

'Or?' I asked quietly.

Ben sighed. 'Either Sparrow has killed her and dumped the body somewhere we haven't yet found it. He's got himself another girl without delay. That suggests he's not expecting her back. Or the other possibility . . .' He looked at me apologetically. 'I'm afraid, Lizzie, the other possibility is that the Wraith did find her again. Perhaps Clarrie was not imagining he was looking for her. She saw him clearly. He will know that. He obviously disguises himself in that ridiculous shroud and what I suspect is a mask of some sort over his face. But she still saw him clear of the fog, and that may have worried him. He may have sought her out. But we haven't found a body, Lizzie, not that I know of. Keep your fingers crossed.'

He took out his watch and consulted it. 'Almost ten minutes. I'll just walk over to the Conquering Hero and see if the not-so-heroic Mr Sparrow is still there.'

Chapter Nine

Inspector Benjamin Ross

IT WAS a short step to the Conquering Hero. The pub stood on the corner at a junction where two roads formed a right angle. Thus it had two entrances in different streets: an entrance into the public bar from one and that to the saloon bar in the one round the corner. A very convenient arrangement, I thought. If a drinker were to learn someone he didn't want to meet had just come in one door, he could easily make his escape through the other. It was likely Mr Sparrow wouldn't want to meet me, so I had to choose the right door.

The men who lived off the earnings of the girls on the streets generally fancied themselves as flash coves. They wouldn't want to mix with draymen and labourers. I made for the saloon bar entrance.

A question to the barman identified Jed Sparrow. From the little I knew of him I had imagined a burly brawler of a thug. But no, he matched his surname, a little shrimp of a man in a bowler hat and suit of houndstooth check. I saw that he had only one eye. Where the other should be was only a sunken cavity indicating that eyeball was missing altogether. The remaining orb seemed to miss nothing, for it darted around the bar-room taking in everything. It had already, I was sure, taken note of me. Certainly it flickered warningly at my approach.

I saw that not only had he suffered no business loss from the disappearance of Clarrie Brady, he seemed to have prospered since then. He sat between two young women in bright clothing, one wearing a mauve silk bonnet and the other a hat with trailing ostrich plumes that reminded me of Daisy and her feathered hat.

When I reached the table, Sparrow gave an exaggerated wink to the girl with the mauve bonnet.

'Well, look at what just blew in! Here's the p'lice, all dressed up in plain clothes, if I'm not mistaken – what I don't think I am!'

He laughed heartily and the two girls joined in but not without nervous glances at me. How did he know my calling? Not for the first time, it puzzled me. But they always did seem to know.

'I believe I'm speaking to Jed Sparrow,' I said to him. 'I'd be obliged for a word. I am Inspector Ross from Scotland Yard.'

'How do you know my name?' he demanded at once, an ugly glint in his single eye.

'Oh, you are a very well-known man, Mr Sparrow,' I said cheerfully, seating myself opposite to him.

Sparrow seemed unsure whether to be offended or pleased to learn this. Then he jerked his head towards the door and told the girls to 'Hop it! Get out there and earn your keep!'

They both scrambled to their feet and hurried away.

'Not sending them out to work as prostitutes, I hope, Mr Sparrow?' I asked mildly.

'Bless you, no, they're good girls. They go round houses collecting rags. I'm in that line of business, you see.' His crooked yellow teeth flashed a grin at me. He didn't expect me to believe that nonsense, of course.

'Rubbish,' I said briskly. 'But it's not those two girls I've come to talk to you about. You know a girl called Clarissa or Clarrie Brady.'

The Cyclops eye squinted at me alarmingly. 'What if I do? Here, what's she been saying about me? It's all lies. You don't want to believe a word she says. Born liar, that's Clarrie. Wouldn't know the truth if it jumped up and bit her nose.'

'She's said nothing, Mr Sparrow, because she hasn't been seen for over a week. Friends have looked for her in vain. I'd like to find her and you, I understand, are the person to ask.'

'I don't know who told you that,' he grumbled. 'It's no use you asking me about her now. I ain't seen her either, not for, oh . . . must be near on ten days.' He put his head on one side and the eye fixed me with a baleful stare. 'What are you accusing me of? If she's gone, she's gone. I don't know nothing about it.'

'At the moment, Sparrow, I'm not accusing you of anything. I'd like to talk to her, that's all,' I said.

'So would I,' said Sparrow. 'She owes me money.'

'She earned you money, you mean. Did you look for her?'

He decided to be conciliatory. 'Well, you know how it is, Inspector. I'd like to help but I can't. Yes, I asked around when she first took off, but well, there's always another one. I was getting tired of her, anyway. She gave me too much lip.'

And it had got her face cut by a broken glass on one occasion, I thought, but didn't mention. He would be curious to know where I'd got my information and I didn't want to lead him to Daisy.

'But her disappearance left you out of pocket,' I pointed out. 'I would have thought you'd be out there hunting her high and low.'

'Like I said, there's always another one.' Sparrow eyed me coolly. 'And what, if I might ask you a question, would Scotland

Yard want with Clarrie Brady? She's magistrate's court fare, she is. She's not into the sort of business that interests *you*.'

I ignored the question to ask another of my own. 'Did Clarrie ever mention to you that she had encountered a creature the girls call the River Wraith?'

Sparrow burst into a shout of laughter. 'So that's it, is it? Listen, Inspector . . .' He leaned towards me confidentially and I tried not to draw back. 'Here's what I can tell you. There ain't no such person – or monster or ghoul or whatever you'd like to call it. It's an excuse the girls make when they don't come back with much money – I mean any rags, they've not collected any rags, you understand!' he added hastily.

'Collecting the rags, if that's what you choose to call it. Did Clarrie tell you that, while she was out "collecting rags", she met this Wraith?'

To my great relief he leaned back. His breath hadn't been the pleasantest. Now he hooked his thumbs into his waistcoat. 'Yes, she did and I clipped her ear for being so stupid.'

'Stupid for being frightened out of her wits?' I snapped.

'No, for thinking I'd believe such a cock and bull story.'

'Can you remember exactly what she told you?'

He shook his head. 'She was jabbering away about it, and piping her eye. She always knew how to turn on the waterworks. Something about the fog clearing and he was standing in front of her. They imagine things, Inspector, those girls. None of 'em is very bright.'

I left him there and went out to see if I could spot one of the ladybirds that had been drinking with him. But neither they nor any of their sisters were to be seen anywhere. The two in the pub had spread the word that 'plain-clothes was snooping about' and they had all prudently decided to 'collect rags' elsewhere.

★

It was my intention, on Monday morning, to request all constables on the beat to ask around for Clarrie Brady. The constables on the regular beats know all the girls who work the streets and, when not actually arresting them for plying their trade too obviously, indulge in fairly spirited banter with them. With luck one of them might have seen her. Or, failing that, might have heard from one of her sisters where she'd gone. I also intended to send Biddle to check the records of the various magistrates' courts to see if Clarrie had appeared before the bench lately. But when I reached the Yard, all thought of Clarrie was put immediately out of my head.

Sergeant Morris once more grabbed me as I stepped through the door and announced, 'Superintendent Dunn wants to see us both immediately, sir!'

'Morris,' I said ruefully, 'this is becoming a habit. I wonder if I shall ever again reach my office without you intercepting me with some new problem. You're not going to tell me there's been another murder, I hope?'

'I don't know, sir,' said Morris. He lowered his voice. 'But Mr Dunn's got someone with him, a chief inspector of Railway Police from Waterloo Bridge Station.' Morris gave the rail terminus its full title to lend weight to his words. 'Both of 'em very agitated, sir.'

Now what was a chief inspector of the Railway Police doing so far from his domain at Waterloo? I wondered. I hurried to Dunn's office, Morris on my heels.

Dunn was scowling ferociously as I entered, but not at me. The recipient of the glare was a man of about forty with a ginger moustache. Some lively discussion (or some might have guessed 'argument') appeared to have been in progress. The first words I heard were spoken by the visitor.

He was saying, 'Of course we cannot investigate it alone but you can't do it without us . . .'

'There you are, Ross!' Dunn exclaimed with obvious relief as he spied Morris and me. 'This is Chief Inspector Burns, London and South West Railway Police, based at Waterloo Bridge.' He turned back to Burns. 'This is Inspector Ross, who is heading the inquiry into the River Wraith and the Green Park murder. And Sergeant Morris.'

Morris stood to attention. Burns nodded acknowledgement of the introduction.

I had no time for social niceties. 'River Wraith!' I exclaimed. 'There's been another murder?'

'Yes, but not in the park. This one was found on a train.' Dunn gestured at Burns. 'Perhaps you'd care to explain, Chief Inspector.'

'Thank you, sir,' said Burns to him. He turned to me. 'About an hour ago a body was discovered in a compartment of a train arriving at Waterloo on the Chertsey line.'

'Chertsey line? Forgive me, Chief Inspector,' I interrupted, 'but where does that stop along the route?'

'Several places, at Egham, Staines . . .'

'Egham!' I cried. My heart gave a painful leap. Was it possible? No, no, surely not, I tried to tell myself. But I felt the cold hand of foreknowledge close round my heart.

Dunn cleared his throat warningly.

Burns, after a glance at him, continued. 'Discovery of the body, that of a woman, was made by the ticket inspector. The train is still standing at the platform but the public are not being allowed access. This is playing havoc with the timetable along the entire route, as you can imagine. As soon as the body has been moved, the train will have to be put back into service. If necessary we can isolate the carriage where she was found. It will require some manoeuvring and take a while.'

'How about the other travellers on the train?' asked Dunn. 'Did they see or hear anything?'

Burns shrugged. 'Unfortunately it wasn't possible to detain any of the passengers. They had left the train and were gone before the body was found. They waste no time when they get to Waterloo! There is always a rush for the available cabs. The unfortunate woman appears to have been strangled with a length of cord or stout twine . . .'

I jumped up again. 'I must see the body at once!'

'Personally, I shouldn't think this has anything to do with your Green Park murder,' said Burns. 'But given the publicity – it's been in all the newspapers – and the method used to kill, I thought I would come over here and ask whether you'd care to come and have a look.' He cleared his throat. 'We have, of course, already set our own investigation in motion. But the help of the Metropolitan Police would be much appreciated . . .'

'Of course,' I assured him. 'I am obliged to you, Chief Inspector, for realising our possible interest and calling on us. I should very much like to see the body and realise you must clear the platform for use as soon as possible. I'll come at once.'

Waterloo is a large and busy terminus with trains arriving and leaving continually. Its platforms and concourse heave with a throng of humanity of every description. Even a discovery as grisly as the one we were on our way to investigate could not close the whole operation down. Nevertheless, it was obvious that a considerable amount of disruption to the smooth running of the services in and out of the station had already occurred. Some of this was unavoidable and some of it might have been avoided if the travelling public had not been so ghoulish in temperament.

An area of platform had been cordoned off by a number of uniformed officers of the Railway Police. They were struggling to hold back a crowd of avid onlookers. These included passengers, some holding bags, porters and other station staff; to say nothing of the usual riff-raff hanging around large public areas anywhere in the city. Some of these were probably drawn to this crowd, as to any, because of the opportunity of picking pockets or other opportunist thievery. Any owner of a piece of baggage rash enough to put it down, distracted by the commotion, might well find when he looked for it again that it had gone. Some would-be travellers, even if they did not miss their wallets or watch and chains, would no doubt miss their trains. At the moment they did not care. All were consumed by their eagerness to know the details of the macabre discovery and oblivious to the risk.

I wasn't surprised to see the throng and feared it would become worse rather than better. There was obviously no way of keeping knowledge of what had happened from the public, nor of rumour carrying the story outside the station. It was only a matter of time, I thought sourly, before the press would hear of it and then they would descend as well.

Burns strode forward, muttering and cursing under his breath. I followed closely as he forced a way through the crowd. A constable, recognising him, saluted and let us through.

'We've told them to move along, sir, but they won't,' he complained nervously to his superior.

'Threaten to arrest a couple!' snarled Burns.

The constable gazed miserably at the crowd. I doubted that, even if he plucked up courage to follow Burns's order, it would do any good.

Free of the mass at last, we made our way on to the platform and past the great chocolate-brown-coloured monster of an engine, still emitting wisps of steam like a slumbering dragon. Behind the engine was a luggage van and behind that was a carriage, the door on the platform side hanging open. Beside it, on the platform, waited a group of people, including the unlucky ticket inspector who had found the body. There were also a couple of curious cleaners with mop and brush, and a medical man, gripping his professional bag. He gave every sign of being extremely angry, red-faced and scowling; what I could only describe as 'simmering'.

Burns introduced the furious medical man first. 'This is Dr Holland. He's taken a look at the body and certified death.'

'Strangled with a cord,' confirmed Dr Holland in a growl. 'A foul deed, gentlemen, a foul deed! Is a lone woman not safe in this country? And on the railway? Who is responsible, eh?' He thrust his red face towards us.

I guessed Burns wanted to retort, 'Not the railway!' But he wisely gave the only reply that would be acceptable. 'I agree with you completely, doctor.'

'Well, well, well . . .' muttered the doctor, deflected from accusing the London and South Western Railway directly of the crime. 'At least it would have been quick. She appears to be a woman of middle age and relatively frail build. She could not have put up any resistance.' He gathered a new head of steam. 'The fellow, whoever he is, is a monster, a fiend in human shape, nothing short of it! I trust you will find him and he will hang.'

'Thank you, Dr Holland, we'll do our utmost,' Burns assured him.

'Do you want me any more?' asked the doctor.

Burns looked at me.

'Tell me, Doctor,' I asked, 'you say the victim was frail. Could a woman have done this by any chance?'

'A woman?' roared Holland. 'Strangle someone – another woman – with a cord? Out of the question!' He paused and added grudgingly, 'I don't say it could not be done. But it is not a woman's crime, take my word for it. Women are subtle creatures, sir. Arsenic in the sugar bowl, that's their style.'

'Indeed,' I murmured, wondering what experience of this he had. 'As you say. I only wanted to know the degree of strength involved.'

'Very little,' snapped Holland. 'A child could have done it, come to that. But I trust you are not suggesting that is the case?' He grunted and marched off.

'He was on hand,' explained Burns a little apologetically. 'So we asked his help. He's not our usual medical man. This is Williams.' Burns now turned to the ticket inspector. 'These gentlemen are from Scotland Yard, Williams, so tell them your story.'

'I can't understand it, sirs,' said Williams. He was a young man of spindly build and looked distinctly unwell. He mopped his forehead with an oil-stained handkerchief. 'I never thought to come across anything like it. It's horrible, sirs . . . and in a first-class compartment, too.'

'You can explain it while we inspect the scene,' I said impatiently.

Burns and I scrambled aboard, Williams on our heels.

The woman's body, dressed in mourning black, was slumped in the corner by the window on the far side. Her black silk bonnet had a mourning veil attached. When the veil had been drawn down over her face, it must indeed have appeared to anyone casually looking into the carriage that she was asleep. It had taken Williams's closer investigation to reveal she was not. I did not need the sight of the gold pince-nez hanging from a ribbon to tell me who she was. Poor Isabella Marchwood. Had she decided, too late, to confess the truth? I would never learn her secret from her now. Someone had made sure of that.

'I thought she was asleep, sir,' whispered Williams, confirming my thoughts. 'I looked into the carriage as I came past and saw her. Sometimes a passenger does drop off to sleep and miss his stop. This is the terminus, so I opened the door and called out to her. When she didn't respond I made so bold to lean over and shake her shoulder.'

He gulped and patted his mouth with the handkerchief. 'She didn't reply and I couldn't see her face for her veil. I wondered if she was ill, fainted or something. So I made even bolder, as you might say, and lifted the veil over her bonnet and I saw—'

Williams broke off his account with a moan.

'Pull yourself together, man!' snapped Burns.

'Yes, sir, sorry sir. I saw the ends of a cord or string dangling down, sir. It was tied round her neck. Her eyes were open and bulging something horrible . . .' He drew a deep breath. 'I saw she was dead, gentlemen.'

'What do you think, Inspector?' Burns asked me. 'Any connection with your Green Park murderer?'

'Every connection,' I said heavily. 'This lady is – or was – Miss Isabella Marchwood. She was a most important witness in the case we are investigating, the Green Park murder you refer to. I interviewed the lady myself twice, both times at Egham at her place of residence.'

'Her ticket was from Egham,' said Williams helpfully. 'I saw that when I checked it.'

'We'll get enquiries going at Egham at once,' promised Burns. 'Someone should remember her getting on the train and whether she was accompanied. Also if any other traveller followed her on.

We'll make similar enquiries at each stop down the line to find out if anyone was seen entering or leaving the carriage.'

I turned to Williams. 'Forgive my ignorance,' I told him, 'but what exactly do you do, how do you perform the task of checking the tickets?'

'I get into each carriage in turn, sir,' said Williams. 'I start at the end of the train and work my way up to the front, then I go back to the end and start again. I ask to see all tickets and clip them.'

'So, between stops you travel in the carriage with the passengers?'

'Yes, sir, until I can leave and proceed to the next one.'

'There is talk,' said Burns, 'of building railway carriages with a connecting corridor, so that a defenceless female like that is not shut in with whoever chooses to enter the carriage after her. After this dreadful affair the public demand for that will increase, and for some other means for a passenger to call for help, some kind of chain, perhaps, running the length of the train, if it could be rigged up conveniently. A tug on it could sound a bell to alert the driver or fireman. I'm all for it myself. Although I have to say, a steam engine is a noisy place to work and I don't know that anyone would hear it.'

'At what point on the journey did you check this lady's ticket?' I asked Williams.

'Between Twickenham and Richmond, sir. I remember her clearly because of her being in mourning, and she was the only passenger in first class. She handed me her ticket and I saw it was in order.'

'Did she speak?'

'No, sir, that is to say, she said "thank you" very quietly, when I handed the ticket back to her. I do remember that. I felt sorry for her, sir, her being in such deep mourning. I wondered if she'd lost someone close. When we got to Richmond I jumped out of this carriage. It was the last before the engine, so I ran down to the end of the train to begin again, as I explained. I do try and keep an eye open to make sure no one tries for a free ride between two stops. The lady was alive and well when I left her.' Williams looked distressed and pointed vaguely down the length of the train to indicate the direction in which his duties had taken him.

'So when you say you are watchful of platform activity, you mean you are watching to see if anyone gets on, not who gets off?'

Williams reddened. 'Yes, sir, but I think I'd have noticed any one acting oddly.'

'You travelled with this lady between Twickenham and Richmond. What stops lie between Richmond and London?' I asked next.

'Clapham and Vauxhall, sir.'

'Can you say if any passengers entered or left the train at Clapham or at Vauxhall?' I urged again.

'Yes, sir. No one got on at Vauxhall, to my knowledge. But four or five people at least got off.' He frowned. 'Mostly it was gentlemen at Vauxhall, I fancy. There may have been one lady. At Clapham two or three got on, but I didn't notice anyone go into first class. Quite a few passengers left, male and female. None of them were acting suspicious. But that's the best I can tell you. I know I must have missed someone, sir, because the murderer must have boarded after Richmond.'

'You saw no one running away from the train towards the exit from the stations you mentioned?'

'No one running, sir, I can be sure of that.'

But our murderer was too clever draw attention to himself in so obvious a way. He'd have descended in a normal manner and just walked briskly away. He may have walked alongside another traveller to give the impression he was not alone.

'Go on,' I urged Williams.

'We reached Waterloo here. Everyone got off, or I thought they did. I began to walk back up the platform. I always look into the carriages as I pass by, just to see if any one of the passengers has left some item of personal belongings. I hand those in to our Lost Property Office here,' added Williams firmly with a glance at Chief Inspector Burns.

'When I got to the head of the train, here, the first-class carriage, I looked in and – and there she was. I was surprised she'd fallen asleep. But, as I was explaining to you, that's what I thought she'd done.'

I turned to Burns. 'Let's assume the murderer was probably among those who got off at Vauxhall or at Clapham.'

'He was a quick worker,' remarked Burns sanguinely.

'He'd had practice!' I told him. 'And this was no random target. He had it all planned.' I looked back at the crumpled figure in its black dress and bonnet.

'We'll start immediate enquiries at Vauxhall and Clapham and all stops along the line,' Burns promised. He pulled a wry grimace. 'He's not your River Wraith, anyway. He dresses up in a shroud, I understand, and he'd be spotted immediately if he did that and tried to travel on a train in the middle of the morning! Anyway, I understand he operates only within walking distance of the Thames in the centre of London. Perhaps this murderer was inspired not by that story but by the reports of the Green Park murder. He read about the method used and it gave him the idea to use a cord.'

'I agree the murderer wouldn't have been in fancy dress,' I said, 'but we don't know who lurks under the disguise – or his motive.

Miss Marchwood was with Mrs Benedict the day they travelled to London, became parted in the fog, and Mrs Benedict met her death in Green Park. Whoever killed Mrs Benedict, I am sure he killed this lady, too.' I sighed. 'But don't ask me if he is also the River Wraith, because, frankly, I don't know.'

'How about her purse?' Burns asked, picking up a point I should have noticed. 'Did she have one, Williams? Where did she keep the ticket?'

'She had a little black bag, sir . . .'

Williams suddenly dropped on his knees, and stretched his arm beneath the seat on which Marchwood's collapsed body was propped. He emerged in triumph, holding up a small jet-beaded black purse. 'Here it is, gentlemen! She must have dropped it, poor lady, in the struggle. She or her killer kicked it under the seat, perhaps, without him noticing.'

'Then it wasn't robbery,' remarked Burns, pulling open the jet purse. 'See, here's some money and here –' he pulled out a small oblong card – 'here's the ticket from Egham.' He handed to me. 'You're satisfied here, Ross? If so, I'll order the body removed. It will be taken to St Thomas's hospital mortuary.'

'Yes, yes,' I agreed, staring down at the little ticket in my hand. A return ticket, but she was never to make the journey back.

'What sort of person,' I asked, 'tries for a free ride, as Williams mentioned?'

'Youngsters mostly,' said Burns. 'And the odd rough type or a young flash fellow who's taken a drop of drink.'

I turned to Williams for the last time. 'And that's the sort of person you were looking out for?'

'Yes, sir,' said Williams unhappily.

But our murderer had surely been respectably dressed and that, in its own way, can be as much of a disguise as a shroud.

Chapter Ten

Inspector Benjamin Ross

'THE QUESTION that enters my mind,' rumbled Superintendent Dunn when I reported to him on my return to the Yard, 'is not just where the wretch got on or off the train, but how the devil he knew that the Marchwood female was travelling on it.'

'It's entered mine, too, sir,' I agreed, 'and the only satisfactory answer I can give is that he saw her board the train at Egham.

'Of course, I'm not ruling out other possibilities. He could have got on later at Richmond, after Williams left the victim's carriage. He could have slipped in unseen behind the inspector's back. He could then have got off at Clapham. Or he could have got on at Clapham, and got off at Vauxhall, or boarded at Vauxhall and descended with the majority of travellers at Waterloo. That holds good if this was a random killing.

'But if it was planned, as I believe it was, then the easiest explanation is that he boarded the train at Egham. He kept an eye on the direction the ticket inspector was moving in, watched and waited until Williams had checked tickets in the first-class carriage where Miss Marchwood sat. He made sure no new traveller had joined her there. Satisfied she was alone and that they could not be interrupted, he then, at that or a subsequent stop, hopped out of the carriage he was in, walked quickly down to first class, and slipped in after Williams left. Williams was either on his way down to the other end of the train, facing in that direction, or already there.'

There was a pause during which Dunn rubbed his head, and then folded his hands on his desk. 'So he lives at Egham too, our murderer? Is that what you are saying? Are we talking of Benedict? The finger would seem to point at him, if you are right.'

'Not necessarily,' I said quickly, 'even though a suspicious and jealous husband is an obvious suspect. But we don't know how many people are involved in this. Another person might have been watching the house, The Cedars. He – our murderer – travelled down to Egham, walked up the hill to The Cedars and hung about there. He could easily conceal himself. The house stands in large grounds. There are trees, bushes . . . If he wished to watch the house unobserved he could have done so. When he saw Miss Marchwood leave, he followed her and boarded the same train. Unless . . .' I added, struck by a thought. 'The murder was committed by an accomplice. The first man, watching the house, followed her to the station and could then have telegraphed ahead to someone that she was on that train in first class. The second person could have been waiting on the platform at Richmond or any of the stations between there and Waterloo, and joined Miss Marchwood there.'

'Why kill her at all?' asked Dunn bluntly.

'Because he – they – feared she would eventually confess whatever facts she was hiding to us. I believe she was on her way to do so. Or she may have intended to seek out my wife.'

Dunn raised his eyebrows.

'Lizzie spoke to her last night, Sunday, after the meeting at the

Temperance Hall,' I explained. 'She urged Miss Marchwood to confide in her but the lady didn't want to talk to Lizzie. However, the conversation, brief as it was, may well have led her to change her mind about speaking frankly to the police. Whatever secret she carried, it was a dreadful responsibility and worry. She was a religious woman, highly respectable. She wanted to unburden herself. The murderer knew that. It worried him. He decided she must never reach the police.'

'Or, I repeat, are we looking at Benedict himself?' Dunn's stare challenged me.

'I don't count him out, sir,' I said with a sigh, because I could see Dunn had got the idea fixed in his head. 'Benedict did take a sudden violent dislike to Isabella Marchwood after I first called at his house. But he didn't immediately turn her out, bag and baggage, as might have been expected, given his wish not to set eyes on her. What was his purpose in keeping her there? Was it simply because, as he said, his wife had been fond of the woman? Or because he preferred to know where she was and what she was doing?' I paused. 'I can't help but think of something that wretched Scully said to me about Benedict.'

'Who is Scully?' asked Dunn.

'Dr Carmichael's assistant, sir. You probably haven't met him. He is an unpleasant sort of fellow, gives you shivers up your spine to look at him. He enjoys working with corpses, I do believe. However, what he said was, did I think the husband had killed her? Why do it in the park, was Scully's comment. Why not kill her at home? But of course to do it at home, would be too obvious. He'd be arrested at once and all the servants would be witnesses. But he might have followed his wife to London that afternoon.'

'And today he followed Marchwood? You may be betting on someone watching the house. My money is still on the husband.

175

You had better get down to Egham and talk to him again.'

'Yes, sir. I wonder, is there something I could ask of you?'

Dunn raised his bristling eyebrows. 'Go on, then, man. What is it?'

'The preacher, Joshua Fawcett, who is the main attraction at the Temperance Hall Isabella Marchwood attended. I suspect he may have been the man Allegra Benedict was going to meet, although I have not yet any proof she knew him personally. But she almost certainly knew of him through her companion. She had a large sum of money with her. The purse and the money have not been found. I think Fawcett may be a confidence trickster, preying on lonely women, persuading them to give him money for his claimed good works. If so, he may have plied the same trade in other cities. My wife describes him as young, about thirty or possibly a few years older but looking thirty. He is a dapper dresser, with a diamond stickpin in his cravat. He has long hair and blue or green eyes. He is extremely eloquent and adept at controlling his audience. My wife, who is a shrewd judge of character, considers him a fraud.'

'I'll make enquiries,' Dunn promised. 'I am glad Mrs Ross is so observant.' He allowed himself a smile. 'But I know Mrs Ross has her wits about her. It is a pity we can't enrol a few women like her in the Metropolitan Police!'

The gardener was sweeping up fallen leaves and garden debris near the entrance to The Cedars. He looked up as I passed and greeted me with a bright, 'Good afternoon, Inspector!' I had not interviewed him myself on my first visit; Morris had done that. But someone on the staff had obviously pointed me out to him. Servants observe all comings and goings at a house and generally know what's happening. I wished even more fervently that Morris would be successful in tracking down the former butler, Seymour. His sudden voluntary departure must have had some fairly drastic cause.

The black bow still adorned the knocker on the front door, but the window curtains were no longer drawn. I wondered if, when the household learned of the death of Isabella Marchwood, they would be drawn again in respect.

Parker opened the door to me and greeted me cheerfully this time with, 'Oh, Inspector Ross! Are you here to see the master, sir? You'd better come in.'

I was glad to see her no longer tearful, but feared my news would return her to her former state of distress. It had been agreed with Burns that I would be the bearer of the sad news. I had already interviewed Benedict in connection with his wife's murder and he must remain a suspect in that case (at least in Superintendent Dunn's mind). He was now, given that this new victim had also been part of that enquiry and lived in his home, part of this. I could well understand Dunn's argument. It was going to be very interesting to see the effect of my present news on Benedict. He was intelligent enough to realise that circumstances were beginning to build up a case against him – and many a man has been hanged on circumstantial evidence before now.

Benedict was in his study. An easel had been set up on which rested a large oil painting. It was one of those compositions usually called a still life, which means everything in it is dead or otherwise inanimate. There were lifeless game birds with lolling heads, an unlucky hare hanging upside down, a pair of glassy-eyed fish I identified as trout, a pewter flagon or two and a bottle of wine in a raffia jacket. I wouldn't have wanted it in my home, but I dare say there is a call for that sort of thing in large country houses.

'Well?' Benedict greeted me, turning from his inspection of his new acquisition. 'You have brought news of some progress at last?'

'I have unfortunately brought more sad news,' I confessed. 'Miss Marchwood has been murdered.'

He stared at me. 'Nonsense,' he said curtly.

'I have seen the body with my own eyes, earlier today, sir. At Waterloo Bridge Station.'

He moved away from the painting now, but still stared at me in disbelief. He was either an excellent actor or the news was simply so extraordinary and shocking that his mind could not accept it. Then he turned and pulled a bell cord.

Parker appeared.

'Where is Miss Marchwood?' Benedict asked her.

'The lady's gone out, sir,' said Parker. 'She went out early this morning. I think she meant to go to London. She said she wouldn't be back for lunch.'

Benedict dismissed her with an irritated wave of the hand and turned back to me.

'How on earth could Marchwood get herself murdered at Waterloo Station? It's a busy place, full of people. Besides, who on earth would want to kill her?' He was beginning to sound bewildered and even, I fancied, betrayed a touch of panic.

'She never reached Waterloo alive, I'm afraid. She was murdered on the train from Egham, at some point after Richmond.' I watched carefully for his reaction. 'We know this because the ticket inspector spoke to her between Twickenham and Richmond, where he left the carriage. Miss Marchwood was then alone in it and very much alive. But at Waterloo the same ticket inspector discovered her dead.'

'Heart attack?' Benedict whispered. I could scarcely catch the words.

'No, sir, most certainly not.' I hesitated. 'Nor any other natural cause.'

Benedict sat down with a thump, and stared up at me, his hands gripping the arms of his chair. His expression was briefly quite wild. I think he only now fully believed me.

He didn't know before now, I thought. *He's not our killer. Dunn is wrong.*

'Who killed her?' he asked huskily.

'I don't know, sir. She died in the same way as Mrs Benedict.'

An expression of pain crossed his face and his features twitched.

'Why?' he asked.

'I don't know why, sir. I suspect she may have been on her way to Scotland Yard. Perhaps she had remembered something and wished to tell us.'

'She could have told *me!*' Benedict shouted, leaning forward in his chair, his face suddenly red with anger. 'But she did not – because she was ashamed, Ross, ashamed! You and I both know why!'

He fell silent but the anger seemed to flow out from him. He looked at me with real hatred. He believed his wife had betrayed him – and that I shared the knowledge. To him, in my eyes he was the cuckolded husband, that stock figure of fun through the centuries.

'We cannot be sure why,' I said gently.

It was true, after all. I had a theory that Marchwood had been on her way to me, just as I suspected Fawcett to be the man for whom the purse of money was intended. But I had no proof. Fawcett would not admit it. I had to have more on him and that's why I had asked Dunn to help find it. I still did not know who had killed Allegra and it would be a dangerous mistake to assume that the two crimes, obtaining money by deception and murder, were automatically connected.

Fleecing the public does not make a man a murderer. If anything, it suggests otherwise. Confidence tricksters' boldness only extends to extorting money from the gullible. They are seldom if ever violent, relying instead on the ingenuity of their fertile imaginations and resourcefulness. If discovered, they melt away and try again elsewhere, working their charms on a new mark. And that's what Fawcett would do, if I confronted him without proof. He would vanish and reinvent himself elsewhere.

As to whether there was more than money involved, who could say? Perhaps Allegra was not actually having an affair with Fawcett. Was it only the knowledge that her employer was selling her mother's jewels to fund the man that her devoted companion had wanted to hide?

An alerted husband does not need proof, however, only suspicions and an instinctive knowledge that he is being deceived in some way. He easily presumes it to be the worst. Benedict knew his marriage had not been a love match, that he was older than his wife, that she had been a beauty and he, on the other hand, very ordinary. Perhaps he had feared from the first that one day some dashing younger rival would come along and sweep Allegra off her feet.

'My wife was untrue to me,' Benedict said now in a bleak tone. 'Marchwood, who might have persuaded her from her folly, or come to me to tell me of it, kept silent. She was complicit in my wife's deception. She encouraged it. Well, I cannot say I feel any sorrow at the news of Marchwood's death. It is shocking, of course, and unexpected. But do not expect me to display a hypocritical grief. I doubt I could do it convincingly, anyway.' His mouth twisted in a mirthless grimace.

I appreciated his honesty. Dunn might have said he was clever. It was better to confess to no sorrow than to feign sorrow and be detected as, at best, a humbug – and at worst, a liar.

'I have to ask you, sir, where you were earlier today,' I said.

Benedict raised his eyebrows and gave a bark of laughter. 'So now I am a suspect? Well, I was here, Inspector Ross. The servants will tell you so and in case you doubt their testimony, this –' he waved a hand at the still life – 'this was delivered here this morning. I was expecting it and took care to be here in order to inspect its condition on arrival. There is always a risk when transporting works of art that they will be damaged. I signed a receipt for it. You may check with the carrier's man.'

'Thank you,' I said awkwardly.

Benedict fixed me with a steady gaze. 'Nor, Inspector, did I kill my wife. You have not asked me that, but I know you and your superiors will have discussed the possibility. You will say, I had cause. But until I spoke with you, after her death, I had trusted her. Trusted her implicitly!'

He threw up his hands in a gesture that was un-English and had perhaps been acquired in Italy.

'Had it not been for Marchwood's furtive manner and obvious hiding of some unpalatable truth, I would have continued to trust her. You, too, Ross, helped plant the seeds of suspicion in my mind, as I said. But let me tell you something.' He leaned forward again. 'If I had learned that my wife was deceiving me, before her death, I would have confronted her with the fact. If she had been willing to show penitence, break off the sorry affair, return to being my loyal wife, I would have forgiven her, taken her back. I loved my wife, Inspector.'

Perhaps he believed it himself. It was love as he understood it. I thought that perhaps his willingness to take Allegra back would rather have been the act of a man from whom a precious object had temporarily been stolen, gratefully accepting its return to his possession. But we know little of other people's hearts. We have enough trouble understanding our own.

'May I ask,' I turned to a practical subject, 'if you know who Miss Marchwood's next of kin would be? Someone we should contact regarding her death?'

'I have no idea.' He shook his head and looked at me as if I had suggested something socially unacceptable. 'I never discussed personal matters with her. She was an employee. However, I can give you the name and address of the agency from which she came. They may have some record.'

'Thank you.' As Benedict scribbled the address on a slip of paper, I added, 'I have one more request to make of you. I am sorry to have to do it, but I would like you to return to London with me and make formal identification of the body.'

He gasped, looked up at me and blanched. 'You want me to return – to that place where I saw Allegra . . . You want me to go there again and gaze on another woman's body?'

'She was in your employ for nine years, sir, and you knew her well. You cannot give us another name, a relative's. She was, I believe, friendly in a minor way with a widow lady she saw at the temperance meetings she attended. But I hesitate to ask a woman . . .'

'Yes, yes!' he said testily. 'I am obliged to do it. You leave me no choice and it is my duty. I'll come with you now. Just give me a few minutes to get ready. Perhaps you'd wait downstairs?'

'I'll wait for you outside,' I offered. 'By the gates.'

The gardener was still working where I'd seen him on my arrival. I strolled over to him and asked him if he had seen Miss Marchwood leave that morning. He gave me a curious look, puzzled by my question, but agreed he had seen her, though only in a cursory way. He had said good morning to her. She had returned the greeting. There had been no further conversation. She had drawn the veil down over her bonnet and he couldn't see her face well. He thought she had walked off down the hill towards Egham. He had not seen anyone follow her.

'I was busy, sir. I didn't pay any attention. But she's that sort of lady, sir, if you'll forgive me, a very quiet lady. You don't notice her or pay much attention to what she does. Then, not long after she left, the carrier came with a package for Mr Benedict. I went up to the house to help him carry it in and upstairs to Mr Benedict's study. It looked like another of those paintings.'

The arrival of the carrier's cart had occasioned a welcome diversion in the gardener's day. But not the coming or going of the companion. Why should it? No one had ever paid any attention to Isabella Marchwood, a quiet, self-effacing but tormented soul. She would not be missed.

The carrier's cart may have saved Miss Marchwood from being attacked on her way down the hill, I thought. It must have been on the road at the time.

Benedict and I made the return journey to Waterloo in silence. While he stared blankly from the train window, I turned it all over in my mind. Surreptitiously I took my watch from my waistcoat pocket and timed the journey between the stops. Where had she died? On the stretch before Clapham or after it? Had her murderer got off the train at Clapham, Vauxhall or at Waterloo? I peered out when we stopped at those stations as if I might spot some evidence from the train. At both Clapham and Richmond I saw uniformed Railway Police officers on the platform, questioning people. Burns was doing his bit.

Benedict appeared to be paying no attention at all. He, too, was lost in his own thoughts; perhaps steeling himself for the gruesome task ahead of him.

I was reminded, as we drew out of that station, that Mrs Scott lived at Clapham. Possibly Fawcett did too, since Lizzie had told me he left the meetings with Mrs Scott in her carriage. Now that might mean something or it might mean nothing, just like everything else.

Theories! I thought with a sigh as we pulled into Waterloo and I put away my pocket watch. All I have is theories to account for two brutal murders of respectable ladies. I still thought of Allegra as such. Fawcett's tawdry seduction of a vulnerable woman, if that was what had taken place, did not destroy her image for me as it had done for her husband.

Benedict stood up well to the ordeal. This time he did not faint away or mutter incoherently. He looked resolutely at the uncovered face of the sheeted body and said, 'Yes, that is Isabella Marchwood, who was companion to my late wife. Do you need me any more?'

'Not today, sir,' I said.

'Then I'll return home.' He began to walk towards the door, not waiting for me, but paused before leaving. 'I hope you will not be requesting me to come a third time to identify the victim of a murderer you appear unable to catch.'

From the corner of my eye, I saw Scully grin. But when I turned towards him the smirk had gone.

'The gentleman appears to be bearing up, sir,' he said blandly.

'He can do nothing else,' I retorted.

There was sound of voices in the corridor outside. Dr Carmichael walked in. Scully, as usual, ran forward to help him off with his street coat and on with his dissecting one.

'Good day to you, there, Ross,' Carmichael greeted me. 'I understand the gentleman has identified the deceased. I met him on the way out.'

'Isabella Marchwood,' I said. 'As we already knew, of course.'

'Hum!' said Carmichael. He walked to the marble table and turned back the sheet, which had reached to the corpse's chin. 'You may wish to see this, Ross.'

A little queasily, I went to look. I never get used to it. The familiar red line scored her throat.

'I took the liberty of removing the cord,' Carmichael said, 'as you had already seen it in place round her throat, in the railway carriage. There is something rather interesting about it.' He produced a folded piece of paper and opened it out flat. Two lengths of cord, identical in type to that round Allegra Benedict's neck, lay side by side. Carmichael looked at me and raised his bushy eyebrows, waiting for me make an observation.

'They are not knotted together,' I said, 'as the other cords still were, after you cut them from the victim's neck.'

'Indeed they are not. I did snip the cord to take it from her neck. But it fell apart quite easily; I found myself with two separate lengths, as you see here. It had not been tied in a double knot as on the previous occasion. I suggested to you, at that time, the murderer had wished to make sure the noose did not slip and release the victim. But this time he either did not bother, or perhaps, as I understand the murder occurred in the course of a railway journey, he did not have time. He tied it once, pulled it tight, was satisfied she was dead and left his victim in a hurry.'

'Yes,' I said slowly, staring down at the two short lengths of cord. 'To murder in the park, unseen in the fog, was one thing. But in broad daylight, in a railway carriage when someone might have got in at the next stop . . . that must have been a rushed affair.'

Or a desperate one. And yet . . . I stretched out my hand and touched one of the cords with my fingertip. 'I like patterns,' I heard myself say aloud to Carmichael. 'And there is no pattern in this business, only a number of events and people who touch at some point but then spin away on a different path.'

Carmichael gave a short, unexpected chuckle. He was not usually given to humour so I was surprised and looked at him.

'Have you never seen Scottish country dancing, Inspector? The couples join hands, part, turn, go in, go out, exchange places, move up to the head of the queue to replace another pair . . . for anyone who has never tried it, and finds himself caught up in it for the first time, it is bewildering. But there is a pattern to it, oh yes, and once the novice has worked out the pattern, then he is away, spinning merrily around with the rest.'

'We should have found him before now,' said Morris sadly. 'Then the poor little lady would still be alive.'

He was only saying something I had said to myself a dozen times since seeing Isabella Marchwood's body slumped in that railway carriage. But there was no point in my giving way to despondency.

'Come, Sergeant!' I admonished him. 'We will find the wretch.'

'I can't even find that butler, Seymour,' growled Morris. 'He seems to have vanished. I've been round all the central London employment agencies for domestic staff. I think I must know the whereabouts of nearly every butler in the country except Mortimer Seymour.'

'Ah, there perhaps I can help,' I was able to say. I handed him the piece of paper on which Benedict had written the name and address of the agency where he'd originally found Miss Marchwood. 'This one, as you see, is a little out of town in Northwood. If he contacted them regarding a companion, he may have done so because previously they'd supplied his butler, and he was well satisfied with Seymour. So satisfied that he was angry when the butler left his household! So try them. At the same time, find out if they have any next of kin on record for Isabella Marchwood. They must keep files on all the people who pass through the establishment.'

Morris took the paper and sighed. 'Like as not a wild goose chase, like all the others I've been on this week,' he said.

After Morris's gloomy appraisal of our situation, it was a relief that Lizzie and Bessie bore the news well when I broke it to them that night. Bessie, I'm sorry to say, even displayed a certain relish, reminding me of those in the crowd at Waterloo.

'What an awful thing! Poor Miss Marchwood. In a train carriage, too? Just imagine. Cor . . .' Her eyes shone with excitement.

Lizzie turned a little pale and said very quietly, 'It is dreadful news. I was so afraid for her.' She hesitated. 'I wonder . . .'

'Yes?' I encouraged.

'I was worried for her safety on Sunday evening, because she was intending to walk quite alone to the station from the Temperance Hall, after nightfall. Of course London streets are well lit, but on a Sunday there are fewer people around. Yet it puzzles me that, if there is any connection with the hall in all this, she wasn't followed from there and attacked on her way to Waterloo. Especially if it is the Wr—' Lizzie broke off with a glance at Bessie. 'But she wasn't,' she resumed. 'Doesn't that seem to rule out anyone who was at the hall that evening?'

'She was also talking to you for a few minutes outside the hall,' I pointed out. 'If anyone there had noticed that, they could have been put off. They would have to have waited until you and Bessie were out of sight before they set off in pursuit. Miss Marchwood would have been well ahead of them by then. There are always people and traffic around stations. It might not have been so simple.'

Lizzie looked unconvinced. 'I do wish I knew what she and Fawcett had to discuss privately.'

'I think I can guess at that. But I need to be sure.' I also glanced at the listening Bessie.

Fawcett and Miss Marchwood had probably been discussing the money Allegra Benedict had been giving the man. He wouldn't want that known. He would have elicited Miss Marchwood's promise not to tell anyone. She had kept her word. Her killer had made sure of it.

'I'm also thinking,' said my wife slowly, 'what a very great shock this will be to Mrs Scott. She and Miss Marchwood were very much involved together in the running of the temperance meetings. I wouldn't like her to read of it in the newspapers, unprepared. I could call on her first thing in the morning, before she has a chance to see the papers, and break the news. It would be the kind thing to do.'

'She lives at Clapham,' I reminded her.

'It's only a step to the station from here and there are plenty of trains to Clapham. It must be a short journey. I should imagine she's well known and I can find the house.'

'I know the address,' I admitted. 'I saw it in Angelis's ledger.'

'Oh, that's a good thing!' said my wife brightly. She knew that already, of course. I'd told her about Angelis delivering a painting to Clapham.

'Yes, isn't it?' I said a little sarcastically. 'Well, go by all means. I know I can trust you not to talk unwarily.'

My wife gave me a look.

'The house is called Wisteria Lodge,' I said hastily. 'That seems a fanciful name for the home of the rather fierce female you've described to me.'

'I ought to come with you, missus,' announced Bessie. 'There's a murderer loose on the railways. He might jump into your carriage and strangle you! If there were two of us, he couldn't do it. He might try it, but I'd jump on his back and pull him off you.'

'Thank you, Bessie,' said Lizzie. 'I appreciate you wanting to protect me. But I don't think that's necessary or an attack likely.' She relented as Bessie's face fell. 'However, you can come with me.'

Bessie beamed, before turning down the corners of her mouth with comical haste. 'That's right, missus. Better safe than sorry!'

Chapter Eleven

Elizabeth Martin Ross

ALTHOUGH I knew Mrs Scott would consider it both impolite and ignorant to pay a social call before noon, nevertheless Bessie and I arrived before the gate of Wisteria Lodge a little after ten, in pale sunshine.

Three years earlier, when I had arrived in London from Derbyshire, my Aunt Parry, to whom I was to be companion, had handed me a guidebook. She said she had found it helpful when she had arrived in London from the provinces many years before.

The guide must already have been out of date even then, because it was entitled *The Picture of London for 1818*. I had nevertheless consulted it the night before, since I knew nothing of Clapham. I found it listed among places of interest in the environs of London. Clapham, the guide informed me, was 'a village in Surrey, three miles and a quarter S. from London, consisting chiefly of handsome houses.' Well, London's tentacles had spread out far further since the guide was written. The coming of the railway had placed Clapham within the orbit of those whose business was in the centre of the capital, but who had made enough money to move away from the city's smoke, fog and smells and take up residence somewhere more comfortable and discriminating. There were many more houses here than fifty years before, nearly all of them solid, middle-class dwellings. But still much of the countryside remained about the area together with a feeling that we were out of town. This was due in large part to the spacious area of grass and woodland popularly called 'the Common' that we had observed on our way to the house. It had been busy, even this early in the day, with people strolling or riding, or with nursemaids who had brought their young charges to run about in the open.

'It's nice, isn't it?' Bessie had observed, and she repeated this comment as we gazed at Mrs Scott's residence.

Wisteria Lodge was a substantial red-brick villa, not more than twenty years old. There really was some wisteria, climbing across the façade, although at this time of year it showed only bare brown branches, here and there festooned with yellowed leaves. The thickness of them suggested it had been planted when the house was new, and in spring they would make a fine show with their trailing purple sprays of flowers. Certainly it had always been called Wisteria Lodge, or named that before the gateposts were built, because the name was chiselled into them.

'She might not be ready to receive, missus,' Bessie warned me. 'Mrs Parry never received visits before twelve. Mrs Scott might not be dressed and most likely she won't have breakfasted.'

I nearly replied that my Aunt Parry was never dressed for the day before noon, having risen from her bed, where she had breakfasted, about eleven. To see her downstairs before half past twelve was rare, although she always appeared in good time for the substantial meal she called a light luncheon at one. But I couldn't say that to Bessie. I was confident Mrs Scott would have considered such a timetable idleness; and we would find her at least dressed, if not expecting visitors.

'I know,' I said. 'But I hope she'll realise, from the early hour, that only something very important could have brought me.'

'She might send down word by a maid that we should leave a note,' continued Bessie. Now that we actually stood before the house, her enthusiasm for the visit the evening before had changed to a marked reluctance to beard the ogre in its den.

'Come on!' I ordered and we marched briskly through the gates, up the short drive and the three steps to a square porch and rang the bell.

After a few minutes a dour, respectable female in bombazine, who could only be a housekeeper, opened the door and surveyed us with some surprise.

I had come prepared. 'Please take my card in to your mistress,' I said, handing over the little white oblong. 'Tell her, if you will, that I apologise for the early hour, but I have brought some news I thought she would wish to hear without delay.'

Curiosity alone, I hoped, would make the lady agree to see me. The housekeeper read the card carefully and invited us to wait in the hall.

While we were alone, both Bessie and I took the opportunity to look round us. There was certainly plenty of Mrs Scott's favourite kind of painting, according to what Angelis had told Ben. Most representations were of Middle Eastern scenes, but some might have been Indian. I wondered if it was one of these that Angelis had been seen delivering by Mr Pritchard; one bought to replace a more valuable picture, sold surreptitiously. Other oriental items indicated the travels of the late Major and Mrs Scott. A bronze many-armed figure stood on the hall table, next to a box for the reception of outgoing letters in some dark wood inlaid with ivory.

The hall itself, indeed the whole house, was very quiet. Only a long-case clock ticked softly in the corner. I felt uneasy, not only because being here uninvited and so early was a social solecism, as Bessie had aptly pointed out, but because this was unknown territory in so many more ways than one. I had only met the lady twice. Both meetings had been brief and neither had been cordial. Apart from what Bessie had told me of her past history, that her late husband had been a soldier, I knew almost nothing of her. Ben had learned from Angelis that she had survived the dreadful siege of Lucknow. So I could deduce one thing: Mrs Scott was battle-hardened. My only poor weapon was surprise. I was sure she would soon dismiss that.

The housekeeper returned. 'If you would care to come through to the morning parlour, ma'am? If your maid waits here, I'll take her down to the kitchen afterwards.'

Bessie, lurking in the shelter of a recess containing a potted palm, perked up at being taken for a lady's maid and emerged. I followed the housekeeper.

The back, or morning, parlour at Wisteria Lodge was a pleasant sunny room, even on this bleak early winter day. A fire had been lit to take the chill off the air, but within the last half-hour; it still crackled and spat as the kindling took hold and the smell of smoke was noticeable. On an opened writing slope lay a half-written letter. A pen protruded from an inkwell. I saw no sign of the morning's newspapers.

Mrs Scott, in a plain, silver-grey skirt and bodice, came to meet me. She wore a little lace widow's cap over her hair and detachable muslin cuffs over her wrists to protect her sleeves while she was busy with her morning tasks. She greeted me with a schooled politeness.

'Mrs Ross? How very nice to see you. How have you come from town?'

'By train,' I told her. 'And I must apologise for what will appear an extraordinary intrusion. I see I have disturbed you at your letter-writing. I hope I won't keep you from it for long.'

'Not at all . . .' murmured Mrs Scott, gesturing towards a chair. 'Would you care for some tea after your journey?'

I declined the tea but sat down. My hostess sat down opposite and folded her hands in her lap, half covered by the muslin cuffs. I saw she wore her wedding band but no other jewellery. She was waiting for me to explain myself. Her face told me nothing.

'I have come to convey some sad news,' I said. 'I learned it last night from my husband. I was afraid it might be in this morning's newspapers, or if not, in tonight's evening ones. In any event, I thought I should come and tell you of it in person. I did not want you to read about it. I'm afraid I have to tell you of the death of Miss Isabella Marchwood.'

Within the muslin cuffs I saw her hands whiten as they were clasped more tightly. After only the merest pause, however, she replied. 'I am obliged to you for your thoughtfulness. As for your news, I am more than sorry to hear it. Are you able to tell me how and where this happened? You say you learned it from your husband. Am I to understand, then, that the circumstances were – unusual? It is certainly unexpected. When I saw her on Sunday night she was in poor spirits, but otherwise of good health.'

'Miss Marchwood,' I said carefully, 'was on her way to London from Egham yesterday morning by train. On arrival at Waterloo, a ticket inspector, glancing into the first-class carriage at the head of the train, saw a woman he thought was asleep. He went to waken her and found she was dead. She had been murdered.'

'Murdered?' Mrs Scott's face at last betrayed some emotion. 'How can this be? Who would want to murder Isabella Marchwood? She was a pleasant person but of no importance.'

I really did not like this woman and struggled not to show it. 'The police are investigating,' I said.

'I think we will have some tea, after all,' said Mrs Scott. She got up and went to ring a bell. Returning to her chair, she continued. 'Do you know how she died?'

'She was strangled.'

There was a silence. 'As was her late employer, Mrs Benedict?' Mrs Scott asked.

'In exactly the same way.'

The housekeeper appeared and received her order to bring the tea tray.

'There is always an element of danger in a lady travelling alone, especially by the railway. It's why I go to the expense of keeping my carriage.' Mrs Scott had used the interruption to regain her composure and her tone was brisk. 'I take it she was robbed?'

'No,' I told her with a shake of my head, 'her bag was found under the seat. There was a little money in it, my husband told me, and she still had her gold-rimmed glasses.'

'She would have had little to interest a thief, anyway,' Mrs Scott observed. 'But I suppose, having entered the carriage with the intent to steal, he did not know it until after he had killed her.'

'I am not a party to what the police think,' I said apologetically. It was true. I knew no more than I had told her.

The tea tray arrived and was set down on a table whose top was made of beaten brass, intricately engraved. Mrs Scott poured me a cup and handed it to me, ironically in a repetition of the gesture she had made at the Temperance Hall after the meeting.

'The police do not know exactly why she was coming to London,' I began carefully, feeling I was walking 'on eggs', as the saying went. 'But I did chance to overhear you invite her to visit you here in Clapham.'

Mrs Scott raised her eyebrows.

'After the last meeting at the Temperance Hall,' I reminded her. 'I was outside on the pavement. She spoke to you through the carriage window, and I heard her.'

'You are sharp-eared, Mrs Ross, as well as observant,' Mrs Scott said coldly. She raised an eyebrow. 'I did not see you on the pavement.'

I had been hiding, along with Bessie, under the arch. But I was not going to explain that.

'It was getting dark,' I said vaguely. 'I wondered if you had been expecting her and she might have been on her way to you yesterday.'

'No, she was not,' said Mrs Scott. 'She would not have called here without sending me a note first.'

She gave me a very direct look as she said this. Even the despised Miss Marchwood had known better than to burst in unannounced as I had.

'Will you tell Mr Fawcett?' I asked. 'And her other friends at the Temperance Hall?'

She stirred her tea without so much as a quiver of the teaspoon. 'I cannot be driving around informing everyone. Besides, as you say, it will doubtless be in the newspapers. The public has a fascination with the sordid.' She set down the teaspoon. 'But I will certainly write a note to Mr Fawcett at once, and tell Harris to saddle one of the carriage horses and ride over to his lodgings with it. He will be very sorry. Isabella Marchwood was a staunch supporter of our cause.'

'So I observed,' I said blandly. 'Apart from attending the meetings, what else did she do to help?'

I didn't deceive her and had not expected to. She looked at me with that expression I'd seen on her face when we had first met. She was perfectly aware that my being here was more than a courtesy.

'She always brought biscuits,' she said. 'That was very helpful.'

'It must have been. Mr Fawcett will find it difficult to conduct next Sunday's meeting with this sad knowledge on his mind.'

'Not at all!' she said sharply. 'His work is more important than any inconvenience such as the loss of Isabella Marchwood!'

She must have seen shock in my face at her brutal turn of phrase, because she added quickly, 'Distressed though he will be on a personal level, you understand, his work must always come first. You can have no idea, Mrs Ross, how dreadful the scourge of drink is among the poor. Even if a man has but a few pence in his pocket, he will spend it on beer or spirits and let his family starve. I wish I could say the women did not do the same, but many do. When Mr Fawcett had just begun his ministry among the London poor, I had the good fortune to hear of it. I heard him speak and was immediately convinced of the value of his work and the difficulty of the task. He wished me to see the problem for myself. I accompanied him to a place where cheap drink was sold. He assured me that I need have no fear for my safety; because he was already so well known and respected in the district, no one would offend us or offer us violence while I was in his company. I told him I had no fears as I had been in many dangerous places in the world at times of great unrest and knew how to stand my ground before a hostile mob.

'The place Mr Fawcett showed me was a gin palace. I have seen some terrible sights in my life, Mrs Ross. I was in India with my husband during the Mutiny. But when I entered that place of alcoholism and despair, and saw the depravity stamped on the loutish faces of those there, I thought I had entered hell!'

I was taken aback by the ferocity in her voice. She, at least, believed in Fawcett and his 'cause'. It would be hopeless to try and persuade her that he was a fraud, as I believed him to be. He had picked his acolyte well. He had cunningly shown her the enemy, drink, face to face. He had told her they must fight it. She was a soldier's widow. She knew about fighting. She had immediately thrown herself into the fray.

'I was filled with disgust, Mrs Ross, as I am sure you would have been. These were British men and women who should have been supporting themselves by honest toil and raising their families to be God-fearing and hard-working. They lounged there in every kind of abandoned attitude. Some were only half con- scious, so stupefied were they by drink. This cannot be allowed to continue or the entire country will go to the dogs! Where will the sturdy young men come from, to fill the ranks of the British Army and Navy? Who will work in our great industries? Where will be the strong hardworking mothers to raise healthy families? Feebleness of character must, like feebleness of body, be expunged from our society!'

Her cheeks glowed red and her eyes sparkled. She leaned forward and clenched her fists. She saw Fawcett as leading a cavalry charge, and she was there at his side.

'And what does Mr Fawcett do to make them change their ways?' I asked.

'He organises gatherings among them to urge them to reform and see their error. He helps by finding them gainful employment.

If they will accept to take work he also, if necessary, provides them with strong boots and work clothes, as many are destitute and in rags.

'He organises classes for their children where they may be taught their letters and so be better fit for employment. Those who are starving he helps with food. Money is never given directly, because that would encourage them in their idleness. Of course, the help is dependent on every member of the family turning aside from drunkenness and debauchery.

'He took me to see a family who had been saved by his efforts. The father was now in employment as a porter. The wife was decently dressed, her children washed and the room in which they lived tidy. They could not praise their benefactor highly enough.'

'If he does all that,' I said, 'it is worthy work indeed. Does he only preach in London, at the Temperance Hall? Or elsewhere? Here, for example, in Clapham?'

'I have been able to introduce him to a good many people here in Clapham,' she returned proudly, 'at my regular soirées.'

And the residents of Clapham, those who lived in the comfortable large houses and villas I had seen, had money to spare for a worthy cause. How much, I wondered, had Fawcett managed to raise in the time since he had begun his 'ministry' at the Temperance Hall? Surely a great deal of money. And what checks were made to ensure it was spent in the way Mrs Scott described?

I knew how these schemes worked. As our town's doctor, my father was aware of everything that went on, and in his additional role of police surgeon got to hear many details of crimes. I was not only his daughter but his housekeeper and companion. We would sit of an evening and he would talk to me freely of his day. He told me of cases where the public had been gulled and parted from its money by an elaborate façade of deception. There would be no difficulty in Fawcett producing a 'reformed family' for inspection, if so required. The interested visitor would be shown a neat, clean room, a newly employed and redeemed head of the household with decently dressed wife and children, all smiling and praising Mr Fawcett, just as Mrs Scott had seen.

The 'reformed family' would be in Fawcett's pay. Each interested visitor would see the same scene, with the same people in it. In the same way, the proprietor of the gin palace described by Mrs Scott would have been paid to allow a potential donor to the cause to view his dreadful premises. A little money had perhaps been dispensed among the drinkers beforehand to make sure that by the time Fawcett brought Mrs Scott there, they were all in the sorry state she had described. But she would not believe me if I told her any of this.

I could not extend my stay any longer. I wasn't sure I had learned anything other than to confirm Ben's suspicions that Fawcett had been raising money from wealthy people, met at the 'soirées', and my own that he was a charlatan.

Nevertheless I was about to learn another interesting detail as we travelled home.

'What did the housekeeper have to say?' I asked Bessie. 'Did you tell her Miss Marchwood was dead?'

Bessie nodded. 'Yes, I did. She was that cut up, really shocked. Said it was awful and Miss Marchwood was a very nice lady who had been lots of times to the house for the swarries.' Bessie darted a look of triumph at me. 'And so had the Italian lady who was strangled, Mrs Benedict.'

Mrs Scott had taken care not to tell me that!

'Are you sure?' I asked Bessie eagerly.

'Mrs Field, that's the housekeeper, told me that a very beautiful lady used to come with Miss Marchwood sometimes and she was Italian. What's more she was murdered, too, and Mrs Field read about it in the newspapers. Mrs Field says it seems a decent woman can't set foot out of the house now without being set on by some murderous ruffian. Mrs Field has a sister who lives in Cheapside; and now she's afraid to travel up to town to visit her on her day off. Mrs Field is a soldier's widow, too, missus. Her husband was a sergeant and he served in India at the same time as Major Scott and that's why she's now Mrs Scott's housekeeper. Mrs Field says that there used to be people in India called Thugs. They used to befriend travellers and then murder and rob them. She says it is getting as bad as that here in England. I asked her what Mrs Scott had said when she'd heard about the murder of the Italian lady.'

'And what did Mrs Scott say to Mrs Field?'

'That it was disgraceful that such a thing could happen in a respectable part of London in broad daylight. Only it wasn't broad daylight, as we both know, because it was that bad fog,' added Bessie pedantically.

'It's a figure of speech,' I said. 'Mrs Scott meant, during the daytime.'

'And Mrs Field let slip –' Bessie smiled at me in triumph – 'that she had the impression Mrs Scott didn't like the Italian lady very much, so she was shocked but not what you'd call sorry. She heard Mrs Scott say once, to Miss Marchwood, that Mrs Benedict was "not devoted to the cause". Which meant, Mrs Field said, she didn't go to the temperance meetings. I asked Mrs Field if she had ever gone to the meetings. But Mrs Field said, "Certainly not." So I asked her why and she said she was a good Catholic and didn't go in for that kind of tub-thumping. She thought that probably the Italian lady had been a Catholic too, and didn't go to the temperance meetings for that reason. But it was not her place to suggest that to Mrs Scott.'

Bessie paused and looked thoughtful. 'You know what, missus? I don't think I'll ever be able to go to the meetings any more; not and really enjoy them, like I did. In my mind I'll always see Miss Marchwood sitting there, or helping with the teas. I hope the inspector finds out who the murderer is quick.'

Chapter Twelve

Inspector Benjamin Ross

'THERE IS absolutely no doubt in my mind that Fawcett is a fraudster,' I said to Dunn the following morning, after I had given him Lizzie's account of her visit to Clapham. 'The woman Scott is in thrall to him. Others will be as completely convinced. He must be investigated.'

'The matter is already set in hand,' said Dunn. 'I have contacted several other police authorities and passed out the description Mrs Ross gives of him. We shall have to tread carefully, however, or he will guess the game is up here and he'll be off to pastures new.'

'I am aware of that, sir,' I said dolefully.

I was frustrated that we could not stop Fawcett and his profitable enterprise at once, but Dunn was right. At the first sign of our suspicion, he would slip from our grasp. He would reinvent himself elsewhere and it would not be until he came to the notice of yet another police authority that anything could be done. Plenty of his sort kept themselves 'in business' for years before the law finally caught up with them. Even then it was always very difficult to prove anything against them. The problem often was that those deceived by such tricksters were unwilling to stand up in court and admit how they had been fooled. Mrs Scott, for instance, even if she were ever to be convinced of his falseness, would never make public admission of it. Her pride would not let her, and more. The Fawcetts of the world survive because not only money has been taken from the victims. The fraudster is protected because the gullible have given him something much more precious: their trust and, in that way, their hearts. For them, discovery of the deception is more akin to finding a lover unfaithful than just a robbery. As police officers, we just have to hope that knowledge of the truth engenders enough rage to make some of them speak out.

I left Dunn feeling that things were not going our way. But, as often happens, the unexpected offered a gleam of hope.

'There you are, sir!' declared Morris, for once wearing a broad smile. 'Found him, that Seymour chap. Like you said, he's on the books of the same agency for "upper servants and superior staff" out at Northwood.' Morris gave a snort of derision. 'No use going to them if you just want a housemaid. Governesses and companions, best sort of lady's maid and gentleman's gentleman, and butlers, that's what they deal in. Well, Mortimer Seymour is butler at a place down near Newmarket now. He works for a Colonel Frey. I have the address here.' Morris waved a piece of paper. 'Shall I get down there and talk to him?'

I took the address slip from him. 'The Manor House,' I said. 'We may have to go through his employer to speak to him. It's better I go. No offence, Morris, but the colonel will appreciate my rank.'

Morris nodded. 'You're right. I'd be sent round to the back door!'

★

'You appear to be conducting this investigation by railway,' grumbled Dunn. 'If you exceed your daily expenses allowance it will be no use asking me to justify it. The department's budget is not limitless and plenty of your colleagues are doing their work on foot within the boundaries of the capital. Let's hope you turn up trumps this time.'

I hoped so too. I had plenty of time, as the train took me down to Newmarket through the peaceful East Anglian countryside, to think out a strategy. There was no knowing how the colonel would react to a police officer turning up at his door, wanting to interview a member of his staff. I did not want to cost Seymour his place. I decided that, when I arrived, I would hire a cab to take me out to the village where the colonel lived and on arrival, find the most prosperous-looking tavern or small hotel if they had one, there to eat my midday meal. I would have to find a way to include that in my expenses. The landlord or landlady, or failing them, the waiter in the dining room or even the potman, would be able to tell me about a local landowner. Forewarned is forearmed.

As I was driven out to the place, I realised that here I was in racing country. There were plenty of signs of that, from strings of thoroughbreds on the skyline to the names of the pubs, all of which seemed to have some direct connection with the turf. The tavern in which I found myself was a spacious, comfortable place by the name of the Finishing Post. Very droll, I thought. A roaring fire heated the dining room and the menu offered a choice of pork chops or mutton stew. I settled for the mutton stew and it arrived, pleasantly bubbling and colourful, with carrots, swede and turnip bobbing about with the meat, and dotted with silvery globes of pearl barley. The smell was mouth-watering.

'All cooked in ale, sir,' promised the waiter, as he set down my generous plateful.

I tucked in, as did the other two diners, a pair of fellows wearing loud check jackets, whose conversation was unintelligible to me. I have never followed the horses. Luckily these two finished before me and left; so that I was alone when the waiter brought my coffee.

'Can you by any chance tell me how I can find the Manor House, the residence of Colonel Frey?' I asked.

The waiter's face brightened. He leaned forward conspiratorially. In lowered tones, although we were now alone, he hissed, 'You'll be the police officer from Scotland Yard, sir!'

I didn't bother to ask how he guessed my occupation, although out here in the country that was more surprising than, for example, Jed Sparrow recognising me in London.

But the specific '*the* police officer' . . .' startled me considerably and I couldn't help but show it. 'You're expecting one?' I asked. How could this be? Surely no one had sent word ahead that I was on my way?

'We all know the colonel has sent for an officer to come,' said the waiter smugly.

'Really?' I replied as I mentally reordered my whole approach to the colonel. 'It's common knowledge, then?' I added. I have found that is always a good conversational gambit for getting people talking.

'This is racing country, sir, and has been since good King Charles the Second's time. If it concerns the horses, everyone knows,' said the waiter.

The horses! I should have guessed, perhaps. It wasn't some ghastly murder or major house robbery, but something to do with the stables. As for the Merry Monarch, he was cropping up all over the place in this investigation. When not strolling in Green Park, it seemed he was watching his horse run here at Newmarket.

'Awkward business,' I said to the waiter in a confidential undertone, to match his.

'Very, sir. If word gets out that anyone's been near the horses, well, the security at all the stables has been increased. The colonel has a couple of men patrolling his premises night and day – with shotguns! But I did hear he was thinking of calling in the police.'

It occurred to me I had to be careful here. I didn't want to find myself face to face with the real officer called in by the colonel and have to explain why I was using his visit as cover.

'We didn't think you'd be here so soon, though,' said the waiter with admiration. 'You've got to hand it to you fellows, right off the mark. You weren't expected until next week.'

Thank goodness for that!

'That's why the colonel's gone away for a couple of days,' said the waiter. He really was an excellent informant. We could do with a few like him in London. And the colonel was away from home? Better and better. After so much frustration were things at last starting to go the way of our investigation?

'He'll be sorry to have missed you,' said the waiter.

'His, ah, lady is at the Manor House?' I enquired.

'Mrs Frey has accompanied the colonel. I believe they are visiting their son. He's away at the university. Oxford,' concluded the waiter. 'We had expected that the young gentleman would have gone to Cambridge but his father wished it otherwise.'

There is not much privacy to be had in small communities and it seemed that Colonel and Mrs Frey had no secrets from anyone local, at least not concerning their general business and movements.

'Another officer will come when the colonel returns,' I assured the waiter. 'In the meantime, I'd like to go out to the Manor and make some enquiries.'

'Half a mile down the road,' said the waiter. 'Turn right as you leave here. You can't miss it.'

Just as well I wasn't planning to nobble the horses, and no surprise that the colonel had posted armed guards. I might find it more difficult to get past them when I reached the Manor House than I'd found it gathering all the background information here!

I certainly could not have missed my destination. A white board painted with the information that this was Manor Stables gleamed at the roadside for all to see. The colonel, obviously retired from a military career, had turned his hand to either breeding or training racehorses.

I turned down a lane and found myself approaching a considerable establishment. To my right was the manor house itself, a square, grey building with tall chimneys, which looked as though it might date from the reign of that same King Charles. To my left were several stable blocks around a sizeable yard; beyond them I could see a manicured track, winding out over the nearby landscape. The gallops, I thought, digging into my scant knowledge of the racing world.

I had had time only to observe these generalities when a very large man wearing a bowler hat jammed down over a pair of cauliflower ears, and carrying a fearsome-looking blunderbuss, stepped out from behind a tree and barred my way.

'Good afternoon, sir,' he said, 'might you be looking for someone?'

The words were friendly enough but the blunderbuss wasn't.

'I am Inspector Ross from Scotland Yard,' I said hastily. 'If I might show you my warrant card?'

I handed the document over and it was very thoroughly

studied. He then nodded and returned it to me. To my relief, he turned away the muzzle of the blunderbuss as well.

'We've been expecting you, sir,' he said. 'But the colonel isn't at home.'

'That is a pity,' I said calmly. 'In that case, as I have come from London, perhaps I might just see the stableyard and talk to whoever is in charge? Then one of my colleagues will return next week when the colonel is at home.'

'It's Mr Smithers you want,' said the man. 'If you'd follow me, sir.'

I did as bid and we arrived in the large cleanly swept yard where a boy was leading a horse round in a circle observed closely by a stocky, red-faced man in gaiters.

'Who is this, Kelly?' demanded this individual as I appeared with my armed escort.

'Inspector Ross, Mr Smithers, from Scotland Yard, as the colonel ordered,' said Kelly.

Well, well, we are here to serve the public and if Colonel Frey had ordered up a detective, here I was.

The red-faced man, whose purple nose suggested to me a close acquaintance with strong spirits, turned back to the boy and ordered briskly, 'Keep leading him round, Jim!'

He then nodded at Kelly to dismiss him and addressed me. 'You'll want to see the layout of the place.'

'Indeed, yes, thank you.'

I followed him as we went around, asking what I hoped were suitable questions, and gathering as I did that the reason behind all this activity was that known members of a notorious gang of horse dopers had been spotted in the area.

'We know which one they are after,' said Smithers to me. 'It's His Eminence here.'

I was temporarily bewildered by the sudden introduction of a clerical figure. But a snort and snuffle, the stamp of a hoof, and the head of a chestnut horse appearing over a stable door, identified His Eminence. He pricked his ears and gazed at me enquiringly. I was glad he couldn't speak. He looked more intelligent than his handlers.

'Is the season not over?' I asked.

'Well, yes sir, but as I thought the colonel would have explained, that is not the problem,' Smithers replied, a flicker of suspicion in his eyes.

'I did not speak to Colonel Frey myself,' I said quickly. 'I only understood this was to do with doping horses.'

'More than that,' said Smithers grimly. 'This is poisoning, sir. They mean to murder His Eminence, or so they say, if the colonel will not pay. The loss of the horse would be a blow. The stud fees, you understand.'

'Blackmail!' I exclaimed as all now became clear.

'The colonel took all the letters to Scotland Yard with him. But he will not pay, sir!'

'Of course,' I said firmly. 'No, no, certainly not, never pay. But we will get the villains, never fear.'

'Whoever it is, they will have hired these doping tricksters to do the work for them,' Smithers informed me.

'If they were seen and recognised so easily,' I said, 'then I would guess it was intentionally. The blackmailer meant to underline the threat by letting it be known his hired desperadoes were close at hand, should the colonel stand firm.'

'The colonel will stand firm, sir. He is a military man.'

The time had come to extricate myself from what was becoming a very interesting case. But not *my* case. When I got back to London, I thought, I would straight away have to find whoever of my colleagues was dealing with all this, and inform him of my activities and the freedom I had taken with his investigation for my own cover.

'Obviously you yourself, and the men under you, are alert and doing an excellent job,' I said. 'But what if a member of the staff at the house were to see anything suspicious, would he or she go straight to the colonel?'

'More likely to Mr Seymour, the butler, sir. Then Mr Seymour would take it to the colonel if he thought the matter serious.'

'Then perhaps, before I leave, I should speak to Mr Seymour,' I suggested.

So that was how I found myself very shortly thereafter seated comfortably in the housekeeper's private parlour, with its flowered wallpaper and glowing fire in the grate, tea at hand, and the elusive Seymour, at last run to ground, seated opposite me.

Seymour was a small, neat man, with black hair brushed straight back from a pale forehead. His black clothing was formal to the extreme and he reminded me very much of a small black and white cat. He was watching me with a cat's wary gaze. I suspected he sensed already I was here about more than the blackmail threats to the colonel.

'I will be frank, Mr Seymour,' I said, setting down my cup. 'I have a second purpose in being here.'

'Indeed, sir?' he said blandly.

'You may even have been expecting a visit from the police, perhaps? I'm not suggesting you are, or have been, involved in anything criminal, please don't think that. But recent events, of which you can't be unaware, may have led you to wonder if we would want to speak to you. I am not referring to the blackmail letters received by the colonel. I lead the team investigating a recent murder in London.'

'I thought as much, sir,' answered Seymour in a bland butler's manner. I might have been referring to some unexpectedly inferior wine delivered by the colonel's regular supplier. He inclined his head. 'I was surprised when Smithers said Scotland Yard had sent an inspector. I had not expected anyone of that rank to come about the matter of letters the colonel has received. It followed that some other, particularly grave, matter had brought you.'

The butler was not a fool and considerably more a man of the world than the groom. Good.

'Then we may cut to the chase,' I said briskly. 'In your previous place, I understand you worked for some time for Mr Sebastian Benedict, of The Cedars, near to Egham, in Surrey.'

Seymour inclined his head and showed neither surprise nor curiosity at my words. 'Yes, sir.'

'For how long were you with Mr Benedict?'

'For nearly ten years, sir.'

'It was a good place?'

'Yes, sir. Mr Benedict was an excellent employer.'

'And Mrs Benedict, the lady of the house? How would you describe her?' I waited for his answer with some eagerness. This was the whole reason for my being here. I did not want to return to Superintendent Dunn and confess I had drawn a blank.

'As deceased, sir,' replied Seymour with an unexpected dry humour. 'I read of the event you referred to in the newspapers and was very distressed. She was a very pleasant lady.'

'It is the death of that lady we are investigating, as you may have guessed,' I continued. 'We had hoped that her companion, a Miss Isabella Marchwood, might be able to give us much useful background information. But unfortunately, before she could do so, Miss Marchwood was herself murdered, on a train. You read of that too, perhaps?'

Seymour nodded and his watchful look returned.

'We are therefore casting our net wider in a search for such information. As butler in the household for such a long time, you would have been aware of most things going on, I imagine.'

'It is my business to know what the staff are doing,' Seymour answered carefully. 'It is not my business to enquire into my employer's private life.'

'Come now, Seymour,' I urged. 'We are trying to find a double murderer here. How many more women do you want to see slaughtered in this dreadful way?'

Seymour flushed and his stiff manner became slightly agitated. 'None, inspector! For goodness' sake, what do you imagine? I had the greatest admiration for Miss Marchwood. She was a woman of the most respectable background reduced to seeking positions as a companion by her straitened circumstances. She gave offence to no one and I can't imagine why she was killed on that train. There is no possibility, I suppose, that it was a case of mistaken identity? The killer thought she was someone else? Or perhaps a robbery that got out of hand?'

There was definitely a note of desperation in his voice now. Aha! I thought. Mr Mortimer Seymour does know something. It is something he would much rather not have to tell me. But he does have to tell me and I think, when he realises it, he will.

'There is no possibility. This was a deliberate murder of a specific victim. The lady's purse was found in the carriage, still containing money. There are other details we need not go into now.'

Seymour sighed.

'You spoke to me of your job and its duties just now,' I began. 'I have a job and duties, too. They are different from yours but place equal obligations on me. I often have to do things I'd rather

215

not do, and ask questions I am embarrassed to put. I am determined to find this killer. I need all the help I can get. But perhaps I can help you a little. I realise that there was a difference in age between Mr Benedict and his wife, that she was not English and quite possibly not entirely happy in her marriage. Would you agree with that?'

'Yes, sir,' said Seymour after a few seconds' pause.

'You left the employment of Mr Benedict very suddenly. Mr Benedict was upset about it. He has not employed anyone to replace you.'

Seymour now began to look distressed. 'Has he not? I am sorry to hear it. I would not have left Mr Benedict in the lurch like that, if I could have stayed. But it had become impossible for me.'

'Because, like me, you had learned things you had rather not known?' I asked gently.

He sighed and nodded. 'I told you, Inspector, that it was not my place to enquire into Mr Benedict's private life. But, given my position in the household, it was difficult not to become aware of certain things.' He hesitated, seeking his way forward, and I did not press him. He had decided to talk now and he would.

'The household staff here report to me,' he said. 'You were asking earlier, as I understand, whether anyone who had seen anything suspicious around the stables or the house would have reported it to the colonel; and Smithers told you it would be reported to me in the first instance.'

'Yes,' I agreed. 'And I'd be grateful if you continued with the pretence that I am here solely about the blackmail threats to the colonel.'

'It would suit me, too,' Seymour said frankly. 'Murder upsets people. I have told no one on the staff here that I was butler at The Cedars. The colonel knows where I was previously employed, because Mr Benedict was good enough to give me a reference. But the colonel's attention is entirely taken up with the blackmail attempt at the moment and I doubt it has yet occurred to him to match the name of the victim to that of my former employer.'

'Then we have a pact.' I smiled at him encouragingly.

Seymour almost smiled back. 'Thank you, sir. You mentioned Miss Marchwood. She was a religious lady. She somehow or other became involved in some temperance meetings in London. She travelled up to them each Sunday and got to know a Mrs Scott. The – the preacher at these meetings is a Joshua Fawcett. Mr Fawcett often spoke at private gatherings at Mrs Scott's house. It is in Clapham, I understand. To my knowledge, Mrs Benedict never went to the meetings in central London on a Sunday. But she did go several times with Miss Marchwood to the private gatherings at Clapham. They were by way an outing for her. She had no interest, I imagine, in the temperance movement. But you are right: she was lonely and unhappy. All of us, all the staff, could see it.'

He sighed. 'Mrs Benedict was impressed by this fellow, Fawcett. I never met him but I understand he makes a very striking figure. Miss Marchwood was also impressed and let us know about it. She – Isabella Marchwood – was normally a very level-headed woman, Inspector. If *she* lost her sense of judgement regarding this Fawcett, then it is not surprising that Mrs Benedict did the same. Mrs Benedict came to this country as a very young bride. She was inexperienced in the world and – I will be frank – Mr Benedict kept her somewhat cloistered away at The Cedars. I firmly believe his intentions were the best possible. He wanted to protect her from the dangers of society. But by so doing, he left her unprotected against someone like Fawcett; do you understand me, Inspector?'

217

'I understand you perfectly, Mr Seymour,' I assured him. I had put Benedict's jealous guardianship of his beautiful young wife down to possessiveness. Seymour put a kinder interpretation on it. Either way, it had left Allegra vulnerable.

Seymour raised a hand in a gesture of resignation and then let it fall again. 'You are a man of the world, Inspector. You can guess what came about. A sordid entanglement. I don't doubt Mrs Benedict imagined it a great love affair. The poor lady was entirely carried away. She had no thought for the future, where it would lead. Where it *could* lead! And indeed, there was nowhere it could lead but to disaster; but she rushed on headlong.'

A sudden vivid and painful image leapt into my mind: The Triumph of Death, that gruesome masterpiece shown to me by Sebastian Benedict. Like the young men in the painting, Allegra fled from the inevitable towards the false shelter of Fawcett's arms.

'If I blame Isabella Marchwood for anything, it is that she did not realise the danger in it either,' Seymour was saying sadly. 'We all saw the difference in Mrs Benedict. She was happy, sir. Really happy, and excited, like a child. There were letters . . . Miss Marchwood sometimes carried them, I believe, or posted hers for him for Mrs Benedict. And there were replies from him, which were definitely not posted because they could so easily have fallen into the hands of Mr Benedict. Those Miss Marchwood must have brought by hand. I cannot understand her complicity. She was such an upright woman!' Seymour flapped his hands again in distress.

'Such people are often the first to fall under the spell of a man like Joshua Fawcett,' I told him. 'They are themselves good and see only goodness in others. But these letters, between Fawcett and Mrs Benedict, you saw them?'

'Mrs Benedict's maid Henderson did, Inspector. She twice came upon Mrs Benedict reading them and once found her mistress kneeling before the grate in her bedroom, burning them. Then there was . . .' Now Seymour reddened and pressed his lips tightly together.

'Go on,' I said gently.

'Mr Benedict will learn of this, I suppose?' he said, gazing at me hopelessly.

'I believe he already guesses. It may be he will not learn the details you are telling me. I can't promise it.'

'It is a wretched business!' Seymour burst out. 'Can you understand now why I left the house so suddenly, why I couldn't remain once I had been informed?'

'By Henderson, the maid?'

'Yes, as I explained, she came to me, as head of the staff, to ask my advice. She did not know what to do. She was worried, frightened . . . Most of the household linen went out to a washerwoman in Egham. But Henderson washed some of Mrs Benedict's more personal and delicate items. That included her . . . underlinen.'

Seymour was now so miserable that I had to encourage him. 'I do understand what you are about to tell me, and how difficult it is for you. But, you understand, as the investigator gathering evidence, I have to hear you say it. My guess at what you mean is not enough.'

'No, Inspector, I do understand that. I am making a statement, am I not? Well, Henderson was distressed at finding – stains – on her mistress's undergarments, after she had returned from some shopping visits to London. Or so-called shopping visits,' Seymour added bitterly. 'Don't think, Inspector, that I simply packed my bags and ran from the situation without trying to attempt some late remedy. I spoke seriously to Miss Marchwood, pleaded with her! But it was no good. By then she was in too deep, to put it frankly. Mrs Benedict fancied herself in love. She wouldn't give up Fawcett and Miss Marchwood could do nothing but stand by and let things run on to the wretched end. She was afraid; by then of course she was. She had begun to realise far too late . . . But she *would* do nothing and I *could* do nothing. With much regret, I handed in my notice.'

Seymour fell silent and after a moment, took out a handkerchief and mopped his brow.

'You did all you could, Mr Seymour,' I soothed the wretched man. His situation had been impossible.

'I could not speak to Mr Benedict. How could I? It would have been the end of my employment there whether I had been believed or not.' Seymour waved the handkerchief around helplessly.

'Mr Seymour!' I urged. 'I can only repeat, you did all you could reasonably do. You couldn't speak directly to either Mr or Mrs Benedict and Miss Marchwood was your only hope. She failed you.'

Seymour tucked away the handkerchief and some of his former stiff manner had returned.

'She failed Mrs Benedict!' he said tersely.

How deep Isabella Marchwood's complicity had run. Not just surreptitious meetings in the parks. Not only girlish love letters. No wonder the companion had been unable to confess it all to the police, or that Seymour's pleas had come too late. Benedict's wrath would have known no limits. Isabella's own reputation would have been in shreds. No one would ever have employed her again. Not only Allegra had rushed on to her doom. The wretched companion had been tugged along in her wake.

'Tell me, Inspector,' Seymour said quietly. 'Do you think this wretch, Fawcett, killed Mrs Benedict to protect his own sorry reputation?'

'I don't know,' I said frankly.

And I did not. It would not have been the first time a lover had become a dangerous embarrassment, to be removed by any means. But I did not think that Isabella Marchwood, however frightened for her own future, would deliberately have led Allegra Benedict towards a meeting in the fog with her murderer. Towards a meeting of some kind, yes, almost certainly a lovers' tryst beneath the oak in Green Park. But to her death? No, there was another element here and we had not yet discovered it.

This was pretty much the gist of what I later told Superintendent Dunn on my return to Scotland Yard.

Dunn, to my alarm, immediately relegated Benedict as a murder suspect to secondary status, and installed Fawcett in his place. We had our man! We could be sure of it. He became quite agitated, rubbing his bristling hair until it looked like a hedgehog's spines as he strode up and down his office.

'We shall bring the fellow in for questioning. We now know he and the Benedict woman were having an affair. He had motive, powerful motive, Ross!'

'Yes, sir, but I am not convinced that alone makes him our man. I believe him to be a quick-thinking, ingenious confidence trickster. However, would he kill? Do something so crass? He is a thinker, sir, not a bully boy.'

'If pushed to it, why not kill? It's not the prerogative of the thug. How many quiet, apparently inoffensive men, well respected in their neighbourhoods, have you seen hanged for murder? There again, how many flash men-about-town, who have found themselves in an inconvenient entanglement, have resorted to the ultimate way to rid themselves of the problem? More than a few, as you and I well know. Would that not describe Fawcett? He's a gambler and sooner or later a gambler's luck runs out.' Dunn snapped his fingers and sat back in his chair, well pleased with his own argument.

'He will run for it,' I said. 'We don't have enough to hold him. To pull him in for questioning, perhaps, but nothing more. What evidence can we put before him? Do we accuse him of this affair on the basis of letters half glimpsed by a barely literate lady's maid? Or stains of unknown origin? We can be reasonably certain Allegra Benedict had a lover, but if Fawcett denies it was him, how can we prove otherwise? The one person who could have told us about it all was Isabella Marchwood; and she won't speak now, poor woman. And what of Marchwood's death? Are you saying Fawcett killed her, too, as well as his mistress?'

Dunn leaned forward and gave a positively evil grin. 'To kill the first time is difficult, Ross, but to kill a second time or a third . . . that's a different matter. It becomes progressively easier, especially when it seems to the killer the deed can so easily be got away with!'

'He will run,' I repeated obstinately. 'We know he's adept at reinventing himself. He's surely played his present game elsewhere. You have no news from your correspondents in other forces, I suppose?'

'If I had,' said Dunn sharply, 'I should have told you. No, not yet, but I trust the expense in sending out so many telegraph messages will not be without result.' He sat down and placed his stubby fingers on the desktop. 'Besides, we are not bringing him in to question him about his activities at the Temperance Hall. We'll be questioning him about a murder and if he *then* runs, he *will* look guilty.'

There was no point in arguing with Dunn about it any further. I still thought it premature to bring in Fawcett. At the same time, I admit I was curious to see the fellow. In any case, the decision was Dunn's and he had made it.

I left Dunn's office and went along to find the colleague who had been given the job of investigating the blackmail attempt on Colonel Frey. His name was Phipps. I explained about my trip to Newmarket and how I had been taken for someone sent by him.

'I hope,' I said, 'I have not jeopardised your own enquiries. I didn't seek to pass myself off under false colours. They just assumed . . . I went along with it. I couldn't do otherwise without explaining myself to all and sundry. I didn't want to frighten Seymour; and I didn't want to meet the colonel face to face if I could avoid it. The opportunity presented itself and, well, I took it.'

'If you had wanted to meet Colonel Frey face to face,' Phipps said irritably, 'you could have done so here a few days ago. He is a peppery old gent. He came marching in here with his bundle of letters and addressed me as if I were a subaltern. Pretty illiterate letters they are, too. I told him, don't reply, don't pay and set an armed guard, which he apparently has done. What does he expect of us? I have set enquiries going among all the known racecourse tricksters. We may find the writer of the letters. But my guess is that if it proves too difficult to get to the horse, or to frighten the colonel, they won't bother. Besides, with so many Scotland Yard men crawling over the place, they will keep well away!'

He gave me a meaningful look.

I apologised again.

'Oh, well, I would have done the same,' said Phipps graciously. 'Obviously you didn't want to speak to the colonel if you didn't have to. You did well to avoid him. I will brief whomever I send down next week to follow up your story. It may do no harm, after all, if Colonel Frey as well as the blackmailer thinks we are sending every available man.'

I left Phipps's office, relieved that he had taken my interference so well. I returned to my own office and there I found Constable Biddle.

'Oh, Mr Ross, sir!' he called out eagerly as soon as he set eyes on me. 'They have found the girl, Clarrie Brady.'

'Found her? Thank goodness! Where?' I exclaimed.

'In the river,' said Biddle.

Chapter Thirteen

Inspector Benjamin Ross

CLARRIE BRADY lay in the morgue reserved for bodies pulled from the river, at Wapping. Morris and I stood beside the table on which she lay, together with Daisy who had been brought to identify her friend. A sergeant of the River Police stood by, watching us with a dispassionate eye. He had seen too many girls like Clarrie dragged from the watery embrace of Father Thames.

'That's her . . .' snuffled Daisy. 'That's poor Clarrie. Who done that to her, Mr Ross? Was it the Wraith?'

'That' was a reference to the cord tied round the dead girl's neck. It was difficult now to say if she had ever been pretty. Immersion in the river had not helped the ravages of death and of strangulation. The scar where Jed Sparrow had cut her with a broken glass showed up lividly on her swollen face, as did the mole on her forehead. She had very black hair which I guessed was not dyed, as were Daisy's scarlet tresses. Other than that she was tiny, a broken doll cast out by a thoughtless child.

'Thank you, Daisy,' I said, 'for coming and confirming her identity. I do understand how sad this is for you. I wish I could tell you who killed her; but the truth is, I don't know. Of course I haven't forgotten what you told me about the River Wraith. I have him in mind, but perhaps I should be looking for another.'

The day was a cold one. Winter was setting in seriously and here, in this grim, dark room with the water scarcely a stone's throw away, there was an unwholesome clamminess in the air. Daisy had thrown a blue woollen shawl over her light dress and, with her bright red hair, struck a colourful note, but it jarred. She had been shivering since we entered, I guessed both from the chill and from fear. She pulled the shawl more tightly about her thin shoulders and looked up at me, her eyes bright with unshed tears.

'What will they do with her now, Mr Ross?'

'Do with her?' The question took me by surprise. But Clarrie had been Daisy's friend and it was natural she should want to know about a funeral. 'Well, there will be an inquest—' I began.

She interrupted me. 'No, I mean, will they give her to the anatomists?'

This also hadn't occurred to me. Daisy's question had not been prompted by a wish to attend a burial, but by a fear there wouldn't be one, or not one in any normal sense of it. I stammered awkwardly, 'I have no idea, no, I shouldn't think so . . .'

She grasped my sleeve and peered up at me urgently, the feathers on her hat nodding and making her look like a bedraggled cockerel. 'Don't let them give her to the learner doctors, Mr Ross! They do that with bodies of people like us who are poor and ain't got no one to claim 'em!'

'Has Clarrie no one who will claim her body? How about her mother?'

'Oh, she's long gone!' said Daisy dismissively. 'Clarrie was a workhouse brat, like me. We run away together, the two of us. They never got us back. Well, I expect they didn't look very hard. There are plenty of others in the workhouse. So Clarrie and me, we finished up on the streets making our living the only way we could. We shared our money at first, so that whatever happened, we both ate. But then Jed Sparrow got a hold of her. He'd have liked to get hold of me, too, but I managed to keep clear. I dare say you don't approve of none of it, Mr Ross, nor your wife. But see, the business has kept me from ever going back into the workhouse. Anyway, Clarrie's mother wasn't never married, I shouldn't think, none of our sort ever is. If the workhouse ever had any record of her name, I expect they've long lost it. So if it ain't a legal relationship they won't give you the body anyway.'

'Perhaps Sparrow could claim her?' I suggested, knowing this was a foolish suggestion.

'He won't!' snapped Daisy. 'He don't care and anyway, he's not legal either, he wasn't her husband and he won't pay for any funeral.' Her grip on my sleeve tightened and desperation entered her face. 'Oh, Mr Ross, if they cut her up she'll never be able to rise up at the Last Day!'

I was now completely taken aback. 'At Judgement Day, Daisy? Whatever made you think of that?'

'How can she rise up if she's been chopped up into pieces by the anatomists?' demanded Daisy wildly. 'There will be bits of her all over the place! It's in the Bible. I've never read it, but I've been told about it. There will be an angel blowing a trumpet and all the dead folk will get up and dance around. But you can't dance around if your head is in one place and your legs is in another, your insides is pickled in jars and someone's gone and lost your arms . . . No matter how hard that angel puffs away at his trumpet! That's how it will be for poor Clarrie, if the learner doctors get at her!'

She was in such real despair at this idea that I said soothingly, 'I doubt very much the body is in a good enough state to interest the medical schools, Daisy. She has been too long in the water.'

Daisy's grip on my sleeve slackened. 'I 'ope so,' she said sadly. 'Can you speak to the coroner, Mr Ross? Ask that she's not chopped up?'

'I will,' I promised. 'But I think it is unlikely it will come to that, as I told you. The bodies for the medical school are required to be fresh.'

Daisy sniffed and rubbed her nose vigorously with the back of her hand before muttering, 'I'll be going, then. Thank you for finding her, Mr Ross. You said you would and you did.' With that, she ran out of the room.

'I wish I could have found her alive,' I said, to no one in particular. I glanced at Morris. 'What was all that talk about Judgement Day, do you think?'

The River Police sergeant, silent until now, answered. 'The poor are very superstitious, Inspector. It's not the first time I've heard of a lot of distress being caused when an unclaimed body's been taken to a medical school. It's because of the fear that somehow the dead person will miss out on the Resurrection, like that girl was saying. A lot of 'em believe the body should be left in one piece, you see. It's no use arguing with them; they've got it in their heads. But you are probably right, sir. I don't think the medical school will want this one.'

Morris, who had been staring down at Clarrie's body with wordless sympathy, now asked, 'Think this is the work of the River Wraith, sir?'

'It's possible. May we have the cord round her neck cut, Sergeant?'

The River Police man stepped forward and snipped the cord. It came away to reveal the double knot at the back.

'I will take this with me,' I said to the man. 'We have seen this before. This is identical to the cord that strangled Allegra Benedict in Green Park.'

Morris rubbed a forefinger over his moustache and rumbled, 'Think he killed this girl first? Before Mrs Benedict?'

'I do,' I said. 'Daisy Smith told me no one had seen Clarrie since the Friday morning, before the Saturday of Mrs Benedict's murder. If the same man killed both women, then possibly he killed Clarrie at some time during Friday. But perhaps he did not kill her until the next day, that same Saturday as the Green Park murder occurred. Our killer will have had the bloodlust up and, after killing Clarrie, went straight on to kill Allegra. That is my reasoning, at any rate.'

'Why would he kill the poor little scrap?' asked Morris, nodding at the body. 'Especially if it is the Wraith. He'd been contenting himself with just frightening the girls before, with putting his hands on their necks. Why go and kill one of 'em? Because this one saw him once? He was wearing his disguise at the time. Anyway, her testimony in a court of law wouldn't be taken very seriously.'

'Practice!' I said tersely. 'As Mr Dunn said, to kill the first time is difficult, to kill after that becomes easier. He intended to kill Allegra Benedict; but he wanted to know that the method he'd thought of would be easy to operate and effective. So he tried it out on this poor girl, and when that presented no problem tipped her into the river and carried on his way to kill Allegra. He did not, as we first thought possible, come upon Allegra in the fog and mistake her for a prostitute. He set out that day to kill her specifically and there is a reason for it. He is a cold-blooded monster, Morris, without any normal trace of human feeling.'

'Or mad,' said the River Police man lugubriously.

'Not mad enough not to know what he is doing,' I told him. 'He planned Allegra's murder very carefully. Now he has a way that is effective and he has used at least three times, if we include Miss Marchwood. He will not hesitate to use it again. No woman is safe.'

Joshua Fawcett was tracked down to his lodgings in Clapham and brought in for questioning at the Yard that very evening, although he was left sitting in a cell overnight. Dunn thought it might impress on our guest the seriousness of his situation. I said nothing to Lizzie about it when I got home. If we kept him in, the news would get about soon enough; but I didn't think it would reach my own house this same evening. Soon enough to tell her when we'd charged the fellow – if we did. Dunn was sure an interview or two would elicit all the confession we needed. I was not.

So, early the following day, I found myself at last seated opposite the preacher and saw our man for myself. Sergeant Morris and another officer had carried out the arrest the previous evening. Morris said he had come very quietly. A night in the cells did not appear to have disconcerted him any further. (It occurred to me he probably had earlier acquaintance with the interior of police stations around the country.) On entering the room he gazed about him with mild interest and seated himself uninvited. He had not shaved, but he was still dapper, his linen clean; only his footwear was slightly scuffed. His long hair lay curling on his collar but the diamond stickpin normally glittering in his black necktie was missing. It would have made a handy weapon, and had been taken from him for his own safety – and that of any officer approaching him. But otherwise he looked much as he probably normally did.

Not only did he appear unabashed, his attitude was almost as if he were to interview me.

'I suppose,' he said calmly, as I took a chair opposite to him, 'it is little use my protesting at this outrageous treatment. But I protest anyhow, and I wish it to be put on record.'

'It will be,' I said in a tone I hoped let him know he could protest as much as he liked and it would not impress anyone here. Every petty thief and whoremonger, every Jed Sparrow of the world, is quick to protest.

Biddle, seated nearby with paper and pencil, began laboriously to write what I suppose was Fawcett's protest for the record. Fawcett glanced at him and a slight smile briefly touched his features.

But he was not smiling when he looked back at me. 'You have no possible reason to do this. In what way can I help you with anything?'

'I hope you will be able to help us a great deal in our investigation into the murder of Allegra Benedict,' I told him.

He shook his head, as if bewildered. 'I am at a loss to follow the process of your mind, Inspector Ross.'

'You are not going to deny you knew the lady?'

'No, but I would hardly say I knew her well. I had met her. She attended one or two evening parties at the house of Mrs Jemima Scott, a loyal member of my congregation and a tireless worker in our cause. Miss Isabella Marchwood, another stalwart of our cause, also sadly deceased now, brought her there. Mrs Benedict was, I well recall, a charming woman, either Italian or French I believe. I was naturally distressed to hear of her tragic death, as I was to learn of Miss Marchwood's. Mrs Scott was also very sorry about it. Anyone with normal feelings would be. A dreadful case!' He leaned forward slightly. 'But I cannot help you find the villain responsible.'

Dunn was mistaken in ordering him brought in! I thought to

myself furiously. He knows we have nothing on him but speculation. He is prepared to sit there and let me make a fool of myself. But I had to go on with it.

'We believe that your acquaintance with Mrs Benedict was rather more extensive than you say, Mr Fawcett. Let me ask you a blunt question.'

A sharp look briefly entered his eyes. Lizzie had talked at undue length about their remarkable colour, a sort of bright greenish-blue. To my mind they were very strange, like glass eyes in a doll's head. But women are impressed by such things, I suppose. At any rate, the sharp flicker was gone almost at once and the irritating serenity returned. I could not help but feel the hackles rising on my neck at the sight of such smugness and struggled to conceal my dislike of him. Not that it mattered. He fully realised how I felt.

'Ask away, Inspector.'

'On the Saturday before last, the day of her death – please don't say you don't remember it.' (He had frowned. But I wasn't about to let him interrupt with some nonsense.) 'It was exceptionally foggy and the news of the murder was commonplace the next day, Sunday. It meant that Miss Marchwood, the helper you mention, did not attend the temperance meeting. She was Mrs Benedict's companion. On that Saturday then, had you arranged to meet Mrs Benedict in Green Park? Let us say at around four o'clock?'

'No.' The faint smile returned. 'Why on earth should I? What an extraordinary question.'

I did my best to ignore his complacency but my voice was gruff when I asked, 'Where were you?'

'At my lodgings, in Clapham,' he replied promptly.

'You seem very sure,' I pointed out. 'You gave my question no thought.'

'I did not need to. I am always in my lodgings on a Saturday afternoon. You see, Inspector,' he leaned forward to draw my attention to some serious point he was about to make. 'For most men Sunday is a day of rest. For men of the cloth, however, it is our busiest day for we are about the Lord's work. It is also the day when we preach our main sermon of the week. On Saturdays, Inspector Ross, I write my sermon for the following Sunday. As today is Friday, I can safely say that tomorrow afternoon I shall be engaged on the same task. Week in, week out, Inspector, that is the pattern of my life.' He sat back, surrounded by an air of saintly forbearance that made me want to reach across the table and choke him with my bare hands.

However there was an irrefutable logic to his reply. Probably every Saturday of the year, clergymen up and down the country were toiling away at the same duty. But nevertheless I pressed on.

'Did anyone see you there? Your landlady? Any visitor?'

He looked hurt. 'I impress on my landlady that I am not to be disturbed. The writing of my sermon takes me all afternoon. I don't dash it off in a few minutes! It requires thought. The examples illustrating it must be carefully chosen. The preacher must reach the hearts and minds of his listeners, Inspector, without confusing them. He must explain, illuminate and inspire. I have often laboured late into the night at the writing of it.'

I refused to be distracted by the image of Fawcett toiling away by candlelight.

'But there was a meeting that afternoon at the Temperance Hall, not far from Waterloo,' I put to him. 'Our maidservant, Bessie Newman, went there to collect some pamphlets.'

'So I believe. I am sorry she was given the pamphlets to distribute without your express permission. I have told your wife of my regret. But I was not present myself at the hall on that

Saturday afternoon, nor indeed on any other Saturday. Mr Walters conducted the meeting that day. Perhaps, if you care to ask your maidservant, she will confirm it.'

'You have a loyal band of workers,' I said to him, still trying hard not to show how much he irritated me and miserably aware that I was failing and that, even worse, he enjoyed my frustration.

He nodded graciously.

'But you had not persuaded Allegra Benedict to join them.'

'No, she was of another religious persuasion. But you are quite right. She was not one of my congregation, so I am at a loss to guess why you think I should have arranged to meet her. And in Green Park?' he shook his head. 'You grow fanciful, Inspector.'

'Let us see if I am!' I snapped back at him and saw that fleeting smile. He had me really rattled and I had all but given up trying to conceal it. I forced myself to regain my self-control.

'I believe that, although she did not attend your meetings at the hall, nevertheless you were in contact with her. She knew of your so-called good work because she had heard you talk of it at Mrs Scott's house. She had been encouraged to contribute to your funds, either because she believed the money would be put to good use, or because she had another reason for wishing to please you. At any rate, she met you that day to give you money from the sale of a piece of family jewellery. She had just concluded the sale in the Burlington Arcade. We have spoken with the jeweller.'

He blinked at the mention of the jeweller. That was not speculation on my part. Allegra had indeed sold the piece.

'I have no idea why the lady needed money but it was certainly not to give it to me. You may search my lodgings. You will not find it, or any other sums of money, in my possession. All is spent on my work.' He pursed his lips. 'I understood her husband to be wealthy. This selling of a piece of jewellery privately seems a surprising thing for her to have done. But if you say she did it, then she did so. But I cannot even guess at her purpose.' He shook his head. 'There are many troubled souls out there, Inspector. Who knows what was in her mind?'

I drew a deep breath. In for a penny, in for a pound. 'What is more, I believe that you and she were conducting a clandestine affair.'

Now he stiffened, flushed and a frown creased his brow beneath those Byronic locks. He looked every inch the wounded innocent. 'That is a most offensive suggestion, Inspector Ross! Naturally I deny it. I deny it vigorously! Not only because I am a man of the cloth, dedicated to his work and bound by the requirements of religion; but she is – was – a very respectable married woman. I take it you have not suggested this scandalous and, I don't doubt, *actionable* theory of yours to the lady's husband? Casting aspersions on the reputation of someone who cannot respond? Is this what our police officers have come to?'

But he was disturbed. The vigorous denial was delivered with a real passion suggesting to me it sprang from alarm. You might say anyone would be troubled by my accusation even if, or particularly if, he were innocent. But I have interviewed a good many guilty men. Aha! Mr Fawcett, I thought, you had not reckoned on your amorous entanglement becoming known.

'I must insist,' he was saying, 'on knowing on what basis you make these lurid accusations. You cannot possibly have *any* reasonable argument for them.'

'We believe,' I said, ignoring his demand, 'that Miss Isabella Marchwood carried your correspondence to Mrs Benedict.'

But now he was on safer ground. I saw him relax and cursed my clumsiness. Miss Marchwood could no longer be called in witness.

'She told you this herself? Miss Marchwood, I mean. She made this ridiculous claim?' His eyes gleamed.

Again, I ignored his question. 'There is supporting testimony from Mrs Benedict's personal maid and a former butler employed by Mr Benedict.'

Morris had made the expedition to Englefield Green and interviewed Henderson, the lady's maid, fortunately still living at The Cedars. Morris has a way with below-stairs members of the household. Henderson had happily told him all when informed of Seymour's claim. She had definitely twice come upon her mistress burning letters and on one occasion (this confessed with a deep blush) rescued an unburned scrap from the grate, out of curiosity. It had been signed *Jos* . . . The last part of the name had been reduced to ash but she was quite certain of the first three letters. Unfortunately for us, she had not kept the charred fragment.

Fawcett threw up his hands. 'Gossiping servants! Goodness, Inspector, a man of your experience surely places little reliance on such so-called information. I am surprised at you. To believe a poorly educated lady's maid with a mind heavily influenced by cheap novelettes? And a *former* butler? A dismissed servant with a grudge?' He shook his head sorrowfully at my gullibility. 'No court of law would place reliance on such testimony, Inspector.'

He was right. I could not prove it. He knew I could not. If I persisted now I would sound increasingly as if I were grasping at straws.

'Let me get this quite clear, Inspector,' Fawcett continued carefully. 'Are you suggesting – I can hardly believe it, but it seems you are – that I had a hand in the murder of the unfortunate Mrs Benedict?'

'We are only asking for your cooperation in our investigation,' I heard myself say woodenly.

'And Miss Marchwood? Do you imagine I can help with that dreadful business, too? Are there any other crimes, at present unsolved, that you would like to lay at my door? I begin to feel a little like the scapegoat of the Old Testament, sent out into the wilderness laden with the sins of the children of Israel.'

'I have no further questions at this time!' I snarled.

He had me on the run. 'Am I to be charged with *any* offence?' he asked.

'Not at present,' I confessed.

'Then I am free to leave?'

'Yes, you are free to leave,' I said. I could see Biddle in his corner giving me a startled look. Well, Biddle was young and had a lot to learn.

Fawcett rose elegantly to his feet and dusted off his sleeves. 'I take it my diamond pin will be returned immediately. I should not like to think it could be lost in police custody.'

I leaned across the table. 'You are pushing your luck too far, Fawcett. Yes, you may go. But don't leave London.'

'Why should I?' he replied. 'Good day to you, Inspector.'

Shortly afterwards, I watched from my window as he strolled off down the road. Dunn was probably right and he would not run, at least not straight away. We had played our hand and shown it to be weak. He had admitted nothing and we could prove nothing. But still, he must be concerned that we knew of his liaison with Allegra. A man like Fawcett would be making plans for his future. What, I wondered, would he do now?

Chapter Fourteen

Inspector Benjamin Ross

I made my way home that Friday evening deep in thought as I headed south towards the river. I was wondering how to explain the latest turn of events to my wife and to our maid of all work, as explain to them I eventually must. There was a faint chance they hadn't yet heard the news and then I would need to say nothing tonight. That would buy me a little time but I couldn't pin my hopes on it. It was far more likely that word would already have got about the congregation and the news carried to my own home by some eager talebearer. They knew Lizzie was married to me. Someone might have hoped to glean information, another reason for not telling Lizzie before; not that she would be indiscreet but Bessie might be.

Most men, I reflected ruefully, would not have found it necessary to explain anything to a servant. It was my bad luck that our maid was both an enthusiastic member of Fawcett's congregation and outspoken as well. So, Ben Ross, I told myself, you can't win. Bessie will probably be dismayed to hear Joshua Fawcett was arrested in the first place, and obliged to spend a night in the cells; Lizzie will be disappointed to hear he's subsequently been released (and piqued that I hadn't told her of his arrest the day before).

Rain had begun to fall in a steady drizzle. Already pavements and road surfaces glittered wetly in the glow of the gas lamps. People were hurrying to be home, as I was. Even so, the ubiquitous London prostitutes were out and about seeking the first customers of the evening. As I passed a doorway I heard myself hailed as 'dearie' and an invitation was extended to let the speaker 'cheer me up'. The voice sounded young. I paused and peered into the shadows, with half an intention to arrest the girl for her own sake and lock her away from the streets and their dangers if only for the one night.

There was a gasp. The light from the nearest lamp-post was shining on my face and the girl could see me far better than I could see her.

'It's you, ain't it?' she said. 'You're that inspector what came to the Hero to speak to Jed.'

'Come out!' I ordered sharply. 'Let me see you.'

A figure emerged and I saw the girl in the mauve bonnet who had been with Jed Sparrow in the public house. She still wore the same bonnet, despite its unsuitability for the time of year, and a light gown equally out of season, with petticoats short enough to reveal her boots and mud-splashed stockings. For warmth she had draped round her shoulders a small cape edged with some fur that looked to me as if it had last been worn by a cat. She also carried a brolly and now put this up to shield herself from the rain – and perhaps also to put a barrier between herself and me.

'I remember you,' I said. 'You sat at the table with Sparrow and another girl. So, out collecting rags, are you?'

She gave a nervous giggle. 'That's Jed's little joke,' she said.

'Sparrow would do well not to jest with the law. What's your name?'

She hesitated. 'Rose,' she said at last, adding in a frightened voice, 'Here, you're not going to run me in, are you? I only just got here, I ain't earned any money yet.'

'And Sparrow, in another of his little jokes, will black your eye if you go home empty-handed,' I said. 'As he used to beat Clarrie Brady.'

'You found Clarrie, didn't you?' she said quietly.

'I viewed her body in the morgue. I didn't find her. The River Police did that. She was taken out of the Thames.'

She sighed. 'It don't seem fair,' she said. 'It was the River Wraith who did that to her, wasn't it?'

She said this with a kind of dull certainty that was sadder than any more dramatic tone.

'You're afraid that, one night, he'll find you, too,' I said.

'I already saw him,' was the reply.

I hadn't expected this. 'When? Where?' I demanded. 'Not tonight?'

'No, it was a couple of weeks ago, just before Clarrie disappeared. I saw her that day and after that I never saw her no more. I knew the Wraith had got her. She was afraid of him. We're all of us afraid of him, but Clarrie, she knew he was looking for her.'

'Daisy Smith said the same,' I said.

'Daisy and Clarrie, they were good friends.'

'Rose,' I said gently, 'tell me where you saw the Wraith and how it came about.'

'It was during the week before we had that really thick fog, I think it was the Thursday.' She paused. 'But the weather wasn't good. The river mist had come up, nowhere near so bad as it got later, but still bad enough. Down near the water it was swirling

about and sort of confusing for anyone out and about in it like I
was. The cold got into your bones. I stopped and bought a hot
potato from a seller. I stood by his stove to eat it and warm meself
up. I know that seller; I often buy a potato from him in cold
weather. Just after I moved off, hadn't gone very far, I heard
footsteps hurrying along behind me. I turned quick – but not
quick enough. He was there, all white robes, like a burial shroud,
with staring black holes instead of eyes . . . He spoke to me.'

This was the first information I'd had that anyone had heard
the prowler's voice. I asked eagerly, 'What did he say? What was
his voice like?'

'Very soft,' she said. 'Strange that, you'd think it would be
harsh, croaking. But it was very soft and would have been quite
nice if it hadn't been coming out of that face. He called me a
harlot, a daughter of sin, and he sort of . . . hissed. I let out a really
big yell, and the potato seller, further down the road, he heard and
he came running. He was shouting out, "What's up?" because he
guessed it was me screaming. When the old Wraith heard someone
coming he took off too, just vanished into mist. By the time the
potato seller got there, I was shaking. But the Wraith had gone.'

Rose had seen Clarrie on the Thursday – and met the Wraith
that same evening. But if he'd been looking for Clarrie on that
Thursday evening, he'd not found her, because Daisy had seen
Clarrie on Friday morning, at a coffee stall.

'You were fortunate,' I told Rose. Indeed she had been, because
she too had seen him close at hand and heard his voice – and
perhaps only the approach of the potato seller had saved her. If
the Wraith had wanted to practise his skill with a cord that night,
it would have been Rose's body I'd seen at Wapping.

'Maybe.' Her thoughts were echoing mine. 'Maybe it would
have been better if I hadn't seen him. Clarrie saw him and look

what happened to her. Perhaps he is looking for me, now.' She peered up at me from beneath the umbrella. 'You going to run me in? Don't, please!'

'No,' I said wearily. 'I'm not going to arrest you. But take care and try and stay where there are plenty of people around.'

'Daisy said you were all right,' she confided.

'I'm obliged to Daisy,' I said. 'Goodnight, Rose.'

'Goodnight, Mr Ross.'

I set off on my way again but the meeting with the girl, and her youth, had depressed me. Perhaps it was the thought of that scoundrel Jed Sparrow waiting for her to bring home any money she earned. Whatever the reason, I turned my head and looked back.

She was standing where I had left her, beneath her brolly, but now she had apparently snared a customer. A well-dressed man was talking to her and some discussion, probably over price, taking place. Then he looked up and in my direction, as if he sensed that the pair of them were observed, and I saw in the gaslight that it was Sebastian Benedict.

I would say that my initial response was surprise. But then my surprise faded, to be replaced by a mixture of feelings. To put the best interpretation on his presence, it was possible he was simply unhappy and lonely following the death of his wife, and that had led him to come up to town and seek out one of the ladybirds working about the streets. Or, and now my emotion was turning to one of anger, this had always been his habit. Despite a beautiful wife at home, he was one of those men who find more pleasure and excitement with prostitutes. There are plenty of well-to-do men of that sort. But it still shocked me that Benedict was turning out to be one of them.

I turned on my heel in disgust and walked on, but soon I heard footsteps rapidly overtaking me and a voice called, 'Ross!'

I stopped and waited. Benedict caught up with me, rather out of breath. I noted that although still clad in severe mourning, he had removed the silk scarf from his top hat. His servants would have noticed if he had changed his dress to come up to town so he was obliged to seek his pleasures still clad in deepest black.

'You are astonished to see me,' he said, his manner and voice both defiant.

'I am a police officer,' I told him. 'Very little surprises me, Mr Benedict.'

The coldness of my tone had impressed him. I fancied that even in the gaslight, I could see him flush. 'You censure me!' he said angrily.

'I am investigating Mrs Benedict's murder,' I said. 'Your behaviour is only of interest to me in as much as it touches on my enquiries.'

'Damn it!' he exclaimed, 'I am not the only man—' He broke off.

'Indeed not, sir.' I kept my tone bland.

'But I am in mourning, and you disapprove of my being here on that account,' Benedict said. When I made no reply to this, he went on, 'When I told you I loved my dear late wife, that was the truth.'

'Yes, sir,' I said.

He hesitated. 'I would like you to understand, Ross, I want to explain . . . You see, my wife was . . . She was a work of art. No sculptor or painter could have produced more perfect a form. I always feared that . . . that she would become pregnant.'

Now I was startled enough to show it. 'You feared it? Most couples hope to start a family.' As I supposed that Lizzie and I would one day, if all were well. 'But that's not my concern, sir,' I added apologetically, because odd though it seemed to me, it was truly not my concern.

'You see,' he said, 'I could not have watched that perfect body become distorted and bloated with child. I have seen pregnant women with their puffy faces and awkward gait. That Allegra should become like that? No!' He paused. 'So, you see, my wife and I seldom shared a bed.'

This unwelcome and distasteful confession did touch on my investigation. Could it have been this very lack of a physical relationship within the marriage that had driven Allegra to seek love elsewhere?

I heard myself ask, 'How did your wife feel about that?'

Angrily he snapped, 'A woman of refinement does not entertain base cravings!'

Confound the fellow! I thought. Does he truly believe that? Then he is stupid, deluded, or simply callous and making a sorry excuse for his habit of frequenting common prostitutes. But I'd been right in my judgement; he did look upon Allegra as a possession, something to be added to his art collection, not a real living being with human emotions and vulnerability. Too late now to argue that out with him. After all, I told myself, I'm neither his medical adviser nor his father confessor. Let him believe such nonsense if he wants to. It has brought him grief once already and very likely will do so again. I just hope he doesn't ruin another woman's life as he did Allegra's. In the meantime, he doesn't like me and I don't like him. There is no need for any pretence.

Aloud I said, 'Well, then, you had better get back to your ladybird. However, it is my duty to warn you that such women are not always only what they appear to be. If you have valuables on you, take care. She may act as decoy for some ruffian who is lurking in the shadows waiting for you. I need not mention the diseases such girls often pass on.'

With that, we parted company. At least I might have given him something to think about.

I arrived in my own house to find myself confronted by two pairs of eager eyes. As I suspected, the news of Fawcett's arrest and his overnight stay in the cells had got about. My faint hope that it hadn't was instantly dashed.

'Well?' demanded my wife.

'What have you done with poor Mr Fawcett?' asked Bessie, less subtle and more partisan.

'The devil take your Mr Fawcett!' I snapped irritably. What with encountering Fawcett and Benedict on the same day, it really was too much.

'Ben . . .' murmured my wife, with a glance at our maid.

'I have had to let the fellow go,' I told her.

'There,' said Bessie smugly, 'I knew poor Mr Fawcett couldn't have done anything.'

'Go and peel the potatoes, Bessie!' ordered Lizzie.

Bessie went, not without a last triumphant look at me.

'You didn't tell me, when you got home last night, that you'd arrested him,' said Lizzie, as I'd known she would. The look in her eyes fell somewhere between reproach and accusation.

'We hadn't charged him,' I said feebly. 'It's a tricky moment when you bring a man in for questioning. I thought it better to be silent on the matter last night and wait until I'd spoken to him today.' I threw myself down in an armchair. 'And, as I told you both just now, we have had to release him.'

Lizzie perched on the edge of the chair opposite. 'He could not tell you anything, then?' she asked.

'Could not, would not . . .' I muttered moodily. 'I knew it was a mistake to bring him in, but Dunn would have it. He wouldn't even confess to the affair with Allegra Benedict although we have testimony from two servants that it was going on.'

'Wretch!' exploded Lizzie. I assumed she meant Fawcett. 'So, what will happen now?' she added.

'We have to hope he does not run for it. Dunn may be right and he won't do so immediately. It would make him look guilty of a capital offence. It is one thing to run to avoid being detected as a swindler. Quite another to present yourself as a candidate for the hangman's noose.'

'Do you think he killed her?' Lizzie lowered her voice, although much clattering from the kitchen announced Bessie's location. She was not a quiet worker.

I sighed. 'I have no idea. Dunn thinks he did. The man had motive. Allegra was in love. For Fawcett that would normally have meant that she was under his sway, but in this case the lady was Italian. She had a Latin temperament; she was passionate and unpredictable. Her whole demeanour had changed. She wanted the world to see how happy she was. We know that the servants at Cedar Lodge had already guessed the truth from her altered manner; and it would only be a matter of time before her husband's suspicions were aroused. I do believe Fawcett had got himself into a situation from which he would gladly have extricated himself. But kill to do it? That's something quite different. In my view it is far more likely that, if it came to a moment of decision, Fawcett would simply have packed his bags and vanished. It would have meant abandoning a profitable enterprise raising money for his so-called work. But given the possibility of some indiscretion on Allegra's part revealing the scandal, well, that's what he would have done. No, I don't think he killed her.

But I am prepared to find out I am wrong. She may have said something, done something, particularly rash and Fawcett may have panicked.'

'I shall go to the Temperance Hall on Sunday afternoon!' declared Lizzie after taking a moment to consider all this.

I wasn't altogether happy about this. 'You will find yourself unwelcome on my account,' I warned her.

'I was not particularly welcome there before, I fancy,' said my wife serenely. 'But I shall be interested to see how Mr Fawcett conducts himself now, after his little adventure in the cells.'

And, I had to admit, so should I. As for my recent encounter with Benedict, and what I had learned from it about the nature of his marriage, I had not and could not tell Lizzie about that. That Benedict had in some way been the author of his own misfortunes did not excuse Fawcett, who had taken advantage of a lonely and desperate woman.

I think Superintendent Dunn was a little discomfited by our having been obliged to let Fawcett go. If so, his good spirits were soon restored. On Saturday morning I headed for my office, only to be waylaid by the eager Biddle.

'Mr Dunn's come in today, and got visitors, sir,' he whispered. There was no reason for his lowered tones. Biddle has a sense of the dramatic. With luck, he'll grow out of it.

'Visitors from the North!' went on Biddle, gesturing vaguely towards the window and what he probably hoped was a northerly direction. 'And he wants to see you, sir, straight away, in his office.'

'Now what?' I muttered to myself as I set off. Dunn did not normally appear on a Saturday. He must have been summoned.

I could hear voices before I got there and when I went in I

found Dunn entertaining, if that's the word, two gentlemen obviously from out of town. They wore top hats and bulky winter overcoats and a faint smell of soot and engine oil hung about them that suggested they had come directly from one of London's great railway termini.

Dunn was looking really pleased with himself. 'Ah, Ross,' he greeted me. 'Just the man. Now then, I think our luck has turned!' He indicated the two men. 'This is Inspector Styles and that's Sergeant O'Reilly. They are from the Manchester force and have just come from Euston Station where they arrived on an early train, carrying with them . . .'

Biddle wasn't the only one with a sense of the theatrical this morning. Dunn picked up a sheet of paper and waved it triumphantly at me.

'A warrant for the arrest of Jeremiah Basset.' Dunn leaned forward. 'Known to us as Joshua Fawcett.'

'We were interested to receive Superintendent Dunn's telegraphed enquiry with a description of the man in question,' said Styles. His voice seemed to emerge from his boots. He was a solid, red-faced fellow with a fine beard. Despite this newly fashionable hair growth, there was something of the countryman about him. In this way he shared his appearance with Dunn, suggesting a pair of farmers met to discuss cattle prices. 'We guessed it was our man. We've been chasing Basset for some time. There are a lot of folk anxious to talk to him in Manchester.'

'Not only there,' put in O'Reilly, his voice contrasting alarmingly with his senior officer's, being rather light and reedy with the soft echo of an Irish brogue. 'They want him in Preston, Sheffield, Bradford and Leeds.'

'But we have got here first!' rumbled Styles with an air of triumph. 'And we'd like to take him back with us, if that's all right with you,' he added, with a look at Dunn, who was preening himself in the background.

'It is, as far as I'm concerned,' said Dunn. 'But since you wish to take the fellow out of London I suppose I should take it higher and get authority first. It should not take long.'

'We are certain, are we, Basset and Fawcett are the same man?' I asked. 'There's no doubt? He's a slippery fellow and we don't want him wriggling off the hook. I expect Superintendent Dunn has told you that we had him in here for questioning in connection with a murder case we have on our hands. We were obliged to let him go.'

Dunn looked disconcerted before saying testily: 'We were unable to hold him for lack of direct evidence. We couldn't get anything on him despite our best efforts and our belief that he may well be our man,' he added with an apologetic look at the visitors. Turning to me, he went on, 'But see here, Ross, these gentlemen do have something on him and a warrant to back it up! They can charge him; and if he's sitting in a cell in Manchester, we need have no fear he'll disappear. We'll know for sure where to find him if we want him again.'

'All the more reason,' I insisted, 'to be certain we are talking of the same man.'

'He's very good at disappearing, is our Mr Basset,' growled Styles. 'But I'll show you this, Ross, as I showed Mr Dunn here.'

He delved into his pocket and produced a small rectangular piece of card that he passed to me.

It was a photograph and showed a small group of people, apparently in the garden of a large house. They were all dressed in their best, gathered into a ragged line, and smiling self-consciously at the camera lens, with the exception of the man at the end who looked as though he'd rather be elsewhere. As well he might. Being caught by the modern medium of the camera was not to his taste. I saw he had already acquired the diamond stickpin.

'That is Fawcett, or Basset, as you call him, without a doubt,' I said, handing back the photograph. 'Who took this?'

'Ah now,' said Styles, tucking the photograph away in his pocket safely again. 'Our Mr Basset – and your Mr Fawcett – has been successfully swindling his way around the country, a very plausible gentleman by all accounts. When he got to Manchester he must have thought he was on a winning streak. We have some wealthy citizens engaged in the manufacture and supply of both cotton and silk. Their mills are a wonder of modern production methods with every invention by way of machinery known to man. Our air is very suitable for spinning cotton. You may not know that.'

Both Dunn and I shook our heads.

'It's damp,' said O'Reilly gloomily. 'Cotton threads break easily in a dry climate. No one could say Manchester has that.'

Styles took back control of the conversation. 'We call our biggest manufacturers the "cotton kings". Somehow Basset got himself introduced to the wife of such a man and, once she had taken him up, and persuaded her husband what a fine fellow Basset was, well, he got to know all the others and their families. The ladies in particular liked him.'

O'Reilly gave a broad grin but wiped it off his face before Styles spotted it.

'We believe in philanthropic institutions in Manchester,' declared Styles.

I could have said that from what I'd heard of the harsh conditions in the mills, wonders of modernity though they might be, philanthropy was not the impression I'd gained. I just nodded.

'So along comes Basset with some plan for saving the children of the poor, who might otherwise be hanging about in our streets at risk of drink and petty crime, and training them up to do an honest day's work.'

'In the mills,' I could not help but say.

Styles nodded. 'Just so. Successful industry needs a trained workforce, Inspector. Naturally, people listened to him . . .'

'And parted with their money!' piped O'Reilly.

Styles frowned at his underling. 'But that photograph was his undoing, you might say. Some of the ladies concerned decided to hold a garden fête to raise funds. Quite a party, it was, anyone who is anyone was there. An account of it even appeared in a local newspaper. And someone had the idea to invite along a professional photographer to make a record of the event. You know how it is; everyone likes to have his picture taken, especially in fine company! This photographic image,' Styles patted his pocket, 'was the result, and very nice, too. Everyone in it was very pleased with it, except our Mr Basset or Fawcett. Now, as it happened, one of the ladies involved has a married sister living in Leeds. The sister came on a visit shortly after the event, and the lady was anxious to tell her about it. She showed the visitor a copy of the photograph, and what do you think?'

'He was recognised,' I said impatiently.

'He was, that. Straight off. The sister cries out, "Why, that's Mr Denton who charmed folk here out of a small fortune to build a hospital for consumptive factory children; and then disappeared with the money when questions began to be asked as to when the first bricks were to be laid!"'

'The lady was horrified and told her husband and he came directly to us. We set out to arrest him immediately. But Basset (or Denton or Fawcett, as you will) had got wind of it somehow and the bird had flown. He had done a moonlight flit, left his lodgings without a word and his rent not paid. I dare say once that photograph was taken he knew the game would soon be up. The good citizens got none of their money back. You can guess how anxious they are to see him again!' Styles added grimly.

'So, he is known as Denton, too,' I mused.

'He's got half a dozen names,' O'Reilly told me. 'We tried to the best of our ability to track him down. Our enquiries of other police forces soon informed us of his previous activities but not his present whereabouts, not hide nor hair of him . . .'

'As I say,' broke in Dunn who had been fidgeting during this long recital, 'it should not take long to make the arrangements for you to take the man back north with you. I suggest you take yourselves off to one of the excellent chophouses hereabouts and come back when you have eaten.'

This idea seemed to find favour and our visitors departed.

'He's a suspect in a murder inquiry,' I said energetically to Dunn when we were alone. 'There may be some objection to his being spirited off by our colleagues to face the lesser charges of fraud, and so far away. And what about the police in Leeds and all these other places? They'll want him too.'

'That's why I'm taking it higher,' declared Dunn, his jaw set obstinately. 'They have evidence and witnesses willing to identify him and tell their story. You were unable to get anything from him when you interviewed him. You have been worried he will leave London. So let Manchester hold on to him. I'll go and see the commissioner and get his approval. He won't mind being disturbed on a Saturday for this.'

So, apparently the fact that we had wasted our time bringing in Fawcett was not Dunn's fault: it was mine.

'Well,' I said, 'at least I know where to find him. It's Saturday and this afternoon our preacher will be penning tomorrow's sermon at his lodgings in Clapham. That is,' I couldn't help adding, 'if he was telling me the truth about that. As he lied about everything else, we shall just have to hope, shan't we?'

Dunn gave me a somewhat hunted look.

Chapter Fifteen

Inspector Benjamin Ross

I HAVE to confess I was a very worried man as I set off for Clapham that afternoon in the company of our two northern visitors. If Fawcett wasn't at his lodgings I would both look a fool in the eyes of Styles and O'Reilly and be blamed for losing the quarry by Dunn. Fawcett would be alerted by his landlady that we'd been at the house asking for him and would pack his bags and leave on the instant. The superintendent would rightly point out that I would have made Scotland Yard look a set of bumbling incompetents. All this might come to pass because I was far from sure we'd find Fawcett at home.

My two companions, on the other hand, appeared in high spirits. Perhaps this was because they had eaten well at the chophouse or just because they had every confidence in me and didn't doubt for a minute we'd find the man where he was supposed to be. Or just the prospect of taking Fawcett home in triumph appealed to them. They probably looked forward to getting a vote of thanks from the city fathers – and those cotton kings whose families had been so comprehensively hoodwinked. I just prayed we were not all on a fool's errand.

'Well, well, Mr Ross!' said Styles jovially as we made our way to Waterloo Station in a hired growler (the urgency of our mission having got Dunn's agreement to the expense). 'So your Superintendent Dunn thinks our man may be a murderer as well as a clever confidence trickster. Is that your opinion too?'

As he spoke, he fixed me with a sharp look that belied his casual tone.

'As it happens,' I replied, 'no, it is not. Fawcett certainly had a role to play in the murder of Allegra Benedict. If I am right, his name was used to lure the unfortunate woman to her death in the park that Saturday. Whether he *knew* about it, that's another matter. In any case, until he decides to confess to an involvement with the murdered woman, I can get no further. I don't think he tied the cord round her neck and strangled her. On the other hand, if he didn't do it, who did? That is much the superintendent's argument. I should very much like to question Fawcett again before you take him back to Manchester.'

'I'm sure that should be possible,' rumbled Styles. 'Although I doubt you'll get the truth out of the fellow. He is a clever and compulsive liar. If you ask me, he's one of those deceivers who enter so fully into whatever role they've adopted, they believe they really are whatever they claim to be. Like an actor, you know, on the stage. Here in London our man's been playing the role of a preacher against drunkenness, so Superintendent Dunn told us, and has proved a pretty effective one. It's a great pity, perhaps, that he never turned his abilities into something legitimate.'

Or a blessing. I remembered Lizzie's opinion that Fawcett could persuade anyone to do almost anything.

It was a very short distance from Waterloo to Clapham by the train. As we rocked along, my mind turned again to Isabella Marchwood who had met her death somewhere along this stretch of line. We had made no more progress with that investigation. Burns had not come up with anything, despite exhaustive enquiries at all the relevant stations along the way from Egham to Waterloo.

'Why not?' I muttered and my two companions glanced at me and then at each other. I must endeavour to keep my thoughts in my head. But why had Burns's hard-working team of Railway Police constables not found a single person who had noticed anything odd on that morning Isabella Marchwood died? I found myself thinking of the beadle at the Burlington Arcade, Harry Barnes. He had not been able to give us any specific information but by that very fact had suggested to me the story told by Miss Marchwood was not quite the truth. Had the Railway Police not found a single traveller or staff member who had noticed anyone behaving suspiciously because the person who killed Isabella travelled up and down this line all the time? The face was familiar. The killer boarded and descended from the train regularly. He crossed the platforms and passed through the booking halls with the confidence of habit. Was I, after all, looking at Sebastian Benedict?

Benedict had been Dunn's first choice of murderer although even the superintendent had abandoned that theory in favour of Fawcett as villain. But would Fawcett really have ventured to take the risks involved in boarding the train and strangling his victim in broad daylight? Of course, Isabella would have welcomed him into the compartment with her. She would have had no fear and no reason to expect attack. The foul deed would have been easy to carry out.

'Tell me,' I said to Styles; since he'd asked my opinion I was entitled to ask his. 'Your acquaintance with Fawcett predates mine. Would *you* say he was capable of murder?'

257

'Not of planning it,' Styles opined after some thought. 'I don't mean because he hasn't the ability to plan just about anything. He's as artful as a cartload of monkeys. Despite that, I don't see him sitting down and making the decision, "Well, I will commit a murder and this is how I'll go about it . . ." It's not his way. He's a fellow who depends on his charm and oratory to get him out of scrapes. But you know as well as I do, Ross, that not all murders are carefully planned. Almost any rogue, finding himself in an unexpected corner and panicking, might kill. What if our trickster felt himself threatened?'

'I am not sure whether you agree with the superintendent or with me,' I told him moodily.

O'Reilly piped up. 'Whatever he tells you, if you do question him again, be prepared to take it with a good pinch of salt, sir. He's got a very active imagination, has Jeremiah Bassett – or Joshua Fawcett, as you know him.'

I was very much afraid he was right. But was he our killer? That is not the way a fraudster works! I told myself again. I think so. Styles thinks so, even though he was hedging his bets in his answer. But are both he and I wrong? A man desperate enough, as Styles had just said . . .

'You're not a Londoner, Mr Ross, I fancy?' observed Styles suddenly, breaking into my thoughts.

'No,' I told him, 'I come from Derbyshire.'

'Indeed? What brought you down here?' Both he and O'Reilly stared at me puzzled.

'I hoped to make my fortune,' I told them wryly.

'As a policeman?' put in O'Reilly and whistled.

'I have not done badly,' I said crossly, 'for a boy who began work down the pit!'

'As it happens, I have an aunt who lives in Derbyshire, in

Ashby-de-la-Zouch,' rumbled Styles. 'When she was a young woman she had a most unfortunate accident resulting in her having to wear a wooden leg.'

I steeled myself to listen to the history of Styles's aunt and her missing limb. Fortunately we arrived before he could properly launch himself into it.

We found the house where our man lodged without difficulty and stood outside, staring up at its bay windows, wondering whether he was sitting at the upstairs one, observing us and getting ready to flee.

'Is there a back entrance?' asked Styles, suddenly less cheerful. 'O'Reilly, you had better go and find out. If he spots us, he'll run for it.'

'There may be an alley running along the rear of the gardens,' I said, thinking of my own house. 'To give a back entrance to the houses.'

O'Reilly obediently trotted off to secure any escape route from the rear of the building. Styles and I approached the front door. He checked the presence of his warrant in his overcoat pocket and I raised my hand to the polished brass knocker. It was in the shape of a horseshoe. Perhaps it would bring us luck.

At first it did not appear so. The door was opened by a plump respectable-looking female in an apron. The appearance of this garment suggested we had interrupted her while she was mixing cakes.

We asked if we might speak to Mr Fawcett.

'Oh dear, is there more trouble with someone he's saved?' asked the landlady. 'Poor Mr Fawcett was away from home all Thursday night after two officers came to see him here. He told me when he got back home that he had been required to give character witness to one of the poor wretches he had persuaded to mend his ways, but who had fallen back into his drunken habits and turned to crime. Mr Fawcett had done all he could to help the poor fellow.'

I exchanged glances with Styles who raised his bushy eyebrows. Like me he was no doubt thinking that Fawcett's ingenuity had not failed him. He had been taken from his lodgings by police officers, spent all night in police custody, and still managed to persuade this trusting woman it had been in a good cause.

'Don't be alarmed, madam,' I said, 'we only wish to discuss something with him. So if you could just tell him we are here and would like to speak with him?'

'Lawks, gents!' said the landlady comfortably. 'In the normal way of things of course you could . . .'

My heart began to sink. Styles muttered something into his beard.

'Is he not at home?' I croaked.

'No, sir.'

'I understood,' I said desperately, 'that he was to be found at home on a Saturday, writing his sermon for tomorrow.' How lame it sounded! How could I have believed such nonsense?

'Why, sir, usually he is, but today he has just stepped out.'

'Stepped out where?' burst out Styles.

'He has gone to take tea with a lady who is a member of his congregation,' she told us. 'She lives in Clapham and sometimes has meetings at her home. There's one today.'

'Mrs Scott!' I cried. Turning to Styles, I hurried on, 'The house is called Wisteria Lodge and I know where it is to be found, my wife has called there.'

I thanked the bewildered landlady, cutting short her praises of her excellent lodger and his tireless efforts on behalf of poor lost souls, while Styles retrieved O'Reilly from the alley where he had been lurking in ambush. We set off at a brisk pace for Wisteria

Lodge. Both my companions were by now as tense and apprehensive as I was. The three of us fairly ran there.

We stood before the villa and discussed how best to go about things. O'Reilly was once again dispatched to the rear of the building. Styles and I approached the front door and as we did, we heard from within the sound of chattering voices and the chink of bone china.

'She's got a lot of people there to listen to him,' whispered Styles. 'How's she going to take it when we turn up?'

'Badly,' I said. 'Have that warrant ready. She will be bound to ask to see it.'

The housekeeper opened the door to us and showed no surprise. She even stood back to allow us inside, with smiles and welcoming gestures.

'The reverend gentleman has not long begun,' she said.

I realised she thought we had come to join in the meeting, sounds of which had increased. I could now make out Fawcett's mellifluous tones, holding forth. My heart leapt. He was here!

'We would like to speak to Mrs Scott privately,' I said. 'Would it be possible, do you think, to ask her to step out here without drawing attention to it? I wouldn't wish to disturb your speaker,' I added duplicitously.

Fawcett would be on the alert, though. If he had the slightest hint of our presence he would know at once we had something new on him. I hoped O'Reilly was ready in place.

The housekeeper hesitated. She was realising something was wrong.

'I am Inspector Ross,' I said, 'my wife called here recently to see Mrs Scott.'

The housekeeper relaxed. 'Oh yes, Mrs Ross, I remember. Just wait a moment, gentlemen, would you?'

261

She made towards a door on the left that must lead into the drawing room and whence came the noise of talk and tea-taking. I moved quickly out on to the front step again and made so bold as to take a quick peep through the window. The room was full of people, mainly ladies. And there was our man! He stood in the midst, fortunately not looking towards the window. A regular dandy he was, too, in his frock coat, pantaloons and cravat with stickpin, gesticulating widely as he made some point. I saw the housekeeper cross the room and stoop to whisper discreetly into Mrs Scott's ear. Fawcett, well into his speech, took no notice.

Make the most of it, Mr Fawcett, I thought to myself. This is the last meeting you will address for a very long time.

I rejoined Styles in the hall. He raised his bushy eyebrows and I nodded in response. Styles smiled broadly within his beard, revealing a set of strong white teeth, a predator ready to pounce.

There was a flurry of silk skirts and suddenly Mrs Scott was bearing down on us, a militant glint in her eye.

Rightly identifying me, she ignored Styles and addressed me. 'This is not a convenient time for you to call, Inspector Ross! Both you and your wife appear to think it acceptable to arrive on my doorstep at any time of the day and expect entry. I am entertaining a party of friends. Go away.'

Well, that was plain enough. Styles didn't like it. He was scowling ferociously and digging in his pocket for his warrant.

'This is Inspector Styles who has come down from Manchester,' I told Mrs Scott.

She stared hard at Styles, who stared back. 'Indeed?' she said dismissively. 'And in Manchester they make house calls at any time of the day or night, I suppose?'

A deep rumble suggesting a volcano about to erupt emanated from Styles's beard.

'Inspector Styles,' I said hastily, 'has a warrant for the arrest of a man we believe is present at your party.'

Styles held out his warrant. It was snatched from his grasp.

'Pah!' said the lady, having read it. She held it out to Styles who quickly took repossession of it. 'That warrant is for the arrest of someone called Jeremiah Basset. I know the names of all the people in that room, Inspector, and none of them is called Basset.'

'You know the fellow as Joshua Fawcett,' I said.

An audible intake of breath greeted my words and a tide of red began to creep up her neck and cheeks. 'Nonsense!' she snapped.

'By no means. He has been recognised and identified. He has gone by various names in the past. I must ask you to allow us to perform our duty.'

Styles was not waiting on niceties. He simply barrelled his way past her and made for the drawing-room door.

'You may not disrupt my guests!' barked Mrs Scott in a voice well audible within.

'Damn!' I muttered and darted past her after Styles.

The door flew open and we burst in upon the gathering. The resulting mayhem was predictable but still impressive. Ladies shrieked, the few gentlemen present leaped up, china fell and shattered, tea and cake flew everywhere. A parrot began an ear-splitting barrage of furious squawks, flapping his wings and ricocheting off the wire bars of his cage.

In the midst of it all stood Fawcett, who reacted as might have been expected. At the first sight of Styles's burly form and beard, and not attempting any denial, the preacher bounded towards a door at the far end of the room. Styles and I raced after him but we were impeded by the agitated crowd and obstacle course of small tables and cake stands. These we sent toppling to either side. More shrieks and wails arose and at least two ladies fainted away. Two men present tried to grab at us but we brushed them off and one of them fell over, too, knocking against a display cabinet and sending that and all its contents crashing to the floor.

The door through which our man was trying to make his escape led into a room at the back of the house. We rushed through it after Fawcett and were in time to see him climbing through a window into the garden.

It was a narrow window and Styles and I collided in our eagerness to follow. I was slimmer and more agile than my companion and scrambled through it first. Behind me I could hear the heavier built Styles cursing as he struggled through the opening.

Fawcett was sprinting across the lawn towards some rhododendron bushes. He seemed to know where he was going. *There is a gate somewhere . . .* I thought as I panted along behind him. *He knows of it and is making for it. Where is O'Reilly?*

As if in answer to my silent plea, O'Reilly stepped out of the rhododendrons. Fawcett, carried onward by the impetus of his flight, had no time to avoid him. They collided with a terrifying *thump!* The sergeant was bowled over and Fawcett lost his footing. They fell together to the ground where both lay winded unable to do anything before Styles and I were upon them. We grasped Fawcett and hauled him upright, leaving the gasping O'Reilly to get up unaided when he could.

'Jeremiah Basset!' boomed Styles, 'I have here a warrant for your arrest –'

Fawcett's wild gaze was fixed on me. Gone was any vestige of urbanity. This was a hunted creature that had been trapped, panting and dishevelled. His fine coat and pantaloons were smeared with mud and grass stains. He had caught a sleeve, probably in climbing through the window, and ripped a long rent in it.

'I didn't do it!' he howled.

'The warrant,' I told him, 'is for your activities obtaining money by deception in Manchester. A similar trick to the one you have been playing here, I fancy! Denying it won't help. The Law has caught up with you!'

'I did do that!' he almost sobbed, 'But I had nothing to do with the other! I swear it, Mr Ross! I had no hand in the death of Allegra or of Isabella Marchwood. Before God, I am not a murderer!'

O'Reilly had found his feet and produced a set of handcuffs from his pocket.

'Slap the derbies on him,' ordered Styles.

Fawcett gazed at his cuffed wrists in bewilderment and then looked up at me. 'You believe me, don't you, Mr Ross?'

Chapter Sixteen

Inspector Benjamin Ross

IT HAD been agreed that Styles and O'Reilly should take Fawcett back to Manchester to face the charges they had prepared against him there. Before that Styles let me take the opportunity to talk to Fawcett again about Allegra Benedict while we still had the wretch in our custody. I continued to call him by the name he had used in London. We had yet to get him to admit to his real one. Perhaps Styles would persuade him to own to it, or possibly Fawcett had used so many names over such a time, he was himself confused. He was an actor who had played too many roles.

The fine man of fashion was a sorry sight on Sunday morning. This was normally the day on which he reigned supreme over his flock, basking in their adulation, thrilling to the power he held to manipulate their emotions and bend them to his will. Instead he sat in a bare cell exuding its miasma of despair and stared desperately at me. No dandy now, but hardly recognisable: a dishevelled, haggard, twitching caricature of what he had so recently been. This was to be a very different sort of interview to the previous one.

'I am not a murderer,' he repeated. 'I swear it.' The man was almost in tears.

'I am not accusing you of murder, not as yet, anyway,' I told him. 'But I am accusing you of obstructing our enquiries into *two* murders, that of Allegra Benedict and also that of Isabella Marchwood. To impede the police in that way, as you will know, is also an offence.'

'How am I obstructing you?' he exclaimed, clutching his head in his hands. 'I know absolutely nothing about it!'

I leaned forward. 'Fawcett, I must know for sure whether or not you were conducting an affair with the victim, Allegra Benedict. You probably thought you were being discreet. But some other person or persons certainly knew of it, in addition to Isabella Marchwood who was a party to it from the first. It is possible that other person, or persons, used the knowledge to send a false message to Mrs Benedict, luring her into the park that afternoon. Do you want the true murderer found?'

'Of course I do!' he shouted at me. 'Until the murderer is convicted, I remain a suspect! How you think that makes me feel? I don't want to swing on the gallows for another man's crime!'

'Then help me find our villain, Fawcett,' I said and sat back, waiting.

He sighed and shrugged his shoulders, sagging in defeat. 'Very well, I'll admit it. Yes, it was a stupid thing for me to have done but – I became involved with Allegra Benedict. Normally I wouldn't have taken the risk. I have never done so before. It is not for lack of opportunity.' He gave me a wry smile. 'I am not boasting. But you should understand, Inspector Ross, that there is a certain type of woman who falls under the spell of a successful preacher, or any man in any kind of authority. It is not just that she believes his words implicitly, but she develops a passion for the man himself. Don't ask me why or how. But not infrequently that is what happens. I have always been aware of it and the danger it presents so have always tried to avoid it. But Allegra was different.'

He fell silent for a while. I did not press him to continue. There was something in his face I had not seen before and, I dare say, few people had: a genuine expression of regret.

'You did not see her when she was alive, Ross. She was not just very beautiful, although her beauty was remarkable, but full of some hidden desire, a – a yearning; and possibilities no one had yet discovered.' He gave a shame-faced little laugh. 'I sound like a writer of lurid fiction but in her case it was so. You know the fairytale of Sleeping Beauty, I expect. She was in some ways like that. Any man would long to kiss her and bring her back to life.' His smile was now a sad one. 'And that is what I did.'

'But you found you had awakened a dangerous sleeping creature,' I suggested.

He nodded. 'Oh yes, it was only a matter of time before the husband realised what was going on. The situation, had it become known to him, would have led him to drastic action. He was a man with influential connections, in a position to bring a divorce action against his wife. I would be named.

'I tried to impress on Allegra the serious nature of the risk, the need for absolute discretion and the necessary deception that required constant awareness. But she had no understanding of any of these words. Both discretion and deception really meant nothing to her. The risk thrilled her.' He sighed. 'Despite all that, I really did think that others had not yet become aware of the affair.'

He gave an irritable shrug. 'Oh, Isabella Marchwood knew and was necessary to our plans, but otherwise I thought I had a little while still. I knew that eventually I would have to cut and run. But I did not think that moment had yet come. I persuaded myself it had not.'

'You were in love,' I said softly, surprising myself as well as Fawcett.

He thought about it. 'Yes,' he said, 'I suppose I was.'

'Did you ever meet her in Green Park?'

'Yes, several times. We would then take a cab to a small hotel I know of where they are discreet.'

There were several such establishments in London, hotels only in name. Some were as good as brothels, with girls supplied if needed. Furtive lovers and other people in need of a private place to discuss very secret business might also go there. At any rate, those who took rooms often stayed only an hour or two during the day. But a blind eye was turned and no member of the 'hotel staff' (as the brothel madam and her bully-boys called themselves) would pass the knowledge on.

'When I heard of her death, I was utterly dismayed,' Fawcett was telling me earnestly. 'But I couldn't show it. I had to appear calm and normal. You cannot imagine how difficult it was, Ross. You will say I have plenty of experience at deceiving others, but that required an effort from me that took all my talents. I did speak to Miss Marchwood, impress on her that she must not tell anyone about – about my friendship with Allegra. Marchwood was the weak link, if you will, but I believed she was too frightened ever to speak.'

Yes, I thought, that is the little scene Lizzie witnessed at the meeting. You were not consoling the distraught woman but giving her what amounted to an order. Be silent. Say nothing. Lizzie later tried to get the wretched companion to confide in her without success, probably because Fawcett's instructions were too fresh in Isabella Marchwood's mind. But on the following day, that of her murder, she had taken the train to London with some express purpose. Overnight she had had time to reflect. I strongly suspected she'd meant to come to the police . . . or to try and find Lizzie.

'Did Mrs Benedict ever give you money, for your so-called work or for any other reason?' I asked Fawcett, who was staring glumly at his fingernails.

He looked up and hesitated.

'Come along,' I urged him. '*I* don't propose to charge you with anything in that regard. You'll face those kinds of charges in Manchester and all the other cities where you've persuaded gullible people to part with money or valuables. I only want to know if Allegra Benedict would have accepted a suggestion that she sell some jewellery, for example, to fund you.'

'I made no such suggestion!' he shouted. 'She never had such an idea from me!'

'But did she ever do such a thing, sell some jewellery and give you the money?'

'Yes, she did but it was her own idea.' He leaned towards me. 'She once sold a string of pearls. But not, I repeat, not at my suggestion. That is the truth, I swear. She told me the pearls had belonged to her mother. She said her husband knew nothing of them, would not miss them nor ask where the pearls were. She did it without a word to me, and then brought me the money, as pleased as a child. I – accepted it. Yes, I did that, unwillingly, though you will not believe me. I was afraid, you understand, that if I refused, she would be upset and there would be an argument. She would go home in distress and Benedict would observe it and want to know what had upset her. I was even more afraid what would happen if she started making a habit of it. I had already learned, you see, how unpredictable she could be.'

He pulled a wry expression. 'In fact, it set me thinking that perhaps the time was at hand when I'd have to leave London and return to the provinces. Provincial ladies are not above making eyes at the preacher, but they live in smaller communities where everyone's business is known. They have sharp-eyed family and friends all around them. They are less likely to behave foolishly. Gossip is meat and drink to small town society, Inspector! They flirt but it goes no further. If they commit adultery, it is only in the mind.

'But Allegra, well, I wasn't sure what she'd do next. After all, a sale of jewellery involves two parties, the seller and the purchaser. She might not have told her husband; but the jeweller who had bought the item might take it on himself to do so. I couldn't be sure.'

'Did you ask her to sell a brooch; or did she ever mention to you she intended to do so?' I asked.

He shook his head, his long hair flying. 'No, no! I told you. I was afraid the husband would find out. Perhaps he wouldn't have noticed the jewellery was missing, as she said, or perhaps he would. I wasn't prepared to risk it. After I accepted the money from the sale of the necklace, I told her she must never do such a thing again.'

I thought he was probably sincere. Missing jewellery that his wife could not explain might well have set Benedict on the track of the truth. Or a jeweller, suspicious that Mrs Benedict had fallen into the hands of a confidence trickster, might well have contacted Benedict, just as Fawcett described. Old Tedeschi, who had known Allegra since her childhood, would not have done that. But Fawcett didn't know it. Despite his pleas to Allegra never to do such a thing again, she had gone ahead, selling the brooch in order to surprise him with the money.

'You have done the right thing in telling me all this,' I told Fawcett. 'I think I have a good idea now of what happened up to the moment Allegra Benedict walked into the park.'

'I have thought about what must have happened there a thousand times,' Fawcett said quietly. 'But I am not to blame for it. If someone else had discovered our secret and made a dreadful use of the knowledge, that is not my fault.'

I was not prepared to argue this point with him. It was not in his nature to accept blame for anything and it would have been a waste of time. Instead I stood up and prepared to take my leave of him for the moment.

'I am to be returned to Manchester today, then?' he asked.

'You will leave for there this afternoon in the custody of Inspector Styles. I will accompany you and the inspector – and Sergeant O'Reilly – to the railway station and see you put on to the train. Once you are aboard, you are no longer the responsibility of Scotland Yard. If it is any consolation to you,' I added grimly, 'you have deprived me of my Sunday rest.'

Elizabeth Martin Ross

Ben's absence that Sunday certainly made it a quiet day for me and for Bessie. Perhaps this made me decide, even though Fawcett was now again in custody, that I would walk as far as the Temperance Hall, and find out if they had heard the news there and how it was being received. I supposed they *had* heard the news, since Fawcett had been rearrested so publicly in the middle of an afternoon meeting the previous day at Mrs Scott's house. But I suspected the ladies and gentlemen who had been taking tea at Wisteria Lodge were not the same as the people who attended the meetings at the hall. I certainly didn't expect to see Mrs Scott at the hall today, after her humiliation in her own home. She was the only one who might be really difficult to handle.

'We're not going to be welcome, are we, missus?' said Bessie, on hearing of my decision. Since learning that Fawcett was a well-known rogue up and down the country, she had been in decidedly low spirits and her mind had not been on her work.

'You need not come, Bessie, if you don't want to,' I told her.

Her eyes sparkled indignantly. 'I'm not going to let you go on your own, am I? What? Face them all without me there to back you up? I should think not!'

I appreciated her loyalty but wasn't sure how she intended to 'back me up' in the event of an argument. Perhaps she feared they'd pelt me with hymnbooks and drive me out from their midst.

'They ought to be grateful,' I said firmly. 'They have been deceived, led astray. They ought to be very glad someone has told them the truth.'

'Well, missus, they won't be,' said Bessie, more attuned than I was to the ways of the London masses. 'It's bad news as far as they're concerned and no one wants to hear bad news, do they? Especially if it makes them look a lot of silly sheep.'

'No, they won't be happy,' I agreed. 'But somehow I feel I have a duty to face them.'

So, with Bessie grumbling and protesting alongside me, we set out for the Temperance Hall.

As we neared it we became aware of some hubbub. A crowd of people had gathered outside the entrance, all gesticulating and shouting. They had certainly heard the news, all right! Among other members of the congregation I saw Mr Walters, framed in the doorway at the top of the steps. His whiskers quivering with emotion, he held forth to the crowd on the injustice done to Fawcett and, paradoxically, at the same time pleaded in vain for calm. Next to him stood little Mrs Gribble in her bright garments, wailing and waving her hands. There was Pritchard the choirmaster, shaking his head sorrowfully. The Sunday gatherings had been moments of minor triumph for him, a paler reflection of Fawcett's glory. There, too, were the members of the infant choir, to whom presumably no one had told the news. They had come along to sing their improving ditty for the day, unaware the meeting was cancelled. They were now enjoying all the disruption immensely, hopping about with beaming faces. A group of little boys had already realised that, if the pennies their parents had given them for the collection were not to be requested of them, then they were unexpectedly in funds. They were gathered together to count their spoils and discuss what to do with the money before their parents found out and asked for it back. As expected there was no sign of Mrs Scott, brooding over her embarrassment and feeding the fire of her fury in Clapham.

Bessie tugged at my sleeve. 'I don't know about this, missus! It's not a very good idea. They're not going to listen to anything you say. They're all in a bit of a state.'

I thought 'a bit of a state' was an understatement and began belatedly to think that quite possibly Bessie was right. Discretion is said to be the better part of valour and we ought to withdraw. But it was too late. We had been spotted.

Mr Walters, higher than the others on his improvised podium at the top of the steps, saw us over the heads of the gathering. He raised his arm and pointed at us like a prophet of old.

'Traitors!' he cried.

Traitors? I couldn't believe my ears. Fawcett had deceived them for weeks and he was not the villain of the piece, but I was?

'Run for it!' gasped Bessie, preparing to do just that.

'Certainly not,' I said sharply. 'This is nonsense.'

I picked up my skirts and strode briskly towards the throng. They appeared nonplussed and unsure what to do. Some looked at Mr Walters for his guidance. He looked surprised to see me advancing on him and hesitated.

It was little Mrs Gribble who reacted first. She ran towards me, tears streaming down her face. 'Oh, Mrs Ross, Mrs Ross! What have you done?'

'I haven't done anything,' I said loudly. 'But your Mr Fawcett has been very active.'

'It's not a question of what you've done, madam,' cried Mr Pritchard, 'but of what the police have done with the minister, isn't it?'

'He is *not* a minister!' I returned vigorously. 'He is a confidence trickster who has lied to you and played the same miserable game in other cities in England.'

Mrs Gribble turned her tear-stained countenance up to me. 'But he was *our* minister, Mrs Ross.'

'Yes, yes, a fine preacher!' bawled Mr Walters from his perch. 'A man with a rare gift used for a noble purpose!'

'Indeed, yes,' cried Mr Pritchard, 'he has a wonderful way with words!'

'And he misused it,' I insisted.

'Never!' boomed Walters, 'I am not persuaded of his guilt, no, I am not!'

This appeared to be the general opinion. The crowd murmured together and was taking on an aspect I didn't like at all. Images of the Parisian mob gathering about the tumbrils on their way to the guillotine entered my head.

'Well, it's not Mrs Ross's fault, is it?' yelled Bessie, suddenly leaping to my defence – quite literally because she placed herself between the crowd and me.

'Shame on you, madam!' roared Walters, ignoring Bessie. 'Shame on you for coming here today! Are you so bold, so brazen, to show your face despite the knowledge of what you have done?'

'Are you out of your mind?' I shouted back, losing my temper with them all. 'The wretched Fawcett abused your trust, took your money and fed you all kinds of lies—'

'But he didn't, Mrs Ross,' interrupted Mrs Gribble, tugging at my sleeve. 'It wasn't lies. Drink is a terrible sin. It brings people to ruin. That's true.'

'Yes, yes!' cried her supporters in the crowd.

'Will you deny that?' demanded Walters.

'No,' I said, 'of course not. But Fawcett didn't use your money in the way he led you to believe.'

'But we *wanted* to help,' said Mrs Gribble. She then added with heartrending honesty, 'And I did so enjoy doing the teas afterwards.'

I had destroyed their illusion, their belief they were working for something good. Fawcett had made them feel better about themselves and now they felt lost and bewildered.

'I am very sorry,' I said, 'that you all feel this way. I am sure that, when you have had time to recover from the shock, you will come to see that Fawcett had to be stopped. Come along, Bessie.'

We withdrew in good order, watched by the now largely silent, but still hostile, congregation.

'Phew!' said Bessie when we reached the safety of the next street. 'I wouldn't like to go through that again.'

'I can't blame them,' I said. 'I should have understood how they would feel.'

We walked in silence for a short way.

'Missus,' said Bessie, who had obviously been mulling something over. 'I know Mr Fawcett wasn't a good man. I knew he took people's money. But that doesn't mean what he said wasn't true. It's like they were all saying back there. He made them think about drink and the terrible damage it does to people's lives. So, although he didn't do it for the right reason, it had the right effect, if you know what I'm trying to say.'

'Yes, I think I do.' I sought an answer. 'But in the end it will have brought disillusionment. Saddest of all, when they are over their shock and anger, they will lose all desire to listen to any crusading preacher, good or bad, ever again. They won't trust any reformer. What of those little children in the choir? They will grow up thinking that no one can be trusted and what appears a good cause is only a way of getting money. That is a terrible thing, an awful distortion of the truth. I think Fawcett was and remains a very bad man. What he has done will continue to cause harm for years.'

Bessie appeared very down in the dumps, so I continued: 'As there is no meeting to attend, Bessie, you may as well take some time for yourself. You need not come home with me. Is there no one you would like to visit?'

'Not hereabouts,' said Bessie. 'I only knew people in Marylebone where I lived before with Mrs Parry.'

'Well, then . . .' I searched in my purse. 'Look, here is the money for a cab. Take one to Marylebone and go and see Mr and Mrs Simms. I believe they are still butler and cook for my Aunt Parry. They will be glad to see you and hear your news.'

Bessie cheered up. The thought that she had such dramatic news to tell the entire domestic staff not only at my Aunt Parry's house, but at every house in Dorset Square where she resided, provided a wonderful opportunity to be the centre of attention.

'I'd like that,' she said. 'Thanks ever so much, missus.'

I watched her hurry off and went on my way homeward alone. Light was fading. The lamplighter was making his rounds. I wondered whether Ben would be at the house by the time I got there, having seen Styles, O'Reilly and their prisoner safely away. But he had not yet returned and the little house was empty and very quiet.

I took off my mantle and bonnet, checked the parlour fire and went out into the kitchen. I did not know whether Ben would have had an opportunity to eat at lunchtime. Probably he had waited until the train for Manchester had drawn out and then gone to find a chophouse near Euston Station. But in case he had not, I should have something ready here. I looked into the larder and saw a boiled hock that was hardly touched. If I cooked some potatoes they would go well with a few slices of the meat. I tied on an apron, took out a saucepan and sat down to peel the potatoes.

Behind me the kitchen door, leading into the backyard, opened and a draught of cold air struck the back of my neck.

'Is that you, Ben?' I called, not looking away from my task. 'I am just getting supper.'

There was no reply and I swivelled on my chair to see who had come in.

It was neither Ben nor Bessie, but a creature from a nightmare. The Wraith! It had crawled from its lair and now it was here and I was trapped with it in my own kitchen with no way out. The apparition, for I don't know what else to call it, was wrapped from the neck downward in a bloodstained sheet or shroud. Its face was a white mask apart from two glowing dark pits where there should be eyes. An air of menace and evil hung about it that was beyond description. As I froze in horror, it began to sway hypnotically from side to side, its shroud rustling. The whole spectral form seemed to shimmer in the gaslight and took on a truly ghostly aspect. Then it began to utter a series of low growls and dropped into a crouched attitude as if about to spring.

My initial paralysis disappeared. I jumped up, the chair falling to one side with a tremendous clatter. As I watched, horrified, unable to flee because of the table behind me, it began to move towards me. I could not take my eyes from the unearthly sight. I could smell it now. It emitted a foul odour of dried blood, river water and something rotten. Slowly it raised its swathed arms and stretched out its hands, the fingers bent like claws, towards me.

I still had in my hand the little knife I had been using to peel the potatoes. Though a poor weapon, its stubby little blade only some three inches long, it was all I had. I found my voice.

'Stay back!' I ordered and jabbed the knife towards the creature.

It hesitated and let out a long hiss of anger. I could see now that its face was indeed a mask made of *papier mâché*. It had been painted, or whitewashed, to a matt uniformity broken by two holes cut out for eyeholes and rimmed with something that looked like the blacking Bessie used on our kitchen range. Through the holes the eyes burned with hatred as they remained fixed on me.

I knew I was in great danger and it meant to kill me. But at the same time my superstitious fear of it, as a monster, had quite gone. However much of a threat it represented, it was a man and not a wraith. It had no unearthly powers, but was someone dressed up in an amateurish costume. Where I came from, children made similar masks at Halloween and went around the houses demanding 'trick or treat' and extorting sweets and biscuits from householders.

'You may frighten the street women and make them believe in the River Wraith,' I told it briskly. 'But you don't impress me, whoever you are. You look ridiculous.'

At that it let out a great screech and leaped towards me, a crazed thing composed of anger and of hatred. These two emotions had taken over from any other reasoning power it possessed and drove it to superhuman efforts. The little knife was knocked from my hand. The creature gripped me now and was trying to get its hands round my throat. I grappled with it and we both fell to the ground.

None of the street girls had ever fought back and it had not counted on a wrestling match. We were both disadvantaged. My skirts hampered me, but its voluminous shroud, too, hampered it. These impediments to action reduced us to equals. Had it not been for that, I think it would have been successful in clasping its fingers round my neck. I knew I must not let that happen or I would soon lose consciousness and it could throttle me at leisure. All the time it was panting and hissing. It seemed to be growing in strength and I really do not know what might have happened.

Suddenly the commotion increased and, at the same time, the creature's grip slackened. I was able to break the grip of his hands and knock them away. The creature suddenly jerked backwards, away from me, and gave me space. I took the opportunity to scramble away. Inexplicably, other bodies had thrown themselves into the fray and the battleground had moved elsewhere. I could hear a screaming that came neither from me nor from the Wraith. I was panting and sobbing and my hair had come loose and fell about my face. But when I had scraped it back with both hands and looked again, I saw an extraordinary sight.

The Wraith lay on the kitchen floor on its back. Both Bessie and Daisy had appeared from somewhere and were pummelling the creature unmercifully.

'You ain't hurting the missus!' screeched Bessie.

'You killed poor Clarrie!' bellowed Daisy in tones that would have outdone any fishwife.

The wretched Wraith tried to fend them off but it hadn't a chance, attacked now by Furies as bent on vengeance as it had itself been. They looked as though they wanted to tear it to pieces. The mask had become loosened and slipped to one side so that the eyeholes no longer corresponded to the eyes and the creature must now be blind. It flailed its arms wildly and kicked out with its feet, but it could not see its assailants and half the time struck only the air.

When I was a small child, my father had bought a tortoise for me from a man who had appeared one market day in our town and quickly collected a crowd around him fascinated by his exotic specimens. My tortoise had been an adventurous little beast, given to scrambling over obstacles and occasionally falling off and landing upturned on its shell, its scaly legs waving in just such a fashion. It had not been able to righten itself any more than the Wraith could now. The shroud had wrapped itself even more securely round the fallen man as he threw himself from side to side in a vain attempt to escape the blows. He uttered inarticulate cries from behind the crooked mask, and all the time he was subjected to that merciless buffeting from the clenched fists of the two girls.

I realised they meant to do him serious harm and I shouted, 'Wait, wait!'

Bessie paused, looked up and demanded, 'You all right, missus?'

Daisy, for her part, immobilised the prey completely simply by sitting on him. Now he couldn't even roll about but lay on his back, his head and ankles emerging from beneath Daisy's skirts, gasping and gurgling in a horrid way.

'I am all right,' I panted. 'But I thought you had gone to Marylebone.'

'I started out,' Bessie explained. 'But before I found a cab, I met Daisy on the way and stopped to tell her about Mr Fawcett.

Then she said she wanted to come and see you and thank you; because if you hadn't brought her home that evening, the inspector wouldn't have gone looking for Clarrie. So I came back with her – and here we are.'

'I am very grateful to you both!' I said in heartfelt tones.

The Wraith squealed and gasped, 'I can't breathe!'

'Perhaps you had better not sit on his chest, Daisy,' I suggested.

'That's all right,' said Daisy. 'Let's have his mask off and see if he's turning blue. If he ain't, he's breathing.'

She reached out and ripped off the mask.

'Well, well,' I exclaimed, 'Mr Pritchard!'

His larded kiss-curls were in disarray; the fat had melted and run down his face. It was twisted in hatred as he glared up at me.

'It is all your fault!' he snarled. 'You set your husband on to persecuting the minister. You have done the work of the devil!'

'*You're* a devil, *you* are!' Daisy told him furiously. 'Wasn't it bad enough you went round frightening all the girls into fits? You had to go and kill poor Clarrie! What harm had she ever done?'

'A harlot!' croaked Pritchard. 'A scarlet woman! Like you, with your dyed hair, painted face and indecent dress! I should have found you and killed you. You are all the same, daughters of sin!'

'What?' shouted Daisy. 'My hair ain't dyed and it ain't plastered with half a pound of dripping, neither!' She grasped him by his ears, raised his head and banged it back down on the kitchen floor.

'Bessie,' I said hurriedly, 'you had better run out and find a constable.'

Chapter Seventeen

Inspector Benjamin Ross

I HAVE met murderers of all kinds. Some have been arrogant, some sinister, others defiant, a few remorseful. Some confess, others deny it even to the scaffold. Some, occasionally, seem bewildered at how they had got to such a sorry state. But this murderer was one of the strangest of the lot: an insignificant little man with hair plastered to his scalp with lard, a nervous tic at the side of his mouth, rolling eyes and twitching hands. By turns boastful and self-pitying, he was above all convinced of the rightness of his dreadful actions.

This was indeed our murderer: Owen Pritchard, butcher by trade. I had been wrong in dismissing the possibility that the Wraith and the killer of Allegra Benedict could be one and the same. I reflected that I had learned a lesson. Until you know your man and how his mind works, you can make no facile assumptions.

We had now searched the rooms in which he lived, above his Clapham shop, and there we had found a ball of thin cord of the type used to strangle Clarissa Brady, Allegra Benedict and Isabella Marchwood. It might have been used to strangle my wife if he had

had it with him at the Temperance Hall that Sunday afternoon, but he did not. He had brought his Wraith's shroud and mask with him because, as he admitted, he had intended later that evening to seek out the street girls on his way back to Clapham, as he had made his habit. But he had not brought the cord and that had made all the difference.

It could all have been so dreadfully different. My blood ran cold at the picture my mind insisted on serving up to me: Pritchard in his Wraith's disguise, creeping up behind Lizzie with a length of twine at the ready.

But it had not happened like that. Lizzie had turned her head fractionally in time, and Pritchard had been obliged to try and use his bare hands. He had not killed with his hands before. He had not practised this as he had practised on poor little Clarrie Brady with his length of cord before he killed Allegra. Lizzie had put up a vigorous defence . . . and Bessie and Daisy had come on the scene in time.

All this I know, and repeatedly tell myself, but the image has never left me. Sometimes I still dream that it's happening. In my nightmare I am standing by, a horrified spectator of the scene, but unable to prevent it. I want to shout a warning, but my voice sticks in my throat and I can only whisper. I want to run towards them, seize Pritchard and save Lizzie. But my feet are apparently glued to the floor. That's when I wake up sweat-drenched and panicking. Then Lizzie wakens too, and asks me what is wrong. I tell her it was just a dream and blame the porter I drank with my supper.

A ball of cord, such as we had found in his Clapham rooms, may be found in any household and no court would have considered that evidence of his guilt. But what we had also found, hidden beneath a floorboard in his bedroom, was Allegra's pink suede purse, still containing the money Tedeschi had paid her for the brooch.

It was this that would hang him. Benedict had identified it as his wife's and the jeweller, too, remembered it. The widower had been brought up to London by a telegraphed message in order to make the identification. Dunn had calculated this was less expensive than letting me once again board a train for Egham.

Benedict had been visibly moved at the sight of the purse but his voice had been bitter when he said, 'Yes, that belonged to my wife.'

As he left the office, he paused by me to say, 'So you found him, then, Ross.' He couldn't quite keep the note of relief from his voice. He knew that until we had our man, he, too, remained a suspect.

'Yes, sir,' I said.

He gave me a look in which I saw clearly he was thinking of our previous meeting when I had seen him picking up a prostitute. It was one more piece of knowledge I had about him for which he would always hate me. I wondered if he would say something more. But he only nodded and walked out. It would be the most I or Scotland Yard would ever get from him by way of thanks.

Dunn now showed the little suede purse to Pritchard in the room set aside for the interview.

'You stole this from your victim, Mrs Allegra Benedict,' declared the superintendent. 'She carried it with her when she went into Green Park and we have been looking for it since.'

Pritchard stopped twitching and declared with surprising force, 'I am not a thief! How dare you say I am a thief? I stole nothing!'

'Then how did you come by this?' thundered Dunn.

Pritchard subsided and became sullen. 'It was bad luck. It was not my intention, no, never! She must have dropped it. My foot kicked against it as I was leaving. I picked it up without thinking. My only wish was to get away. I put it in my pocket. When I got home, I found I still had the wretched thing. I didn't know what to do with it, so I hid it. I meant to get rid of it later, you see. I would have got rid of it eventually if you hadn't interfered and gone looking around my home *without* my permission, mind! I never meant to keep it.' A note of defiance returned but it rang unconvincingly. 'Count the money. It is all there, all of it!'

'We had a search warrant,' I told him. 'We did not need your permission to search your premises, either your shop or above, where you live.'

'I am a respectable citizen,' Pritchard insisted, the tic at the side of his mouth working feverishly. 'Everyone will tell you. Ask anyone in Clapham. They all know Pritchard the butcher. I have never sold poor quality meat. My shop is spotlessly clean. There is no smell and no flies.'

'We are not interested in your trade as a butcher!' exploded Dunn. 'You are here charged with a most serious matter, murder. Three counts of murder, may I remind you! Let's deal with the first murder to come to our attention. You were in Green Park, as you admit, in the fog, and there you met and killed Allegra Benedict. Had you followed her there or was it by chance you met her? *Why* did you kill her?'

Pritchard looked up, his dark eyes gleaming. 'But it had to be done, didn't it? She was an adulteress! A scarlet woman. She had led the minister astray, with her beauty and her foreign wiles. She would have been the ruin of him. She had to be stopped!'

'Stop calling him "the minister"!' I ordered. 'He has no theological qualifications.'

'What has that to do with it?' demanded Pritchard. 'He's a wonderful preacher.'

'Let us begin at the beginning,' I suggested, refusing to be further drawn into argument about Fawcett. That gentleman would soon be breaking stones on Dartmoor and his silver tongue would avail him nothing there.

I suppose, since he had attacked my wife, I ought not to have been present in that room with Pritchard and Dunn, and Biddle scribbling furiously in his corner. But this man had occupied my days and haunted my nights. It had been my investigation from the start and I held all the pieces in my hand. Now, at last, I would be able to put them together.

'You dressed up as a wraith or ghoul in order to frighten the women who worked as prostitutes near the river,' I said. 'Is that right?'

'Harlots!' spat Pritchard. 'They would not turn aside from their evil ways. They might be frightened out of it!'

'And one of them you killed, Clarissa Brady, known as Clarrie.'

'I knew none of their names,' he said pettishly.

'But you strangled one of them with a length of cord and pushed her body into the river?'

He gave me a cunning look. 'I had been searching for that one and I found her. It wasn't difficult to put the cord round her neck. She hardly made any resistance, you know. Only stood there, sobbing. Well she might lament her sins!'

'She was petrified by fear!' I snapped.

'She deserved what she got,' mumbled Pritchard.

'The murder of Clarissa Brady allowed you to try out the skill as a strangler you wished to use on Allegra Benedict, did it not? How exactly did that come about?'

'I waited, and when she came, I killed her,' he said simply.

'You knew she would come to that oak tree in the park? Did you send her a message, perhaps pretending it was from Fawcett?'

He shook his head. 'No, no, I had nothing to do with that. My part was only to be there and be ready for her.' He frowned. 'We could not have expected the fog. That was sent to help us. Sent from above!' He nodded in satisfaction and pointed skyward.

'Us?' I asked quickly. 'Who are "we"? Who wrote the note or sent the message asking that Mrs Benedict come to the park that afternoon?'

He was shaking his head furiously. 'Nobody wrote a message. Miss Marchwood told her that Mr Fawcett would be there, would be waiting for her. That was what she usually did, you know, take a message by word of mouth. She was guilty too, Isabella Marchwood. She aided and abetted the woman Benedict in her seduction of the minister.'

'Isabella Marchwood was a party to it?' Dunn exclaimed in dismay. 'To the murder of her employer?'

Again Pritchard was shaking his head crossly. 'No, no, of course not. She only thought we meant to talk to the Benedict woman, persuade her she must cease troubling the minister and leave him in peace.'

'So,' I burst out impatiently, 'you and Miss Marchwood were in this together? She passed on a false message. You waited by the oak tree and Mrs Benedict found you instead of Fawcett, as she had expected. But you had decided, unknown to your fellow conspirator, that you would kill Mrs Benedict. The murder was your idea?'

'No,' he said regretfully, 'it was not mine. It was hers.'

'You make no sense, man!' growled Dunn.

But it was beginning to make sense to me. 'It was not originally *your* idea to kill the lady, nor did *Miss Marchwood* have any idea, poor soul, that you meant to do it. There is a third person in all this. You and *another* hatched that devilish plan. The unfortunate

Miss Marchwood was your pawn. You were directed to kill Mrs Benedict, weren't you, and later you were directed to kill Miss Marchwood for fear she would tell the police the truth?'

'That's it,' agreed Pritchard, nodding, 'I carried out my orders.' He smiled proudly.

'But,' roared Dunn, 'who gave you these orders?'

Pritchard stared at him in surprise. 'Why, she did, Mrs Scott.' He brightened. 'Mrs Scott is a very fine lady. She has very high principles.' He paused for thought. 'And had always been a very good customer.'

He had succeeded in silencing both Dunn and myself. Biddle sat with his mouth agape. Then he dropped his pencil. The clatter as it landed on the floor, and Biddle's mumbled apology to us as he retrieved it, broke the spell.

'What happened next?' I asked.

'Nothing,' said Pritchard. 'I went back to my shop.'

'And Mrs Scott, what did she do during your attack on your victim? What did she do afterwards?'

'Mrs Scott was not there,' he said. 'I was alone.'

'But you reported what had happened to Mrs Scott?' Dunn asked. 'Surely you didn't leave her to find out from the press whether you had been successful or not?'

'Oh, yes, indeed,' Pritchard agreed, nodding. 'I went that very evening to her house and told her.'

'And she said . . .?' Dunn and I chimed together.

'I think she was satisfied,' Pritchard told us, looking mightily satisfied himself. 'She told me to go back to my business and say nothing to anyone.'

Dunn and I exchanged glances. So Mrs Scott had not been surprised. She had known Pritchard waited to kill Allegra Benedict.

'Tell us about the next murder, that of Isabella Marchwood,' Dunn invited our prisoner.

Pritchard's smugness evaporated. 'I was very sorry about that, indeed I was. She was a good religious woman. But she had strayed from the narrow path of virtue. She had carried messages between the Benedict woman and the minister. Then she was overcome with remorse and knowledge of her wrongdoing! Mrs Scott feared she would speak, perhaps even to the police, but more likely to Mr Benedict. Miss Marchwood was still living in his house, you see. The Cedars, it's called, and a very fine house it is, too. Well, the husband was there, and she was weighed down by her guilt. So it was likely, wasn't it? That she would speak to him about it?'

'Tell us what led up to it,' I invited.

Pritchard was more than willing to do so. 'Well, now, you see . . . I take the train home from Waterloo to Clapham after every meeting at the Temperance Hall and that Sunday was no different. I saw, as I was about to leave the hall, that Miss Marchwood was talking to Mrs Ross outside . . .' Pritchard looked at me severely. 'A very interfering sort of person, your wife, if you don't mind my saying so.'

I did mind but before I could say it, Dunn urged the prisoner, 'Get on with it!'

'So I went back inside and waited until Mrs Ross and the girl, Bessie Newman, were out of sight because I didn't want Mrs Ross asking me questions. I thought she might. I didn't know what went on in her head, you see, your wife's . . .' Again that severe look at me. 'But then I hurried off to Waterloo, anxious to be home.'

'You had no plans to dress up and frighten the street girls that night?' I asked.

He shook his head regretfully. 'No, I thought the Wraith might lie low for a little. There had been so much fuss and so much written in the papers!' He could not repress a little smile. Clearly his notoriety had given him great pleasure.

Then he gave a little sigh. 'But I did miss it, you know, going out and about in my shroud. I took a lot of trouble making that. I used blood from the shop to stain it. So soon I began to think I would let the Wraith loose again. That's why I took the costume with me to the hall last Sunday. Mr Fawcett couldn't do his godly work; you'd got him locked away. But I was free to do mine.

'Anyway, when I got to Waterloo that Sunday, there I met Miss Marchwood again. She was waiting for the train to Egham. She was pleased to see me and asked if I would take a note to Mrs Scott for her, if we could find pen and paper. Well, I had no pen but I did have a pencil I could lend her. Neither of us had writing paper to hand, but I had some of our leaflets with me . . . the leaflets we had had printed about meetings at the hall. She wrote on the back of one of those, trusting, she said, Mrs Scott would excuse such unusual letter paper. She folded it up and gave it to me.

'I promised I would take it over to Wisteria Lodge – that is Mrs Scott's home in Clapham, another very nice residence indeed – and give it to the lady that very same evening. Then I took my train to Clapham. Several trains out of Waterloo stop there and I took the first. On my way, I unfolded the letter and read what she had written. It worried me, I confess.'

'And you took it to Mrs Scott that very evening, Sunday?'

He nodded. 'I went straight there from the railway station. I did not go home first. I thought it was important. Mrs Scott agreed. She had not long been at home herself, having first taken Mr Fawcett to his lodgings in her carriage. She told me Miss

Marchwood must be stopped, just as the Benedict woman had to be stopped. Miss Marchwood told her, in the letter, that she would come the next day, Monday, to Clapham to see Mrs Scott. She wrote the time of the train she hoped to take from Egham, so that Mrs Scott should know about what time to expect her at Wisteria Lodge.'

'"You know what must be done, Pritchard!" Mrs Scott said to me. I certainly did know. The next morning, very early, I left my assistant in charge of the shop and took the early train down to Egham. I intended to wait outside The Cedars, the Benedict house, and intercept Miss Marchwood on her walk down the hill into Egham to catch the train. That would have been the best place to waylay her. She would have died well away from London, you understand, and probably the police would have suspected Mr Benedict. There would be nothing to link her death with the Temperance Hall. But I was out of luck.' He went on sadly, 'There was a carrier's cart on the road, well laden, and making very heavy weather getting up the steep climb. The horse was really struggling. I thought the beast might slip and fall. Most of the time Miss Marchwood was walking down the hill – and I was following behind discreetly – one or the other of us was in sight or sound of the carrier. It meant I could not hide but had to walk openly and I feared, you know, that she would turn her head and see me. I had a sort of story ready if she did – that I had come out there hoping to talk to her. But I didn't have to use it.

'At the station, she got into a first-class carriage; there was only the one of them, just behind the engine. I got into a third-class carriage much further down the train. At each stop I put out my head and took note who got on or off, and whether anyone else got into first class with Miss Marchwood. No one did. It was not a popular time of day for people of means to travel. There was a ticket inspector, however. He was working his way from the back of the train to the front, entering each carriage, one at a time, between stops. He could have presented a problem. But at Twickenham he reached the first-class carriage and got in there. That meant that he got out again at Richmond, the next stop after that, and began to walk down the whole length of the train to begin again. It was my chance. I slipped out of the train, hurried along to first class and got in, behind the inspector's back, as he was walking down the train. He didn't notice me.'

'Miss Marchwood was surprised to see you, I don't doubt,' said Dunn heavily, 'and alarmed, too, perhaps guessing you, and not some other person wandering in the fog, had murdered her employer, that afternoon in the park?'

Pritchard gave that smug smile again. 'Ah, but, you see, the train had started moving again and she could not get out.'

So it had been easy for him. Until trains were built with a connecting corridor running along them between carriages, as Burns had told me was under consideration a single woman alone in a carriage would remain vulnerable.

'It was a cowardly attack!' I said fiercely.

Pritchard looked sullen. 'I had my orders.'

So that was how I found myself again at Wisteria Lodge. Mrs Scott received me in her drawing room and showed no surprise at my being there. She must have been waiting for me. She knew, once she heard that Pritchard had been arrested, that he would talk freely, proud of what he had achieved. So it would be only a short time before the police arrived to arrest her too.

The drawing room that Styles and I had so disrupted in our pursuit of Fawcett had been restored to order. There was no sign that anything untoward had ever happened here, except the parrot had apparently lost a few feathers when cannoning around his cage in all the excitement. Nor, I fancied, had he forgotten me, the cause of all the hubbub. He had fixed me with a vicious eye since I entered the room. From time to time he shuffled along his perch and uttered a low squawk, indicating that if only he were to be released from his prison, he would delight in getting at me.

His mistress probably harboured much the same feeling towards me but sat rigidly upright on a hoop-backed parlour chair with her hands folded in her lap. The housekeeper had shown me in. She, too, had remembered me and looked at me in trepidation, probably wondering what havoc I would wreak this time.

'You will know why I am here,' I said. 'We have had several long interviews with Owen Pritchard and he has fully explained his part in it all – and told us of yours.'

She made no reply other than to raise one eyebrow.

I gestured at the room around me. The parrot seized a wire of his cage in his beak and chewed at it, demonstrating what he'd like to do to me. 'Allegra Benedict,' I said, 'met Joshua Fawcett, as you know the man, here, did she not? In your drawing room during one of your private parties at which Fawcett spoke?'

Mrs Scott drew in a long deep breath. 'Marchwood brought her along and I believe had some hope her employer would be able to help our cause. Instead of that, she destroyed it utterly! From the moment the Benedict woman set eyes on Mr Fawcett, I saw she meant to set her cap at him. She was an immodest creature with no natural decency of manner at all. He had no defence against her tricks. Like so many men whose minds are set on higher things, Joshua was an innocent in the ways of such women.'

I think not! I thought but only waited.

Mrs Scott pursed her lips. 'She came twice, I fancy. Then she did not come any more and at first I was very relieved. I thought the danger had passed. But then Isabella Marchwood came to see me in great distress.' Mrs Scott shook her head. 'Marchwood was a well-meaning person after her own fashion, but far from being the most sensible. To my horror she explained that Joshua had been seduced into a tawdry affair that would be the ruin of him. The woman Benedict was without shame or discretion and Marchwood feared the cuckolded husband would soon find out about it. Marchwood herself had been persuaded to facilitate the affair by carrying messages. As I told you, she was far from being the most intelligent of women. Even so, I cannot imagine what made her agree to be their messenger. I can only suppose that Allegra Benedict held sway over her as she now held sway over Joshua Fawcett. Marchwood did not know what to do. She turned to me.

'I saw that there was need for drastic action. I enquired where the lovers met and was told that often it was at a certain oak tree in Green Park. "Very well," I told her. "Tell Mrs Benedict that Mr Fawcett wants to meet her there on Saturday afternoon. I will wait there with Mr Pritchard, as representatives of our little group." I went on to explain we would speak very seriously to Mrs Benedict; tell her that the affair was now common knowledge and that it was only a matter of very little time before her husband became aware of it. The fact that Pritchard and I already knew of it would frighten the woman enough to make her break off the liaison. Marchwood accepted the plan and was only too willing to put her trust in me – and Pritchard.'

She fell silent and I asked: 'Was that what you really intended, to talk to Mrs Benedict, nothing more? Or was that simply the version you told Miss Marchwood to get her to agree to her part in the deception?'

'Of course, nothing more,' she said calmly.

I found I was fascinated by this dreadful woman. She spoke so coolly of their wicked plan. She had had no qualms and now she expressed no regrets. 'And you were prepared to stand by while Pritchard killed her?' I asked in a voice that shook despite my best efforts.

'No, of course not, that was not the intention. As I told you, we would just speak severely to Mrs Benedict. However, as things turned out, I didn't go there on the day. I had told Marchwood I would be there; but a dreadful fog came up and reached out as far as Clapham from the centre of London. I have spent many years in hot dry climates and such weather affects my health. I dared not venture out lest I take a dangerous chill. I stayed here, in Clapham, and Pritchard went alone to meet Mrs Benedict. He took it upon himself to kill her.'

She met my gaze evenly. I could not disprove it. She knew that. It was her word, that of a wealthy woman of some social standing, against Pritchard's. What jury would believe such a woman, living here so respectably and comfortably in a Clapham villa, would plan cold-blooded murder?

Well, she might escape responsibility for Allegra's death; that of Isabella Marchwood was another matter. She would not be able to explain that away!

'What did you think when Pritchard told you, or you heard, that he had strangled her?' I began.

'I thought it was probably for the best,' she said with that same inhuman calm. 'It would cause a good deal of fuss but that would have to be borne. It would die down in time.'

'But Miss Marchwood did not go so conveniently away!' I said sharply.

The parrot let out a harsh squawk at my change in tone.

'No,' his owner said thoughtfully. 'She did not. I realised, of course, she would be distressed. But I thought fear of discovery of her part in it all would frighten her into silence.'

'On the Sunday evening before her death, Miss Marchwood ran up to your carriage door, observed by my wife, and asked to talk to you. You told her to come to see you here in Clapham,' I said.

A faint frown creased her brow. 'Yes, Mrs Ross told me of that. I did not see Mrs Ross in the street. I cannot imagine where she was.'

Hiding in an entranceway to a stableyard . . . but it was not for me to tell the woman that.

'When we found Miss Marchwood's body in the train at Waterloo, my first thought,' I told her, 'was that she had been on her way either to see me, or to try and find my wife. But that was not the case, was it? She was not on her way to central London, but only to Clapham, where she meant to get off and walk to your house to see you.'

Again that raised eyebrow.

'When my wife came to see you here, the Tuesday following Miss Marchwood's murder, you disapproved of her arrival unannounced on your doorstep,' I continued.

'It is not the usual social convention,' she replied.

'Miss Marchwood would never have flouted convention in that way,' I went on.

'No,' she agreed.

'So, when she conveniently met Pritchard again at Waterloo Station on Sunday night, she asked him to take you a note, explaining she would come the next day, Monday, and the time of the train she would take from Egham – so that you would know about what time to expect her. The note was written in pencil on the back of a leaflet of the sort given to Bessie Newman to distribute, advertising the meetings.'

'Your wife objected very unreasonably to your maid distributing the leaflets,' said Mrs Scott. 'But no, I received no message scribbled on one.'

'Pritchard says he brought it here on Sunday evening, as soon as he got back to Clapham.'

'Pritchard came to see me here,' she corrected firmly, 'but brought no letter. He is mistaken in that or, for some reason he alone knows, has invented it. Pritchard spoke to me and expressed his fears. He sought my advice. He was worried about Miss Marchwood and also, I have to tell you, alarmed at the obvious interest your wife was taking.'

I ignored the sly implication that Lizzie was somehow to blame for Isabella Marchwood's death. 'You realised neither Pritchard nor you yourself could be sure she would never speak of the plot you had hatched,' I said.

'I realised she was unreliable,' she agreed. 'A weak brain, I fear, and no backbone! I thought your wife might wheedle it out of her.'

'So you told Pritchard she must never reach this house.'

'That is what he says?' she asked, her gaze sharpening.

'It is. Pritchard received his orders, as he did on the previous occasion, and set about carrying them out.'

'You are wrong. I soothed Pritchard's fears and promised him I would speak to Miss Marchwood and explain that she must remain silent. That is what I intended to do.'

'You would do that when she arrived at your house on Monday?'

She did not fall into that trap. She recognised it for what it was, gave me a strange little smile, and said, 'There was no such arrangement, no letter written on a leaflet or on anything else. I have told you so. That is an invention of Pritchard's.'

I pressed on. 'He has described the sequence of his actions that day to the police in some detail. After strangling the helpless Miss Marchwood, he descended from the train at Clapham. He walked away calmly with other passengers, leaving the dead body of the poor woman in the carriage behind him, and went back to his own shop. The body was not discovered until the train reached the terminus at Waterloo. That must have seemed a stroke of luck to you and Pritchard.'

'She would be alive now, if she had kept her head,' Mrs Scott said dismissively. 'And not alarmed Pritchard.'

She smoothed a fold of her skirt with a careful hand. 'When your wife came to see me so unexpectedly on that Tuesday morning, with the news of Isabella's death, that was the first I had heard of it. I was very sorry. I realised Pritchard might have been carried away and gone a little too far. If indeed it was Pritchard's doing.'

'You certainly put up a cool front,' I said. 'And the girl, Clarissa Brady? Did you know that was Pritchard's doing, as you put it?'

Until now I had told her nothing she didn't know, whether or not she was yet prepared to admit it. But this was a new name to her. She betrayed a momentary surprise. 'Who is she?' For the first time, she sounded just a little uneasy.

'She was Pritchard's first victim, a prostitute. He practised the method of strangulation on her before going on to strangle Allegra. He rolled her body into the Thames, from which it was later retrieved by the River Police.'

'I know nothing of this!' she denied vigorously. 'A prostitute, you say? However should I know anything about such a girl?'

'Did you know that Pritchard had a habit of dressing up in a shroud and, on foggy nights, leaping out and frightening the street girls who work near the river by putting his hands on their throats?'

She looked puzzled. 'Why would he do that?'

'He says he wanted to frighten them away from their trade.'

'Oh,' said Mrs Scott, 'then he meant it for the best, I dare say.'

'Perhaps you did not know he had strangled Clarissa Brady,' I said. 'But I think you did know about his activities as the Wraith and that is why you chose him to kill Allegra Benedict. He was malleable to your will and easily accepted your superior authority. What is more, I believe it is possible that even his activities as the Wraith were originally your idea. You sent him out, wrapped in a bloodstained sheet and papier mâché mask. Before you turned your attention to combating the scourge of drink, you had decided to do something to clear the streets of prostitutes.'

'The police seemed to be doing little to achieve it!' she suddenly burst out. 'The country is going to rack and ruin and the authorities do nothing! It is the duty of every right-minded citizen to fight against every kind of loose living in our society! What was wrong about Pritchard's harmless little charade?'

She clamped her thin lips together, realising she had said more than she intended.

'A right-minded citizen,' I said, 'would surely have gone immediately to the police when Pritchard told her he had killed Allegra Benedict. If what you have told me is true, and you did not intend him to murder the woman, you seem to have taken the news remarkably calmly and to have done nothing to bring him to justice.'

'I decided he had been overenthusiastic, but the result was what we would have wished. Joshua was freed from that woman. That was all that mattered.' Her grey eyes, so cold until now, suddenly sparkled with triumph. 'We had achieved our purpose.'

I could not sit here any longer. I had heard enough. I got up and went to the window to signal to Morris who was waiting outside.

When Morris had joined us I turned back to Mrs Scott.

'Jemima Scott, I arrest you on two charges of aiding and abetting a murderer and of a further charge of concealing information relating to a crime. I must ask you to accompany us.'

The parrot began a frenzied beating of his wings against the bars of his cage.

Chapter Eighteen

Elizabeth Martin Ross

BEN TOLD me everything that evening. We sat before the fire in the parlour, which was obstinately refusing to draw, and I listened to the whole sorry tale. We could hear Bessie in the distance, clashing pots around in the kitchen. I was glad he didn't hide the details from me. I wanted to know everything, though I admit I was very distressed at Mrs Scott's cruel suggestion that I had hastened the death of Isabella Marchwood by attempting to befriend her outside the hall, and being observed doing so by Pritchard.

'If I'd known Pritchard – or anyone else – was watching,' I said, 'I should have followed her down the street a little way and then spoken to her.'

'Pritchard would still have seen you. He was following Miss Marchwood and caught up with her at Waterloo.'

'I should still have tried harder to persuade Miss Marchwood to confide in me!' I burst out. 'I should have walked with her to Waterloo and, along the way, gained her trust. Bessie and I could have stayed with her until she boarded her train that evening; and she would have had no chance to write that note for Pritchard to

305

deliver to Wisteria Lodge. She would not have got into that train up to London on Monday morning and Pritchard would not have been following her.'

'Come now, Lizzie,' Ben replied, taking my hand. 'You were a stranger to her. She didn't wish to confide in you. You couldn't make her.'

'I could have done something!' I insisted.

'You did. You observed her speak to Jemima Scott and overheard the invitation extended to her to go to Clapham. You told me about it. The knowledge of that scrap of conversation was very important to the investigation. Lizzie, Isabella Marchwood was doomed from the start, when she first took Allegra Benedict to Wisteria Lodge.'

I supposed Ben was right and sighed, but then a thought occurred to me that made me say angrily, 'And the dreadful Fawcett will bear no blame in any part for it? But surely, he is the cause of it all! His lies and deception led to his being invited to speak at Mrs Scott's house and meeting Allegra there. He began the affair with Allegra – and don't tell me he was an innocent seduced by a designing woman. That man doesn't know what innocence is!'

'It's a great pity,' Ben returned, 'that for the first time in his life he didn't seek first and foremost to save his skin. He understood the risk of Benedict finding out and was half planning to leave London, as he had left other towns when things got complicated. But though he knew he should cut and run, he found it hard to break away from Allegra. In his own fashion—'

'Do *not*,' I interrupted fiercely, 'I beg you, say he loved her. He is not capable of it!'

'All right then,' Ben agreed meekly, 'let's say he was infatuated with her. He is still a young man. She was a young and very beautiful woman. She made a mistake in trusting him. He made a mistake in wanting to cling to his relationship with her . . . and both of them were being watched by a woman who was, in her own way, just as obsessed with your Mr Fawcett as Allegra Benedict was. Don't you think it possible, Lizzie, that Jemima Scott, despite the difference in their ages, had also developed a passion for the fellow? Allegra was not just a threat to the cause, as Scott calls it, she was a rival for the preacher's affections. Fawcett himself told me how some women fall in love with a male figure in authority. That could be at the root of it all.'

I stared at Ben in horror. It had not occurred to me that Mrs Scott had been more than simply committed to Joshua Fawcett's so-called campaign to save the poor from drunkenness. Had she really fallen in love with him? The thought of that cold woman harbouring secret desires . . . It made me shudder.

'If that's so,' I pointed out, 'then she can't possibly be telling the truth about the plan hatched with Pritchard. How could she really only have intended Pritchard to plead with Allegra to break off the affair? Did she really not know he would strangle her? Did she truly, in what passes for her heart, not want her rival out of the way for ever?'

'She will never admit to deeper feelings or any personal rivalry for Fawcett's affections,' Ben replied. 'So, for practical purposes, let us say her only wish was to protect Fawcett from scandal and enable him to continue his work. I still believe she plotted with Pritchard to murder Allegra. It came as no surprise to her that he had done so. I don't think she would have been so calm afterwards if it had come as an unwelcome shock. She would have been furious with Pritchard and gone at once to the police. Instead, she deliberately shielded and colluded with a murderer, following the crime. She will find that hard to explain to a court.'

Remembering my own visit to Wisteria Lodge after the murder of Isabella Marchwood, and the composed manner in which I had been received by its owner, I murmured, 'She must have nerves of steel and no ounce of pity. Perhaps both things brought her safely through the dangerous days of the Mutiny in India.'

Ben rattled the poker in the hearth then took the tongs and added a lump of coal to the fire. It made a token attempt to blaze up. 'Pritchard himself claims she knew the meeting was arranged for the purposes of murdering Allegra Benedict,' he said. 'It was not his own idea; it was hers. He followed her instructions. There seems to be little reason why he should lie about that, unless he fancies that spreading the blame will save him. It will not.'

He shrugged. 'Personally I believe that she did know and that was the plan from the first. Of course, Isabella Marchwood knew nothing of their true intent, but Jemima Scott, as well as Pritchard, had decided Allegra would not leave Green Park alive. But proving her involvement? Ah, that's a different matter. Scott is a clever woman. She took good care not to be present herself when either murder was carried out. The note Isabella wrote at Waterloo Station on the back of a leaflet and gave to Pritchard to deliver, that was surely thrown into the fire the very same evening. She is too clever to deny he came to the house. Her housekeeper might have remembered that and told us. But Mrs Scott insists he only came to discuss his fears. She told him she would speak to Isabella Marchwood on his behalf and persuade her of the need to stay silent. No more.'

There was another silence during which I stared into the struggling flames and Ben seemed lost in his own thoughts. He was roused from them by a particularly loud crash from the kitchen, followed by Bessie's voice calling, 'Don't worry, missus, no harm done!'

'You know, Lizzie,' Ben said quietly, 'when I first began to unravel this case, I thought I dealt with two separate murderers. One dressed as a wraith and hunted down the street girls like the unfortunate Clarrie Brady. The other had murdered Allegra Benedict and subsequently murdered Isabella Marchwood.'

'And there was only the one, Pritchard!' I observed, as it turned out precipitately.

'It depends how you look at it, Lizzie. Only one pair of hands, Pritchard's, physically carried out the murders but there were *two* minds behind it all. That, I now know, was what confused my thinking. Left to his own devices, Pritchard would have continued to prowl the foggy streets until we caught him, concentrating on the prostitutes whose activities so offended him. He had no reason to entice Allegra Benedict into the park and kill her. *He had known nothing about her!* Don't forget, Pritchard had never been invited to the afternoon tea and cakes at Wisteria Lodge where Fawcett met Allegra. Allegra never attended the meetings at the Temperance Hall. Pritchard had never set eyes on Allegra Benedict before the fateful encounter in Green Park. Pritchard only knew of the liaison between Fawcett and Allegra because Mrs Scott told him of it; and persuaded him that Allegra posed a serious danger to the minister. After that she had little difficulty in getting him to agree that the danger must be removed. One man, you see, but two minds: a double-headed monster, if you like.'

'And will a judge and jury believe that?' I asked, aghast at the image created of the conspirators.

'They will believe what the prosecution can prove in a court of law,' said Ben ruefully. 'Where is the proof? There are no witnesses to the conversations between Scott and her minion. Other than Mrs Scott's shielding of Pritchard after the murder of Allegra, which continued after the murder of Marchwood, it is a question of his word, a confessed murderer's, against hers. She is guilty of criminal behaviour in shielding him after the fact. But that is a lesser charge than conspiracy to murder.'

'Then there will be no justice!' I stormed.

He shrugged. 'Have you seen the newspapers?'

'Not today,' I admitted.

'Well, when you do, you'll see that they have found out Jemima Scott's history during the Indian Mutiny, the privations she and others suffered during the five months of the siege, and how her husband died there despite her efforts to save his life. One or two artists have even illustrated the scene . . . Major Scott dying in his loving wife's arms.' He gave a bitter little smile. 'I cannot imagine a judge willing to don a black cap and sentence to death a heroine of Lucknow.'

I broke the long silence that followed this statement by saying, 'I think Bessie has lost interest in temperance.'

'Thank goodness,' said Ben, 'perhaps now I can have a bottle of porter with my dinner in peace.'

Inspector Benjamin Ross

A few days after my conversation with Lizzie I was again walking across Waterloo Bridge. It was a bright clear day and the skyline as crisp as a painted cardboard silhouette in a child's model theatre. I began to whistle a tune, because when all was said and done we had tied up the Green Park murder (and the railway one, not to forget the killing of poor Clarissa Brady) and although these cases had yet to come to trial, we had been successful. (Lizzie would never be satisfied but that couldn't be helped. A police officer is very often dissatisfied with the outcome of a case but he knows that, in the end, these things are decided by lawyers.)

Even a case that was not mine had been decided. As I left Scotland Yard the previous evening I had encountered my colleague, Inspector Phipps, in the company of a choleric-looking gentleman with magnificent whiskers and a single eyeglass dangling from a ribbon round his neck.

'Ah, Ross,' said Phipps with something of a smug look, 'you will be pleased to know we have the gang who were foolish enough to threaten Colonel Frey here. There's no honour among thieves, they say, and one of 'em decided to turn Queen's evidence when he found out the Yard was on the case!' To his companion he added, 'This is Inspector Ross, Colonel, the first officer to begin the enquiries at your stable yard. You were absent at the time, I believe, and have not met Inspector Ross.'

The colonel screwed the monocle into his eye and studied me. 'Ah, quite so, quite so. Good work, er, Ross . . . good work!'

'Inspector Phipps's good work, sir, I was only standing in for him that day,' I explained with suitably modest demeanour.

'Nevertheless, played your part, I am sure. Good man!'

With a nod, the colonel strode past me. Phipps followed in his wake, giving me a wink as he passed by.

I was thinking of that encounter and smiling when I saw a familiar silhouette coming towards me, feathers bouncing atop its head.

'Well, 'allo, Mr Ross!' said Daisy cheerfully.

'Good afternoon to you, Daisy. Is that a new hat?'

'No . . .' Daisy put up her hand and patted the confection adorning her scarlet hair. 'It's the same one, but I got new feathers to replace the ones Lily Spraggs broke. I got 'em off a poulterer in the market. They're from a pheasant's tail. Nice, ain't they?'

'Very elegant,' I said.

'All the girls are very pleased we caught the Wraith,' Daisy informed me. 'Now they don't have to worry about him jumping out at them every foggy night!'

'Daisy,' I said awkwardly, 'you know that, although one danger has been removed, there will always be others for you and your – your friends to face? This occupation that you follow may have kept you from the workhouse, but it is full of risk. Girls like you get attacked both by their clients and by men like Jed Sparrow. There is the danger of the sicknesses associated with your trade with all their hideous physical effects. You may be brought in off the street and subjected to a forced examination at any time. If discovered to be infected, you'll be locked away until declared no longer able to pass on the disease. But there are plenty of clients out there who will pass it on to you. There are threats enough without men like the Wraith who prey on the girls for warped reasons of their own. There are also the Jed Sparrows who would seek to bully you out of your money. Above all, forgive me, even if you escape all that and the ravages of syphilis, you will still not always be young and pretty. What will you do—'

'You're not preaching at me, are you?' she interrupted.

'Not preaching, only pointing out, as a friend and one very much indebted to you for saving my wife, that you should think seriously of giving up your way of life. Surely you don't want to finish like your unfortunate friend, Clarrie, in the river?'

'It's the only trade I know,' said Daisy, after a moment.

'But you could learn another. My wife knows of an organisation in Marylebone. They have as their object the rescue of girls such as you from the streets. They teach them skills that make them employable and help them to find work.'

'I know all about them!' broke in Daisy with a scornful snort. 'They'd teach me to be a housemaid. What, spend all me life polishing and dusting, with some old woman ringing a bell every five minutes, expecting me to run and see what she wants? I should think not! Don't you worry about me, Mr Ross, and tell your wife not to worry, either. I'm glad I, and that funny-looking maid you've got, arrived in time to pull the Wraith away from her.' Daisy gave me a wicked grin. 'See, your wife is a very respectable lady, but she still got attacked by the old monster in his shroud, didn't she? It ain't being out on the streets like me that makes life so risky. It's just being a woman that's dangerous, that's what.'

With that, she burst into laughter and with a wave of her hand set off past me across the bridge. I turned to watch her go, the new pheasant feathers bobbing bravely in her refurbished hat.